Master Fox

The Immortal

Salahudean Gill

Copyright - © - 2022 - by Salahudean Gill.
All rights reserved.
"No part of this publication may be reproduced, distributed, or transmitted in any form or by any means, including photocopying, recording, or other electronic or mechanical methods, or by any information storage and retrieval system without the prior written permission of the publisher, except in the case of very brief quotations embodied in critical reviews and certain other noncommercial uses permitted by copyright law."

ISBN: 9798351944326

First Edition: September 2022

DEDICATION

This book is dedicated to my beautiful family. I am so very grateful for you.

Table of Contents

SHINY DUMPLINGS	1
NEW VENTURES	22
THE DISAPPEARANCE	49
UNEXPECTED EDUCATION	65
THROUGH THE PALL	83
THE S'LA'MANDA	98
THE FIRST	117
THE SIBLINGS	133
THE DESCENT	152
THE ARKYALA	177
THE FOURTH	194
THE HELLFIRE ROAD	216
INTO THE MOUNTAIN	241
THE SHOMYIRA	262
LABYRINTH	285
SHOGATT	308
SHUI	326
FIRE FORTRESS	347
DANGER, COURAGE, GROWTH	368
THE GAZING GATES	382
CHO CLEI	410
THE NINE STRIKES	420

WEN-YI	432
ESCAPE	439
CONFRONTATION	448
RAGYALA	457
THE ROAD HOME	466

Master Fox

The Immortal

Chapter 1

Shiny Dumplings

Everything changed when Old Fong became successful. There was a saying about men like him. They were young when they moved, but old if they sat still. Old Fong was somewhere between 50 and 75, depending on if he was moving or sitting still. He had always been around our family. Father had done some service for Fong in the past. I knew that Father had saved Fong from some trouble when they were young, but neither ever mentioned what actually happened. But, after saving him, Father felt responsible for Fong. So, Father made sure to look after the old man and invite him over often.

He and Father never talked about what had passed between them, but it was clear he had great respect for Father. Fong once told me that he had met Father when they were both boys, so it was a long time ago.

Even though Fong is older, he has always looked up to Father and sought his advice. Fong wasn't around every day, but his presence was a constant throughout my youth. Even when I was very little, I remember Old Fong coming to feast days and birthday celebrations.

I can never imagine him being young, although he must have been at some point. I do remember that he was always kind and usually smiling. The only time he wouldn't smile, was when he was cooking. When he cooked, he became intense and serious. It seemed strange to me, because cooking was the one thing he clearly enjoyed more than anything else.

Father said Old Fong was the 'most talented' cook in the whole province. Anyone who had tasted Fong's cooking agreed. Whatever he made was *always* delicious. Father said that Old Fong's family had been very skilled carpenters. He would point out a beautiful and elaborate bookshelf that my great grandfather had bought from Old Fong's grandfather.

It was clear that Fong's family had been skilled at woodwork. But it had been equally clear that Fong had no interest in continuing the family business. Fong only enjoyed preparing food. He enjoyed eating too, but only ate enough to make sure it tasted good. He had 'tried' throughout his twenties to support himself with carpentry, but had barely been able to pay for his necessities. Neither his heart nor his mind were interested in woodwork. And because he never wanted to look for carpentry work, his family called him 'Lazy Fong'.

Eventually, when Fong had grown up, his father arranged a marriage for 'Lazy Fong'. In truth, Fong was not very pleased at his father's choice of wife for him. She had an abrasive manner and liked to argue. So, he disliked working as a carpenter, and he disliked what he came home to, after an odious day's work. This was just too much for him. Something had to give, and Fong reached his breaking point. I had just turned fifteen when this happened.

Fong decided that he would not work wood any longer. Enough people in their area came to him if they needed something repaired, so he would be able to feed his household. He decided that he would only be a handyman occasionally and continue to cook.

He was good at cooking, and he loved it. Besides, his wife knew she was a bad cook. She honestly preferred his cooking to hers. (In truth, everyone who had sampled Fong's cooking preferred it to any other food.) He had promised himself that he would never work in wood again, but it was a promise he would not keep.

So Old Fong cooked. And on Sundays, when Old Fong made dumplings, word spread fast. People would come from all over the whole town to get some. They would knock on his door, compliment him on the aroma coming from his house, and after giving him a few copper coins, they would leave with a package of his dumplings. Between the occasional handyman job and this 'dumpling money', he was able to pay for his family's few needs.

Old Fong was married, and they had one daughter later in life. She seemed to be the exact opposite of her father. She was rarely kind, never smiled, and by all accounts, she was a terrible cook. His wife had taught the daughter to cook, but she could only teach the one style of cooking she knew.

Everything Fong's wife made was overcooked and over-seasoned with burnt garlic. Where she grew up, garlic was farmed very heavily. All of her region's dishes tasted overwhelmingly of garlic. Garlic wasn't Fong's favorite seasoning, but he had tried to learn to enjoy it. Perhaps it wouldn't have been so bad, but she always cooked the meal for too long. So, in addition to being over seasoned with burnt garlic, the texture of the food was either mushy or leathery.

Maybe it was because she never showed any talent for cooking that made Old Fong an even better cook. He got plenty of practice. And if his wife ever asked if he was hungry, he would reply, "Not for burnt garlic!" She would storm off and be mad at him for a while, but at least he didn't have to eat her food. He considered that a good deal. Enduring her ire was worth it.

When Old Fong made his first batch of shiny dumplings, people's reactions were different than they had ever been before. As usual, townspeople would knock keenly on his door and ask after the delicious aroma. They would pay him and leave with dumplings. However, without exception, everyone who bought dumplings was irresistibly tempted. They ate them on their walk home and immediately returned for more. Every single person who bought Fong's dumplings returned that same day for another helping. They were so impressed with the flavor that they each pressed him for his 'secret'. They were convinced that he had some special technique because normal cooking couldn't explain the extreme tastiness of the dumplings.

Of course, by late afternoon, Fong had sold all of the dumplings. And, with a twinkle in his eye, he refused to tell them his secret. Every single person left disappointed, but Fong promised that he would make the dumplings again soon. They asked him to set some aside for them, and he agreed. That first batch of shiny dumplings was the beginning of Old Fong's Dumpling Shop.

Later cultures would say, 'Do What You Love, And Success Will Follow'. That was never truer than with Fong. When he decided to make a proper business out of cooking, a change came over Fong. He seemed even happier to everyone who saw him. There was energy in his eyes and, for a while at least, he even seemed younger.

Father was the one who had suggested that Old Fong look into opening a dumpling shop. Old Fong immediately seized this vision and decided to make his house into a dumpling shop. His wife was unconvinced, but lacking any genuine objection, she did not try to stop him. He decided to make his kitchen as professional as possible. He asked Wei-Yon Yon, the house builder, to help him make his kitchen bigger. Wei-Yon Yon had agreed to supply the materials and be paid in future dumplings. (They were that good.)

Soon, Old Fong's kitchen could make three times as many dumplings as before. After that, he emptied his house's living room and garden. Then he borrowed Wei-Yon Yon's cart and old donkey. He collected a piece of charcoal and an axe, and then came to see me. Technically, he came to see Father.

He asked Father if he could use me as muscle to cut down trees. I was fifteen at the time. I was big and had large shoulders, for my age. Father thought that any exercise was a good idea and sent me off with Old Fong. Father and I had just finished talking about my future when Fong had arrived.

I remember it was an anxious time for me. Like every boy my age, I was trying to figure out what I wanted to do with my life. For generations, our family had been soldiers. But during the time of my grandfather, there had been a massive change throughout the land. The Emperor had been forced to disband the military. Somehow, war itself had been outlawed.

Mysterious and powerful men had come down from the mountains, dealing with conflict situations before anyone went to war. If there was a problem, they solved it. Or rather, they motivated the people involved to solve the problem- peacefully. They were so powerful that they stood between the arguments of nations. They did not let the arguments grow into wars. Neither the warriors of the armies nor even the Emperor himself dared to challenge these men. They made lasting peace, and kept that peace. Father said that the Emperor himself answered to these people, not the other way around.

I had never seen any of these people, but Father told me that they existed. He verified that these special and powerful 'Mountain Men' were the reason our family had to change its profession. My grandfather had told Father bedtime stories that featured warrior heroes. Naturally, Father had wanted to be a great General when he grew up, but life (and these 'Mountain Men' had given him a different situation. With no army, and no place to *become* a General, Father had spent his life as a policeman. And now, he was pushing for me to do the same.

And while I was not sure what I wanted to do with my life, I *knew* I didn't want to spend it as a policeman. I didn't want to be stuck in this little village forever. I knew every person here. I had known them my whole life. I knew every street, every house... Somehow, I knew it would never be enough.

To become a policeman, a person first needed to pass an examination. These exams were held in various cities across the Empire, since the land was so vast. Because we lived relatively near the capital city, that's where the exams were held for our little village. A person had to be at least 15 years old to take the exam. And I was 15. Father rarely missed a chance to remind me that later in the year, I could start my police education.

I had the impression that Father resented these 'special people'. But peace had been made. And I know father is a peaceful man, but when he talked about 'their' peace, he sounded like he was conflicted. According to him, these special people came down from 'the mountains' and (after demonstrating their power) disbanded the armies.

Father always took my questions seriously. When I pressed him about what he really thought of these 'Mountain men', he was quiet for a long time before he answered. "Kwan, the purpose of a warrior is to fight. But the purpose of fighting is to *protect* the innocent and *preserve peace*. I have to admit that the 'Mountain men' did something good.

"But I've never gotten over the feeling that they robbed me of my childhood dream. And it is clear they robbed you too." I had prepared to speak up, to tell him that I did not want to become a policeman. Those people never robbed me of any dreams. I wanted to tell Father that I had no dreams of soldier life or police work! But I knew that he would ask me what I wanted to do with my life instead. And the truth was that I didn't really know. And for him, if I didn't want to follow in his footsteps, I was indecisive, bordering on simple-minded. But Father had gone on, "But fortunately, you will still have the police." He nodded. I didn't. "And the examination in Capital City will be here before you know it!" That's what I was afraid of.

***

Together, Old Fong and I walked the cart and donkey out to the forest. I didn't mind. Fong and I had always gotten along. Since he had been a regular figure throughout my life, we could (and often did) enjoy a comfortable silence.

When we had travelled some distance into the forest, Old Fong pulled the donkey to a halt. He walked straight to a tree half as thick around as my waist. I picked up the axe and followed him. He used his piece of charcoal to make a complicated mark on a tree. Then he told me to cut it down.

While I was cutting, he was marking the next trees. Physically, I have always been strong, so swinging an axe was not a big challenge. It felt good to use my strength, and I gave myself over to it. I worked up a sweat, attacking the cutting enthusiastically. Fong busied himself stripping the bark from the fallen trees. When we took breaks, we talked.

"Is he still giving you a hard time?" Fong asked. I had known Fong my whole life. He had witnessed Father's growing pressure on me throughout the years. He had heard me tell him over the last few years that I did not want to grow up to be a policeman. I was tempted to talk about it, but I knew that nothing would come out of the discussion. First, I would complain. I would say Father's mind was made up.

Then Fong would ask me about my few friends at school. I would tell him that nothing had changed. In fact, it had gotten worse. I had begun feeling like my friends were destined for dull village life. They were actually glad that their futures were predictable! And I dreaded the thought that I would end up the same way. Friends, well at least the friends I had, seemed less and less fun to be around.

Fong would respond that all boys are interested in the same things. I would smile and agree, letting the subject drop. But I felt that some people seemed easily… satisfied. Or something like that. I tried and tried, but I needed more than they did. And the other boys' fathers probably weren't pressuring them about what they were going to do with their lives! He treated me like a child… who wasn't living up to his potential. I rolled my eyes to myself.

But then we would be back where we started in the discussion. Instead, I saved us time, and skipped to the end. Chatting about it wouldn't solve anything. "You know Father." I said. He nodded and I kept swinging.

I already knew the course of the conversation I would have had with Fong. I already knew that it would not end up in any place new or useful. I already knew that by the end, Fong would feel sorry for me, but my situation would not change. Then he would encourage me to pay attention to my cutting.

He knew how frustrated I was. But he also seemed to know that he couldn't really do anything about it. Father had been shaped by life, and Fong did not have the power to change him.

So, I paid attention to my cutting. I focused all of my attention on swinging the axe. But no matter how much wood I chopped, no matter how hard I swung, my future looked bleak.

Grimly, I cut. As the day passed, I had felled the trees he marked and cut them into manageable pieces. I worked for several hours, cutting down trees and helping Fong to saw them into flatter pieces. Then we had a lunch. Fong had made and brought a soup and we shared it in silence. The soup was delicious, naturally, because Fong had made it. Once I had sat down, I realized that I was tired, and we ate in silence.

After eating, we hoisted the wood into the cart and I asked Old Fong, "Why did you make those complicated marks on the trees? I could have seen a simpler mark."

He replied, "I respect nature, Little Kwan. I make a mark of blessing on the tree, and I thank it for its sacrifice. There are many good spirits in nature. But there are also bad spirits too. Not many people still hold these beliefs, I suppose. I learned them from my father. And he learned them before I was born." I nodded, still not understanding. Fong had never struck me as a particularly spiritual man. He had never given me the impression that he had studied with anyone. In truth, Fong had always struck me as funny, but not serious or wise. Father had always been the holder of those qualities.

Soon after that, we finished loading the wood and headed back home. The sun set as we walked the donkey back to the village. The donkey knew the way better than we did, so we let him lead us. Fong was pleased, and wanted to talk. I was tired, and the sky was lit with fiery colored clouds. My memory of this walk is still, to this day, somehow clear.

When Old Fong dropped me off back at home, the sun had set. It was dark and only the light at our front door was lit. Exhausted and sweaty, I walked into the house. I looked in on my little sister. She was sleeping quietly.

Then I bathed and went to bed. Just before I blew out the candle, Father walked to my door. He nodded in approval at my obvious fatigue and grunted, "Good night Kwan." Then he went to bed too. Father was a hard, monument of a man. His will was like iron. Naturally, Father approved of most things that made me tired.

Over the next weeks, we made several more trips out to the forest to acquire wood. Frequently, we talked about how Father was unmovable. But by the end of each trip, we would only have lumber, not solutions. Father's mind was made up. I was to become a policeman, and that was decided. Once we had enough wood collected, Old Fong used his meagre woodworking skills to make tables and chairs. At first, he tried to make the furniture beautiful, but gave up on that goal quickly. The furniture he made was never beautiful, but he knew enough to make the pieces sturdy and level.

While he was building his shop, nobody paid much attention to Fong. His neighbors only complained a little when Fong and Wei-Yon Yon started rebuilding the kitchen. Everyone knew Fong was an extremely good cook and secretly hoped they would eventually benefit.

When Old Fong's Dumpling shop first opened its doors, it was a Sunday. That Sunday, when people came to ask after his delicious dumplings, they found a shop instead of a house.

Father had sent me that morning to help Fong with the opening. He sent me with a gift. It was a tiny bell to hang over the door, for luck. Fong could use some encouragement, Father said. The bell would be a symbol for Fong. It would ring whenever a new customer came in. Father had instructed me to be positive, no matter how the day turned out.

Honestly, I was just excited to help. Life can seem dull in a small village, so any diversion was welcome. Fong's house and restaurant was small but clean. Initially, there were only two items on the menu. Old Fong sold his shiny dumplings, and tea.

The usual dumpling enthusiasts came and took the dumplings off to their homes, but no one wanted to stay and eat. At first, Fong was full of nervous energy, pacing around, and fussing over details. But eventually, when no one came in, Fong sat down. He and I sat in the empty shop, just waiting. Over the next two hours, Fong's movements became more and more subdued.

Fong had begun to despair. He wanted people to stay. He wanted to be a real restaurant. He wanted to justify the work that he had done to build the shop. I wanted success and happiness for Fong. And I wanted the restaurant to be a success too. After all, I had helped a little.

As the day passed, I started to have doubts too. Then I remembered what Father had said, and tried to inspire Fong. Back then, I was not much of a speaker. I was still a boy, but I felt the need to encourage Fong. I tried to be cheerful, saying optimistic things, but I had the impression that I was making matters worse.

That was when our luck changed. Before I had finished speaking, the bell rang. The door opened and the first customers walked in. They were two old men who waved and smiled at us, then slowly settled at a table. I looked at the customers, then looked at Fong. He nodded and a wide smile spread across his face. He rushed off to greet the elderly men.

In the end, there were a total of seven customers who stayed to eat on that first day. There were the first two old men. They both were stooped over and must have been 100 years old each. They talked incessantly, smiled often, and ate their dumplings slowly.

Then a family stopped for lunch as they were travelling through town. The family consisted of a man, wife, and two boys, around 8 years old. They were dressed in rich black silk clothing with silver buttons. Their mother wore a large pearl necklace. It was clear that they were visiting our village on a journey from the capital. No one in our village had the riches to dress like that.

The father ordered their dumplings and they were soon eating with abandon, shoveling the delicious dumplings into their mouths. They ordered a second helping, then a third. The father complained that there was no wine. The mother complained that the chairs were ugly. I had the impression that they were the type of people who liked to complain, but they could find nothing to complain about when the food had arrived. Their mouths were too busy enjoying the dumplings to complain.

The last man came at the end of the day. He was a big man, both tall and fat. However, when he moved, it was apparent that he had muscle under the fat. He looked large and cumbersome, but he moved gracefully. He wore a rosary of heavy stone beads around his neck. The beads on the necklace were large and round, the size of plums, and were made of different colored stones. There were two dozen stone beads on the necklace, and though they were different colors. Most of the beads looked highly polished. The stone rosary must have been very heavy.

The man's wide head was shaved and he was dressed in common clothes. They were the simple and practical clothes of a traveling monk. Actually, at that point in life, I had never seen a monk. The closest I had ever seen was the traveling priest that visited every few months from the capital. Something in his manner seemed 'priestly' to me, so my first thought was 'fat priest'. His robes did not look new, but they were clean and well maintained. I had noticed that travelers were usually dusty when they passed through town.

The fat priest wore an old satchel over his shoulder, and carried an odd staff in his hand. The staff was gnarled and twisted at the top then straightened toward the bottom. It was made from wood from a tree we called 'ironwood'. The wood was very strong and had a bronze- colored sheen to it. It took much longer than other trees to catch fire. It would catch on fire, but this would take several minutes on the fire before it would light. Only the strongest saws could even cut ironwood. The staff was as thick as a man's fist at the top and narrowed toward the bottom. At the bottom, the staff tapered to a perfect circle the size of an egg.

The strange part was a grain of silver metal running through the wood of the staff. It looked almost like lightning, flashing when it reflected light. But to make a staff like that, a blacksmith would need to pour molten silver into the ironwood. I remember wondering how the fat priest had put metal into the wood without burning it. I knew ironwood was strong, but I didn't know how strong. Father had told me about ironwood weapons, but I had never seen one. Seeing the golden metallic sheen on the wood, I immediately identified it.

When a huge priest comes into a room, it certainly makes an impression. Since our village didn't have a regular priest, seeing him was even more striking. But, it was his face that was most memorable. His eyes twinkled as though he knew a wonderful joke. He had a wide face- with a wide nose, vast cheeks, and a broad smile. It was a contagious smile and I couldn't help smiling back.

His cheeks were rosy and he looked around curiously. At first, he just stood there, and I could now see some dust from the road as I looked him over. His robes were brown, with an under-robe of lighter brown. A piece of gray rope tied around his waist served as a belt. Over his left shoulder, he wore a bag made out of some kind of tan cloth.

On his wide feet, he wore flat leather sandals. He was a big man and he walked in slowly. He closed his eyes, leaned his head back and inhaled deeply through his nose when he walked in. He slowly let out the breath and lowered his head. His smile was, if possible, even wider. When his eyes opened, he was looking directly at me.

When the priest came in, I could immediately feel something different. It seemed to me that he brightened the room, bringing energy with him as he entered. He stopped, a few feet in from the door and looked around slowly. The fat priest inhaled deeply again, his barrel-chest chest expanding. Then, his head rolled back and he started laughing. His laughter was deep and booming. It was a big, but pleasant, sound.

The family of four was just finishing their meals. They looked over at the big priest. The wife of the family flashed an irritated and hostile expression at him, before they returned to eating. I could see the priest notice her, but he was unconcerned. She had given him an unfriendly look, clearly wanting him to be silent. He smiled pleasantly back at her, utterly untroubled by her hostility.

I hurried over to the priest and offered him a table by the window. He nodded his head appreciatively, bowed his head, and sat. I turned to speak to him, but just then, Fong walked out from the kitchen. He waved me away and began speaking to the priest. I went to the kitchen to make more tea. The family was still eating, and I was sure they would be expecting tea to be ready soon.

I took the empty plates away from the family and poured them tea. Then I retreated to the kitchen. A moment later Fong met me in the kitchen. He was chuckling. Apparently, the priest had made a good impression. Fong busied himself in the kitchen checking the dumplings. "Maybe so, but THAT gnat will never make babies! Ha!" Fong shook his head, clearly retelling himself some joke. "We need more customers like him! He is funny and he is hungry! Ha!"

I walked softly over to the door of the dining room to sneak a look at the priest. As I did, he turned and looked directly at me. He gave a small nod and raised his tea cup. Startled to be discovered, I jumped a little. I straightened and hurried out to see what he wanted.

He smiled and spoke without preamble. "Hello Kwan. Please get me another pot of tea." I nodded, picked up the empty tea pot and hurried back to the kitchen.

There was something different about this priest. Something was unusual about him. As I moved around the kitchen, tried to figure out what it was. Then it came to me. The air around him faintly hummed! And the closer I got to him, the louder the humming became. I had never met a person who made a sound in my ears when I got close to them. This was something new. I wasn't normally given to an overactive imagination, so I had no doubt that there was something strange going on.

I made the tea. Fong only looked over and nodded at my careful treatment of the pots and cups. Fong only had three teapots. Only after I had ladled boiling water into the teapot did I wonder how the priest knew my name. He had called me by my name, Kwan. I resolved to ask him when I brought the tea out. I would also ask him about the humming in the air. I stirred the leaves in the pot and replaced the lid.

Maybe the air hummed around all priests? I just didn't know much about priests. Or the world, for that matter. We honored our ancestors that had come before us, like every other family that we knew. However, because Father was not a 'religious' man, we were not a religious family.

I had only heard about priests from Mother, not from any experience in a temple. Mother had made them sound exotic and holy. So far, I only had a vague understanding that priests were different. This fat man was certainly different. His looks were different, but the energy he radiated was the most startling part. I had never thought of myself as sensitive to these types of things, but I could *feel* something different about him.

I brought the tea out to him. When I set down the pot, I glanced over at the family of four. They didn't speak and all looked at their plates, still intent on eating. They didn't even seem to notice that there was anyone else in the room. I glanced at the kitchen. The priest read my mind. "Don't worry, Fong won't mind you stopping to talk."

His smile reassured me and I relaxed. His ironwood staff was standing up, leaning against the side of the table. He offered to pour me a cup of tea, but I just looked down and shook my head. That would be too much! A priest serving tea for a village boy! I felt my cheeks burning. I looked at him a moment later and saw that his eyes were twinkling. He was amused by my discomfort! And he could read my mind! "You're a good boy, Kwan."

I nodded tentatively, and asked him a question, "How do you know my name, um, Honorable Priest?" Fox looked at me for a second before throwing back his head and giving a deep, full laugh. The bass of his voice rang out in the shop. The mother of the family again threw a dirty look in his direction.

"I'm not a priest, Kwan." His eyes twinkled. Still amused, he continued, "Though people do keep making that assumption. There are few of us, so I would expect you haven't seen one of my order before." He paused, looking thoughtful, then continued. "Do I look like a priest to you? Oh, you've never seen a priest before! Your mother only described them." He *was* reading my mind! "But I'm not a priest. How did I know your name? Fong mentioned your name when he was talking."

He took a sip of his tea, but never took his eyes off me. I nodded. It made sense. I don't know why I hadn't thought of it. Of course, Old Fong would have mentioned my name. I was the serving boy, after all.

"If you're not a priest, what are you? Some kind of holy man?" I was a little embarrassed at my mistake. I was at an age when I was very self-conscious. The mysterious man was not unkind, but it was clear that, whatever he was, his position was above mine. I didn't have any experience. And my ignorance was clear to him.

He looked into his tea for a moment, apparently lost in reflection. I thought he wasn't going to answer me, but he did. "I'm just a helper. It's difficult to explain Kwan, but sometimes there are special problems in the world. Sometimes, certain people can help. That's what I have been trained to do. I am called Fox."

I thought about what he had said. My mind was immediately filled with questions, but I wasn't sure how many of them I could ask. What kind of order? What kind of 'special problems' was he talking about? He had a sense of credibility around him, so I immediately trusted him. I could feel that he told the truth. He was a helper. But help with what? At least I knew what to call him now. I began to think of him as Lord Fox.

"So, um... Lord Fox, you solve crimes? Like catching thieves?" I asked nervously.

He smiled patiently. (He appeared to have an ocean of patience.) "I'm not a lord, Kwan. In truth, Fox is not the name my parents gave me." He paused, as if deciding how much to tell me. "After beginning our training, we are given a new name. If we distinguish ourselves, we earn titles, but none of them are 'Lord'." He paused again, seeming to read my mind again. "Before you ask, I do have titles, but knowing them would not be useful to our relationship. At least not at this point. Just call me Fox." He seemed cheerful and humble.

He paused, while I took time to digest what he had said. He wasn't a lord, and I should just call him Fox. But the way he carried himself seemed like a Lord to me. True, I had never met a lord, but I couldn't imagine someone more confident than him. He naturally projected a power that I couldn't ignore, as though he knew all the world's secrets. He gave the clear impression that titles were negligible, and was unwilling to discuss them further. Still, I was curious. What was his title? I put that question away to find out later.

He went on, "Sometimes I solve crimes, Kwan, but they rarely involve the laws of men. Once you have understood human nature, the regular crimes of men are not a challenge to solve. Whatever men plan, it ends up being transparent." I looked confused, so he clarified his statement. "What one man can do, another man can figure out... I tend to reserve my efforts for the 'special' problems in the world." He put emphasis on the word 'special'. Then he waited again.

If he didn't deal with the laws of men, what kind of problems did he deal with? And where did he come from? I wasn't coming up with any answers. I could only make more daughter certainly enjoyed their new wealth and status. Her full name meant 'Golden Flower'. But behind her back, the people of the village called her 'Garlic Flower'. (Her manner did not invite kindness.) After she had walked passed them, showing her unfriendly attitudes, people in the village would joke about having indigestion.

Still, a newly wealthy Old Fong was able to arrange an advantageous marriage for her to a man from the capital city. She was not particularly grateful, but Fong felt pleased. Old Fong's new son-in-law, Ozei, appeared to be quite driven and was from an old family. Their line was not wealthy, and had fallen from its once lofty status. However, the family was very old, and that conveyed a sense of stability families like Fong's wanted.

Ozei was seen in some circles to be rising in the imperial bureaucracy. He expected great success and wealth very soon. He announced it loudly and frequently. Ozei told Fong that he planned to buy a grand manner house for all of them soon.

It was very likely that Fong's grandchildren would have a good life. At least, this is what Old Fong thought. In truth, Fong was trusting by nature, and wanted to believe.

Fong was now well known at the moneychanger's office. His dumpling shop had been open for less than a year, but he was already wealthy. Clearly, his wealth would only grow. He was treated with more respect.

By this time, people had started calling him Big Fong. And while many people changed their attitudes when they got rich, Fong never changed. He still hated carpentry. He still loved cooking. Big Fong's main pleasure was being in his kitchen, making his shiny dumplings. He cooked, periodically taking a break to serve some dumplings and talk with the patrons.

One day, not long after a visit by 'Garlic Flower' and her husband, Big Fong was talking with a few patrons, having just delivered their orders. They were two workmen who were very excited about news they had recently received. According to them, the Emperor had decided to vastly expand the palace in the capital. They had heard the news from their foreman and, as far as they knew, he had never, ever been wrong.

If the workmen were right, the huge project would guarantee a steady flow of work for years. Fong was a simple man, but he was not stupid. He would not normally be called 'ambitious' or 'enterprising', but even he recognized the opportunity.

He saw how attractive the idea was and decided to expand. The capital city was only a half day's travel. Why not open a new shop? His business was too new, he reasoned. He had no business trying to expand! But if he had more dumpling shops, he could do more cooking, he also reasoned. He wrung his hands for a moment, before he finally nodded. He would talk to Father. He had made up his mind. He wanted to do it. Just like that he had decided. Fong had found ambition.

With his mind made up, Fong went about making his plans. He began to envision the new location. New recipes even began to occur to him! His mind was filled with new ideas. He was anxious at the risk he would be taking on. But eventually, his excitement began to outweigh the anxiety.

He went to check exactly how much money he had saved. He routinely went to the local moneychanger and had small coins changed for gold pieces. He then put that gold in a heavy wooden box.

He knew that it had been a substantial amount. The last time he had checked, the box was nearly full. He prepared himself for several hours counting.

When he opened the heavy box, he was shocked to find it empty. It was empty, except for a small piece of paper. In shock, Fong stooped down and picked up the note. It read:

Father,
I have taken the gold. Ozei says we need it. Don't try to find us. You owe this to me. Accept it.
-Flower

Fong sagged into a nearby chair, staggered by what he had read. It took some time for Fong to understand what he was reading. Flower had *stolen?* From *them*??? What was she talking about? What did he owe her?

It's true that they had never been very close, but he had always tried to be a good father to her. How could she do this? She and her husband had departed only a few days ago. They had seemed strange when they left, but Fong did not understand it at the time. He assumed that it was the normal awkwardness of newlyweds. People rarely married for love. It was usually arranged, and so it often took years for deep feelings to develop.

Don't try to find them? She wanted nothing to do with them?? Accept it!?? He could not believe it, much less accept it! When Fong discovered the theft, his wife had been out at the market. She came home and saw him sitting, still slumped in that same chair, holding the piece of paper. Although they had never had a particularly strong emotional connection, a feeling of dread immediately hit her. He pointed to the heavy wooden box, held out the note, and in a quiet tone, said, "Look what she's done."

··

For several days, Old Fong did not come to the shop. He did not talk to his wife. He would barely eat, and customers at the shop agreed that the taste of the dumplings was not up to its usual standards. Only a happy Fong could make the shiny dumplings right.

However, when the patrons saw how dejected Fong was, they did not hold the lapse against him. In general, our culture prioritized the collective. People were expected to be loyal to their family. I certainly was. I would have done anything for my family, and knew that I wouldn't exist without them. All of them, were more important than any one of us. Of course, I write this with the benefit of later education. At that time, I could not have articulated it very clearly.

No one in our village would do anything to cause someone else public embarrassment. Shame, and a person's reputation, were taken very seriously. The villagers had known each other their whole lives. They valued Fong, so they kept any negative opinions to themselves. I assumed that people treated each other the same everywhere.

A few days after Garlic Flower's theft, early one morning, there was a knock at our door. It was Fong's wife. She had come to see Father for advice. Surprised at the visit, Father invited her into his small study and closed the door. Her voice was very loud so I didn't have to put my ear to the door to hear what she was saying. She was worried about Old Fong. She told Father what their daughter and son-in-law had done. I was shocked at the news, but did not show it later. I did not want to shame Fong either.

Father was a man of direct action. After only short consideration, Father made a plan. He and Fong would travel to the capital city. Father had retired from running the police force by that point. Father would become business partners with Fong, and get a location in the capital. Then Fong would devote all of his energies to the new location. Father reasoned that by getting out of the village, and having a new project to focus on, Fong would have an easier time accepting his daughter's betrayal.

Father went to Fong's house and proposed the plan. Fong's wife sat there, quiet at first. Initially, Fong did not want to accept. He felt great despair and shame about his daughter. He was ashamed that his wife had come to Father, without consulting him. Fong's wife looked down, but she had no regrets about her actions.

It was a delicate point of pride, but if Fong was honest with himself, he was glad that she had told Father. Father was Fong's most valuable advisor and oldest friend. He needed help to deal with this foul twist of fortune. Fong was glad that Father knew, and could share his shock and give him advice.

Fong didn't want to take charity from Father. But, as he and Father had been life-long friends, Father brushed the matter aside. Father had a plan.

Fong was afraid that he would fail in a new location. Father patiently addressed each obstacle. After some discussion, Father dismissed these concerns.

Father declared (with a finality Fong needed to hear), that the shame belonged to Fong's daughter and her husband, not Fong. Father was not giving charity, he expected success in return. Everyone knew what a good cook Fong was, so there was no question about his future success.

Still Fong wavered. But eventually, with Father's calm, forceful nature and his wife's vocal agreement, Fong accepted the offer. He was still dejected, but his trust in Father let him follow. Father had a powerful will and when he was determined or excited, it was contagious.

First, they had to train a chef to carry on making dumplings in Fong's absence. I perked up at this. I was interested in learning from Fong. The dumpling shop, and the dramatic developments afterward, were something new in my small world. For a boy who had been stuck in a dull and predictable village-childhood, anything new was exciting.

I think it was because the plan was Father's idea, he suggested they choose me to learn the dumpling recipe. I was surprised to hear Father speak in complimentary terms of me to Fong. Father proudly declared that I was mature and responsible, old enough, and most importantly, to be trusted.

***

Chapter 2

New Ventures

Feeling proud, I started to wake before dawn and was at the restaurant/ Fong's house by sunrise. Fong was a patient teacher. In fact, he was much more patient than Father. And Fong had known me since I was born. He and I were already comfortable with each other.

There was indeed a difference in the way that Fong made dumplings. It wasn't a 'secret ingredient' so much as a 'process'. Fong had been asked his secret several times, but he had just thought it idle praise. At first, he would have told anyone every detail of how he cooked. But not any longer.

In the beginning, he didn't know what made his dumplings special. Only after years of cooking, did he realize the one thing he did differently from other dumpling makers. He began to test the idea, and quickly confirmed it. He explained to me every step, including his special technique. He even demonstrated the difference to me, making me taste the results. After his restaurant became famous, Fong's wife asked him to make the recipe "Top Secret".

She had taken their daughter's theft harder even than Fong had. She was not a friendly person to begin with. But after her daughter's betrayal, she became especially paranoid and suspicious. Fong agreed and made me promise not to tell anyone about his secret dumpling process.

Father also agreed that it was wise to protect their business from competition. But I think Fong mainly enjoyed having a secret. Even though Fong is long dead at the time of this writing, out of respect, I will not disclose his secret.

In short order, I had learned to make the shiny dumplings. According to the plan, I would run Fong's local dumpling shop while Father and Fong travelled off to the capital. Since the restaurant was not unmanageably busy, I would be able to take care of the shop by myself. I found myself looking forward to the responsibility.

Before I felt ready, the time had arrived. In preparation for the journey, Father had bought two horses. Both of them were a dark chestnut brown and heavily muscled from plowing the farmers' fields. Both horses were docile and friendly.

My sister, Cho Clei, immediately loved them. The farmer who had sold the horses to Father had named them. But when Father saw her reaction, he suggested she give the horses new names to fit their new lives. Joyfully, she did. Their names escape my memory.

Father and Fong went to the capital city and their project developed very quickly. Father promised to send messages to us whenever he could. He knew Mother would worry, since he had been present their whole marriage. But she did her best not to show that worry.

There was so much to do. They had to find out first if the construction rumors were true. If they were, they had to find a location to open the shop. They might have to expand the kitchen, like Fong had done with his house. It depended on the available locations and what facilities they included. Father and Fong then had to find suppliers to sell them the food to serve. They had to acquire pots, pans, dishes, furniture… everything. There was so much to do!

Fong could have been overwhelmed by the bustling frenzy of city life. Fortunately for him, Father's force of character calmed Fong (and usually impressed anyone he met). I suspected that Grandfather's martial training was a large part of Father's character.

While they were in the capital city building shop two, I was running Fong's Original Dumpling Shop. Before they left, Father had joked that this little village dumpling shop would someday be famous as the *original* shop. (It was unusual to have Father make jokes.) I was excited at the responsibility. There weren't a tremendous number of customers, but there was a growing group of regulars who came frequently. Some of them came almost every day.

That time in life became a blur to me. I was fully engaged in running the dumpling shop. I took care of the cooking, the accounting, and the upkeep of the shop. When Fong or Father arrived home for visits, I wanted to be prepared to show them my hard work. I woke when it was still dark so I could I arrive at Fong's every day by sunrise. Every day I left after sunset.

The hours were long, but I found myself enjoying them. Fong's wife would have been the obvious choice to replace him if she showed any talent for cooking. She wasn't interested enough though, so that left me. She found a reason to go out every day. She often had not returned by the time I left the shop. I had not remembered her going out so much before.

When I asked Father why she was always gone, Father explained that she now had money to entertain herself. Her daily excursions suited me fine, since she was often in a bad mood.

***

That period of my life was a blur of constant motion. It was punctuated by two types of events. The first was that Father sent letters from the capital. The second was that I began to see Fox on a regular basis.

For the first month, Fox would come into the dumpling shop every few days. He always ate large amounts, and was always ready with a genuine smile, humor, and insightful comments. His visits quickly became the best part of my day. When I was around Fox, I had the feeling that I was a student around a patient and wise teacher. He had information on every subject I could mention.

It was clear that he had travelled extensively, but he was hesitant to talk about his past. His reluctance to talk about his past did not bother me. I was less interested in his past than I was with the many other subjects he knew. I had the feeling that I learned more when he came in to eat than in entire seasons at school. The best part was that Fox did not act superior even though he clearly knew more.

However, every time he appeared, the hum in the air came with him. Every time we talked, I forgot to ask him about the hum in the air. Every time I left, I resolved myself to asking the next time. But then I would forget again. Between the talks with Fox and running the dumpling shop, most of my time was filled.

During one of Fox's visits, the hum in the air was starting to give me a headache. "What is that ringing?" I blurted out. I shook my head, trying to clear the sound. Fox's eyebrows went up and he looked carefully at me.

"What ringing? Are you feeling alright, Kwan?" I looked at him looking at me. I somehow knew that he understood me.

"You know what I'm talking about!" I tried to keep my voice low. "When I get closer to you, I can feel something... a sound... in the air. What IS that??" Fox did not get upset at all. Instead, he leaned in to peer at me and squinted his eyes.

"Can we do an experiment?" Fox reached for his ironwood staff and brought it closer to my head. The charged feeling increased. I winced, and Fox took the staff away.

"That's interesting. You are having a strong reaction. But the reaction isn't to me, it's to Shui." He nodded to the staff. His staff had a name? He paused at my look of confusion and leaned his staff against the wall. "My staff holds a substantial source of energy, Kwan. You are apparently sensitive to it. If you are sensitive to Shui, I wonder..." He trailed off, but quickly started again.

"Anyway, this sensitivity is easy enough to harmonize. An introduction should work well. Just hold still." I realized that I had not known Fox for very long. He was a familiar patron of the dumpling shop, but in truth, he was a stranger to me. For some reason, however, I found myself trusting this strange man.

He murmured something under his breath, and brought the staff over towards me again. As he did, I could have sworn I saw the silver grain in the wood start to glow. Before I could examine the silver grain more carefully, the ringing sound made me wince, then close my eyes and grimace.

The ringing in my ears got louder as the staff approached me. Fox's arm slowly extended the staff and he seemed to be softly mumbling something under his breath. The hair on my arms was standing up and a feeling like lightning filled my body. My whole body was getting warmer, and I felt like jumping up and running around.

But then the staff touched my forehead, above my left eye. Several things happened at once. My head instantly cleared, the 'noise' immediately stopped, and the hair on my arms all lay back down.

After the 'noise' from before, the quiet was almost a shock. I looked at Fox as he withdrew the staff. He was squinting his eyes at me again. I felt like I was waking up. And I felt wonderful. The only sounds I could hear were the loud chewing and slurping of the family. At length, after peering into my eyes, his face relaxed into a smile. "Feeling better?"

***

News soon came from Father. His first letter confirmed that the Emperor was planning large constructions; a series of pavilions, gardens, and stables. This had been the biggest question, the 'gamble' as far as Father was concerned. In his letter, he admitted that he had been anxious about this key piece of information. He would only have lost out on the price of the two horses, but Father actually seemed excited. He had *wanted* the news to be true. He expected this to be the beginning of a 'dynasty of dumplings'.

According to him, the rest of the process would be straightforward. Father had found and secured a good location for the restaurant, with a kitchen they would not have to expand. He asked about the family and the dumpling shop. Mother wrote a letter back to him, and the days fell into routine.

After a few weeks, they had launched the second of Fong's dumpling shops. After arranging the location, Father quickly arranged for furniture, dishes, teapots, and food supplies. He arranged everything a dumpling restaurant would need. The tone of Father's next letter was cheerful. He seemed to be enjoying decorating the new restaurant. The original shop, where I was working, had almost no decorations. I remembered hearing about Father's interest in art when he was young. I wondered if decorating the new restaurant appealed to his artistic side. (Though I had never seen this side of him, I liked the idea that Father had it.)

A few weeks later, a letter arrived from Father. It proclaimed that the new shop was a success. The success was quick and profound. Father had found a location that was on the main road to the Imperial palace. He had Fong make free dumplings early every morning. They made small packages that they could give out to the workers in the mornings. The steady stream of foot traffic had taken the free samples without thanks.

But, without fail, every worker who had tasted Fong's dumplings, returned at some point during that week. They became very busy, and had to get rid of the tables Father had bought. There was only room to stand and eat your dumplings. Despite the crowd, none of the diners seemed to mind. They appreciated that it was so crowded. It only made sense, after all. Fong's dumplings were the best. Very quickly, the dumpling shop had made a name for itself.

Father's plan had worked almost too well. His goal was to start a robust lunch business. But the free morning samples had made many of the workers associate mornings, work, and dumplings. So almost immediately, they had a robust morning-dumpling trade too. Soon, they were so busy that he and Fong had to hire a full staff. Father determined reasonable prices for the dumplings, but the materials to make dumplings were inexpensive. Soon they were making more money than they could believe.

In fact, it was such a success that they were already half-joking about opening a third location. Mother laughed at the idea and said, "When your father gets excited…" She was not surprised.

The only limit to their success was how many dumplings Fong could make. No matter how many dumplings he could make, they could always sell more. It was a problem they wanted to have. In short, he needed to share the 'secret shiny dumpling process'. Fong had developed some trust with one particular worker at the new dumpling shop. He expected to eventually be able to train the worker in the 'Top Secret shiny technique'. Father agreed. A replacement chef was needed, and he agreed on the worker Fong chose.

Word of Fong's skill spread very quickly. Soon, his name was known all over the capital. Occasionally, people from the big city would even come to our local dumpling shop and ask me if this was where Fong started. They had made a pilgrimage to the birthplace of the 'shiny dumpling'! They talked about how much they loved his food and promised to return one day. It seemed strange to me, but Fong's dumplings were just that delicious. They inspired loyalty and enthusiasm, bordering on fanaticism.

His shiny dumplings became even more well-known than Fong himself. The first location in the capital city was a large building that had been an inn. Father described the place very thoroughly. There was a large space downstairs with the kitchen, and rooms upstairs for Father and Fong.

In the next letter from Father, he told of a problem. The arrangements Father had made for food turned out not to be acceptable. A bad shipment had arrived. The meat was not very fresh, and the vegetables were wilted. A change needed to be made. They closed the shop for a few days to solve the problem. The workers complained about the shop closing, but neither Father nor Fong would compromise on quality.

Father and Fong had taken several days to wander through the markets. It did not take them long to identify where the best meat and produce were to be had. Father made new arrangements and soon they were back in business.

The business flourished as no one could have expected. Fong's shiny dumplings were so popular that people lined up early every day, from sunrise to mid-afternoon, to buy them. The dumpling shop was the most talked about place in the capital. 'It's good like shiny dumplings!' the people would say. In his letters, Father joked that 'shiny' was becoming synonymous with 'good'.

Quickly, Father and Fong were making a fortune. And though they were busy, Father made time to write every few days.

Occasionally Fong sent me a letter too. He asked after the shop whenever he wrote. He asked about the dumplings every chance he got. Occasionally he asked about his wife. I assumed that he was sending her letters too.

He never, ever mentioned his daughter. He must still be dwelling on her, but he never asked if I had heard anything from her. I hadn't, but he never asked. Still, the tone of the few letters he sent me, showed that he was improving and becoming cheerful again.

My conversations with Fox continued too. He sometimes gave me riddles to test me. He said that I was cleverer than the average village boy. He seemed so very different from the rest of the people in the village. He was interesting and had an open mind. During these conversations, I realized again that I would never be like the other men (in our village) who came before me. In our village, the people thought in small terms and were slow to take to new ideas. But Fox played with new ideas like a child plays with toys. He seemed open to talk about anything. I remember them as conversations, but in reality, I was both the cook and the waiter, so when it was busy, I didn't have very much time to talk.

Still, I was becoming steadily more and more impressed with Fox. He was different and impressive in so many ways that I wanted to be like him. I doubted that I would ever know as much as him, but I wanted to learn. Getting an educated visitor was unusual in a small village like mine. And Fox seemed beyond educated to me. His mind was like a library of knowledge and experience.

During that first trip, Father was gone for three months. He had left in the autumn, but did not return until the end of the year. The new business still needed him, but Mother had been anxious to see him again. In truth, we all wanted to see him.

In his last few letters, Father had described how Fong had been moving past Garlic Flower's betrayal. He was excited opening the new shop. The whole process distracted Fong, as Father hoped it would. The immediate success of the shop had given Fong back the confidence, (and the money that was stolen).

Being responsible for their capital dumpling shop was something new, and I could imagine Fong getting overwhelmed. I only thought of Fong as an excellent cook. I wondered if dealing with a busy shop in the capital might be too much for him. But Father wrote that Fong was well on his way to recovering from his daughter's actions, and had even begun to grow more assertive. Father had been giving him lessons. I thought back to Fong's letters and could see the evidence of Fong's revival. According to Father, he was healing and growing into a more capable Fong.

Two weeks later, a letter arrived from Fong. He wrote that he was training his replacement chef and would come home for a visit soon. Father had chosen the replacement, judging that he had the right character to be trusted. Neither Fong nor Father wanted to stay in the capital. But until that chef was trained, Fong would need to be at the new shop.

With horses to ride, the distance between our village and the capital was not an obstacle to visiting. Father wrote that Fong was getting tired, and needed to rest. The new chef had completed his training with Fong. Now there were three of us who could make the shiny dumplings. Father was sending him back to the village, and they would take turns overseeing the new shop.

A few days later, Fong returned home. He seemed somehow older to me. The challenges of being in the big city seemed to have aged him. However, he no longer seemed sad. He stayed long enough to check on the dumpling shop, see his wife, and sleep for a few days. Then, after only two weeks, Fong rode back to the city, so Father could come home.

***

When Father returned, it was a joyful day. It was early afternoon, not long after lunch. He had left Fong at sunrise to see us earlier. According to him, Fong was ready for this, so Father did not worry.

When Father had first left the village, he and Fong had disappeared down the road, each on one of the chestnut horses. When Father returned I was surprised to see two horses, but only one rider. Then I noticed that one of the animals was not actually a horse. Father had ridden up to the house on the large brown horse that he originally rode. But behind the horse was a gray and white mule, heavily packed. Father had brought many presents. He had brought many comforts from the big city for our home. (More comforts, in fact than our little house could accommodate.) He had brought clothes for mother. He had brought a knife for me. Like all the other boys in my village, I was excited about a knife of my own. He also informed me that, since I was needed at Fong's original dumpling shop, I might need to wait until next year's Imperial examinations so I could become a policeman. I was flooded with relief at Father's decision.

For my little sister, Father had brought a doll that looked almost exactly like her. We all marveled at the similarities. The doll's straight black hair was cut in the same style as my sister. The features were similar. The doll was wearing a long, gray tunic, and that day, my sister was also wearing a long, gray tunic. It was uncanny. Cho Clei loved the doll on first sight, and named her Zao Clei.

Father later told us about the persuasive peddler who had sold him the doll. He and Fong were walking back from the market when a wild-looking, unkempt man rushed out into the street to stop them. The man only had three teeth left, but they were gold. He looked like he had never bathed or used a comb before. His pants and his tunic were in tatters. His hair stuck out in all directions and he was laughing hysterically.

When Father recounted the story to us, he said the wild-looking man seemed crazy. Father told him to get away, but the man wouldn't budge. Only when Father threatened to beat him with his fists, did the man stop laughing and get to his point.

The man claimed to be a homeless mystic. (But father admitted it was strange that a 'homeless mystic' would have gold teeth.) He was a doll-maker, and made only one doll each month. He claimed that he knew, in advance, who would buy the doll. He claimed that they were magically imbued with energy and made for specific children. Father had lost patience, and would have chased the man away, but the wild-looking man pulled out the doll. As I said, the doll looked exactly like Cho Clei. The man said it was a powerful talisman. He promised it would protect the child while her father was away.

Father had no intention of buying the doll. But the mystic had known that Father had a daughter at home. And since the doll so closely resembled my sister, Father relented and listened to the beggar. It was too much to be a coincidence. Maybe it was good fortune, disguised as a dirty beggar? So, in a rare moment of spontaneity, Father bought the doll.

***

On the day that Father had returned, he announced that we would be building a new house. It was no secret in our family that Mother wanted a bigger house. She and Father were always debating whether or not it was necessary. Father said that Mother had been right, and we did need a bigger house. With the wealth that came from the dumpling shops' success, they would finally build a new place to live.

As Fox and I were later able to piece together, it was a series of unfortunate errors that unfolded. The tragedy of errors started with one misstep, followed by another and another. The trouble started when Mother mentioned that since they were going to be building a new house, we would certainly use a Compass Master.

A Compass Master is often hired by a person or family wishing to consult nature before setting up a building. The people who did this wanted to be in harmony with the land. They used a system to calculate where to build a new construction, so that the flow of favorable energy is maximized. A Compass Master had tools that let them read the energy of a place, or so they said. Father considered their entire science, at best, as mere superstition. At worst, he thought it was a confidence scheme to trick gullible people.

Also, even though our family now had money, Father was still frugal. He also thought the way Grandfather had taught him to think- like a warrior. He believed what he could see. Anything else, gave him doubt.

He thought a Compass Master was a waste of money. "Why waste money on wishful thinking?" Father had said one night. They had been going back and forth after dinner.

I had come home from closing Fong's dumpling shop. After I got home, I went to the bowl in the kitchen and washed my hands, made a plate of food, and brought it out to the main room. I had found my parents still sitting at the table. My sister had cleared the dinner and was sitting, reading in the corner, ignoring my parents. Being only seven, she had to practice reading every night after dinner.

"Why waste money on wishful thinking?" Father repeated, furrowing his brow and spreading his hands. "What about all the generations that had successful and long lives before they used that compass superstition? The people of the past proved that a family could have wonderful lives without indulging in any wishful thinking!"

I remember Mother replying that in the past, it was all luck that determined your life. "It isn't wishful thinking, Shao. Luck falls like rain," she had said. "Sometimes it falls here, sometimes there. Now we have a chance to build a house in a spot of *guaranteed* luck! What could be a better use of money?"

Eventually, she cast her eyes down and quietly said, "I believe. Isn't that enough? You used to believe and have an open mind, Shao. Now you only believe what you can see. So you only can see what you already believe." I think Father would have been offended, if not for the disappointment and sadness in Mother's voice.

They talked into the night. Each one kept repeating their same arguments. But I was always aware that they held respect for each other. Even though they 'argued', their tenderness was apparent. They let me watch them, so I watched. I found their discussion interesting, but the outcome was never really in doubt. Father always let Mother have her way. Or Mother made Father give in. I was difficult to tell the difference.

According to Mother, Father used to be a carefree spirit that longed only to paint and make art. Grandfather, a member of an outlawed warrior class, argued those dreams out of Father. Even though we weren't allowed to practice war anymore, Father was absolutely not allowed to be an artist. (Unless it was a martial artist!) He stopped making art. Mother didn't blame him, Father or Grandfather though. She could only imagine how hard it had been growing up in a family that had to break *all* of its traditions. Father became hard, in response. In fact, according to Mother, Father eventually stopped thinking in abstract terms.

Instead, Father took on a simple but hard view of life. He was strong and disciplined, but always kind to Cho Clei and me. But as I got older I noticed that he was disdainful of other belief systems if they did not seem practical enough. At the time, I did not understand that Father was conflicted about the path he took in life. He had been a budding artist at one time, but now, just as Mother had said, he only believed in what he saw.

So, when he decided to build the new house, Father was fully aware that people (if they could afford it) consulted a Compass Master before building. Of course, Compass Masters were paid for their calculations. Since he didn't believe in their 'science' to begin with, Father considered it waste of money to worry too much about nature's energy. If it were only up to Father, we would not have the benefit of an expert telling him the best place to build a house.

However, Mother knew Father well. She knew, in advance, that Father would want to skip this step. She argued that it was crucial to follow all precautions to guarantee the best future for our family. Father thought that she was just being superstitious, but, in the end, Mother got her way. He finally agreed to find 'a compass master'. As I said, the outcome was never really in doubt.

Immediately, once Father had agreed, a practical obstacle came up. When a town is being built, it is common to have a Compass Master at hand. They would be summoned for the occasion, analyze the landscape of the town, and make a general plan for all of the buildings. But after a village construction was complete, they would move on. Father had never heard of how to locate a compass master when a single house was being built. People did it, but Father had no experience with the issue.

As I have written, this is what Fox and I have been able to learn about the events that led up to our first journey. At first, it was clear that Father was not very serious about finding a good Compass Master. It was clear because he wrote to Fong to ask about finding one.

Normally, Fong was the one coming to Father to ask advice, not the other way around. Fong wrote back and promised that he would find one, or at least find out how to get one. It wasn't that Fong was incompetent. Far from it, he was good when clearly given direct tasks. But he was, at heart, a simple man. He wanted happiness and harmony. His virtues were simple loyalty, a hard working spirit, and a good character.

Fong came home the following week when Father returned to the city to oversee the shop.

***

At this point, several things happened without Father knowing. The first thing was that Fong's daughter, Garlic Flower, returned. She brought back the gold that she had taken. She begged for forgiveness, and after enduring Fong's wife's shouting and Fong's stony silence, the daughter was allowed to stay. Fong, being very soft-hearted, forgave her a few days later.

Fong, however, knew that Father would never trust her, no matter what he said. Once a person had shown they could betray trust, Father never forgot. He might forgive, but he never forgot.

So Fong knew to hide his daughter's return from Father. For a man that did not naturally have guile, Fong did a remarkable job of it. Father didn't know she came back. I would not have known either, but one morning I saw her.

I had come to the shop to open it as usual. Fong let me in when I arrived. I glimpsed a feminine figure peeking out from the back room. I immediately recognized Garlic Flower and stiffened in surprise. She quickly disappeared from view, but I had seen her.

Fong found me a moment later, holding a carton of eggs in the dark hallway. He saw the shocked look on my face and immediately confessed. He knew that I would not lie if Father asked me directly, but he nervously pleaded with me not to tell Father *unless* he asked.

It seemed harmless to me, at the time. I remembered all of the times when I was very young that Fong was always a safe and understanding place for me. Fong had always been a kind uncle to me. I respected him, so I agreed.

Garlic Flower had made many claims when she returned. Among other things, she claimed that she had studied to become a Compass Master. (Later, I found out that she had not been away long enough for that to be true.) She claimed to be first in her class. She talked about how she had been extensively trained to sense the way *all* energy flowed in *all* places *all* of the time. She claimed that although it usually took several years to become a Compass Master, she was such an amazingly exceptional student that she finished in a matter of months. She even had the Official Seal of a Grand Compass Master. She had shown it to him. She kept it in a silk pouch, Fong said.

Since I knew, Fong had begun to confide in me and tell me the claims Garlic Flower was making. He believed her. Or, I felt, he desperately *wanted* to believe her. To me, Fong often sounded like he was trying to convince himself about her.

Even though I was only a teenager, I doubted her claims. But I was still a boy at that point. I figured that it wasn't my business. Not really, not unless something put Father, or our family, or the dumpling shop at risk. So, I stayed quiet, keeping Fong's secret.

Eventually, Fong believed his daughter enough that he decided to help her. Father had put Fong in a position where he could help his daughter. He could arrange for his daughter to be Father's Compass Master as our house was built.

This was largely possible because the owner of the house rarely met the Compass Master until the house was finished. Before that, the builder was usually the only one who met with the Compass Master. Fong understood how little Father thought of Garlic Flower. So Fong and Garlic Flower made a plan. To Fong, the goal was to sneak his daughter into an opportunity to show her immense talent, and redeem herself.

On more than one occasion, I heard the younger carpenters say that 'superstitions are for old chickens.' They thought that most of the 'old ways' were nonsense. In the old times, everyone thought in terms of gods, and energy, and fortune. Now, people took much less on faith. It was a strange time, and the 'old ways' were being lost.

The process of building a house during my youth was this: first, the Compass Master looked at available lands and offered three choices. The Compass Master sometimes accompanied the Owner to the prospective locations. Once the owner chose the land, a builder then made the architectural plan for the house. Then that plan was submitted to the Compass Master. The Compass Master then offered corrections to the plan, and the carpenters proceeded to build it. The Head Builder oversaw the whole construction. When the building was complete, the owner, the Compass Master, and the builder would meet to review the final construction.

Fong then wrote to Father to tell that he had arranged for a Compass Master for our new house. Father was pleased (or more accurately, Mother was pleased.) and the process began. In truth, only Garlic Flower knew the depths of her own lies.

However, I had known Fong my whole life. I knew that he might be weak, but he was good and loyal. I also knew that Fong was a simple man. So, in my mind, because Fong was attached to the deception, it couldn't go very deep. Thinking up a devious plan was impossible for the man I knew. Later, discussing it, even Fox, who had only met Fong a few times, doubted that Fong was involved with what followed.

Fox and I never found out where the girl came from, but Garlic Flower soon had an 'assistant'. Fox expected that the assistant and Garlic Flower were not the masterminds of this plot, but rather, they were tools. The assistant appeared one morning not long after Fong had decided to help. Garlic Flower had an accomplice.

The 'assistant', a young woman named Yi, would pretend to be the Compass Master. Since Father did not believe in their science to begin with, they imagined it would be easy to trick him. Fong reasoned that only people who already believed in compass science would ask difficult questions. Also, Father had no idea of their deception.

Fong participated in the deception because his daughter would 'authentically' apply Compass Science for Father's house. He imagined they were only deceiving Father about the identity of the legitimate Compass Master.

Fox suspected that Garlic Flower had just picked the potential locations at random. He also informed me afterwards that no one ever achieved Grand Compass Master status before the age of sixty. Because of this, we could be certain that she had come across the seal by some dishonest means. With only that stolen seal and a clever plan, Garlic Flower and Yi set out to deceive father.

What follows is the account that Mother gave me. (I was making shiny dumplings when the whole business began.) Fong had told Father and Mother that the Compass Master would meet them one morning. On the appointed morning, Yi arrived at our house. She was only a dozen years older than I was, but she carried herself like an old woman. Over tea, she told Mother and Father that she had selected three properties where the energy would be positive for our family. I can picture Mother nodding in agreement the whole time, while Father crossed his arms and waited, clearly impatient to be done. Then they departed to view the sites. Father had brought three horses for just this occasion. Our next house was going to have a small stable, and Father was well on his way to filling it.

Mother wanted to see all three properties. But Father didn't. He seemed to take a dislike to Yi immediately, treating her with cold formality. According to Mother, because Father was not enjoying the process, he just picked the first one, so he could be done with it. According to Mother later, she got a bad feeling from the place, but 'Assistant Compass Master Yi' insisted that the land was perfect, so she kept silent. Mother also knew that the only reason Father was going along with this was to make her happy.

As for the land, it was on the outskirts of the village. Father liked the idea of already being established when the town grew out to meet them. While there was a central flat area where a house could be built, that land was surrounded by a dark forest that ran the length of the horizon. The forest was like a large hand, reaching out to enclose the flat 'building' space. There was also a deep, rock-strewn ravine some little ways into the forest.

Father was a decisive man. And he wanted to be done with the consultation. Those two factors led to a speedy decision on what, in retrospect, was a large matter. After only a cursory look at the land, Father agreed on that first place. He declared that he liked the land and they had found the location. He said that it was even handsome, in a dark and dramatic way.

He told 'Compass Master Yi' to have the builder start drawing up the plans. She must have been very pleased that Father had fallen for their ploy. It was the beginning of spring when Father gave Yi that initial approval.

Later that spring, as the house was being built, I asked Mother more about why she didn't like where Father had chosen. She said that it was the dark woods in the distance behind the house. She mentioned it to Father, but he thought that it was just her being nervous. Uncharacteristically, Mother doubted her feelings and didn't insist, so the process continued. Garlic Flower and Yi continued with their plan.

They found a builder in town and claimed, this time, that Yi was the 'assistant' to the Compass Master. She told the builder that contacting Fong's wife would be most direct way to reach the Compass Master. Living in the same village, the builder knew Fong, but only as a spectacularly gifted chef. He didn't actually know Fong's wife, but knowing Fong was enough.

He hadn't thought of Fong as having those kind of connections, but the builder believed her. He had no reason not to. Father was known in town. Father and Fong being friends was also well known in the village. So, the builder assumed that Yi's story was legitimate. The builder, Wei-Yon Yon, started on a design.

As Father had directed, Wei-Yon's plan called for a large house and a few smaller buildings. The entire grounds of the house would be walled-in. In the center of the walled-in area was a large open garden. The garden was nearly as large as the house, taking almost half of the enclosed space. The house itself would consist of three stories. The first floor would contain the kitchen and common spaces. The second floor would contain 3 large bedrooms for me, my sister, and a guest. The top floor would all be rooms for Mother and Father.

When he completed the design, Wei-Yon had the plan sent to Fong's wife, who in turn passed them to her daughter. Garlic Flower likely pretended to do some calculations, and finally wrote her approval on the plan. The name she signed was small and sloppy. The brushstrokes were erratic and she covered them with several unnecessary seals. Fox told me later about seeing a copy of the house plan. He said it showed clumsy attempts to hide her identity.

Regardless, Fong felt like he had witnessed the genuine application of Compass science, and Garlic Flower would be able to continue to use her father. His goodwill was necessary for their plan to work. She lied to her father so he would continue to hide her plot. It seems clear to us that Fong was their tool. It may sound cynical, but Fox and I agreed that our theory seems most likely.

Yi brought the 'approved' plan back to Wei-Yon Yon, and the builder put the process in motion. So far, Garlic Flower and Yi had been successful in their plan.

It wasn't my decision. But in my opinion, the land Father chose seemed nice enough. It was filled with trees, and I enjoyed being out in nature. One hundred paces behind the house was a rocky ravine. Its walls were steep and there was a small stream at the bottom of it. The area around the house was so dense with foliage that few people ever wandered there. So even though we were only at the outskirts of the village, it felt like the house was remote.

Some people in the village thought the woods were dark and somehow forbidding, but Father didn't mind. To Mother, the woods looked sinister and ominous. But Father instead called them 'mysterious and handsome'.

Father would distract my sister whenever she called the forest 'scary'. Since she had received the doll from Father, Cho Clei always carried her doll. It was with her wherever she went. She slept with it too. They were inseparable.

Soon we took strength and confidence from Father's certainty. If he was not scared, we would not be scared. With Father's part done, it was now up to the builder, Wei-Yon. Father returned to the capital to focus on the new dumpling shop. One week later, Fong returned. They continued this pattern, taking turns being home in the village, then off in the capital. Throughout that spring the tradesmen worked to build the house.

It was to be the same basic layout as our present house, only bigger, and with a large garden. The outside was stone and wood. All rooms were arranged around the central garden. There were four bedrooms; one for my parents, one for me, one for my little sister, and one for when Grandma Lan came to visit. There was a kitchen and separate rooms for eating and sitting.

Dark wood and bright screens would make the house look very warm and inviting. Father had brought decorations home from the capital. He was clearly planning where every new piece would go. Because he had real artistic talent, Father's decoration ideas were always in good taste.

We visited during construction. Mother liked to see the progress. As the house took shape, my sister and I explored the grounds and got to know the area. We saw several dead birds when we were walking, but disregarded it as part of natural life in the deep woods. Other than the occasional carcass, the land looked typical.

We went to the ravine and looked down at the stream. My sister imagined she saw something move and called, "Come out!" But I couldn't see anything. She started forward aggressively to confront whatever she had imagined, which was very unlike her normal behavior. She was not a timid girl, but she had never been confrontational either.

No sound or movement responded to her call. The only answer was the pleasant sound of the stream winding its way through the ravine. The riverbed, made of mud, rocks, and dead sticks, extended far to either side of the stream.

As far as I could tell, the landscape looked normal but I had an odd feeling. I looked around again, slowly and carefully, but didn't see anything unusual. Still disquieted, I collected my sister (and her doll) and we headed back.

The new house was a half of an hour's walk from our old house, so Mother, Cho Clei, and I would often go to look at the house and come back later that same day. Each time he returned home, Father seemed pleased with the progress. Before long, the house would be complete. My mother was collecting our belongings and packing them away. Soon the new house would be complete and we would be ready to move.

I did notice something unusual as the house was taking shape. Whenever Fong came back to the village, he acted strangely. If a person did not know him well, they probably would not have been able to see the change. But I could. Fong had been a fixture in my life since I was born. I knew his character and mannerisms very well.

On reflection, I decided that Fong was probably feeling guilty. Fong was part of a plan to deceive Father, his life-long friend. He knew about Garlic Flower and Yi but didn't say anything. This guilt often showed itself by Fong being nervous and distracted. Father probably noticed the difference in Fong, but likely attributed it to the stress of multiple businesses and memories of his daughter's betrayal. That was my theory, at least. As soon as Fong left to return to the capital, the thought left my mind.

Soon, Father had returned back home. The day had come and the movers came to help carry all of our things to the new house. I had been willing to move our things, but Father had made other plans. With new wealth from the capital dumpling shop, Father decided to hire workers to carry our belongings.

The day had a rough start though. Cho Clei, hurrying to look for something, knocked a cup off of the table after the morning meal. When it hit the floor, the cup shattered. I jumped at the sound. Father was surprised, and frowned as he looked down at the pieces of the cup. Cho Clei was very startled, and spun around when she heard the sound. Her surprised expression immediately gave way to tears.

Mother was concerned about my little sister, watching her carefully. I could see it on Mother's face. Cho Clei had been acting strangely and was unusually irritable. She was either quiet and sulking or complaining or aggressive these days. All of which were unlike her.

Father was busy directing the hired men. He directed all of us, instructing where to put everything. He was assertive, but none of the hired men seemed to think he was overbearing. I clearly saw how Grandfather's training had made him a natural leader. Or maybe people preferred being told what to do? Regardless, our belongings were brought to our new home.

***

The clouds had slowly been moving in for two days. That day, they became darker, and darker, going from dark blue, to purple, to almost black. The sky was a sickly greenish yellow, filled with dark purple/black storm clouds.

Shortly after lunch, several people in town came in to eat. Every single diner remarked (around mouthfuls of dumplings) that it looked like it was going to be a fierce storm. I had to agree. I could *feel* the storm coming. Apparently, everyone could.

It was late afternoon when I made the decision to close up the dumpling shop. The sky was clearly preparing for a severe storm. It was going to rain and, since the small flow of customers had tapered off to nothing, I decided to go home early. I wouldn't normally leave early, but I felt like the storm made for an exception to the rule.

Father was off in the capital city with Fong. He had left three weeks ago. I knew that Mother would want help managing the house if it turned into a big storm. She had gotten used to making due when Father was in the capital, but having a strong son around was always useful. I certainly wanted to work as hard as I could for Fong, but my feelings of responsibility to Mother were greater.

Fong's wife was nowhere to be seen, so I went through the same closing process that I did every night. As I was cleaning the floor, the rain began to fall. It started as a mist that grew until it was a steady shower. I remember enjoying that the rain made a soft, calming 'sshhh' sound as I cleaned up.

When I was done, I dashed out into the light rain and hurried home. The street had gone from dusty to muddy and was spotted with the beginnings of puddles. I passed close to houses whenever possible, moving under the eaves, trying to stay out of the rain.

The way to our new house was different from my old way home. There was a fork in the path, and I had always taken the right way to get to our 'old' house. I remember that it struck me as strange that my way home now was on the left. The rain soaked through my shirts. And even though it was not cold, a shiver ran through me. I was impatient to get home. The new way was longer and crossed a small bridge on its tortuous path.

As I looked ahead, I saw a tall, fat figure on the little bridge. I recognized him, even from a distance. Fox was looking up at the sky, but otherwise stood unmoving. Then he bent down to the ground and, a moment later, stood again and tilted his head back. I ran up, and called to him in greeting, but he didn't answer. I was only a few paces from him before he realized I was there. He was holding something flat and metal in his hand. He turned to me in mild surprise. The rain was dripping in rivulets down his wide face. He wore a vague look of anger. "Is everything ok, Fox?

Instead of answering, he turned and looked down at the ground. He dropped what was in his hand. It landed, clattering unceremoniously to the ground. It was awkward feeling a bad mood from Fox. At a loss for words, I stared down at what he had dropped. At his feet, appeared to be two connected pieces of metal. One piece was a golden ring, large enough for a big man to fit around his wrist. The flat ring had a straight spike running through the center of it. A second piece of metal, shaped like a star was mounted in the center of the ring. The star and the surrounding ring were connected by the spike that ran through both of them.

He bent down and stared at the metal he had just thrown down. He picked them up and again dropped them. Again, they fell to the ground. He shook his head and scooped the metal back up.

He stood and turned back again to look up at the sky. Fox closed his eyes like he was praying, but almost immediately opened his eyes. He looked like he had just been rudely insulted. I stood there, puzzled, staring at him.

He must have been standing there for some time. He was even wetter than I was. Small rivulets of water ran down his wide face, but he didn't seem to notice them. He squinted up through the mist, muttering to himself. I thought that I heard him mumble the words, "… element twisted…but… why?"

I was beginning to think he didn't even know I was there. But then Fox spoke. He did not look at me as he warned, "Get home, Kwan. Now." He said it quietly, but I nodded instantly and did not ask any more questions. Relieved at being dismissed, I rushed past him and continued my trip home. I was already soaked, and I didn't want to be out there any longer than necessary. But even if I wanted to stay out or ask questions, Fox's tone brooked no argument. Fox had always been calm and cheerful. But now he seemed disturbed and somewhat… angry.

Fox normally gave the impression that he was relaxed. Both Father and Fox had a masterful quality, but it was based on different characteristics. Fox gave me the feeling that he was calm and in control because he always understood his surroundings. He was knowledgeable and cheerful, but even his cheerfulness was based on having a deep understanding of everything happening around him.

Father's power came from a different place. Father had great force of will. Father could move a mountain if he put his will against it. So Father being masterful came from confidence in himself, not from having more information.

They were very different but they both seemed powerful to me. They both inspired me. Some part of mind saw that Fox was joining my father in becoming a role model for me.

When I got home that afternoon, my sister was playing with the doll that Father had brought her. She was reading to the doll, and pausing occasionally to talk about what they read. She would pause as though listening to the doll's response.

Cho Clei was reading a children's book Mother had read to me when I was little. As I passed her, I patted my sister on the head. Cho Clei looked up at me with a serious expression and held out the doll to me. I smiled and patted the doll's head too. Cho Clei went back to reading.

Mother was cooking, and smiled up at me as I came in. Then she noticed I was dripping water onto the floor and frowned. She sent me off to wash and change into dry clothes while she finished cooking. The storm was closer and darker than before.

I washed quickly, ate, and started walking around the house. I tried to do the same activities that Father would have, like making sure the window shutters were closed and in good order. They were in good condition, being new, but checking them made me feel useful. After that, Mother made tea and we all sat together. Mother and Cho Clei read. I listened to them and the steadily increasing sound of rain.

In my memory, the darkness fell quickly that night. The sun had not been visible all day. But, as night approached, the sky quickly darkened to the same purple black as the storm clouds. The sun had seemed to hurry away in the last hour before setting.

As soon as the light faded, the rainfall became heavier and heavier. It had started as a steady 'ssshhhhh' sound in the background, but quickly became louder. Soon, it was raining harder than I had ever seen. But I imagined that rain this heavy could not go on for long. I checked the windows and doors a few more times, as I knew Father would have done.

Even with lantern candles lit, the room held an oppressive feeling. We had eaten dinner, and should be relaxed, but both Cho Clei and I were somehow nervous. The sound of the rain got progressively heavier, and gave no signs of losing strength. There were occasional flashes of lightning and booms of thunder, followed by brightness that momentarily lit the sky like midday. It sounded like 'nature' itself was somehow upset and the storm was getting closer.

Cho Clei got frightened by one particularly large clap of thunder and scooted closer to Mother. Mother placed an arm around her and continued reading. After a while, Mother said that it was time for my sister to go to bed.

Cho Clei came over to me. I put my hands on her shoulders. I was close to my sister and, according to my parents' encouragement, had quickly taken to the 'big brother' role. She always came to say good night before bed.

While I was big for my age and physically strong, my sister had an entirely different type of build. She was thin and small for her age. Her shoulders felt small and fragile to me. I felt a strong protective impulse. I patted her head like Father did and told her to sleep well.

Cho Clei seemed worried somehow. I was going to ask her what was wrong, but Mother repeated that it was time to sleep. Cho Clei gave me a single glance over her shoulder as she and Mother disappeared into the hallway. I suddenly stood, feeling that I was missing something important. But they were gone. I shook my head to clear it, and sat down.

I had planned to stay up after dinner. In my mind, I had some vague plans to do something interesting. It was unusual for me to close the shop early, so I wanted to make use of the extra 'free time'. But as I listened to the rain, I quickly became drowsy. I was working now, and it had been a long day. Suddenly sleepy, I couldn't remember what I had wanted to do.

Sleep seemed like the only good idea. Even the startling thunder and lightning did little to fight the overwhelming urge I had to sleep. I remember having the strange sensation of needing to find my bed before sleep took me. It felt like, if I didn't, I could fall asleep sitting there.

I stumbled down the hall to my room and lay on the bed roll. I lay there listening to the growing storm, surrendering myself to the overwhelming need for sleep. The lightning and thunder got closer, but seemed to be muted. I felt sleepier and sleepier until I could barely even hear the thunder. My consciousness faded, the thunder fell away and sleep took me.

Chapter 3

The Disappearance

My dreams were troubled that night. They were filled with fleeting impressions of shadows. One shadow was larger than the others. That shadow radiated menace and, in my dreams, I was terrified. I tried to shrink away from it, but I was somehow trapped. I tried to run, but I couldn't move. It felt like a heavy weight had pinned me down.

The strangest part of all happened when I woke up. My heart was hammering in my chest. I was panting, like I had just run a long way. And while the moments before sleep are filled with some confusion as the mind gets oriented for the day, I saw something I couldn't understand.

I clearly saw symbols written in the air, floating above me. They were written in a glowing red ink that seemed to burn like a thin trail of fire. I could not recognize any of the writing, but it was clearly some kind of language. The symbols disappeared after a few seconds, burning out. It was fleeing my mind by the time I stood. I told myself it was just my imagination. I shook my head and did not think of it again.

As I started my day, the sky was just lightening. I got up at my usual time, before sunrise and dressed quickly. I would eat breakfast at the dumpling shop. As was my habit, I tried to leave the house quietly so that Mother and Cho Clei could stay asleep a while longer. Once I got to the door, I slipped on my shoes and started the walk to Fong's.

There was still a light rain falling when I set out. The morning was cool from the night's heavy rain. Although I barely got damp, the light morning rain gave me a chill almost immediately. On my walk, the sky went from a dark purple to a light gray. I did not see anyone on the way to the dumpling shop.

When I opened the door, and walked into Fong's house, I had an uneasy feeling. I disregarded the feeling as a remnant of poor sleep. It was time to work. I knew the process and followed it... By that point, operating Fong's dumpling shop was a routine for me. I set my lantern on the counter and started to make the dough.

***

It was later in the morning when Mother came into the shop, frantic that she couldn't find Cho Clei. My little sister had disappeared. She hadn't been in the house when Mother woke up. Immediately, like Mother, I began to worry. I knew that Father would have been logical as he processed the problem. So, I tried to be logical, but I could only come up with obvious ideas. Father was a mountain of stability, but I only felt growing panic. Something was horribly wrong.

I tried to calm Mother, forcing myself to think clearly (like Father) and ask her questions. Father had always said to take any problem step by step. But I had never dealt with anything like this before. As soon as I began questioning her, I felt like I was out of my depth.

Mother had woken up and gone to make her morning tea, as usual. She started breakfast, and gone to wake Cho Clei, but the bed was empty. Mother assumed that Cho Clei was out in the small back shed, using the toilet hole in the ground. But when she did not appear a few minutes later, Mother went to look. The shed was empty.

The house was empty. Mother started to call out, but that quickly turned into panic. She hurried to the houses closest to our new place, which were within sight, but took several minutes to reach by foot. She and Father had introduced themselves when we first moved in. They were not close, but they were the closest people around.

Mother, clearly distressed, announced that Cho Clei was missing. The wife tried to calm Mother while her husband went outside to look for Cho Clei. But Mother soon joined him in searching the surrounding area. After an hour with no success, and becoming more worried, she came to see me.

There are few techniques to deal with worrying about another person. I looked into it when I got older. There are techniques for a person to calm fear for themselves, but I never came across a way to stop worrying about others.

When Mother burst into the shop, I had immediately caught her panic. Fear and panic were contagious. Visions of my sister being hurt jumped to my mind. But Mother was in worse shape. And she clearly needed me. I tried to reassure Mother that Cho Clei would be found shortly.

I kept trying to think like Father. What would he do? Our new neighbor had gone to the local administrator and lawman, Captain Bao. He told Captain Bao about the disappearance. The captain immediately arranged a search party. They searched the village and a small distance into the woods, but they did not find any sign of her.

After a while with no new ideas, I suggested that we dispatch a letter to Father. Mother immediately agreed, and I realized that was the main reason she had come. She had already written the letter, and she had wanted me to agree that it was the next necessary step. She rushed off to send the letter and I tried to go back to work. I was more upset than I had ever been. Confirming Fong's theory about his process, my dumplings that day did not come out well either. Apparently, only a happy cook could make the shiny dumpling.

Several customers came in that day. At first, I asked if anyone had seen Cho Clei, but after receiving only pity, I stopped asking. No one knew where she was, and asking them was just making me worry more. I felt like I was trapped in a nightmare. It wasn't until Fox came in that I awoke from my worry.

By this point Fox had become a regular at the dumpling shop. He always sat at the same table from his first visit. He always ordered the same thing; six orders of shiny dumplings. (As I said, he was a big man.) He had a large appetite and was always pleasant and talkative. Actually, that wasn't quite accurate. He was always positive. And while he was talkative, the talk was not aimless chatting. It was insightful, and thoughtful, and always carried constructive ideas or poignant questions.

This visit was no different, except for one key element. I had grown very used to seeing him walk in smiling. But when he walked in that day, he looked serious, even grim. He leaned his staff against the wall and sat down heavily. His heavy brows were furrowed in a stern expression.

I had a brief feeling of dizziness when I saw him. Something was wrong with Fox too! So many key elements were out of place. Everything in my predictable little village-world felt strange and disturbed. My sister was missing. My calm mother was panicked. Father, the family anchor, was away. And now Fox, who had always been cheerful, seemed disturbed. I walked up to him, intending to be cheerful, myself. But by the time I had reached him, after Fox looked me in the eyes, all thoughts of cheerfulness evaporated. Reality came crashing back- my sister was missing.

He squinted his eyes at me and then looked me slowly up and down. Then he leaned in, clearly concerned, and started questioning me. "What is it Kwan? What happened last night?" I pulled back, startled. How did he know that something had happened?

"Today, there have been several signs of trouble. But trouble is plainly written on you. You were happy enough yesterday, but today, your demeanor has changed…" I must have just stared back, uncomprehending. So, he went on, "Sometimes, it is just a matter of looking carefully, remembering what affects you see, and then figuring out causes for those effects. The world of men works entirely on cause and effect. That's how I knew… It was a simple enough conclusion. The 'special' problems that go beyond the world of men, are more… complicated. Now, what happened?"

Before I could think through how I would answer, I had a feeling of reassurance wash over me. I seemed to know instinctively that I should trust Fox and confide in him. If anyone could help, Fox could.

A flood of emotion (and words) spilled out of me. Without hesitation, I told him that my sister was missing. He had a strength and calm that was soothing to my worry. He listened patiently and did not interrupt. He was silent a moment, taking in what I had said. Then after a long moment, when he seemed to have the puzzle in place, he began asking questions about last night and that morning.

When had I last seen Cho Clei? Did I lock the window shutters and doors before I slept? Were they still locked in the morning? Was I sure I locked the doors and windows? What was the weather like around our house last night? When was the last time I had seen Father? The questions went on and on. There was no limit to the details he wanted to know.

Most of his questions seemed logical. But some of the questions seemed not to have any relevance at all. I answered them as best I was could. I spilled out any and every piece of information I could, even if I didn't think it would be useful.

At some point though, it was making me feel better, making me feel like I was doing something as I remembered details. Fox was only getting information from his questions, but it also let me feel better as I talked. I told him everything I could think of. I even rehashed details of things that I had told Fox before. I talked again about my suspicions of Garlic Flower. I talked again about father bringing home the doll as a gift for my sister. I must have mentioned many things that were useless to Fox, but he listened patiently.

Every other customer who heard about Cho Clei's disappearance was politely sympathetic. However, Fox was very different from the rest of them. I had the impression that he actually wanted to help me. He seemed to actually care. But most importantly, the force of his masterful character seemed larger than the fear I felt. For the first time that morning, I felt hopeful and less lost.

I answered his questions. I was about to ask him how he knew that something had happened last night. I was curious what had happened, and what he was doing the last time I saw him. I had an image of him on the bridge, dropping the flat metal circle, looking puzzled, then staring up into the sky and muttering to himself. But before I could speak, he asked for his usual six orders of shiny dumplings. I hurried off to the kitchen.

When I returned with the dumplings, Fox asked me if anything new had occurred to me. Again, I felt useless, unable to remember anything useful. I had turned to go back to the kitchen when I remembered the strange, fiery writing in the air. This made me remember the dreams I had the previous night. I went back to tell him. I blurted out the details of the dream (that I could remember). Then, I mentioned the writing in the air. I did not expect him to believe me, but I knew he would not tease me about it. As I mentioned the writing. Abruptly alert, Fox's eyebrows went up.

Unexpectedly, he set down his chopsticks and leaned forward, staring at me. "Kwan, do you think you could recognize the fire writing if you saw it again?" I told him that I thought so, but wasn't sure. Then he questioned me about the dream. I told him everything I remembered.

I tried to ask his opinion on what might have happened. He declined to tell me, saying only, "It would be a mistake to comment now, Kwan. I have some suspicions, but I need to get more information and perform more tests before I could tell you anything really useful."

After he ate, Fox pulled the red pouch from his cloak and paid for his dumplings. As he stood to leave, he saw me looking at him, and waved me over. I hurried over to thank him, but my face must have been showing worry for Cho Clei. He saw my expression and changed whatever he had been about to say. Instead, he said, "Try not to worry, Kwan. We *will* find her. I have some suspicions. And if my growing suspicions are correct, it is possible she doesn't even know she was taken."

I looked up and him and asked, "What?... I don't understand..." A series of thoughts flashed through my mind. "We...? You mean you'll help? Really?" I asked.

Fox looked me in the eye and did not blink. He said, "Yes, Kwan. Even without the training, I would naturally *want* to help. But if it is a "special problem", it becomes a matter of *duty*, not want. Part of my mission is to help with the 'special problems'. Of course, I will help you."

I was grateful, but some part of me already knew this about Fox. The other thing that he had said was still sticking in my head. I asked, "Wait... you said 'She doesn't know she was taken'? What do you mean??"

Fox replied, "Kwan, this is beginning to look like a 'special problem'. Certainly, there are some troubling indications. I will do everything I can to help you. But I will need to confirm my suspicions before I can tell you any more. Right now, I don't have enough information. Just like you need flour to make your dough, I need information to reach the right conclusions."

He put a hand on my shoulder and turned, walking out of the shop. For the first time that day, I felt that my sister's disappearance could be put right. He turned to leave, then turned back and locked his eyes on mine. He said, "Kwan, there are no problems without solutions. In this place, Heaven, and *all* of the realms, *every* problem has a solution. Every single one." He slowly nodded, without another word, turned on his heel, and strode purposefully out of the shop.

My sister vanishing had already begun to feel more like evil than accident. But with Fox helping, I suddenly had hope again. If it was evil, Fox could help. I didn't know how, but he could. I was sure. He was different from any other person I had met. I don't know why I had so much confidence in him, but I did.

Over the course of the day, I continued to feel that a huge piece of my life was out of place. Not only was part of our family lost, but the things around me were not trustworthy anymore. It is hard to describe what I felt that day, but the sense was definite.

Soon after Fox left, a boy came running in with a note for me. I thanked him and he ran off without saying anything. I stepped to the door and looked out onto the road. I turned and tried to see the boy but he was just turning a corner in the distance. He was very fast.

Stepping back inside, I opened the note. It was from Mother. She wrote that Cho Clei had still not been found. The news struck me like she had just been lost again- the feeling hit me with fresh impact, just like the first time Mother had told me. The woods nearby had been searched. The village had been searched. They were still searching, but there was no sign of her. Mother had sent the letter to Father in the morning. She expected him some time in the evening. I was instructed to come straight home after closing the shop.

Later that afternoon, the village lawman, Captain Bao, came into the dumpling shop. The last diners had just left the shop, so it was empty. He was tall and lean in his limbs and torso, whereas Fox was fat. Captain Bao's body and features were like a weasel. His eyes were dark and small and the sides of his mouth were turned down in an ever-present frown.

Captain Bao smelled the dumplings and his eyes flicked to the kitchen. He wanted some, that was clear. But, considering the situation, it would have been inappropriate to order dumplings. We both knew that he was actively involved in the search for Cho Clei.

I had no experience with any kind of investigation, but I thought he might come to see me. He might ask for more information to help him find my sister. He did question me about the disappearance of Cho Clei, verifying the details Mother had given him. After doing that, he looked over each shoulder to check if anyone was listening. Satisfied that we were not observed, he told me the real reason for his visit. There *was* new information he had learned!

He had received a report from the next village. There was a suspicious vagrant who had passed through that village two days before. The headman and administrator in the next village, Bao's counterpart, had sent a message.

The drifter was wanted for theft. Captain Bao had said that if a man would steal, he might kidnap too. It wasn't a far distance from any one crime to another. He confessed to me that he was keeping this information from Mother. He impressed on me that, as a fearful and anxious Mother, this information would only make it easier for her to worry. He said that her distress would become unbearable if her imagination had more fuel.

I agreed with his insight, nodding absently. I realized that my imagination would also plague me, but since I was a boy, he thought I should handle it. I thanked him for the information, but was already picturing a criminal taking my gentle little sister. He promised to update me with any new information, then turned to leave. I asked him to wait a moment, then ran to the kitchen. I tied up a package of dumplings in a cloth. When he saw the package I handed him, he smiled slightly. I was not worldly at that point in life, but I understood the value of good relations. He left, and I returned to the kitchen.

I looked at the hourglass on the kitchen counter. It was nearly closing time. I went about cleaning and preparing the kitchen for the next day. My last duty before leaving was to put the chairs on the tables and clean the floor.

As I finished the process, I imagined that I heard my sister calling out to me. She sounded upset and impatient. Heart pounding, I stopped and listened carefully. For a moment, I imagined her somewhere very close by… I would find her confused and hungry, with some simple explanation…

I strained my ears to hear, but I did not hear her again. Shaking my head to clear it, I locked the door to Fong's and headed straight home.

It was depressing at home. The house felt empty and Mother was the most worried I had ever seen her. I could see that Mother was trying to hide her anguish. Worry was making her imagine Cho Clei's voice every time there was a sound… The worry was clear on Mother's face. Mother did not want to talk, but she looked nervously over at me every few seconds.

Before long, dinner was ready. Mother and I ate in silence, both of us trying to seem calm for the other. We both avoided looking at Cho Clei's empty place.

I don't remember what we ate, but I do remember Mother's constant looking between me and the front door. I assumed that she was somehow waiting for Cho Clei to return. Every time Mother looked at the door, I did too.

But when Father walked in, I realized what Mother had actually been waiting for. Father looked around as he walked in. His face was a mixture of worry and anger. Mother jumped up and ran to him. He opened his arms to her and she began sobbing, her worry spilling out. Father held her in a firm embrace and spoke quietly into her ear. She began to nod and started to calm down. I could feel relief flooding into me. Only when I started to tear up, did I realize how upset I had been. But now Father was here. He was a source of strength for both of us. Once Mother was calm, Father was able to address both of us. We listened attentively.

Father was certain that someone had taken Cho Clei. He reasoned that the success of the dumpling shop had made us targets for criminals. They knew our family had money now. He expected that we would be contacted during the next few days. He expected that when the kidnapper's letter arrived, it would tell us how much money Father needed to pay them. Father hurried on, before Mother could ask. He said that we would, of course, pay. The horse he had returned on carried two sacks of gold. Then she would be back. He made it sound so simple.

He went on to say that he would, of course, stay at home until Cho Clei was found. Also, after she was found and Father eventually returned to the capital, he would hire some men to act as security for us.

Even though Cho Clei was missing, Father's presence was beyond reassuring. Knowing that Father would be staying at home with us comforted both Mother and me. He had already informed Fong about the kidnapping before he left. We had so much faith in Father that it calmed our worry and Mother and I fell into an exhausted sleep. I was certainly still worried, but I felt confident that Fox and Father would be able to solve the mystery.

***

On the day Mother discovered that Cho Clei disappeared, the search party had set out to find her. The search party was determined and methodical in its search. However, they did not find her. They did not find anything useful; no trace of her, no clues.

The following day, with Father there to direct them, the search party was even more determined. Father dismissed me to go work at Fong's. The business should be maintained too. He said I would be more useful taking care of the shop. He would take charge of the search.

For a moment, I felt insulted that Father had dismissed me. He clearly was implying I had nothing useful to add to the search. It felt like I was being treated like an idiot, who would make things worse, not better. But then, after a moment, I realized I was being oversensitive. Finding my little sister was the only important thing now.

Father was a persuasive man. He started the search by reminding them that Cho Clei might not have eaten and could be very weak and hungry. Most members of the search party were parents themselves. The thought of their own children, weak and starving in the cold, was powerful motivation to every parent in the search party.

Somehow Mother and I expected the disappearance to be resolved quickly. We expected that Father would come home and instantly make everything right. The next day was filled with a flurry of action. But this problem was even beyond Father. By the end of the search, Cho Clei was still missing.

I had sold very few dumplings that day. It seemed clear to me that I was not needed at the shop. I just decided to shut down early when Fox came in. It was clear that he had been in motion. He was not stopping to chat. It was not a social visit. Instead, he came in needing fuel (food) to finish his mission. I hurried to the kitchen and put together a package of dumplings for him to take with him. Then, I passed on the news that Capt. Bao had conveyed to me. I told Fox that a thief had been seen in the neighboring village.

He was not expecting the news. "Hmm… Well, certainly I will check him out…" He said. Then he turned to leave. Before walking away, he turned back and said, "the next time I see you, I should have news for you." And then he was gone, walking away purposefully.

Feeling confused, alternating between defeated and optimistic, I went home. Because I was distracted, I started back toward our old house. The habit was overwhelming. It was only when I reached for the door that I realized I was in the wrong place. So, I turned around and headed to our new home. But in truth, this new place did not feel like "home" if our family was not together. That night I slept fitfully.

The following day, I did not open the dumpling shop. The search party went out again and I went out with them. Again, we did not find anything useful. We formed a line, walking side by side, and entered the forest. We walked through the woods, deeper than they had the day before. We examined the ground carefully, but could not find any trace of my sister.

All that day I kept wondering what Fox was doing. I hoped I would run into him, because I trusted that he would have information for me. I did not need to be told that Fox was the type of man who always kept his word. But I didn't see him.

After a third day of searching without finding Cho Clei, Mother began to lose hope. She had dark circles under her eyes, and began to wear a dull expression, as though her mind was farther and farther away. She had been given to constant weeping and her despair made me also begin to lose hope. Father was losing hope, but he would not say so. He told me, in a heavy voice, that I should open Fong's dumpling shop the next day.

Feeling lost, I went to Fong's house at dawn and made the dumplings. That day, only one person came in for dumplings.

Word had spread around our small village about Cho Clei's disappearance. The people in our village seemed to want to distance themselves from the kidnapping. I cannot remember what made me feel this way, but the people I saw that day would look away and hurry off when they saw me.

Father had once told me that if an animal was sick or weak, the rest of its group would increase their pace to leave it behind. Unable to keep up, the weak prey would be killed off by whatever animal hunted it. Cho Clei's disappearance was a misfortune that the other villagers wanted to leave behind. We were unlucky now and to be avoided. I wondered briefly if I would have acted the same way. I didn't think I would. At least, I never would after this point, now that I knew how miserable it felt.

I sat there on the stool in Fong's kitchen, feeling like an outcast from the village, feeling deeply worry about my sister. I began to think that I was somehow responsible for what happened to Cho Clei. When I had let Fong lie to Father, had I invited misfortune into our family? I *might* have. I might be even more guilty than Fong! The feeling grew throughout the day.

The day had passed without a single visitor. I decided that coming in was a mistake. I prepared to close the shop.

I was about to throw away the dumplings, when the tiny bell over the door rang. I looked over to see Fox walk in. I had been lost in my despair, and had not expected to see him.

He didn't smile, but he did soften his expression when he saw me. He looked me up and down as I emerged from the kitchen. Seeming to read my mind, he spoke, "Don't throw the dumplings away. I'm hungry." Either because I was depressed or in despair, or just accustomed to his ability to 'guess' my thoughts, I wasn't surprised. He looked around the empty restaurant. "Bring me some dumplings, then come sit with me." Without hesitation, I turned to do as he said.

I returned from the kitchen to find him sitting at his usual table. I set the dumplings on the table and sat opposite him. I expected him to start eating, but he waited. Again, he peered into my eyes and seemed to read my thoughts. I imagined that I could feel his influence in my mind. At last he spoke, "I have been looking into what happened to your sister. This business is much deeper than it first appeared. I have been using some of the tools available to me. And, to be honest, it is rarely difficult to find something that has been lost in a 'normal' way.

"So, I went about using some of my tools to find out where your sister was. It was very surprising that my tools could not find her." Fox said

"What kind of tools?" I asked Fox leaning in. He smiled in a kind, but tired manner. He seemed to consider every question I asked very seriously.

"Well, usually my most useful tool is of course the mind. By looking at the world around us, by watching how everything fits together, by watching how people behave, there is very little that you could not 'figure out'. But what I'm referring to is different than my reasoning.

"Where I was trained, where I learned about the Gale, is called the GaleTemple. It is an incredible place high in the mountains, many months journey from here. In the GaleTemple, we were taught a wide variety of subjects by a number of Masters. We were taught about everything from how to use herbs, ways to train the body, and how to manage the mind. We were also taught about how to use energy, and knowledge of things that are 'outside the normal realms of men'... Things that you might think of as supernatural, or paranormal.

"There are other tools I have, but explaining those now would be premature." Fox continued, "So I went about getting more information. But before I go on, have there been any developments since we last spoke?"

I tried to clear my head and think. I thought for a minute and then told him about the message from Captain Bao.

"Tell me every detail you can remember. This is important, so try hard. If this thief is responsible, I will be able to determine it. And, if so, I will certainly be able to determine where Cho Clei is... Men cannot hide evil."

I looked askance at him, "But they can lie." I said.

He replied, "When you work with light, nothing can hide in darkness." That didn't make it any clearer for me, and my expression must have said as much. But Fox shrugged and went on. "Did he tell you anything that would give us a clue to this thief's location?"

I thought back to what Captain Bao had told me. I couldn't remember any more information that I had already told Fox. Also, I didn't remember any clues to the thief's location. I told as much to Fox.

He nodded, unsurprised. "Then, our discussion can wait. I must first find this thief and then question him." Then, as an afterthought, Fox remembered his hunger. Quickly, he ate the forgotten dumplings. He must have been very hungry, because he seemed not to mind that they were cold. He pulled out his red pouch and put several coins on the table. Then, without another word, he stood and strode out of the dumpling shop. In a moment, he was gone.

I went about clearing the dishes Fox had used. I carried them into the kitchen and put them into the wash basin. I was about to begin washing them when the bell above the door rang. Thinking that it was Fox returning, I rushed back out into the dining room.

It was Captain Bao, not Fox. Captain Bao looked tired and drawn. His small and beady eyes were now tinged with red, as though he had not slept.

"Captain Bao!" I blurted out. "Did you find her? Any news?" I could hear the anxiety in my own voice. The Captain shook his head sadly.

"No, Kwan. We haven't found her yet." He sighed heavily, "In truth, we haven't found the thief either. I have been working with Captain Wan, my counterpart in the next village. We have been looking for this thief. I came to keep you informed about what is happening."

My face must have shown disappointment. He immediately went on, "Don't worry, we will not give up! Your father is well known and respected and we will give our best!"

When Capt. Bao left, I did not feel very much confidence or hope, but what else could I do? I wanted to run off into the woods to look for her myself just calling out her name in the forest. But, before the thought had gone very far, I knew that that wouldn't do any good. I felt powerless.

I went home, depleted, and feeling like our family was somehow hollowed out. The house felt empty. I slept fitfully that night, plagued by dreams of my little sister in various dangerous situations.

The next day, Capt. Bao returned without news. It was not good news in that my sister hadn't been found. But more importantly, it was not bad news either. Capt. Bao reported that his counterpart in the next village was pursuing the thief, but the thief was crafty and had eluded them so far. This thief had been witnessed fleeing a pig farm 'red handed' with a stolen piglet. It seemed that he was a "cattle thief". Capt. Bao promised that they would continue to look, but that was all he had to report. So far, there was no good news of any kind.

I had briefly gotten my hopes up when the Captain first walked in. But since I knew that Cho Clei had not been found, I had plunged back into despair.

Some people may have come in that day to eat dumplings. Or maybe nobody came in. I had no idea, honestly. I was so distracted and distraught that I was just going through the motions. I felt like I was in a fog and the day passed before I knew it.

Chapter 4

Unexpected Education

The next evening, I saw Fox. It was just before 'closing time' and I was about to clean up. He looked preoccupied, lost in thought. He came in, looking stern and ordered four plates of dumplings. Then he said, "Sit down after you bring the dumplings. It's time we talk. But first, I need to eat something."

I nodded, immediately feeling more confident in Fox than I had in Captain Bao. Luckily, I had made the dumplings so many times that I did not have to think about it. Balancing the plates on top of each other, I walked out to the table and sat.

When I realized that I had forgotten Fox's tea, I stood back up and hurried back to the kitchen. I sat down and restrained myself from asking questions while he ate. Fox was a big man and clearly, he had a voracious appetite.

In short order, he had finished all of the dumplings. I walked back out to the table. Then he wiped his mouth and poured each of us a cup of tea. "Well, I have been able to find out a few things…. No, don't get excited yet! I don't know where your sister *is*, but I have been able to figure out where she *isn't*." Fox said. I did not understand what he meant, but I was in a situation where good news was desperately needed.

Fox continued, "There were three possibilities at the beginning of this. Either your sister wandered off, or she was taken, or she wandered off and then was taken. So, finding out which one of those possibilities had happened, was necessary before we could figure out how to locate your sister."

"There are certain tests and techniques that are available to me that can determine where something is when it's lost.

Without spending too much time going into it, I can tell you that I have several ways to locate things. In fact, some tools make it very easy. That is, if the things have been lost naturally, I can usually find them. Actually, I have not yet failed in finding something once I have looked for it. Perhaps I'll fail in the future, but it hasn't happened yet."

"Really?" I asked. I was just a boy from the village but that seemed like an extraordinary claim to me.

"The point is that there are other ways that I could have found whatever you might be looking for- if that thing is *here*." Fox said the word 'here' with strange emphasis, but I didn't understand. "After performing several tests, I can say that your sister's disappearance bears several distinct signs of being a... special problem."

I was confused. Anxiety rose in me. What did he mean, if she's '*here*'? "You mean here in the village, right? Did she get taken out of the village?" The feeling in my stomach took on a new dimension of fear.

"It looks that way, yes, but not how you're thinking." He could see the look of anxious confusion growing on my face. He put his hands up. "Slow down, Kwan. Fear will always compromise your reasoning and make it impossible to think clearly. So, when we are afraid, we have to use effort to think clearly. So, calm yourself and let me take you through my reasoning process so far- the actions I have taken."

I nodded and took a deep breath. Then I leaned in, concentrating.

Fox began, "Initially, I was able to determine that the Gale was being diverted in this place. By that I mean the energy of any place flows. There is a natural movement to it. But when force is used to change the Gale, it gets disturbed. And I can detect that disturbance."

I interrupted, "Disturbed?"

Fox did not mind. He seemed to have limitless patience. "Imagine water flowing through a stream. The water is flat on the surface, even though it is moving." I nodded. "Now imagine you put your hand in the water to pluck out one of the stones on the riverbed." I nodded again. "Your hand would leave ripples and currents in the water." I nodded again. I understood so far.

"I have been trained to tell the difference in that water, to that flow of energy."

"How?" I interrupted again.

"I mentioned before that I have certain tools at my disposal. But it didn't seem necessary to show you then." I was still picturing ripples and currents in water, more thinking than looking.

"There are a range of tools and techniques... Before, I mentioned the mind. The mind is always our first tool. At my school, I was taught to quiet my mind enough to detect such things. In truth, it's amazing what you can learn once you get familiar with the mind.

"Could...could I learn how to do that?" I asked, suddenly curious. Fox paused rummaging around in his bag and smiled patiently.

"Absolutely, you certainly could. But I warn you, the training contains a great deal of just sitting in stillness and breathing and keeping your mind blank. Only after that can you begin to perceive the Gale... But we're getting off the point. I perform this practice every day; breathing, making the mind blank, so that I can perceive changes in the energy that moves all life- the Gale.

"A few days before I entered your village, I felt a disturbance in this energy. The awareness was very faint at first. But each day that I got closer to this place, the stronger it became. Something unnatural was happening, or about to happen in your village. There was an energetic potential surrounding this place, when power has been assembled, before being used." He resumed looking for something in his bag.

"I arrived here in your village, but until 'the trouble' happened, I couldn't pin down the problem. But the night your sister disappeared, the 'ripples in the current' increased dramatically. I had checked the condition of the Gale that afternoon and I was certain that trouble was coming.

"That day, I used several additional tools I carry to verify that something unnatural was happening. I travelled around the village to see if I could learn where the trouble was happening. When you saw me on your way back home, on the bridge, I was doing just that.

"How could you see the Gale had been disturbed? And *which* tools did you use?" I asked.

Fox reached for his shoulder pack. It was sitting on the floor, next to his chair.

He reached into the bag. He was clearly searching for something. My eyes must have been playing tricks on me, because it looked like more of Fox's arm was in the bag than the bag could have held. But because I was trying very hard to concentrate, I did not really register what I was seeing at the time. I was busy trying to imagine invisible ripples in the air.

On cue, Fox smiled slyly, finally finding what he was looking for. He pulled a small bag out of his large shoulder satchel. The smaller bag was flat, and made from a shimmering blue velvet.

He set his larger bag on the floor and leaned forward, holding the smaller bag. He opened the bag and took out a flat metal disc. He held flat on his upturned palm for me to inspect it. It was the same piece of metal he had been dropping on the bridge. I recognized it.

But now, with the chance to study it clearly, I looked carefully. The outer disc was a shining golden metal. Inside that disc was a smaller, star-shaped disc. Through the length of both discs, a metal spike ran, just slightly longer than the outer circle was wide. The circle (and the star set in it) fit completely on Fox's palm. But the spike through them extended almost to his wrist.

"I recognize that thing! You were dropping it on the ground, then staring at it, once it was lying on the ground." I said. Fox had clearly cleaned it since that last rainy night.

"Good. That saves us time. You saw it and remember what I was doing. When I dropped this, it fell flat on the ground and just lay there." Fox turned the item over, showing it from all sides. Yes, of course it 'just lay there' I thought. That's what things do. "This is the 'Marwol.' It is a creation from an ancient GaleMaster named Te-Sulu. He had a gift for seeing connections and a talent for making powerful items. He was both a scientist and an artist."

He held the 'Marwol' up for me to inspect as he spoke. "When powerful items have been created or discovered, they are often brought to the GaleTemple."

I couldn't help myself and interrupted, "Ok, the 'Marwol' one of these power items. It does something?"

Fox looked down at the 'Marwol', "Yes, but it has its limits. It is only a diagnostic tool to *detect* change. It is not powerful enough to *make* change. In short, the 'Marwol' is able to verify if there has been an *alteration* of the Gale, if… there are ripples in the water."

"So, it can tell if the energy around us is flowing normally or not?" I asked. To which Fox just nodded. "How?" I asked.

"This device is activated and influenced by the flow of the gale. It gives a visual of how the GaleForce is flowing."

I was closely looking at the inner 'star' on the 'Marwol.' It was inscribed with tiny letters and symbols. There were only four lanterns lit in the dining area, so it was not exceptionally bright. But the inscriptions caught that light and reflected it brightly. They flashed a golden yellow.

"The 'Marwol' will not function if the Gale is being tampered with…" He said.

"Ok, but what is it supposed to do? How does it work?" I interrupted.

"Like this…" Fox dropped the 'Marwol' on the ground between us. My head jerked back in surprise. It took me looking at it for a moment before I could understand what I was seeing. It looked like the 'Marwol' had become a gold and silver ball, standing upright on the spike end. But, looking a moment longer, I could see that the inner 'star-coin' and the outer 'ring' were quickly spinning, giving it the appearance of being a sphere.

It was spinning like a top. The end of the spike that poked out from the ring was the only point touching the ground. The strange part was that I had been looking down at Fox's hands as he dropped the 'Marwol.' He hadn't flipped it, or spun it, before letting it fall. It appeared to land upright, on its own, and spin itself! Maybe it was a practiced trick?

Fox reached down and picked up the spinning 'Marwol.' He said, "The disturbance that was altering the flow of the Gale has passed. Because the gale is flowing again, the 'Marwol' spins when I drop it. It is not registering its 'full' connection though…

"It does more than just spin?" I asked. Fox nodded and gave an amused smiled.

He went on, "It does, but those functions would probably only activate if your sister were home. I suspect that only then would the 'Marwol' connect to the natural flow of pristine, 'unaltered' Gale."

I didn't understand what Fox was saying, but he handed the 'Marwol' to me. "Drop it yourself." He said.

I took the metal object with both hands. It was strange to me that I was supposed to drop it, but I felt like I was holding some 'sacred' thing. Why else would it be in so fancy of a bag?

Carefully examining it, I noticed that the 'Marwol' was heavier than expected. As I stared at it, the golden metal of the outer 'ring' began to shine faintly. The inner 'star' was made from a silver metal. Both parts were inscribed with hundreds of small markings. The rune-markings looked like tiny random scratches until I looked more closely. I brought the 'Marwol' up to my face and squinted at the scratches. Holding it close to my eye, I saw that the scratches were precisely carved markings.

The carved markings reminded me of something, but I couldn't figure out what it was at first. I turned the 'Marwol' over in my hands, when suddenly it came to me. The markings looked similar to writing I had seen before. The morning that we found Cho Clei gone, I awoke seeing a glowing, red writing in the air. These marks were similar, but different from the writing I saw in the air.

"When the flow of the Gale has been 'tampered' with, the 'Marwol' is unable to connect to it- unable to move. When you saw me, I had been testing the flow of the Gale with it. When I dropped the 'Marwol', it did not spin. It fell, and lay on the ground, inert. When it didn't move, I had another confirmation that the Gale was being twisted." He saw me look back down at the 'Marwol' in my hands. "Go ahead, drop it again." Fox said.

I nodded, somehow already doubting what Fox had shown me. It's strange how quickly the mind can turn. I leaned forward and carefully held the 'Marwol' with both hands. I pinched it between the thumb and forefinger from either side of the 'ring'. I extended both hands in front of me waist-high. I would be certain there was no spin on it. Careful to open both hands at the same time, I dropped the 'Marwol'.

It fell neatly and landed upright, spinning. I stared at it for a long moment. I looked up at Fox and he just nodded apologetically. "The 'Marwol' confirmed that something had been done to the GaleForce, but it didn't prove that she was taken. In truth, it couldn't tell the difference between an evil alteration in the Gale and a neutral alteration in the Gale. She may have wandered off the same night the Gale was twisted. It could have just been a coincidence.

I interrupted, "Wait, what do you mean by a 'neutral alteration'? What does that mean?" I might have been asking a silly question, but I wanted to learn and knew asking was the best way.

Fox half nodded at my question. "There could be different reasons the Gale gets changed. Some of them might be harmless. For examples, portals and gates can spontaneously appear. If a portal were to appear in our realm, it would block the 'Marwol' too. I needed to find out more than the 'Marwol' could tell me. So, I moved on to another tool.

Fox took the 'Marwol' back from me and replaced it in its bag. Then he put it carefully back into his shoulder sack.

He lifted the rosary around his neck. Using a thumb and forefinger, he lifted the string of fat beads off his chest. "Have you ever looked closely at my rosary? A rosary is a spiritual tool. But this one is a 'utility belt', or an 'investigation kit' as much as a rosary. It serves a double purpose." He shifted his grip on the rosary, holding up one particular bead. It was a solid milky white color.

"This bead is known as the 'CloudStone'. Its actual name is quite long, so 'CloudStone' works as well for our purposes. It is a 'Feeler'. It is sensitive to energy in ways that most people aren't." Fox said.

"Sensitive? What do you mean? And how does it work?" I asked. Fox nodded, separating the white ball from the rosary. I didn't actually see how it came unattached. One moment it was attached to the rosary. The next moment, it was free and sitting in Fox's upturned palm.

"By sensitive, I mean that the 'CloudStone' can test for very faint traces of things. For example, the 'CloudStone' can test to see if something is, broadly, good or evil. It can determine if something is healthy or poisonous, that kind of thing. It can detect energetic portals and anomalies." I must have looked confused. Fox went on, "Anomalies are things out of the ordinary. Every technique leaves an energetic residue. The 'CloudStone' is able to 'feel' that residue.

"As for how it works, the 'CloudStone' changes color in the presence of different energies. I can see from your expression that my claim seems hard to believe. Let me demonstrate." He gestured to our two cups of tea on the table. Then he reached down and picked up a pebble off of the floor. He handed me the pebble. "Put this stone in one of our cups. Don't let me see which one it is. Feel free to move them around. Fox turned his head away and covered his eyes.

A moment of inspiration came to me. I reached back and grabbed another teacup off of the next table. I quickly poured a third cup of tea. Then I dropped the stone in 'my' cup. Then I changed the location of each cup, scrambling their positions. Then I waited a moment, making sure each cup looked identical.

Fox turned back and opened his eyes. As he looked down at the cups, he smiled at my addition. "Clever boy. So, the 'CloudStone' can test for traces of things. For example, it could tell us if something is good or not, maybe natural or tampered with, that kind of thing."

Fox extended the hand holding the 'CloudStone' over the cup in front of him. Nothing happened. The white ball stayed white. I looked a Fox expectantly, but he moved his hand to the cup in front of me. Again, the white ball remained white.

Then Fox moved the 'CloudStone' over the third cup. My eyes were looking at the cup at first. Then motion drew my eyes up to the 'CloudStone'. A gray shadow, like smoke, was creeping across the surface of the stone. A moment later, the 'CloudStone' had turned fully gray. "The pebble is in this one. You can see…"

An idea occurred to me. "Fox, what would happen if someone put poison in your cup?"

He was not as surprised by my question as I thought he might be. "The 'CloudStone' would have alternated between red and black, not gray. Instead, the gray stone is telling me that the tea is not clean, but it also isn't poisonous. It is a useful tool if you are familiar with how it communicates.

I looked at Fox, dreading the statement I knew was coming. Fox said, "When your sister disappeared and I tested with the 'CloudStone', it turned red. So, we had an indication that something evil had indeed taken place. If it had turned silver, I would have known that a portal had opened. But it turned red, showing that it detected the remnants of some evil process, or spell, or technique. At this point my tools had shown me a few things; something had twisted the Gale here, that thing was evil, and it was not a 'portal' that had taken her. Does that make sense so far?" he asked. He raised the 'CloudStone' to his necklace. As he did, the gray smoke color faded away. The ball quickly returned to white. The rosary accepted the white stone back.

I was mentally following his process, and I said so. I did not say that I felt like I was dreaming, which was also true. What can you say to the wondrous being demonstrated.

"You had given me a puzzle when your sister disappeared. The simple question first struck me when you told me she was gone."

I looked askance at him. "What puzzle?"

Fox replied, "Well, your sister is missing." I nodded in agreement. "But the doors and windows in your house were locked. You were diligent preparing for the storm, like your father would have done. If you remember, I asked several times to make certain. Do you still remember it that way?" I did remember Fox asking me specifically about that point. I still remembered it the same and said so. "So how did your sister get out of the house?" I looked blankly at him. "Think about it, Kwan. She can't fly. She can't pass through solid
walls. How did she even get out?" I could feel the surprised expression on my face. I had never thought of that. "So, our first question was if she wandered off or was taken." I remembered. "But if she wandered off, how did she get out of your house without unlocking a door or window? Or, if she was kidnapped in a 'normal' way, how did the kidnapper take her without using a door or window? At that point, a picture was suggesting itself. But I was still no closer to finding your sister.

"So, I moved on to the next tool. It is substantially more powerful than either the 'CloudStone' or the 'Marwol'. With empowered items, there is a hierarchy."

He held up his rosary again, this time pointing out a bead that was a dull yellowish color. "This is known as the Wandering Light or the Finder's Light, depending on which translation you use. The cave where it was discovered had that written above the entrance."

I interrupted again. Some part of me realized that it was a bad habit. "How does it work?"

Fox nodded again and looked thoughtful. "Let's perform a test now, the same way we did with the tea." Fox picked up his chopsticks and used them to pluck the pebble from the third teacup. Then he moved the teacup away and set down the small stone. "Go into the kitchen and hide the pebble very well. I will stay here. Remember, make it very, very hard to find. Go on, I'll wait."

I dashed off to the kitchen, determined to make the pebble impossible to find. For a moment, I forgot that I wanted to believe Fox. Once I was in the kitchen I walked over to the cupboard where Fong kept dishes. I opened the door and moved a few additions around so they made some noise. Then I loudly closed the cupboard.

Feeling like I had come up with a way to confuse the yellowish bead, I walked to the back of the kitchen, down the hallway, and stopping at a small room were Fong stored flour and oil and vegetables. I walked into the room and looked into the corner to my right. There were two sacks of onions. I moved the onions and put the pebble on the floor. Then I put the two onion sacks back on top of it. As a finishing touch, I put a sack of flour on top of the onions. I gave it a last look and, satisfied with my work, headed back to Fox.

Fox was in the same position, drinking his tea, looking thoughtful. I sat back down. "Finished? You've hidden that pebble someplace very difficult to find?"

I nodded, "Yes, now what?" Fox reached up to his rosary. The dull yellowish bead separated from the rosary, seeming just to appear in his hand. "I will use my energy to start the Wandering Light. Then I will ask it to find the pebble."

"What should I do?" I asked.

Fox smiled, "Follow the Light." Then he closed his eyes. I assumed he was concentrating on the giant rosary bead in his hand. Then he opened his eyes and handed me the bead. I took it, surprised at its weight. I was unsure what would happen.

I did not have to wait long. One moment, the stone was opaque, a dull yellowish color. The next moment, a point of light began in the center of the stone. The light grew in brightness, still visible inside the stone, until it was impossible to ignore.

I watched the light rise out of the stone bead. When the light emerged, it was smaller than it appeared inside the stone. It was much smaller than the stone where it 'lived' but it was very bright, and impossible to miss.

The light hovered above the stone for a moment, in front of my face. Then the light began drifting, slowly at first, then moving faster- directly toward the kitchen. After the 'Marwol' and the 'CloudStone', I wouldn't think that anything could surprise me. I was wrong about that. Mouth open, I stared at the light, watching it drift away. "Well... Follow the light!" Fox said. Snapping out of my trance, I stood up.

"You're not coming?" I asked Fox. The light paused its journey as I hesitated. It floated a few feet away, at chest height.

But he shook his head, "I already know it works. This demonstration is for you." So, I followed the light. It went into the kitchen. I'm not sure what I expected, but the Wandering Light moved at walking speed, slowly pulsing. It did not move at all toward the dish cupboard, ignoring my trick. Instead, it turned and moved down the hallway in the back of the kitchen. Obediently, still holding the yellowish stone, I trailed behind it.

When the light reached the storage room, it floated in through the open doorway and drifted over to the sacks of onions. The light perched on top of the onions, like it was waiting.

Curious, I moved the flour and the top sack of onions. The light sank down to sit on the lower sack, and again waited. When I moved the second sack of onions, the light drifted down to sit directly on top of the pebble. The wandering light had found it. I realized that I wasn't surprised. I already knew that Fox was trustworthy.

I picked up the stone. When I touched the pebble, the light floated back and sank into the yellowish rosary bead. A moment later, the light was extinguished. It appeared that I was just holding a dull and opaque ball of stone.

I walked back to Fox. He was waiting patiently in the same place. I had an inspiration to try the test again, pretending to hide it, but this time to keep the pebble in my pocket. But just as quickly as the thought came up, I knew it wouldn't work. "I saw it, Fox. I believe you. Honestly, I never really doubted you."

Fox nodded, somberly. "I understand, Kwan. This is all new to you. When I was first shown these things, I had the same reaction. I was amazed, even shocked. But I will tell you what my teacher told me then. Master Eclipse said that the world had become bigger for me. I had just learned, and opened the door to a larger understanding.

"Somehow, I felt frightened when I realized how much is out there. Master Eclipse told me that it was essential, now that I had seen what he called 'otherworldly forces', to keep my mind open. I would see much more, before my training was done. He said that 'what was new' was scary, first because we realize how much more unknown is out there. He warned me not to be rigid, trying to hold on to my old views. Be flexible. Adapt, Fox. Be flexible." He repeated it, almost like a chant.

He looked away, eyes unfocused, clearly reliving the memory. Then he turned and focused on me. "You're actually handling it far better than I did. Well done, Kwan." I forced myself to focus, and ignore the compliment.

"Does the Wandering Light work finding anything?"

Fox looked thoughtful at my question. "It will work finding many things, but like all tools, it has its limits. He took the yellowish stone back from me. He held it as he went on speaking, "Naturally, I asked the Wandering Light to find your sister. Its response was... troubling. Observe, I will ask it to find your sister..." Fox closed his eyes for a moment. When he reopened them, the light immediately flared and rose out of the stone. Watching the light closely, I saw it began to shake and vibrate, darting a tiny distance in one direction then another. It didn't seem to know where to go. Then, without any other warning, the light burst apart. It broke into millions of sparkling smaller lights that all faded out, shooting off in different directions.

I was confused. "The Wandering Light… broke?? What… what does that mean?"

Fox said, "That's what's troubling, Kwan. There would only be 2 reasons the light can't find her. First is if some being is actively blocking the Light. The second reason is that she has been taken somewhere that the light cannot travel."

It was surreal, but I couldn't argue with Fox. His proof it was irrefutable. I nodded. "I… see. Cho Clei might be 'somewhere the light can't travel'… You're right, it's a lot to take in at once. You have… otherworldly forces… Oh, and your staff sometimes glows." I shook my head to clear it. I sighed, "Never mind… the light couldn't find her. I think I understand. Go on."

Fox continued, "Well Kwan, yesterday in the evening, I ran into Capt. Bao. He told me about the pig thief. And while it didn't seem likely that he was the kidnapper, I needed to check to make sure. Like we already discussed, how could any kidnapper get in and out of a locked house? So, I went to find this cattle thief this morning."

My hopes soared. "You found him?!"

Fox shrugged his heavy shoulders and nodded. "Sure, that was easy. I used the Wandering Light. It took me directly to him." Fox saw my hopeful expression and said, "No Kwan, he was not the kidnapper, and he had no idea about your sister." But just that quickly my hopes fell again. I must have looked as dejected and disappointed as I felt. Fox gave me a clear look of pity and said, "I understand that you want more information, Kwan. But, at this point, I can't tell you what you want to hear. But, take heart- the investigation continues. It is not the time to lose hope. There is one last avenue for me to explorea source to consult. By tomorrow, I will likely know where your sister is and have a plan to get her back. Not certain, but likely…" He gave a smile and stood. I mumbled my thanks to him, already lost in my thoughts.

That night, after closing the dumpling shop and coming home, I was preoccupied as question after question began to occur to me.

I examined possibilities and reviewed what Fox had told me… again and again, until late. It was hard to sleep that night. When I finally did drift off, my sleep was fitful. I dreamed that my sister was calling for my help.

When I awoke the next morning, the sky was threatening rain. The clouds hung in dark gray layers. I was in a panic, realizing that I had slept in. The dark clouds had made me think it was earlier than it was. I knew that nobody, including Father, would blame me, but it was suddenly a matter of pride. I had given my word. I scrambled to put on my clothes and shoes, determined to hurry.

I didn't normally eat in the morning, but that morning, even though I was in a hurry, I paused as I passed through the kitchen. I had caught movement from the corner of my eye.

I had seen something from the kitchen window. Had a light just flashed in the dim morning? I walked over to the window and looked out. Fox was down on his knees, inspecting the dirt… outside our house! The morning light had flashed off of one of his polished rosary beads. As I watched, he stood up, peered around, then hurried off toward the forest. I ran out the door to catch up with him.

Fox was deceptively quick, for such a big man. I hurried to catch him. The morning dew made my pants and shoes wet as I ran after Fox. I could have shouted for his attention, I suppose. But because it was still early, I didn't feel comfortable yelling.

He turned and watched me approach the last ten paces. I had caught up with him and would finally be able to ask the questions I had thought up.

I began to speak, but was out of breath. I hadn't realized how hard I had been running to catch him. He was alternating between looking up at the clouds and glancing at his glowing staff.

What had he found out about Cho Clei? What had he been doing with the dirt around our new house? And all of the other questions that were coming back to me competed to be asked first.

But Fox spoke first, "I have been able to confirm that this is a 'special problem', Kwan. These are the kind of things that a normal person cannot deal with, Kwan. There are forces at work here. Without the proper training and education, it is beyond a normal man's capabilities to deal with the beings from other realms. I have had that training and education. The sources I consulted with directed me to your sister.

I have to leave this place to go get her. I have to leave in a moment, Kwan. I understand that you will want me to explain, but there isn't time for that now." Fox said.

Hearing that Fox knew where Cho Clei was had made me overjoyed. I didn't have to think before I spoke. Heart pounding in my chest, I said, "Fox, I want to go too! If you're going to save Cho Clei, take me!"

Fox looked down at me and frowned. Only then did I notice Fox's posture. He was standing in front of me, with his arms folded across his chest. The effect was clear- He was barring my path. "Kwan, this journey is going to be dangerous. Very, very dangerous. But with a chance to save your sister, I have to go. The celestial window will be closing soon."

"Celestial window?" I interrupted.

Fox shook his head. "Never mind." He looked around, choosing his words. "When I was younger I took an oath to help, if I can. So, I must go. And Kwan, if I don't go now, there will be little chance for your sister. If I don't go, Cho Clei will probably be lost."

I thought about his words and the ring of truth they carried. After a moment, my mind was made up. "Then I have to come, Fox! This is my fault! I knew that Garlic Flower was a snake! Her lies were a part of this! And I didn't warn Father! I did not do what I should have, and I caused this!!! I can *feel* it. I *have* to come, Fox!"

His expression softened. He held up his hands, palm out, "Hold on, little Kwan. I suspect that there were several elements that conspired to make bring about this situation. From what I can tell, Fong's daughter was only one part of this. But *you* are not responsible. There are several in line for guilt and punishment. But you are not one of them!"

I started to look down, feeling that Fox just didn't understand.

He lowered his hands and his voice became quiet, "Look at me Kwan. I do understand how you feel, but you were the smallest part of this puzzle. I suspect that I have identified the main culprit here. I suspect we are seeing a plan that has been operating for some time now. Now I will confirm my suspicions, while retrieving your sister."

Fox kept looking like he wanted to leave, but I wasn't planning on letting him go without me. Fox continued. "You see, Kwan, all children have intrinsically pure spirits. Since they are closer to the Source of Life, they resonate much closer to the original vibration."

I must have showed that didn't understand. He went on, "Or rather, more of the Light still clings to them. For some evil beings, a child's life is powerful energetic currency. He would be able to use that currency for many things."

"Like what, Fox?" I asked. Fox looked away toward the forest. For a long moment, he didn't answer.

Finally, he said, "Terrible things Kwan..." He swallowed hard. "But I'm not going to let that happen." He sighed heavily, closing his eyes. Eyes closed, Fox took several more deep breaths, before opening his eyes and continuing, "I could force you to stay, Kwan." He let out a long sigh, making up his mind. "I won't though. You have a right to help. Several clues have suggested that... perhaps... you are supposed to come help. But I will tell you that if you decide to follow me, you will never be able to go back to your ordinary life. Do not ignore this warning!

"There are things that once you see them and feel them and know they exist, they change you, and you can never choose to un-know them." He stopped speaking and stared at me, as I thought through his words. If Cho Clei could be saved, I had to help. She was my baby sister. I knew what Father would have done. No matter what it cost me, I would help. I had decided to follow him, but my feet did not want to move.

Fox took a long hard look at me. He seemed to look deep inside and see my resolve, like he was reading my character. I felt like I was laid naked before his gaze all of my secrets uncovered. His piercing eyes seemed to be able to read everything. He nodded at me approvingly and I felt confident that I would be able to handle the unknown. He hadn't wanted me to come initially, but now that he had agreed, he was fully supportive. I could feel encouragement in his gaze. "All right then, let's go.

He turned and started briskly walking towards the woods. Again, I had to run to catch up with him. Either the rain was getting lighter, or I was so wet already that I no longer noticed it.

I didn't know exactly where we were going. Fox was walking through the grass toward the forest so I followed. He would occasionally close his eyes, hold his staff and correct his direction slightly. I could see that he knew where he was going. I couldn't see any difference in where we entered the woods, however.

At the edge of the forest, Fox approached a place where one tree had fallen against another tree. It looked like the tree had been blown over recently, possibly in the recent storm when Cho Clei was taken. The trees had been several feet apart, but were quite tall. The fallen tree was leaning against the standing tree, caught in the upper branches of the standing tree. The upper branches of the standing tree were spread like a man's arms, outstretched. it looked like one standing man had caught another man who was falling. The trees formed the top sides of a triangle twice the height of a man. Fox unerringly approached the triangular opening they made. Apparently, this was our destination. I couldn't imagine why.

When he reached the opening, Fox took his staff and put it through a loop on the shoulder strap of his satchel. It was the first time I had noticed the loop. The staff now was strapped to Fox's back, somehow held in place by the single loop on the strap. It sat up perfectly vertical, parallel to Fox's spine, and invisibly stuck in place as he moved.

His staff put away, Fox then pulled a small red bottle from his satchel. I stood next to him, uncomprehending. He took a wooden stopper from the bottle, and poured a small amount of fine red powder into the palm of his hand. He replaced the stopper in the bottle and the bottle into his bag. Then he swung his arm in a wide arc, flinging the powder out at the triangular opening.

He faced the triangular opening, closed his eyes, and began to quietly speak. I could not hear what he was saying, but it seemed to rhythmically repeat, like a chant. I looked back and forth between him and the trees before us. I was confused. And my confusion was just beginning.

Chapter 5

Through the Pall

He quietly continued chanting, and I began to feel the hairs standing up on my arms and the back of my neck. Alarmed, I looked at him, but his eyes were still closed. I also noticed a sound coming from triangular opening in the trees. It was the sound of dry wood crackling in a fire. Then there was a flash of light from the doorway in front of us. It was so bright that I had to close my eyes for a moment.

When I opened them, the scene before us had changed. Fox had opened his eyes and was staring at the triangular opening. I followed his gaze and looked at the opening. Where before there had been an opening between the trees and the ground, now there was a shimmering, triangle-shaped screen of red light. Something massive was moving behind the screen, but the background seemed to be swirling too.

I stood there next to Fox, peering at the screen of shimmering red light. An enormous shadow moved behind the screen. A massive figure stepped out from the red screen. It appeared to be a giant man, more than twice my height. But even if he had been our size, one difference showed that he clearly was not a man. He had the head of a giant cat!

He bowed his head slightly as he stepped through the door. His skin was covered in a short fur that was a tawny gold and he wore a white gown down to his giant feet. The gown was tied with a gold strip of cloth at the waist. The giant was clearly male, and his muscles were visible through the white gown. He had massive shoulders and a thick neck. His white gown had gold embroidery from the shoulders down the sleeves and encircled his wrists. He looked like a giant, golden, furry man with a cat's head.

I stood frozen in shock and could only stare at him. I noticed several things immediately about this figure. The first thing I noticed was that the proportions of his body were different that a normal man. His arms were longer and his paw- hands were larger than a man's would have been, even considering his height. I noticed, with surprise, that he only had three fingers on each hand. In his left hand, he held a black scepter, shaped like a spike. It was blunt on one end and pointed on the other. Next, I saw the shape of his head. His head, while massive, was smaller than I would have expected. And it was shaped like a cat's head. It was only slightly wider than his neck and it was flattened at the top. Brilliant yellow eyes, large and widely spaced looked down at us. They had vertical slit pupils like a cat.

His face was serene and patient as he stood in front of the door and looked calmly down at us. He stood with his feet wide apart and I had the impression of enormous power emanating from him. That power radiated from him in a way that I could feel. I wanted to study him more, but it took too much effort to look directly at him. It was like I was forcing myself to stare at the sun. By body had the impulse to yield, but I tried to fight it.

I became aware that my legs were shaking. Being in its presence took too much strength to remain standing. It felt like there was an increasing weight on my shoulders.

Fox immediately dropped to one knee and bowed his head. Before I could wonder at the unbelievable situation, Fox grabbed my sleeve and pulled me down to the ground next to him. As I fell to my knees, the pressure seemed to lighten.

The giant just stood there, looking down at us for a long moment before he spoke. Fox reached over and put his hand on the back of my neck, pushing my head down to look at the ground. I understood what he was urging and looked down and away from the giant.

I couldn't resist trying to look up with my eyes, but didn't move my head. All I could see was his wide feet. They were golden and barefoot. Each foot had only three toes.

His voice was the biggest surprise to me. When he spoke, instead of the thunderous baritone I expected, I heard the sound of a chorus of women. "We regard you... GaleMaster, Immortal, ..." Its words startled me as much as its voice had. As I listened to it speak, I could pick out individual tones; some higher, some lower, but all sounded feminine. It spoke slowly, with great rumbling volume and long pauses. No, I realized I was wrong. The voice sounded neither male nor female.

The cat-giant continued, "You have come... to cross the Pall... Passage of the living is forbidden... You know the cost of crossing the boundary..." I looked over at Fox, but his head remained looking down at the ground.

Fox did not raise his head as he spoke, "Great Ragyala..." His voice was more of a singing tone than regular speech. Fox paused. "I know the cost... Our need to cross is great."

The giant took one step forward. "Young Immortal... We have not seen your kind in many cycles..." My mind boggled at the things I was hearing. GaleMaster? Immortal? I couldn't understand. What was this thing? Why did it radiate such power? Why did it look like a giant, golden, furry cat-man but sound like many women? I shook my head to clear it, as more and more questions occurred to me. What boundary? Was Fox really immortal? What were we involved in? I felt the giant look over at me. I could actually feel power coming from its' gaze. "Why bring this little one?..."

I knew he was talking about me. Immediately, I wanted to object to being called little. But after only a moment, I realized the giant was not only huge and powerful, but also ancient. I *was* a little one, young and insignificant, compared to it.

Ragyala the giant stood there, waiting for a response. Fox did not keep it waiting. "Great Ragyala, by the Infinite Light..." Fox reached up and touched his forehead. "By the Sounds of Being..." He touched his forehead again. "And by the Primordial Fracture..." He touched his forehead a third time. "We must pass... My oath requires it."

Ragyala shifted its gaze to Fox. I knew because I felt the weight on me lighten. The weight did not disappear, but I felt a tangible relief as some of the pressure lifted. I wanted to back away from it. I felt like backing away. If Fox had not been kneeling next to me, I might have fled.

The giant spoke, "Truth... The rescue of an Innocent... We see your need is great, young Immortal... The Forms are correct... But the price must still be paid..."

I sensed Fox tensing for a moment as he replied, "Great Ragyala... I request return passage for my small group... And...I request the payment come due on our return... I pledge spirit payment in full..." I was lost, not understanding anything either of them said.

Unable to resist, I sneaked a look up at the giant. He had a thoughtful look on his huge feline face. His luminous eyes flicked over at me, and his expression briefly showed amusement. It reminded me of the look Mother gave me when I was little, if I did something mischievous. Looking directly at the giant felt... like I was taking a liberty I had not been given. I felt chastised and quickly looked down again.

Time froze as Ragyala examined us. Ragyala spoke again, "Aaah, clever Immortal... We see... your mind... But the price cannot be changed. One spirit for one spirit. You may pass and return... but you will owe five spirits when you return... This is the price of passage..." Fox looked as though he expected to hear this.

Fox shrugged and went on, "Then you would allow us to pass?" Fox looked up slowly. I followed his example and did the same.

Ragyala put his hands on his hips and cocked his head, peering intently at us. It was a strange sight. The posture and the cat's head struck me as funny, but I did not dare laugh. "Payment in full spirit... five spirits... We will open the Pall... and allow return passage for your group... Because you come to rescue an innocent... Go with Our Blessing..." When Ragyala said 'blessing', a sphere of light emerged from its chest. It pulsed and flashed, changing colors. The sphere of light hovered for a moment, before the giant. Then it shrank down to a hand-sized ball of swirling light. It floated over to Fox. Still kneeling, and not looking up, Fox caught the ball of light and put it in his bag. "By the Light... by the Sound... and the Fracture..." The giant seemed to be waiting.

Fox immediately replied, "By the Beyond... Great Ragyala, by the Gale, I so pledge it."

The giant nodded and, in the voice of many women, spoke a single word, "Agreed..." There was a crack of thunder and a flash of blinding golden light. I flinched at the sound, shutting my eyes tightly closed, and cringed closer to Fox.

Fox rose to his feet and pulled me up a second later. Hesitantly, I opened my eyes. The giant cat-man was gone. The woods before us looked the same, only somewhat darker than they had been before. Fox was still in place next to me, and the shimmering red curtain remained.

Fox put his hand on my forearm. He kept a firm hold of my arm and pulled me toward the portal, leading me through the shimmering red screen. We were through before I could feel much anxiety about the crossing. Unconsciously, I held my breath and closed my eyes as we went through. My skin felt an uncomfortable tingling as we stepped through the shimmering boundary.

The thing that struck me first, as we stood in the new world, was that the vividness was gone from the scene around us. The world looked like half of the colors had been removed. The sky was gray. The trees were a muted brown and pale green, nearly gray. It looked like the life had been drained from everything in our environment, and only a pale husk remained. I looked down at myself and my clothes. They looked normal. I looked normal. My skin color looked the same as it always did. Then I looked over at Fox.

He was faintly glowing. Fox looked the same as he usually did, but a subdued light seemed to be coming from him. If the environment seemed devoid of life, Fox seemed to positively glow with intense energy.

After a moment, the glow faded and Fox appeared as normal. He looked around, surveying our surroundings. He cocked his head as he noted the faded colors of the trees, but he did not seem surprised.

I took strength from his calm. Only then was I aware I had been suppressing a feeling of anxiety. Fox took a deep, slow breath. Unconsciously, I followed his example. As I let the breath out slowly, the feeling lessened.

Again, I followed his example and looked around. We were in the forest... Or rather, we were in a forest, but... a different forest. This was not the forest around my house. There were several things wrong as I looked around. First, we had been at the edge of the forest before. The shimmering red portal had been between a field of grass and the trees. As I looked around, I could only see forest. The shimmering portal was gone. There was no grass anywhere in sight. I turned slowly in a full circle, but there was forest in every direction.

The next wrong aspect of the forest was the trees. I looked up. The trees that surrounded us were substantially larger than they should have been. The comparison was not even close. In the regular forest by our new house, the trees grew to five times a man's height. In this 'other' forest, the trees looked 20 times a man's height. The trees seemed older too. Their massive gnarled trunks stood like silent pillars around us. Barely any of the gray sunlight reached the ground.

Then I became aware of a vaguely pungent smell. It smelled like it had just rained, like leaves decomposing. I hadn't noticed the smell of the forest before, but I noticed the difference when it changed. Again, I looked over at Fox. He was still examining our surroundings, nonplussed. So, I went back to looking up at the tall trees, trying to guess how high the branches went.

After a moment, Fox spoke. "You must have many questions, Kwan. I promise, you will have the opportunity to ask me all of them, but before that I will need to orient us and figure out which way we are going. After that, it is likely we will be traveling for some time. But first..."

Fox took out his bag. From it, he pulled an amulet that seemed to be made from a dull bluish metal. It was an oval, half the thickness of my hand. The amulet was the size of a man's palm and inset with concentric geometrical markings. There were squares inset in circles, inset in triangles, in stars with varying numbers of points. The carved shapes got smaller and smaller until, in the center, was a pebble-sized, milky-white stone. Fox said, "this will help to keep you safe in this place." He handed it to me.

I looked down at the amulet it had a leather thong attached to it. I looked at the intricately carved shape feeling its weight, heavy in my hand. It was warm to the touch, with a life of its own. I turned it over in my hand, studying it.

Fox gestured towards the amulet, and explained to me, "I know you won't be able to understand all of this, but it is a powerful talisman crafted at the GaleTemple. The shape of this amulet is what's most important. The geometry of those lines is a powerful communication to the fabric of reality. It creates an area around you that will help to keep you safe. Put it on."

Fox took his staff, which he called Shui, out from behind his back. He pulled the staff from the loop on his satchel's strap. Then, he placed the gnarled and twisted top of the staff against his forehead and closed his eyes again. He murmured some words, but I could not make them out. The silver metal grain running down the staff began to pulse with light.

After his brief incantation, Fox released his staff and stepped away from it. I was amazed to see the staff stand there, upright and unaided. It stood by itself. The staff stayed balanced long enough for me to take a few steps to the side and look from another angle. It should have fallen over, but it didn't.

After a moment, Fox opened his eyes to look at the staff. The staff started to fall, slowly at first. Then it picked up speed as it fell and like it was going to hit the ground. I was surprised that Fox did not make a move to grab the staff. From everything that I had seen, Fox valued the staff and always treated it well. And because he did not make a move for the staff, I did not make a move to catch it either. (Somehow, I was beginning to intuit that following Fox was generally my best course of action). The staff fell until it stopped, miraculously, at knee height from the ground. The thin end of Fox's staff was resting on the ground a few feet from us.

The fat, fist-sized end of the staff was hovering at knee height pointed away from us and to the left. Fox nodded and stepped forward. He held out his right hand and Shui rose to it. I probably should have been amazed at his staff moving by itself, but after seeing Ragyala and coming to this place, I must have been in shock.

Then he addressed me, "my staff is showing us our way, Kwan. Your sister is alive. She is in this direction. My heart quickened when I heard him say this. I looked at him hopefully. "I can confirm that your sister is here. I can also confirm several other things but I won't discuss those things yet. There are a few questions I have remaining, and several critical points need to be passed successfully before I should talk about them."

With that, Fox adjusted his shoulder satchel, inspected his sandals, and started off in the direction that the staff had pointed. I hurriedly scrambled to catch up with him. Together, we began our hike into the forest. The rescue had begun.

***

My thoughts jumped all over the place at the beginning of our journey. As I walked beside Fox, I realized several things very quickly. The first thing that I realized was that I was not prepared for a long journey. I did not have a walking stick like Fox had. I had not brought any clothing. I could have found better shoes for a long hike. Also, I had not brought any provisions. I had not brought anything to eat at all, nor any water. I looked over at Fox

My worry about being unprepared must have been plain on my face. Fox seemed to understand with a glance what was bothering me and he waved his hand dismissively. He said, "I can provide for everything that we need Kwan. This will be harder in a mental and spiritual sense that it will be in a physical sense. At least, I hope so…"

I was mystified by what Fox had said but still I knew that my sister was worth me doing anything and everything to help her. Fox and I marched along in silence. His shoulders were relaxed, his gait was even. Fox seemed to take it in stride that they were going to find my sister. He seemed to have confidence that we would be successful. His feeling of confidence gave me a feeling of confidence.

I looked around at the woods around me as we walked. Fox did not seem interested in conversation and so I did not speak. Instead, I looked at the woods around me. Each of the trees trunks was a dark brown and the leaves high up above were faded greens and washed-out browns. The first snap of cold would be arriving soon. When it did, when the cold really set in, the leaves would fall. At least, it would if the seasons even came to this place. The occasional log was strewn on the forest floor. Fox and I walked along for what seemed like hours. I began to get tired.

We had been walking through the forest for the better part of the morning before Kwan said, "You know, Fox, we should have reached the Wan Lau town. We headed west, and on the other side of the forest is the Wan Lau town. With as long as we have been walking, we should have been there by now."

I looked around realizing that the gray forest looked largely the same as it had the entire time. I knew that the forest around our house wasn't that large. I realized that something abnormal was going on. The distances did not make sense to the reasonable part of my mind. We had been walking for hours and still had not made it through the forest. I just shouldn't have taken this long to get through the woods.

Fox turned and explained to me in very patient tones what was going on. He explained that we had crossed through the barrier between realms. That barrier separated the dimension that we normally lived in from the dimension where he believed my sister was being kept. When we crossed over the threshold, we entered a place where the illusions of the demon could be used against us. The demon could use illusions on us once we had passed through the barrier to his realm. The forest, he explained, was just an idea of a forest. The trees, he explained, were not real trees. Nothing in fact was 'real' about it. But he said that most of reality was like that, which just confused me.

"It will take a full day of walking before our minds get adjusted to this reality." Fox explained. "It's about time, and not distance really. After that time, we will start to influence this reality with our minds. But even after that point, other powers that live here will still have more control than we do. Until then, we must push forward." Fox smiled and reached out and patted my shoulder. It was small consolation.

He and I kept walking. The forest seemed very gradually to change. The trees became thicker and denser. The trunks of those trees became gnarled and twisted and their leaves were in shapes I had not seen before. The ground was more and more cluttered with fallen tree trunks and branches. There was a solid carpet of leaves everywhere that we walked. We had been hiking up an inclined slope for the better part of an hour. Our legs were tired. In fact, my whole body was tired.

For the first few minutes of our hike, I expected Fox to start talking. He didn't. Instead, I became aware that he was breathing deeply and regularly. His posture was upright and relaxed. And while his powerful strides were larger than mine, he adjusted so that I would not have to run. Although, in truth, I was very anxious to see Cho Clei. So, I would have been willing to run. Eventually, I couldn't stand his silence any longer. "Well?" I burst out. "I don't really understand. Tell me more about this place! Where... where *are* we? And how did you know Cho Clei is here?" Fox stopped walking and looked intently over at me. He took a deep breath, but did not break his gaze.

He began slowly, "We are no longer in the world you know Kwan. We have crossed a boundary into a different realm. This realm has different rules than the world you are used to."

"New Realm? New rules?" I asked. I wanted to make sure that I didn't miss anything during Fox's explanation.

He explained, "well, for one thing, time works differently here. According to my best current plan, we should be home later today. But it won't still be 'today' for us. Even if we were to stay here and search for a year we could still return back to the village this same morning, in theory." I must've looked alarmed, because Fox went on quickly, "No, don't worry. I don't expect us to be gone that long. I don't expect that it will take long at all.

"Another difference here is the idea of space. Where we are is not such a simple question here as it is in the village. There are a few different ways to look at it, really. In one way, you could think of this realm as though we have entered my travel bag."

I was confused, "We entered your bag? I don't understand."

Fox smiled patiently and explained, "We didn't enter my bag, but this place bears some similarities to inside my bag. I'm sure you have noticed that I carry more inside this bag than it should bag able to hold. That is because my bag is bigger on the inside than it is on the outside. This realm is like that. We could travel a thousand years in a straight line, but might still emerge where we entered. There are several concepts you would need to absorb to fully understand it.

Where we live is like an onion. The thing that you think of as the real world has layers. These layers sit next to each other. But, they are different. The facets of how this world operates will reveal themselves to you. And Kwan, the creatures that live in this realm that have no business in the world of men.

"What…, what kind of creatures?" I asked.

He stopped walking and turned to look at me. "There are things here, that may shock your mind. It is likely that we will encounter different beings- "

"Beings? Like ghosts?" I interrupted. I wasn't a coward, but I didn't like the idea of dealing with ghosts.

"Entities." He clarified, but my expression must have shown that I still didn't get it. He went on, "Spirits… or creatures. Some may look like people. Some may seem like monsters to you. It is likely that we will encounter several different kinds of creatures. Some will impress you more positively. The Ragyala is an example of that."

For a moment, I had almost forgotten about that magical creature. Seeing a golden giant with the head of a cat, was so strange that it seemed easier for my mind to push the idea away. I was filled with wonder as I thought back to it. "Yeah, I still can't quite believe what I saw! Who is Ragyala? Was he a giant?"

A list of questions flooded into my mind. "Why did he have the head of a cat? Why did he have such a strange voice? What was that powder you threw? And how did you make that door to this place?" I knew I sounded like a little kid, but my mind was spinning trying to understand it. I probably would have kept asking questions, but Fox held out his hand for me to stop. He turned back to our course and continued the march.

I fell in step with him, and he began to explain as we hiked. "The Ragyala is not a who, it is a what. 'Ragyala' is the title of an ancient position. It is an office, not the being's proper name. Also, the Ragyala would be neither male nor female. 'It' has no need for male or female parts. It is a spirit from before the time of men, that was made into part of the Foundation.

The Ragyala is a guardian of the boundaries between realms. At the GaleTemple we are taught that the guardians of the reality boundaries are often associated with felines. There are theories as to why, but we don't know for certain." He paused in his explanation and continued hiking. "There are hierarchies of power in the celestial orders."

I must have looked confused. He went on, "There are rocks, and plants, and animals. And above them, men." I nodded, agreeing. He went on," And there are things above men. Many things. And as far as power goes, at least in this place, the demon is above us. The Ragyala is above demons. And of course, there are things above the Ragyala."

It was simply laid out. But it somehow stunned me to have it explained to me so simply. And it wasn't just talk. This was insight that he got from experience. I had seen it! I suddenly felt like I was now living in a supernatural place. It had become fully real in my head now. I was stunned. We walked on in silence.

I tried to understand what he was saying. There was more than one world? Was this where people went after they died? The colors were muted. I would expect a 'dead' realm to have 'dead' colors.

This was all so new. My mind felt awake in a way I had never felt. I surrendered myself to my curiosity. The questions continued.

And what did he mean by monsters? Then I thought back to seeing the Ragyala. I remembered that feeling of pressure and power the Ragyala projected. I imagined if something that powerful had decided to attack us, it would have been terrifying. Perhaps this was what Fox meant when he talked about monsters. I couldn't imagine anything stranger than that.

Fox went on, "Really, you should expect anything that you can imagine. In this realm, reality is bent. It can be… twisted. In our home realm, unless one slips through the boundary, there are no monsters. There are some dangerous animals, and there are some evil people. Aside from accidents, they represent the majority of dangers you could meet at home. But here there can be, what you think of, as 'actual' monsters." I started to tense up, thinking about what he was saying. But he noticed and immediately went on, "Don't let yourself go into fear. Fear will paralyze your mind and block your light. There is danger in our world. If we are careful and alert, the dangers are much *less* dangerous. There are dangers in this place too. It is just a reality here. Just like at home, we will need to be careful and alert!"

I walked along next to him for a moment before I realized that I had been fighting to come with him. And I had succeeded. I had wanted to come with him, and could somehow feel that this was the crucial time when I should act. But I realized that I had jumped into this river of new experience and was severely out of my depth. It slowly kept coming to me that I was actually in a different place. The lack of colors, all of it, forced me to accept the new reality.

As Fox began explaining our situation, his main message came through to me. The message was under every piece of information he gave me. He was warning me this place was dangerous. It was very dangerous. For the first time, I realized that I could die rescuing Cho Clei.

I was making the right choice and I had gotten what I wanted, but now, as I walked alongside Fox, I realized that there was a terrifying challenge waiting ahead.

As Fox and I walked through the woods, it became eerie to me how much quieter it was here. The rain had nearly stopped, and hardly penetrated the trees' canopy. The sound of the rain was muted to barely a hush. The trees of the forest blocked the majority of the rain from reaching the ground. Only occasional drops fell.

As Fox and I hiked through the forest, my mind was largely distracted, considering things that he was telling me. I barely paid any attention to the woods. The woods were changing, however. Smaller trees and bushes began to appear and fill in the spaces between the large trees. The transition was so gradual that we might have gotten lost, but a trail had opened up before us. We followed the trail. Fox seemed to trust that we were heading the right way, and I, clearly, trusted Fox.

As we hiked, Fox pointed out a low hill, off to the right of our trail. No trees grew on the hill. Instead, there were only short gray grasses atop the hill. At the base of the hill, a large shadowed opening was facing us. "There are other beings that use this realm. That is one of the Gartun caves."

On either side of the cave's opening was a statue slightly larger than the Ragyala. Each statue was generally in the form of a man. They stood, with legs together and their arms held at their sides.

On the left side, the statue was massively muscled, and had the head of a lizard. In the statue's right hand was a thick stick with a ball on the bottom end. The statue's left hand was held rigidly with all the fingers in a line.

The statue on the right was slightly smaller, also having a man's arms and legs. It also had the face of a reptile, but this one was smiling and looked almost pleasant. The lizard man statue's two hands were holding a large book in front of it. There was writing on the book, but I wasn't able to read it.

Even though the statues were large, I might have missed them. If it weren't for Fox pointing out the cave, my eyes could have passed right over them. Both statues were covered in a brown moss that blurred some of their features. Still, they were recognizable as reptile figures.

"Gartun?" I asked. I had never heard of them. And Father had taught me about the people of neighboring lands.

"The world where we live is shaped like a child's ball. Many people do not actually know this. They think that the world is flat, like a field that never ends. But it isn't." I nodded slowly, as two impulses fought within me. One impulse was to trust anything Fox said. The other impulse was to argue. Of course, the world was flat. Sure, there were hills and mountains in the world, but generally it was flat. Besides, how could someone live life while balancing on a ball?

Fox went on, "We live on the outside of that ball; the outside of the world. There are several groups of beings that live on the inside too. One of those groups is called the Gartuns."

"How could they live inside?" I asked. I was trying to sound skeptical, but I couldn't see any reason why he would want to trick me. His outlandish claims rang true. But honestly, I chided myself, he had already proven himself by getting us this far.

"The world is hollow, Kwan. Just like a child's ball is empty inside, our world is the same. There are long tunnels that become passages to that world. Those tunnels lead to immense caverns, caverns so large that many even have their own weather. Judging by those statues, the Gartuns use that cave as an access to this realm."

The trail took us up a slight incline and I found that I had to lean into the walk. Fox was somehow very strong and spry for a big man. He was careful not to go too fast though. Still, I was impressed with his ability to keep up such a vigorous pace indefinitely. He never seemed to get fatigued. He had breath to talk and answer my questions, while I was just keeping up.

Chapter 6

The S'la'manda

I was getting tired. I was thinking about what Fox was telling me, so I was distracted too. I was tired and would have missed the danger, completely unaware. Luckily, Fox's sharp senses spotted the trouble approaching.

I was alerted to its arrival by the sound of Fox's sharp intake of breath. I was about to ask Fox another question about the Gartuns. I had been looking down at the ground in front of me, but at that sound, my head snapped up to look at him. He was on my left only slightly in front of me, so I was able to see his expression. His eyes were wide, and his face looked deadly serious.

I tracked where his eyes were looking, and directed my eyes there, scanning. Fox was looking at a space on the forest floor some 20 feet ahead of us. There, I saw a small lizard, no longer than my hand. I think I might've missed it entirely, were it not a bright red color. It seemed to have a flash of yellow at its tail... and something else... a shimmering orange aura around it.

Immediately Fox began chanting again. He placed two hands on his staff at chest height, and dug the butt of the staff into the ground. The little lizard appeared to be running straight towards us. I looked over at Fox, but his eyes were closed.

Again, it seemed like several things happened one after another, in my mind. First, I noticed the fire. In the distance, behind the lizard, the forest was on fire. I guess it can only be exhaustion to explain why didn't see it before. I didn't have

Fox's ability to walk forever without getting tired. Even if I knew it was just my mind here in this place, my mind was tired.

After noticing the fire, I saw that the ground around us was rising. My thought was that Fox was raising walls around us out of the ground itself. It was clear enough for me to see that the fire was coming towards us. My mind was coming to the idea in that moment of panic, Fox could protect us with a wall of dirt. I realized that I would be burned if not for his intervention. I didn't question Fox's many strange abilities. It seemed reasonable enough to me, to think that he could use his powers and make a wall of dirt and stone around us. Why not?

After a moment though, I realized that there was no wall rising around us. Instead, we were rapidly sinking underground. I looked down at the ground around me. It was as though Fox and I were standing on a flat disk that was being pushed into the ground. Then the ground above us was moving, coming together to form a roof over our heads. The roof was tall enough for us to stand without crouching. I was amazed as I realized what was happening. In just a few seconds, Fox and I were submerged in complete darkness. I could hear his breathing, laborious and heavy in the dark. He whispered a word to his staff, and the light began to glow from the metal embedded in it. Fox had stuck the narrow end of the staff into the ground. It provided a central light to our circular space, but cast eerie shadows on Fox's face.

He turned to me, calm again, and said, "That tiny thing was an ancient evil. It is known as the 'S'la'manda'. S'la'manda were banished from the world many years ago. For one to be here, means that one was brought here from the darkest void. This demon is even more reckless than I thought. S'la'manda can burn this realm, and then cross over to ours. The materials they touch begin to burn. Then those things burn other things. And soon, the world has burned." His features darkened as he spoke, "It cannot be allowed."

After a moment, his features relaxed, and he again took on the demeanor of a teacher. "As I said, their power is an ancient evil. It does not obey the normal rules. S'la'manda were actually the victims in an ancient war. They are forever feeling cold, and run in search of warmth. As they run, they set fire to everything around them. But, in a cruel twist of their fate, they can never feel the warmth of the fires they set. Imagine that you are cold and want to put on clothes, or a blanket. And every time you do, the clothing bursts into flames without heat. It is a devious punishment…"

I was unsure what to say to that. The fire lizards were victims in some war? What war? Who punished them? I added it to the list of questions to ask him later. No, I thought. Be Practical. I nodded. "So, what we do now?" I asked Fox.

Fox looked at me for a moment considering my question. Then he sat down on the ground. His staff was still stuck firmly in the ground at the center of our underground room. He was calm, and I determined to be calm too. In the light from his staff, I studied our surroundings. After a moment, I began to realize that the walls of our shelter were not smooth. Somehow, I imagined that the disc platform below us, that got pushed into the ground, was a circle. But then I realized that it was the same oval shape as the medallion I wore.

If it weren't for the light of Fox's staff, I would have been unbearably anxious. As it was, being able to see Fox's calm demeanor made our predicament almost more interesting than terrifying.

Very soon we began to hear a series of pops and cracks. They were muffled because of the dirt between us, but we could still hear them pretty clearly. The pops and cracks grew to a hissing sound and roaring sound. The volume grew. Also, the ceiling became warm. In the grand scheme, I didn't actually know how thick the roof was. I understood that the walls were not high but we were completely surrounded by dirt. The higher up I felt on the wall, the hotter it became. Ceiling of our little room was very hot to the touch. I looked at Fox to see what he wanted our next move to be. To my surprise, he merely made himself comfortable.

"The demon got the drop on us." He could see that I was confused by the term, so he clarified himself. "It caught us before we were aware that the attack was here, before the attack was coming. So, we don't really have that much choice as far as now. We didn't get to choose the time, we didn't get to pick the terrain, but we were able to get to shelter before the inferno hit us. Outside, above us, the forest is on fire." Fox's free hand gestured vaguely at the ceiling.

"By this point, considering how densely packed these woods are, everything is probably on fire by now. I made an emergency safety borough for us. In truth, we were lucky that the attack happened over soft dirt like this. Had it been bedrock, I would not have been able to do it. So, we just have to wait for the fire to burn itself out. The lizard can't be burned by its own fire. In truth, it is absolutely fire-proof, even to much hotter temperatures than fires. Although how we know that is another story…" He trailed off, distracted.

"It was just troubling me that the demon had been so reckless. I suspect our enemy released this evil thing to harass us and interfere with recovering your sister. These lizards were banned from the realm of man for reason. They were too dangerous to be around flammable things." A series of images of fires filled my mind. Worry and tension began to take me. Soon I was worrying about all sorts of things. I began to worry about the amount of air that we had inside the shelter. I started thinking, reasoning that we were breathing, and logically, might run out of air. I brought this concern up to Fox.

Again, he smiled kindly at me, and shook his head. "Part of this technique generates all energies we need to live- like breathable air. There are a few protections that this type of shelter affords us, but that you might not suspect. For instance, the hole we are in would protect us from other dangers too. There are deadly forces in most of the realms; dangers that can't be seen. This realm is no different. Gasses, poisons, predatory spirits, even tiny pieces of radiant energy can kill us. This hole protects us from all of them." With that, Fox lay back and, a moment later, was softly snoring.

I couldn't believe it. Fox had gone to sleep! The forest above us was burning, but he was relaxed enough to sleep! After a while of sitting there watching him, I could see that he was genuinely getting rest, not just making a show of trying. I couldn't think of anything else to do, so I lay on my side and used one bent arm as a pillow. The muted roar of the fire was soothing above us, calming my worry. Surprisingly, I slept too.

I awoke, after what seemed like hours, and the roar above us had died down. Fox was already awake, sitting up, and looking at me. He rose to his feet. I scrambled to my feet too, following his example. I reached up and touched the dirt ceiling. The ceiling of our underground retreat was warm, but not uncomfortably hot…

It seemed that our wait was over. Fox returned his hands to the same positions they had been in, on his staff. He closed his eyes and began mumbling to himself. A moment later, I began to realize that we were rising. There was only the slightest vibration to show that we were moving, but I could feel it.

A small hole appeared in the center of the ceiling. The ceiling parted above our heads. A blinding light began to filter in through the opening in the ceiling. I squinted at the light. In the short time that we had been underground, my eyes had fully adjusted to the darkness. After only light from Fox's staff, the little bit of light coming from the burnt forest above was very bright.

There appeared to be a glowing haze of light around us. The haze was a shimmering icy blue color. A gust of burning wind blew through where we were and the shield flared a brighter blue, blocking the heat. As I focused on the blue shield, I could feel the temperature drop around us. It must have dealt with the smoke in the air too.

I watched, amazed, as we rose out of our hole. Soon, we stood back where we had stood. It was strange to look down and see us standing on an oval of unburned ground. Outside of that oval, the ground was charred and smoking.

The air was sweltering, but I couldn't feel it. There were embers on the ground, and smoke in the air. Peering through the haze, the more I looked around at the devastation, the more I felt like coughing. Fox released his right hand from his staff and made an odd gesture with his left hand.

At the time, the best way that I could think of it was that we were stuck inside a section of bamboo. Bamboo grew in hollow tubes. It was like we were in an invisible tube of bamboo. The disc of unburned ground we stood on, was the 'floor' of the tube. The walls of the tube kept us protected from the heat around us. The air in the forest was hot enough that I could still see embers floating in it.

Fox inhaled slowly and deeply, taking in more air that I imagined possible, and then held that mighty breath. After that, he blew out as hard as he could. Fox was a big man and, I later found out, an adept at breath control. So, it was impressive to watch his 'power breath'. At the same time that he blew out, the walls of our bamboo tube, seemed to expand outwards in a circle of frosty blue light.

The icy blue ring spread out from us. Whenever it encountered the burnt remnants of the forest, it cooled them on contact. Even the air was cooled and cleansed as the blue light passed through it. Smoking tree trunks immediately stopped smoking when the blue light touched them. I looked around in awe.

While I was not an expert on fire, I did realize that this was not a natural fire. I had made my share of fires when camping. Even before Fox's breath had cooled our surrounding, the trees had already been consumed. In the regular world, it would have taken a long time for the fire to consume the forest.

Apparently the s'la'manda created a fire that burned faster than normal fire. I couldn't help but blink when the ring of blue light spread out from us. The point where the energies began was Fox's staff. When I open my eyes, I saw a different landscape from just a second ago. It seemed that most of the reds and oranges had been removed from the landscape. The air no longer felt hot. Even though there was still a heavy smell of smoke in the air, I did not find it unpleasant being there. Just then I noticed that not all the blue light had dissipated. Even after Fox had sent out the ring of cooling blue energy, a second, fainter ring, still remained on the ground around our feet. It looked as though most of the energy had dealt with our surroundings, but that some part of it stayed behind to protect our bodies. I admit that I felt reassured.

It appeared that the freezing energy that Fox had sent out didn't have the same effect everywhere. I say this because when I looked around at the forest around me, I noticed that some branches were still smoking, while other branches were beginning to drip water from patches of frost that had just appeared on them.

Fox looked slightly worried as he looked around, his eyes scanning our surroundings for the s'la'manda. He was still mumbling to himself. He half turned towards me, but never took his hands off of his staff. "We're in trouble Kwan. The s'la'manda only has to touch us for a second to fully set us on fire. If I were to strike it with Shui, there is a possibility that my staff would burst into flames. To be honest with you, I'm not sure what would happen. So that means that we are in a defensive position. If the s'la'manda rushes at us, the shield I've left around us, would only hold out for a few seconds. Which means that I have very few options in the situation. One thing that I can do is to conjure the predator of the s'la'manda. But, in truth, releasing one of them would be as dangerous as releasing the s'la'manda was. The last time one of those flew over land, the entire world was plunged into an age of ice."

It seemed like a neat and obvious solution to me. I leaned in towards Fox and asked, "What is the natural enemy of the s'la'manda? If this is what the s'la'manda can do, whatever you're considering would be worth it."

"It does seem that way, doesn't it?" asked Fox, "but all the records are very clear, when it comes to the hok. The hok is allied, in theory, with the positive force. Unfortunately, not every story is like the heroic tales they tell you as a child. You see, the hok is not very bright. It is powerful bird, but simple minded. It will intend to follow instructions, but, in *every* account, they forget why they were summoned. Their animal nature takes over, and they try to escape. Their instinct to range looks to be more powerful than their minds. Either way, the warnings are clear.

In theory, there is a way that we would be able to get rid of the s'la'manda, but not freeze the world. However, to do that, we would need to capture the hok as soon as it caught the s'la'manda. We would only have one chance to banish the bird. And if we were not successful, it is possible that the ice hok could escape this demon's pocket dimension. In theory, if the bird were to fly straight up, it is possible that he could pass the barrier between realms. If he does that, the world will freeze again. Again, the world will be covered in ice. It will create another ice age."

"Again?" I asked, surprised.

"Yes, there have been many periods when the world has frozen before. Some were caused by the hok, some were caused by natural processes. We are living in the period between these 'ice ages'. The world is warm, and if we can stop it freezing, we should. Whether the world froze or burned, it would be equally disastrous for life now. Either way, we have to prevent it."

He took off, walking quickly and I hurried to catch up. "We have to lure the s'la'manda to us, Kwan. If it wanders too far, it may find a way out of this realm."

I was confused. "How do we lure it to us?" I asked. "And isn't that dangerous? We had to hide from it last time."

Fox nodded, "Yes, but last time it got the drop on us. I hope to change that." He smiled at me. First, we have to choose our terrain. Follow me."

We had barely reached the center of the bowl indentation in the valley when the s'la'manda attacked. Our main advantage was that the s'la'manda was bound to the land. The hok could fly. And controlling a flying thing is a much bigger challenge than it sounds.

As we approached our destination, Fox had broadcast the intense impression of warmth through Shui. Fox explained. The signal had travelled through the ground and attracted the s'la'manda to our location.

A bush off to my right burst into flames, announcing the presence of the s'la'manda. Seeing the approaching lizard, he quickly uttered some strange words, raised his arms wide and clapped them together. When he did, there was a flash of light, and the high-pitched tinkling sound as though ice was being broken. Then his hands immediately rebounded back outward, this time 'holding' a sphere of twinkling light. Fox stopped them about two feet apart, just barely outside of the light. He wore a fierce expression, clearly exerting effort to keep the ball of light contained. A feeling of cold was the next thing I noticed.

I wanted to see what this new animal looked like, but I couldn't see anything. As soon as the light flashed, the area around us was filled with a frosty mist. It was like an ice-cold morning fog. I heard the animal before I saw it. A high, shrill, piercing sound emerged from the Misty cloud at our feet. Before we could decide what to think, the ice cloud dispersed. I stopped and took the time to look down at the hok. The hok, in turn, looked back up at me.

It appeared to be a bird, shaped like any other hawk. It was surrounded by a glowing blue ring on the ground. The main difference was its coloring. Instead of being the normal brown, its feathers were shimmering, constantly shifting between ice blue and a silvery white. Also, instead of a normal bird's eyes, its eyes seemed to glow, radiating a pale blue color. Its claws appeared black, but the tips of them were surrounded with frost. They appeared to have icy white sheaths covering over the talons themselves. It seemed content to study us as we studied it.

"They are beautiful, Kwan. But make no mistake, they are extremely dangerous." Fox warned.

My eyes flicked to the side as I suddenly remembered the attacking fire lizard. It appeared to be stunned, frozen in place.

We were both inclined to admire the ice hok, but Fox had the presence of mind to put a hand in front of me. The bird seemed to understand that Fox did not want me to be hurt. I wondered if he had some way to influence the bird since he was the one who had summoned the bird.

Only then did the hok's head turn to look at the frozen lizard. At that moment, the s'la'manda awoke from its stasis. It shook its little head, then, seeing the hok, it turned and ran from us. For something that had just been frozen, it was surprisingly quick. There was a 'whoosh' sound as a semi-burnt bush burst back into flame.

The ice hok narrowed its eyes and launched itself into the sky. For a moment, I feared that it was trying to escape, but it stopped 20 or 30 feet over our heads.

It started making circles through the air of the forest, clearly searching for the s'la'manda. The bush to my right that had burst into flames was starting to go out. There had not been much to the bush, and the fire was able to consume it very quickly. But, surprisingly, the s'la'manda was nowhere to be seen. The hok had seemed to understand our need as soon as it was summoned. It looked like the s'la'manda also understood that it was being hunted. It understood so well that it had completely disappeared. But, as Fox pointed out, when your passage can't help but set things on fire, it is extraordinarily hard to travel in stealth. Even as I was thinking this thought, a tree off to my left began to crackle and smoke. It appeared that the s'la'manda had brushed the tree. The ice hok did not need to be alerted by us. It turned, wheeling in the air and gracefully fell into a power dive. I did not understand how the hok could move so quickly, but it appeared to fly faster than anything could fall.

The chase was over disappointingly quickly. The ice hok made a few quick turns, avoiding branches that were in its way and swooped down. Light flaring as they made contact, the hok neatly caught the s'la'manda between its claws. It seemed like my senses were enhanced, because I could see that s'la'manda's red coloring and hazy aura were flickering, off and on. The hok, with a fierce look on its face, bent down and, with its beak, neatly snipped the s'la'manda's head off. Immediately, the red drained from the s'la'manda, leaving it a pale gray husk. Then the hok swerved to the side to avoid flames that were climbing up the tree that the s'la'manda had ignited. The hok appeared not to see the fire as a threat, but to see it more as an irritation.

The hok continued wheeling in air and made a second pass towards the tree. This time, I saw just the tip of its wing brush against one of the branches of the tree. Instantly, ice appeared on the branch and started to grow outward. The ice creeped across the surface of the tree, encasing it. A tree which had been burning just seconds before was now being covered with ice. Then it began to brush against all the trees that had been burned. It was as though the burning trees offended it and the hok preferred to leave ice behind. We watched in amazement as tree after tree began to turn white, frozen.

Fox was moaning to himself with urgency as he performed a rapid series of hand gestures, then began chanting something. I sensed that it would be stupid and dangerous to distract him at this moment so I kept quiet. After a minute, Fox's eyes flashed open immediately tracking the progress of the ice hok through the sky. The ice hok still had the body of the decapitated s'la'manda in its claws. It gave piercing shrill cry that was somehow combined with the cracking tinkle of breaking ice.

Making this sound, the ice hok turned in the air and started to climb, flapping its wings powerfully to gain height. The metal grain in Fox's staff flared brightly. "No!" Fox said. "She's forgotten…trying to escape! And I told you what will happen if she gets out." My mind was racing as I tried to figure out how I could help. I was so clearly out of my depth but I was determined not to be a liability the whole time. I imagine that if I had a bow and arrow, that I might be able to shoot the ice hok from the ground. But I didn't have a bow. I realized that I wasn't doing anything useful. Panicked, I looked over at Fox.

He had dropped to one knee, spun his staff, raising the narrow end on his shoulder, and pointed the thick end up at the sky. He followed the hok's flight for a second, then a blast could be felt as the staff pushed Fox, bending him back. His eyes stayed trained on the hok. I whipped my head around, turning from Fox to the hok. It looked like a ball of 'fuzzy air' shot out of the staff and raced to meet the hok in flight. When the ball of 'fuzzy air' reached the hok, I expected some dramatic reaction, an explosion or something. Instead, the hok appeared to continue flying, but in slow motion. It was still climbing, wings still flapping, just very slowly.

I turned back to Fox. He had his hands placed about a foot apart from each other. Between them, a crackling ball of golden energy flared to life, suspended in the air. He looked up and tracked the hok with his eyes. His eyes squinted just for a moment as he threw his hands up, raising them to the sky. There was a 'thump' in the air, a concussion without any sound, as light leapt from Fox's outstretched hands, rocketing into the sky. The light traveled impossibly fast, shooting through the sky to intercept the ice hok. I expected that the energy ball would hit the hok that the hok would surely explode this time. What actually happened was very different.

When the ball got close to the hok, it expanded into two halves of a glowing blue cage. The half-cages flew to intercept the hok, then clapped together, holding it there. Time around the hok seemed to return to normal. It flapped its wings, frustrated, but it could not escape the glowing cage. The hok gave a long angry cry of protest.

His hands still raised and outstretched, Fox began to draw the hok back down towards us. I watched as the cage began slowly to float down towards us. When it was only a few feet away, Fox kept one hand, his right hand, outstretched towards the cage. He knelt down, and with his left hand on the ground, he began chanting something again. A geometric shape of concentric triangles shimmered into being, appearing on the ground under his hand. Then he drew the cage in until it was sitting on top of the geometric shape.

Then, Fox stood up, his staff appearing in his hand. Using it, he pushed the cage down into the geometric shape. To my astonishment, the ice hok and the cage disappeared. Both the cage and the diagram seem to dissolve each other. After Fox staff touch the ground, there was nothing there to tell that anything strange had just happened.

Fox and I stood there, both worn from the ordeal. Although he was worn from actually doing things, and I was just worn from worrying. He looked at me critically for a moment. "Try breathing like this. First fill here." He indicated a point on his belly. Then he performed a series of exaggerated breaths, demonstrating.

Dazed from the encounters with the s'la'manda and the hok, I followed the strange breathing exercise. Some breaths were long and deep, filling the belly, then the lungs, then the mouth. Some breaths were short and quick, like panting. Soon I felt calm again.

Fox nodded and began walking again. I looked around at our scorched, icy surroundings and thought of Cho Clei. She was why I was here, and I would not fail her. Clear minded again, I followed. Our long trek continued.

We walked out of the iced and burned forest and I felt a wave of exhaustion hit me. I swayed on my feet. Fox announced that we would be stopping for the night. I was going to protest that it wasn't even dark, but thinking better of it, I kept quiet. Fox had me sit while he collected firewood. "It's not the element I want to deal with now, but a hot meal is a powerful tonic. So, we need fire. Do you feel hungry?" Before I could answer, he was busying himself with the fire.

After Fox made the fire, he went about preparing dinner. From his bag, he pulled a flask of water, as well as 2 cups. I was surprised to find 2 cups ready in his sack. Perhaps having guests and visitors in his camping was a usual thing? He reached into his bag and pulled out a small bamboo container with a stopper in the top. He also pulled 2 cups from his bag. He opened the bamboo container and poured out a liquid that appeared to already be hot. He handed one of the cups to me.

I accepted the cup with a nod of thanks and look down at it. The cup was made of carved wood that had been polished to a mirror-like finish on the outside. Inside the cup, was a hot tea. Tea had a fragrant, minty aroma. Smoke billowed from the top of it.

After that, Fox reached into his satchel and began pulling out vegetable after vegetable after vegetable. He also pulled out a small board and a long knife to cut the vegetables. He looked around for a moment before seizing on a suitable rock. Then he walked over to the rock, and place the cutting board on top of it. After that he said about diligently cutting up all of the vegetables.

I watched him as he went about these domestic chores. He brought his full attention to even these small tasks. When he did them, it seemed like there was nothing else happening in the world. It seemed as though there was no other reason that he existed. He committed so fully to every action I had witnessed that I could not help but be impressed.

After cutting the vegetables, Fox reached into his bag and pulled out a metal pan. I eyed the pan, partly because it was a metal that I had not seen before. It had a vaguely bluish tint to it. The other thing that was that the skillet/pan was so large that I am certain I would've seen it before then. There's no way that Fox could have had such a large thing in his sack without me seeing the outline of it.

I looked up at Fox, and again he seemed to read my thoughts before I could respond. "Before you ask" Fox said. "My bag has some interesting properties. Not everything is the way that it appears Kwan." He smiled broadly at my expression. I must have looked amazed. He continued, "I suspect that this trip will be *highly* instructive to you. You right now, at this very moment, are in the middle of something like a dream. Part of you is here, connected with me in this challenge against our adversary. And part of you is grounded back in our world.

Now that you have entered this realm with me, I should tell you something about what we face. We are up against a primordial evil being. Not every demon is a great one. But all demons are formidable. And this one, judging by what he has been able to do, is a formidable one indeed."

He placed a few logs over the fire, making a stovetop for the skillet to sit. He emptied the cutting board into the skillet and then he placed the skillet directly on the 'stovetop'.

Then, apparently wanting a place to sit, he started looking around. He spotted a large tree trunk that had fallen over a dozen feet away. He grabbed a branch that was sticking out of the tree trunk with one hand, and pulled the entire trunk over by the fire. Then he sat on the trunk and watched the vegetables cook.

My eyes goggled as I did a quick calculation and realized that the tree trunk had to be as heavy as several men. But Fox looked completely at ease. I looked at Fox curiously wondering at his strength. He was a large and, if you ignored the big belly, muscular man. But this was too much! How was that even possible?

Fox cooked vegetables over the fire. They appeared to be an onion, and some sort of root vegetables I could not recognize. Fox reached into his pack and pulled out a tiny pouch. Carefully he opened the drawstring at the top of the pouch. He reached in this fat thumb and forefinger pulled out a pinch of spice. Then he carefully sprinkled it over the vegetables. He reached into his bag next and pulled out a clean and polished, brown wooden stick. He used this stick to prod the vegetables in the pan.

The smell of the vegetables cooking and the spices on top of them made my mouth water. I hadn't even realized I was hungry. Scared and tired were the only feelings I had been aware of until then.

I sipped the tea that he had given me, and looked into the growing fire. The vegetables were just beginning to make a hissing sizzle sound. I looked over at Fox who was also sipping his tea. I watched carefully as he stared at the fire without blinking, seeming not to notice me. He seemed relaxed, his mind somewhere else.

In fact, his manner was so relaxed that I felt comfortable asking a question. "Fox," I said hesitantly. "Do you really think we are going to find my sister?" I asked him.

What I had known of Fox up to this point led me to believe that he would be honest, but somehow, I was afraid of the full truth. I was nervous that his answer might be different this time. Fox, however, did not look different at all. He continued to look wistfully into the fire.

After a long moment, he spoke. "I have to be completely truthful with you Kwan." He said. "I don't want for you to have unrealistic expectations about your sister. As I said when we first arrived, I can tell you that she certainly is alive. I can also tell you, that I have a good idea where she is within this realm. And Shui can sense her exact location." I let out a breath I didn't know I had been holding.

He went on, "If you asked me how confident I am that we can beat our opponent. Then... I would say I am not sure. I don't know if we can beat it. All indications have been that it is an extremely powerful demon. But the worst thing that we could do at this point would be to underestimate him."

Then Fox outlined his basic plan. "We will need to find this demon. More specifically, we need to find your sister first. That may not be easy, but we have Shui to help guide us. After we find the demon, we will need to force it to let your sister go. I have a few ideas about how to do that. And finally, after all of that we will need to make sure that it cannot do this again. We came to find your sister. And I do believe we will, but now that we're here, I have to be realistic with you. It will be a genuine challenge to deal with this demon. *It* is a special problem."

I looked at Fox with renewed respect and realized how far out of my depth I really was. I was now a pure liability to Fox. I doubted that there was anything I could do to help. I didn't have any of Fox's skills. Doubts and fears began to creep into my thoughts. I was afraid I would just be something weak that Fox had to protect.

I had wanted to be helpful, but I felt like the opposite of that. Maybe I should have let Fox go alone. Maybe his chances would have been better without me. My fervent wish to help save my sister might work against the situation.

A few minutes later, the vegetables were done cooking, then Fox produced bowls, napkins and chopsticks from his bottomless bag. We ate. It tasted better than Fong's cooking to me. I said as much to Fox.

He thanked me for the compliment and said, "The laws of nature are different in this place. It affects both our bodies and our minds. One of those effects is that, while we are here, your body does not *need* food."

"I don't *need* to eat?" I asked, incredulous.

Fox's face broke into a grin. He shook his head. "No, and neither do I, in this place."

"But... then why did we eat? Why did you even make the food?!" I asked. I didn't understand. It had been nice, but my sister still needed us!

Fox's bushy eyebrows furrowed and he gave me a look that was both serious and compassionate. "We will not be able to rescue your sister if our spirits are broken when we reach her. This realm lacks many things that we are accustomed to, like color, sunlight, edible food, clean water... I could continue. The effect of these things missing around us, is that we have to sustain ourselves with our own energy. Does that make sense so far?"

I thought about it. It made sense. My expression must have shown as much, because Fox continued. "There are a few ways we can help ourselves deal with this problem. One way is by participating in routine activities we did in the normal world, like eating and drinking. Our bodies could only tolerate food or drink from our world, so you notice that I prepare food I *brought* from our realm. And while the food doesn't feed our bodies, the familiar activity helps to balance and refresh our minds."

He paused and looked me up and down. "You feel better, don't you?" I thought about how I felt, and he was right. I did feel better. "This is how we sustain ourselves to stay strong enough to rescue your sister." His words made sense, and I relaxed somewhat.

After we ate, Fox cleaned up and produced a teapot. Then he reached into his bag and pulled out a long wooden flute. It was longer than my arm. Fox put the flute to his lips and gave an experimental blow. A pure, mellow tone issued forth. The flute was clearly a well-made instrument.

Fox played as we both looked into the fire. At least fire seemed normal here. The dancing flames and flickering embers were hypnotic. The melody Fox played was beautiful, but made me a little sad. He seemed to sense this and changed the song. He played a new melody that built into a confident, and rousing climax. Where before I had felt sad, now I felt ready to fight, clear in my mind, and resolved in my spirit.

Fox put his flute away and told me to prepare myself to get moving again. Quickly and efficiently he packed away the cooking supplies. Everything disappeared neatly into his bag. I didn't think to notice, at the time, how the cooking tools remained clean. But later, on reflection, I realized that another strange effect was at work. The dishes were always clean, even though I never saw Fox wash anything.

Once Fox's bag was packed, we set out again along the trail. His large bag was slung comfortably over one shoulder, his gnarled staff held easily in one hand. His robes, while unimpressive in the city, looked perfectly natural out here.

We continued on for what seemed like another hour. It was longer than I was used to walking, but I did not complain, especially because I knew that I had asked for this. I also knew that saving my little sister would be worth any hardship.

After another two hours hiking, the terrain under us became rockier. The ground towards the right of our trail began to slope downward. Eventually, the ground to the right of the trail dropped off to reveal a large ravine, a gaping valley. As the ravine came into view, a thin ribbon of river could be seen at the bottom. It dully reflected this realm's pale gray light.

Fox stopped and repeated his incantation from before, making his staff glow, stand up, and fall again. This time, the staff pointed off the trail. It pointed to the right, down the slope, toward the distant river.

Without hesitation, Fox turned and strode off the path. In my mind, the path had come to represent safety in that strange place. Hesitating only for a moment, I followed. We made our way down the slope, occasionally catching sight of the river below.

Initially, when the slope was gradual, we still moved quickly. But as we descended, we encountered steeper parts and had to be more careful not to slip. Gradually, we made our way down to the river.

The trees of the dark woods gave way to rocky terrain. Moving into unburned woods had been a huge improvement. But over time, the woods had become something different. I hadn't realized it inside the forest, but I had been fighting a feeling of oppression under the trees. Now however, it was a relief to see the sky, even if it was pale gray color.

The river was larger and wider than it had seemed from a distance. A lazy current moved the water slowly past us. As we approached it, we were walking upstream. The banks of the river were littered with large rocks.

When we reached the river, Fox and I stood on the bank for a long moment watching the water flow past. I was going to speak, but he held out his hand to stop me. Then he pointed out at the river, pointing out his observations to me too. I began to see a pattern as to how Fox taught. He liked to draw my attention to things I would not normally have noticed.

For example, he pointed out that along the banks of a normal river, a person could usually see small reeds and plants growing. Here, there were no plants growing around it at all. Looking out at the river, Fox warned me not to touch the water. He reminded me that some parts of this world could be very different from how it is in 'our' world. In our normal world, water always supports life. "In this place, water doesn't have that requirement…"

The rocky ground on either side of the river was flat for a few paces, then angled upward toward the woods that topped the ridges on either side of the valley. It was simple, since there wasn't a bridge. There were only two possible paths for us to take; upstream, or downstream. Fox's staff confirmed our direction. We walked upstream, alongside the river. Fox only checked our direction occasionally. As we hiked, Fox explained. We walked along the bank of that river until we met a tributary that was flowing into the stream.

Eventually, after consulting Shui, Fox had us retrace the tributary. As we followed it upstream, it curved back up into the woods. We walked upstream, the trees grew denser. The stream was twice a man's height. I was pretty sure that with a running start, I could have jumped across it. With the riverbed visible, it appeared to only be knee deep, but I heeded Fox's warning and didn't try to check.

Chapter 7

The First

We walked up the bank of the stream. The water flowed past us. Every step brought us closer to bringing my sister home.

Eventually, we heard a growing, constant roar ahead of us. After hiking another few minutes, we saw the waterfall. Fox slowed us to a stop as we approached it. The waterfall faced us, a hundred feet away. The river flowed past us on our right.

Fox held up his left hand (not holding his staff). The silver grain running down his staff had begun to brightly glow. He wore a look of concern on his face. "Kwan..." he said. I stopped immediately, alert and worried. "Shui senses trouble... we are being... watched." Then he started walking again, albeit slower. Warily, I followed him.

We walked on toward the waterfall. It was gracious to call it a waterfall because the water only fell about 6 feet. The sound was more a tranquil than roaring. The volume of water was not impressive. The only thing that really seemed impressive about the waterfall, was the inexplicable Torii gate built over it. Fox and I both paused our steps as we noticed the gate.

The Torii gate was made of two, stout and square, upright wooden beams that stood on either side of the waterfall. Across the top of those two lay a third, larger, square cross-beam. The cross-beam extended over past the upright beams. The upright beams were painted in a shiny black lacquer. The cross-beam was painted a shiny red lacquer. Gleaming iron letters, in a script I could not read, were written across the beam.

Back in school, I had learned that Torii gates were built at temples or shrines. But there were no temples or shrines, here, out in this place, were there? Where were the people to 'use' the shrine? Would there be shrines in this realm? Why would this construction be sitting out in this place? Rather, why would somebody have built this ornate and heavy thing in the middle of the woods if it did not serve a purpose? And why was the hair on my arms and neck standing up? I felt the strange sensation and looked down to look at my arms. Why would my hair be sticking straight out? I was trying to understand what was happening when the world cracked.

Fifty feet ahead of us, between us and the Torii gate, an enormous bolt of lightning sliced down through the sky. Time seemed to slow down as I watched the lightning zig-zag toward the ground. It was too bright for me to watch, but still I was aware of its approach. Part of me responded with panic, while another part of me was observing. The one bolt split into two bolts above the waterfall. Those two bolts sharply turned away from the gate, in our direction. The two bolts simultaneously hit the two largest trees in front of us, on either side of the waterfall.

When the lightning struck the trees, they exploded. One of the trees was only ten paces away. The thunderous boom that immediately followed the lightning was as shocking as the flash. I could feel the crack of the thunder throughout my body. I felt the thump like a punch to my chest. It was a stunning display.

I cringed and cowered, instinctively flinching, covering my head, and closing my eyes tight. Before I could think through what had happened, I realized my ears were ringing. Awareness of the ringing was the first thought. I opened my eyes a sliver.

I saw Fox standing in front of me holding his staff with both hands. He was grasping it, head down, as though shielding us behind the staff. Then, I felt a humming vibration coming from the medallion that Fox had given me. I looked down to see that the medallion was floating slightly off of my chest, pushed or pulled upward by some force.

After a moment, when the ringing in my ears had passed, I opened my eyes fully and looked around. Fox stood in the same position as before, -upright and unhurt. Remarkably, so was I. (Not upright, but unhurt.) I looked around and saw that the air was filled with pieces of wood falling to the ground. A cloud of haze and smoke filled the air. Wood chips and splinters littered the area in an oval around us. And inside that circle, there were no twigs at all. I didn't know whether it was Fox or the talisman that had protected us, but I was impressed. Clearly, the lightning (and the exploding trees) could have killed us. I resolved to ask Fox later about what had protected me. I looked down at the medallion with renewed respect. Fox frowned at me, then warily scanned our surroundings.

Fox told me to wait in that spot, then took a few steps forward. He whispered a few words to his staff, then stood it upright, with the small end resting on the ground. He pulled his hand back from the staff and stepped away. Shui remained there, upright and not falling to the ground. The silver metal grain running through the staff pulsed.

Then, turning his attention away from our surroundings, Fox swung his bag around from over his shoulder. I watched him loosen the rope tie at the top of the bag, and reach inside. He pulled out a small cloth pouch. After a moment Fox opened the string on the pouch and poured out a small mound of powdered blue crystal into his hand.

Fox dropped to one knee. Then he closed his fist and held it upright, oriented like he was holding his staff. Letting the blue crystal dust trickle from his hand and pivoting his body, he precisely laid the dust in a circle around him. The circle he was drawing was just wider than Fox's shoulders, and I marveled at its skillful construction. Even from the first moment's glance, I could see that the circle was perfectly round. Then he stepped out of the circle he had just made and invited me to step into it. I stepped into the circle.

After that, Fox made a second, larger circle for himself right next to the one for me. He stepped into his circle, and reached up to his necklace. Visually, a person couldn't help but notice Fox's rosary. It was made of around three dozen different colored spheres. I watched carefully as Fox pulled three stone beads from his giant rosary. I tried to follow what was happening.

Fox's rosary was a necklace on a single cord. It didn't appear to have any opening. But somehow the stones parted from the necklace without any resistance. It was like they answered Fox's call and released the cord that had been running through them. The beads did not appear to have any holes in them either. He took the first sphere, a marbled blue stone with white streaks, and threw it twenty paces away from us, off to the left. Then he took the second stone, a dark gray smoke-colored one, and threw it twenty paces ahead of us off to the right. Finally, he took the third stone, a dully reflective silver metal, and tossed it a few paces in front of us.

Then he took back his standing staff and again scanned the river and forest. I looked over questioningly at Fox. Fox, without seeming to notice my expression, replied in answer, "now we just need to lure it out into the open."

"H-How?" I stammered. The more I realized what was happening and what had just happened, the more I began to tremble.

The looked back at me and smiled knowingly, "Demons are arrogant and vain. I will insult its strength and challenge its pride."

Then, he began quietly chanting under his breath. I looked over in rapt amazement. Fox's chanting grew, from a low monotone to a slightly louder monotone. I stood nervously in my circle with my arms at my sides, looking at Fox and waiting. The forest seemed even darker around us, as if the light was being sucked away.

Whenever I have gotten scared in my life, I've realized that one of my tendencies was to think about things. Later, Fox told me that that was a positive trait and that I should encourage it.

But at the time, I remember thinking that the habit was not useful. Aside from noticing that the forest was darker, I also noticed that the air seemed charged with electricity. And I noticed that I was terrified.

The evening was quickly becoming darker and the charged feeling in the air grew in intensity. I felt the hair on my arms go up. I felt the hair on my head go up and my scalp began to tingle. In fact, I felt the hair going up all over my body. I looked up at Fox. He looked over at me, and nodded once, acknowledging that he felt it too. While the gesture was not much, it was reassuring. Fox radiated a calm reassurance that provided me a sense of security in this strange place. No matter what was happening, he was the center of the storm, untroubled by what was happening. And his calm was contagious.

As the electricity in the air reached a static pitch, when the air would hold no more, a brilliant flash of lightning came down from the cloudy sky above. It struck the Torii gate.

This bolt of lightning was enormous. I closed my eyes, but I was a second too late. The lightning was blinding, leaving its wide and jagged path burned into my vision. I couldn't imagine how Fox would have been able to see either. Briefly, I opened my eyes, squinting up at the waterfall. The Torii gate was made of iron and wood. I watched, terrified, as the iron on the gate glowed red, impossibly hot, as it was electrified. Behind the iron letters, the wood of the Torii gate burst into flame as well. "The letters are written in the ancient GaleScript. They give the demon's title. Apparently, we are facing ——, the Destroyer of the Weak." Fox made a strange sound, his face contorting with the effort of pronouncing it. It sounded like 'Mal-(grunt/snort sound)-rto'.

"Malgurto?" I asked. I tried to duplicate the sound, but couldn't.

Fox smiled gently, "Close enough. Don't try again. Without the training that I received at the GaleTemple, I could do damage speaking the GaleScript aloud." He spoke in a low tone to me, but didn't take his eyes of the Torii Gate.

"What do you mean damage?" I asked.

Fox looked around, but continued to talk. He replied in a serious tone. "Well, they are sounds that men are not supposed to be able to speak. In truth, no man can speak the GaleScript well. Unless you learn to make those sounds before your tongue and throat are done developing, it is almost impossible. Forcing the sounds can injure your throat.

"But more importantly, the GaleScript is a language of primordial power that can be used to influence reality itself. Remember that all of reality is just an expression of the Gale. Also, language is only a representation of an idea. Some of the ideas that GaleScript conveys can be overwhelming to an unprepared mind. The sounds referring to the demonic ideas are intrinsically twisted. Those who have spent too long examining evil have learned this lesson the hardest way. Take this warning seriously: speaking it has driven people insane before." Fox finished his sentence and immediately began chanting again.

There was another flash of light and then I saw something I will never forget. What stood before us, standing in front of the Torii gate, was roughly a man, if a man were made of lightning. Upon reflection, I realize that this was not a good comparison. This thing was not like a man. It was sort of a skeleton or like a sketch of a man. The sketch was made up of Glowing electric white lines only outlining the barest shape. For the purpose of this report, I will call it a demon, because that is what Fox called it. From Fox's grim expression, I knew it was trouble.

As he looked at the lighting man, Fox stopped his chanting. He looked at the electric being for a long moment. The electric figure, curious, cocked its head to the side and looked back at Fox, perplexed. "Come on." Said Fox.

The lightning demon tilted its head back and an ear-splitting screeching sound filled the air. I clapped my hands to my ears, trying to block the sound out. It was high-pitched and crackled with malevolence.

The sound ended, but the demon hadn't moved. It just stood there facing us. How would we be able to talk to it? "Fox," I whispered. He only grunted to acknowledge my question. His eyes never left the demon. "Fox, can that thing speak?"

He replied, but still never took his eyes off the man-shaped lightning, "It is speaking, in a way…" I waited for him to continue, but he didn't offer any other information.

"Well, what's it saying?" I asked.

Fox shrugged, and answered me, but still, would not look away from the demon. "In truth, he's not *really* trying to communicate. I insulted him, announcing that he was in the presence OF HIS BETTERS!!!" Fox raised his voice and glared at the demon as he said the last three words.

The demon seemed to understand and his lightning flared, growing brighter. Fox continued is his normal tone, "As I said, demons are vain and arrogant. Calling it an inferior infuriates it. It is projecting that fury at us. That's just a rage sound it's making, but the meaning is pretty clear." I had to agree. It was the least friendly sound I had ever heard.

I only slightly understood the situation we were in at that time. I was much younger and terrified of this new place where I found myself. I was ignorant and out of my depth. So, there may be some inconsistencies in how this journal is presented. I can only hope that the brothers who read this can excuse my faults. At that time, I did not know the word incantation. But, in my time with Fox, I came to learn. The incantation he began was one that I later came to know very well.

The lightning demon cocked its head to the other side, still watching Fox as he intoned the strange sounds. Fox stood there, feet firmly planted shoulder width apart, head thrown back, both hands holding his staff in front of him, intoning words. I kept repeating to myself, "This is a demon. This thing in front of me is a demon… some kind of lightning demon. At the time, I could clearly feel that I was in the presence of something supernatural. It felt different from everything in the world of life. It was clearly something 'other'.

Fox called out some phrase in a strange language. At the time, I certainly did not understand. From the demon's response, the words had been a taunting insult. The electrical demon flared in brightness, clearly offended. The singed branches on either side of it began to smoke.

(Even later on, with years of dedicated study under Fox, it was very difficult to understand and duplicate what he was doing. For students of our sect of the Gale school, it would be useful to research my instructional volumes about information that I gleaned in my time with Fox. His knowledge of advanced meditational techniques was substantial. His trans-dimensional exploits and understandings, as well as his improvement of the demon catcher sutra are all worthy of deep study.)

This demon was aware apparently, and knew that Fox was moving against it. Before Fox could complete his incantation, the demon raised its electrical hands/arms to the sky. To say that it raised its hands is not quite accurate. In truth, it moved so quickly that the arms were down one second and in the next second, the arms were thrown up towards the sky. A moment after its arms reached up to the sky, a fierce storm of lightning poured down on us.

The best way that I could describe what happened would be to say it was like a heavy rain but the rain was lightning instead of water. It was a deluge of impossibly bright lightning from the sky. The rational part of my mind had just enough time that I understood that I was going to be destroyed. The other part of my mind could not process what was happening to me. The light was blinding. Then the sound that it made convinced me the world had split apart.

I couldn't help but close my eyes when the lightning struck. All of my senses were overloaded. After the initial noise and blinding light, the lightning continued, but lessened. Nauseated, I squinted to look around me. My knees were shaking and I felt off balance. I was amazed to find that I was still standing in the same spot. I couldn't believe that I was still alive and, though grateful, I wanted to understand why. What I noticed next was as astonishing as the lightning.

A moment before, I had stepped into an empty circle enclosed by a ring of blue powder. Now, I was standing on a solid blue crystal disc. It was a bright and vivid blue, contrasting with the muted colors of this realm. I stared down dumbly, and noticed that the disc was not all one color. Some parts of the disc were a brighter blue than other parts. I puzzled, staring down at the disc that had filled Fox's circle. Above me, a second, identical disc hovered over my head. I was surrounded by a shimmering blue screen that connected the discs. That screen protected me from the lightning and thunder and seemed to absorb them. The lightning was bright, but I could squint and see. The sparkling blue cage must have absorbed some of the sound too, because the multiple thunderclaps were loud, but not deafening. I crouched there, in the shimmering blue tube, confused but deeply grateful for the protection.

Just then, the demon attacked again. It threw a fresh torrent of lightning at us. The attack was overwhelming. It was too much for me. The intense light was overwhelming me. I felt myself losing consciousness, but my vision was fading to a blinding white rather than fading to black.

***

Knowing that I was in danger, I fought to keep my senses. I opened my eyes to find I had fallen to one knee. Kneeling on the ground, I was disoriented, as though I had been roughly shaken awake. My stomach was queasy; ears ringing and head pounding. It was difficult to see. There were disorienting tracers of light on whenever I closed my eyes. While my eyes were still struggling, my ears clearly heard Fox calling out in that strange language.

In response to the taunt that Fox had shouted out, the lightning demon stepped forward down off of the Torii gate. I remember how odd it seemed that a demon made out electricity would walk. But in truth he jerked forward, and the ground charred wherever he stepped. As the demon walked forward towards us, lightning crackled all around it, occasionally arcing out to scorch a nearby tree. It was blinding to look directly at it, but we could look around it. The trees were around it were reflecting a flickering white light.

As it got closer, the lightning demon quickened its pace. Then several things happened at once. Fox widened his stance, gripped his staff with both hands, and lifted that staff off of the ground. Fox stood there, unmoving, with his staff held high, vertically in front of him.

As the demon came closer, now less than twenty paces away, I could feel every hair on my body standing up. Fox threw back his head, shouted some word in that same strange language and stabbed the butt of his staff into the ground. As the staff touched the ground, the stone rosary beads Fox had thrown flared to light. They each sent off a beam of light to the adjacent stones, forming a triangle of light. I had somehow forgotten about the beads Fox had thrown. The lightning demon was within the stones' triangle. The demon, outraged, took the form of a bolt of lightning and shot straight at us. I flinched back, expecting electrocution. But Fox hadn't moved. The demon was trapped and bounced back from the triangle-light-prison. He crackled and shot around inside the triangle like an angry wasp. He hit the walls of his triangle cage, rebounding off, more times than I could count, too fast for me to clearly see. But the triangle of light beams held the furious storm of lightning.

The third rosary bead, made of the dully reflective metal, began to grow brighter than the other two. A high-pitched clear sound could be heard, growing louder as the rosary's light grew. The stone's light and the demon's light vied for brightness. I squinted my eyes down to slits, as the stone's light surpassed the demon's. Its light reached out toward the demon. The lightning demon made that horrible ear-splitting screeching sound as it was pulled forward into the light of the stone. Since the stone was a few paces in front of us, the demon was being sucked toward us.

I watched, terrified and fascinated. The lightning demon's body got smaller and smaller as it was pulled toward us into the rosary bead. The clear sound of the rosary bead grew in volume until it had surpassed the demon's wail. A moment later, the demon was gone.

It had disappeared, fully absorbed into the stone's light. When it did, the high-pitched clear sound, and the light beams from all three stones abruptly cut off. We were left standing there in silence. The electrified air around us smelled burnt, carrying the lingering smell of ozone.

After the ordeal, after the lightning strikes, the exploding trees, the electric rain, and the demon's absorption into the stone, the silence was deafening. I became aware that my ears were ringing.

Then I stumbled backward and fell to the ground. The shimmering tube-cage around me had winked out of existence. I had been leaning back on the wall of the shimmering blue screen. I fell back with force and landed on my backside. Apparently, I had been pushing against the back of my protective tube, trying to scramble away from the demon. With the demon gone, the protection turned off automatically.

My first thought was to look over at Fox, but the metallic rosary bead looked like a tiny lantern, and drew my eye first. The 'stone' still looked metallic, but was somehow translucent and pulsed with a swirling, sparking internal light. It threw off tiny threads of lightning.

I looked up to see Fox extending his hand to help me up. After Fox made sure that I was unhurt, he turned back toward the waterfall. The Torii gate had disappeared just like the demon. It had returned to this realm's version of 'normal'.

Fox spoke to his staff again so that it was standing on its own. The silver metal running through the grain pulsed as it monitored our surroundings. Then Fox raised his right arm, opened his hand, and murmured something under his breath. His left hand was holding on to his rosary at his chest.

At that point, nothing should have surprised me. But I was surprised to see the metallic rosary bead rise from the ground in front of us. It flew up to land in Fox's outstretched hand. He held the glowing, pulsating bead in his hand and the glow faded. It appeared to become solid metal again, no longer leaking electricity or light. He held the bead up, next to his rosary. His hand covered the stone bead and necklace for a moment. There was a brief warm glow of yellow light under his hand. Again, I didn't see the cord open to accept the bead. One moment the bead was in his hand; the next second he covered it, the light flashed, and it was back on the necklace.

Fox repeated the process with the other two rosary beads. They each answered his call and flew back to Fox's hand. Each time the rosary accepted the stones back, rejoining them with the others. I watched as closely as I could, but still couldn't see the cord open.

His staff, Shui, stood next to Fox and pulsed silently. After Fox adjusted his clothing and rosary, he spoke again and the staff fell, stopping at knee height and pointing out our direction. It indicated that we should continue in the same direction.

As we walked, I became aware of a strange sensation. The leather of my shoes was relatively thin, so I was a little foot-sore, and noticed something hard under the dirt of the path. After several steps, I stopped to investigate. There were wooden planks buried just under the dirt. The planks were longer than I was tall and about the width of my hand. As we walked, the planks rose closer and closer to the surface, eventually emerging from the ground. Soon we were walking on a path of wooden planks. The planks sat directly on the ground, crudely inset. The wood was obviously old and dirty, having been buried. The wood that was above ground looked like it had not been walked on in years, and had been left to the elements.

As we walked down the now-paved wooden path, a thick fog began to roll in. It appeared, too quickly and too dense. Thick white clouds swirled in front of my eyes. After only a few minutes, we couldn't see more than a few feet in front of us. "Careful, Kwan. This fog is not natural. Keep your guard up…" Fox said. We stayed on the wooden planks of the path, and our pace slowed to a crawl. The moisture of the fog emphasized the dank, primordial smell of this place. The almost-musky scent of this realm, damp and mossy, pressed in from all sides.

We walked through the thick fog, being careful to stay on the wooden planks. Occasionally, along the way, we would see a wooden post jutting out of the ground to waist high. Fox told me that they looked like they had been supports for a walkway. But the posts were irregularly spaced and seemed incredibly old. Aside from the path itself and the handrail support posts, the fog obscured everything but the occasional, ghostly tree branch reaching out to us.

As we walked through the fog I imagined that I could hear the soft flapping of wings. I had the impression of being watched. As we walked, more of the handrail posts began to appear, and I couldn't see them clearly until they were only a few feet away. It was difficult to judge time in the fog as well. We may have been walking for one hour or six hours, and I would not have been sure.

Walking through the fog, I saw an owl standing on a tree branch through the mist. It was just off the path. The owl, like the ghostly tree branches was only a shadow until I leaned forward to see it better. It was silent, so I almost missed it. It turned its head, tracking me as I walked, looking me in the eyes. I felt a little dizzy at the moment, but I remembered that I had not eaten in some time. I was probably light-headed from hunger.

I stayed on the path, but thought seeing the owl might mean something to Fox. I called him to draw his attention to the owl, but in the second that I turned away to call Fox, the owl silently flew off. Also, Fox was already past me, so I hurried to catch up.

I sprinted down the path, catching him a moment later. Fox turned stopped when I approached. I told him about the owl that I had just seen. With a careless air, he dismissed the matter out of hand. He marched on, seeming to forget about the owl, and so did I.

Fox and I wandered on. He seemed relaxed, so I lowered my guard too. Eventually, our senses became dulled walking through the endless fog. I imagined that I heard more flapping of wings, and mentioned it to Fox, but he said that he could not hear anything.

Fox pulled us to a halt, and produced a gourd full of water from his bag. He offered it to me, but oddly, I wasn't thirsty. So, I didn't drink. Then he drank. He put the gourd away and prepared to consult his staff again about our course. Before he could complete whispering to his staff in the strange language, a crashing sound came from the forest behind us. It stopped Fox in mid-incantation.

Fox and I glanced at each other. Without a word, he turned and fled down the path, away from the crashing sound. Feeling upset that he had left me behind, I took off after him. He was surprisingly swift for such a big man.

Fox darted ahead, so fast on his feet that I could barely keep pace. The sound behind us changed, but still pursued us. Initially, it sounded like a single huge beast crashing through the forest to catch us. But as we ran, the sound changed. Eventually it became the sound of a group following us. Guttural, inhuman voices could be heard yelling and snarling. Metal could be heard jangling against metal. It sounded like they were gaining on us. I imagined that there was a horde of armored, demon soldiers chasing after us.

Moaning with urgency, Fox only hissed, "Faster! Run!!!"

The sound behind us changed again. It became the sound of an army of beasts, led by one massive beast. My mind, my imagination was flooded with images of possible pursuers. The creatures from my nightmares, from childhood stories suddenly came back to me. I fought down panic as I frantically pushed myself to run faster. I tripped and fell hard, bruising and cutting my hands in the impact. But I scrambled to my feet. Vague images filled with fangs and claws filled my mind.

More of the railing posts appeared along the sides of the path. They appeared with more and more regularity. Eventually, a thick handrail appeared atop the posts. Once the railing appeared, it remained, extending into the distance. I stumbled at some point, but fortunately was next to the railing. My hand reached out to grab it, preventing a fall. Despite my fear, I remember thinking that even though the railing was old, it was smooth to the touch.

In my panic, I was aware of four sounds as we ran down the path, through the fog. One sound was the footsteps, mine and Fox's. The second was the sound of our pursuers, the beasts chasing us. The third sound was my own ragged breathing. The fourth sound was the river, consistent, though unseen, off to our right side. Briefly, the sound of the river grew louder. Then, the sound fell away, as though the river had just been cut off. We kept running.

As the sound of the river had fallen away, the handrail on either side of the path grew thicker, now with the supports appearing more frequently. The path was felt much safer with the thicker, reinforced handrail. It felt like we were fleeing on a road to safety, if we could only get away from those beasts. But they were relentless, their sounds seemingly only a few feet from us. I was sure that if the fog weren't hiding us, we would be able to see them. I reasoned that they were either following our scent like a dog, or they were chasing the sound of our running feet. I forced myself to ignore the pain in my side as I sprinted on.

It was a surreal journey fleeing the terrifying sound of the pack pursuing us. The wooden path and its handrails began to look newer and brighter, in better condition. The wood appeared to have aged better in this section. The path that we ran on was like a track. The path itself was wide enough for four men to walk shoulder to shoulder. The railing, on either side, was waist high and sturdy.

The sounds of the things chasing us fell away. Was it possible that they lost our scent? Had they gotten tired? We ran a few minutes longer, even after we stopped hearing any noises behind us. Realizing that the pursuit stopped altogether, Fox and I came to a halt.

The fog began to clear as a wind blew through. As the fog receded, I was astonished to find an entirely new landscape greeting my eyes. The river and the forest were gone. The path that we had been walking on, was now a bridge.

Fox and I stood on the bridge and turned around in a slow circle. Remembering how Fox had instructed me to be observant, so I studied our surroundings. The wood of the bridge, including the railing, had no joining marks. It appeared to be carved from one impossibly huge piece of wood. The bridge extended into the distance ahead of us. Its construction was simple, but it seemed very sturdy, as if appearance was less important to its builders than durability.

The bridge was so long that it disappeared to a single point on the horizon. What we had taken to be a path was the entrance to a large bridge across an impossibly wide chasm. Behind us, the trees of the forest, still visible, were shrouded in mist.

Looking down on either side of the bridge, I did not see any kind of supports for the bridge. Without pillars, how could such a bridge exist? Even more disturbing, I could see roiling purple storm clouds below us. White and yellow light flickered in the dark clouds, but no thunder could be heard. It seemed that the weather below the bridge was taking a turn for the worse. But if the clouds were now below us, how high were we?

I could not imagine how we had gotten as high as we appeared to be now. We had been on the ground just a moment before. We stood on the bridge just at the edge of the chasm. Before I could really process our options, the sound of our pursuers rose again. Both of us turned to stare for a moment at the misty forest. Our pause lasted only a moment. With the clamor of pursuit growing behind us, we again broke into a run and sprinted farther onto the bridge.

Before long, the sound of the pursuit fell away again. The ground below the bridge also fell away. By that point, when Fox and I stopped and turned around, both directions looked identical. The bridge extended, in either direction, to a single point on the horizon. We were stuck on the bridge, impossibly high, somehow above the storm clouds.

Chapter 8

The Siblings

Only now, when not running for my life was I able to appreciate how beautiful the bridge was. The wood was a light sandy color and had been exquisitely carved. It shone with a warm light polished to a glowing finish. Only then did I notice the colors had returned to the world. Rather, they weren't just as bright as the real world, they were even brighter! I didn't question how this was possible. I was just grateful for it. I took a moment to admire the magnificence of the bridge next. I wondered who would have built such a thing.

Now that the sound of the pursuers had fallen away again, Fox and I dropped back to a walk. As we walked, a gust of wind threw both of us off balance, me more than Fox. Then a series of gusts of wind began to hit us, like blows, from different directions. The gusts were so precise that they were clearly 'intentional'. Nature didn't react like this.

A gust of wind hit me head-on. The gust had just hit me, neatly side-stepping Fox. The wind passed Fox by and caught me square across the chest, blowing me back off of my feet. I landed hard on my back and shoulders, but tucked my chin so my head did not hit on the wood planks.

I looked up to see Fox being struck from different directions by gusts of wind. A sustained wind blew him forward, forcing him to use his staff to keep his balance. Then the wind suddenly changed directions, throwing him backward, and a series of gusts from the left and right threw Fox off-balance.

A tremendous gust of wind hit Fox from the side, and he staggered to the railing. The gust continued and picked up force until Fox could barely keep his footing. His clothing flapped furiously in the wind. I couldn't believe what I was seeing, but the wind was actually trying to dislodge Fox! I watched him, from my spot on my back lying there on the bridge. I felt paralyzed in my position. It all happened so fast. I looked up at him and watched as the wind tore his satchel from his shoulder. I watched as it blew away and fell over the side of the bridge. Fox had both hands clutching his staff trying to use it to lean into the wind and resist.

Just then the wind died. Fox staggered forward a few steps, still on his feet. He looked over at me and gave me a scared look. After a moment, just for the split second when Fox lowered his guard, the strongest gust of all came. With an impact like a charging horse, the wind crashed into Fox and threw him. First, he was thrown to the side and smashed into the railing. He clawed the railing, trying to keep his balance.

Then, the wind grew to a fevered pitch and Fox was pitched out over the railing. Time slowed as I screamed and reached out an arm to him, but he was already falling. I saw the panic and fear etched on his face as he disappeared over the edge. His answering scream could be heard in return dwindling down to silence as he fell.

I don't know how long I sat there, mouth hanging open, on the bridge. I couldn't believe what had happened. The wind had immediately died down, as if turned off, and the silence that it left behind only emphasized my shock at Fox's fate. Fox was gone, and a series of even more alarming thoughts was waiting behind that- I was trapped in this realm. I had no idea how to find Cho Clei. And even if I could find her I couldn't get her back. Without Fox, I was lost. Maybe I could have done something with his staff? But even as I thought it I knew that it would not have been enough. Either the lightning demon or the s'la'manda would have easily killed me. That much had been clear.

It was shocking how sudden it had been. One minute Fox and I had been walking along. The next minute Fox had been blown off of the bridge, leaving me stranded and alone in this supernatural place.

I thought about going back the way that I came in, trying to retrace my steps. But I had no desire to face whatever had been chasing us. I couldn't forget the sound of those beasts tramping through the forest after us. And even if I were to make it past whatever that was, I would be back in the realm where the lightning demon had attacked. I think that I could've retraced my steps, but I didn't know what other dangerous surprises might be waiting. And even if I could make it all the way back to where we started, what would I do then? Would I just sit there and wait for the Ragyala to appear?

And what would I do if it never showed up? And how long until I died?

And it looked like the wind had been specifically targeting Fox. I didn't know why Fox had been attacked, but I thought it might not come after me. Either way, taking my chances against wind attacks was more attractive than dealing with a howling pack of armed, fanged, and clawed demon-beasts.

I weighed the choices as best I could, considering that my teacher, guide and protector had just died. My best option was to continue on. I turned back in the original direction Fox and I had been traveling, put my head down, and marched forward.

Walking on the bridge felt light and airy. The wind blew, but there were no dangerously strong gusts. The sky was beginning to lighten and the sun was coming out. Despite realizing that I was alone and had lost Fox, I found myself... surprisingly functional.

While walking on the bridge was very different from walking through the fog, both were disorienting. It became hard to judge how long I was walking across the bridge. The monotonous sound of my footfalls was hypnotic, and lulled me into a trance-like state as I walked.

I stayed on the bridge- there was no other way to go. My only choices were to go forward or back. I fell into the habit of looking down at the wooden deck of the bridge a few feet ahead of me. After walking for some time, enjoying the better weather, I looked up into the distance. Despite the shock and horror of Fox's fate, I felt an unfounded sense of good humor and confidence. I was less afraid than I should have been.

As I raised my head to look into the distance, checking the bridge ahead of me, I saw two figures in the distance ahead of me. They were small, and so far away, that they looked like vertical lines on the path in the distance. At first I thought, with apprehension, that they might be another threat from this place. Then, after a moment of thinking, I realized that without help, I would be here forever. Whoever was approaching in the distance might be my only chance of salvation.

Mindful not to seem frightening or aggressive, I quickened my pace in order to meet up sooner with whoever is approaching. In a few minutes, the two figures came into sharper focus. It appeared to be a man and a woman. Both of them were short and only came up to my shoulder. Both of them had bright white hair, braided neatly. Both of them had large bulbous noses. Both of them were wearing sandals, and pants that came down to just below their knees. Their pants and their tunics were identical and colored gray. Over their tunics they each wore a simple vest. The man's vest was black and the woman's vest was a darker gray. Their clothing was simple, but clean. My nose could detect the pleasant scent of pine. Both of them seemed kind, as they smiled approaching me. As they got closer, I realized that their wrinkled skin had a gray tint to it also.

I held up my hand in greeting and called out to them. "Greetings!" I wave my hand, hoping that I was not making some kind of mistake. There were so many things I didn't know about this realm. I realized Fox had not taught me very much before being blown off the bridge.

Somehow, I was imagining that I was in some kind of story - that an adventure would take place and that somehow, despite adversity, we would overcome. Now, the reality was very different. I realized that the chances of my success were almost zero. I realized that I was, for all intents and purposes, lost in this realm, possibly forever. Even though my situation was enough to give me reason to cry, as I approached the elderly couple, I felt very positive. The couple smiled as they saw me, and the old man raised his hand to wave back at me. Both of them greeted me warmly as they approached.

"Hello, young man." The old man said. The woman echoed his greeting.

I bowed in the old custom. They were clearly old, and I thought they would appreciate the gesture. They smiled, delighted at my display of manners.

"Hello, good Elder. My name is Kwan. I'm lost in this place, and... um, looking for my sister." I said. Before I knew it, I was talking, and my whole story spilled out. Neither of the old gray people's kind expressions changed as I explained my plight.

The old woman spoke, "You're lost in this place, sister is missing, and your master was blown off this bridge. That is bad luck." They clucked sympathetically.

Then I remembered my manners and asked them why they were here. We are looking for our brother, just like you are looking for your sister."

I was completely taken aback. It never occurred to me that there could be someone else in my position. Maybe meeting them was an incredible stroke of luck. Before I could even suggest it, the gray woman spoke, "We should travel together. There's safety in numbers! We can look for your sister while we look for our brother." They took one step toward me. "You see, our brother is lost, just like your sister. Maybe we can help each other?" The old woman smiled warmly at me.

The relief must have been evident on my face. They smiled even wider. "Do you have any idea what's at the end of this bridge? We've been walking a long time..." the gray man trailed off.

I was grateful to have something useful to contribute. "At the end of this bridge is a forest with a river. But there are some terrible things in that forest. We escaped just before a horde of beasts reached us. We were also attacked by a demon there." I didn't mention the little fire lizard or the ice bird. Somehow, it seemed even more unbelievable than the demon.

"A horde of beasts? A demon? An actual demon? How terrible!" the gray woman said. They glanced at each other. "We will not go that way, then." She turned around and looked back at the way they had come. "Oh well, we will just return to the city. It's wonderful there, actually. We just left. We will go back and look there for your sister there. And after we find her, one of the wizards there will be able to send you home. It should be eeeasy!" The gray woman stretched the word out and gave me a greasy smile.

Suddenly something seemed wrong about the situation. It was like looking at a puzzle where one piece doesn't fit. Something wasn't right here. Time seemed to stretch out as I considered. It should be easy? Nothing about this whole thing has been easy! It struck me as a false note in a song, almost like an alarm bell, but I was having trouble thinking. And why was she smiling like that? There was something I was missing. It felt like I was in a dream, or just waking up. I caught snippets of words that the gray woman was saying. "…morsel… not resist… Time returned to normal as I focused on the woman. She had been saying something. "…of your own free will."

I was about to ask her to repeat what she had said, when I had the strangest feeling. I heard Fox's voice inside my head. It said, "Your mind has been trapped in an illusion, Kwan. I'm going to break the illusion and pull you from it, but it is important you do not react to what you will see. Can you do that?"

Fox? Fox!!! I felt a flood of relief that Fox was not dead. I looked up to see the old gray couple looking at me with concern. There was a jolt, like I had been falling asleep and jerked awake. Then the fog in my head was gone.

Before me, everything had changed. The bridge was still there, but the wood was no longer bright and polished. Now the bridge was old and covered with mosses, fungus and rot.

The sunny sky had reverted to the pale, bleak, and faded sheet I had seen before. My eyes flicked to the sides. The roiling purple storm clouds under the bridge were the only thing that remained consistent. The flickering light flashed brightly.

More alarming than the bridge, the old gray couple had transformed into two nightmares. There were still two of them, but they were only vaguely like people. They looked somewhere between fish and reptiles. Their skin was still gray, but now it was scaly and mottled with sores. Their features were very different too. Their round, fish eyes were completely black, whites suddenly gone. Their bulbous noses were gone. Their thick white braided hair had disappeared. Both were piebald, with only sparse patches growing from their scalps. The hair was grimy and gray and hung in limp tangles. Their clothing was filthy, tattered rags. Their smiles, and full lips, were now gone. Their mouths now extended out like crows' beaks. I glanced down and noticed that their fingernails were long, black, and curled. Where before they had been wearing sandals, now I saw that they had hoofed feet like goats. Controlling a rising sense of panic, I realized I stood facing two monsters.

Fox's voice had prepared me to be shocked, but nothing could have prepared me for the smell. A concentrated smell of rot clung to them. I had an impulse to turn and run away. I wanted to sprint back to the forest. Whatever beasts were lurking there would be better than these nightmares. Only Fox's reassuring voice in my head kept me calm. Knowing that he was there, and I was not facing these demons alone, gave me courage. I froze my expression like a mask, keeping a pleasant and calm smile on my face.

The old couple were still talking to me. With my expression frozen, I realized that they were hissing and croaking, rather than speaking. Had they been doing that the whole time?

One of them took a half step toward me, still hissing. Then the other one stepped forward, croaking. I ignored the part of my brain that was translating the monsters' language. Panic rose in me with more force than before. Just when I felt sure that I would crack, I heard Fox's voice again. "Count to four, then close your eyes, and move backward. It's time to deal with these two… Start your count… Now!" I felt a big hand tap me on the shoulder.

"One." I said. With a start, I realized that I had counted out loud, not silently in my head. The first of the demons, the 'woman', cocked her head at me and hissed. Some part of my mind understood the meaning of the hiss. She was asking why I said 'one'.

I didn't trust myself to answer her, so I said, "Two." The 'man' stepped forward. He croaked and then a long, forked tongue flicked out from between his pointy beak. The tongue slowly licked each of the 'man's' black eyes. He croaked again and they each took another step toward me. With one more step they would be able to lunge forward and reach me.

Then I said, "Three." and several things happened in quick succession. I was looking at the monsters and heard a 'thunk' sound at my feet. The old couple suddenly sensed that something was wrong.

Their heads whipped around, sensing Fox's presence, but apparently unable to see him. I glanced down to see what had made the 'thunk' sound before closing my eyes tight and throwing myself backwards. The last thing I saw before closing my eyes, was the metallic silver ball from Fox's rosary rolling to a stop at the feet of the old couple.

As I fell backwards, I heard Fox's clear voice shout that strange word in that same strange language and the resounding thump as he stabbed the butt of his staff into the ground. The part of my mind that had been able to translate the monsters' hissing, understood that language too. The word translated to 'SoulCage!!!'.

Since my eyes were shut, I couldn't see, but my imagination vividly filled in the details. As the staff touched the ground, the dully reflective rosary bead that Fox had rolled, must have flared to life.

I heard the recognizable, clear tone from the metal ball, growing louder as the rosary ensnared the demons. The monsters screamed, making strident and outraged, squawking sounds, as they must have been pulled into the light of the stone.

Unable to control my curiosity, I opened my eyes. I was lying on my back, several feet back from where I had been standing, propped up on my elbows. Fox stood next to me, hands on his staff, glaring at the demons. I looked up at him. I was so relieved to see him alive, but my eyes slid to the pair of demon monsters.

Since I was even closer to the stone than I had been with the lightning demon, I could see the whole process better. The metal 'stone' had thrown out a glowing metallic net around the demons. They were trying to use their crow beaks to 'bite' through the nets, but the netting was unbreakable. Each net was being gathered inexorably into the sphere. I must not have been able to see the net before because of the lightning demon's excessive brightness. The demons screeched and hissed and struggled, but could not escape.

One of them saw Fox clearly. I could see it's scaly facial expression register surprise, greasy gray eyebrows going up. Then it's expression turned malevolent, contorting in fury. It contracted for a moment and started shaking. Then, explosively, it spat at us. Time slowed, like it had with the hok. I watched as the putrid glob flew out at us from between the 'rope' of the SoulCage's net. The net grew a tentacle that whipped out, impossibly fast, and captured the glob of filth before it could reach us. The tentacle dragged its nasty package back into the larger net and dumped it in with the demon monster. The demon's fury doubled.

Again, I was fascinated as I watched the SoulCage operate. The two grotesque shapes shrank down as they were being dragged, screaming, into the metallic ball. The demon couples' bodies got smaller and smaller as they were reeled in.

The SoulCage's clear tone grew in volume until it had surpassed the demon pair's wail. A moment later, they were gone, fully absorbed. The sound from the little metal ball abruptly cut off. Again, we were left in silence.

***

The metallic rosary bead looked like a tiny star, impossibly bright when it absorbed the demon couple, then slamming the door shut on them and cutting off the light. After absorbing the lightning demon, the ball had put off small sparks. This time there were no sparks. Instead, a red haze surrounded the ball for a moment.

I looked over again to see Fox extending his hand to help me up. I got back up on my feet. I realized with embarrassment, that I was always ending up crouching or cowering or flat on my back. I decided I would react better next time. After Fox made sure that I was unhurt, he turned to look around.

Fox spoke to his staff again so that it was standing on its own. The silver metal running through the grain pulsed as it monitored our surroundings. This time Fox walked forward and bent down to pick up the bead. He held the bead in his hand and the red haze around it vanished. It appeared to become solid metal again.

Again, he lifted the bead up to his rosary. Again, his hand covered both the metal ball and rosary for a moment. Again, there was a brief warm glow of yellow light under his hand. I am certain that the cord did not part to accept the bead. But somehow, a moment later, the metal ball was back on the necklace.

"What... What... Fox! How did you... I'm so glad!" I stammered.

He smiled broadly, but his underlying concern was evident. "I'm glad to see you too. Are you feeling all right? You must be feeling disoriented."

"What happened? I... I'm confused." I wanted to make my voice sound more confident, but I was feeling lost for words.

Fox nodded understandingly, "I'm sure you are. Nothing you've experienced would have prepared you for something like that." He gestured with his chin toward where the demon couple had been captured. "The short answer is that those demons captured your mind and pulled you into an illusion." He paused, and with emphasis, said slowly, "None of what you were seeing was real."

"I saw you die!"

"Illusion." He slipped into teaching mode. "Those kinds of techniques are visually based. That means they hypnotize you, eye to eye." He leaned in, peering at me, "Did you see anything that could have hypnotized you? Did you look anyone or anything, other than me, in the eye?"

I paused to think back. "The owl! I saw an owl! It looked me in the eye!" It all came back to me. "Back when we were in the mist!" I had a moment of doubt. "Was the fog real?"

Fox nodded, "It was real. At least it was as real as anything in this place. The fog was very dense." I was getting excited now, remembering. I walked through what had happened.

"I saw an owl... then I felt dizzy and lightheaded... then I told you about the owl but you didn't think it meant anything..." I reasoned.

"Oh, I didn't eh? That's something I definitely would have had questions about. It sounds like they pulled you into the illusion as soon as you saw the owl."

I considered that, and continued my recollection. "Then..."

Fox interrupted, "Then you took off sprinting down the path!"

"We were being chased! And you were running too!" I was sure that was what happened.

"I'm afraid not, Kwan. That was illusion. We were walking and you paused. I thought you might be tired, so I stopped. I had just set my bag down when you ran off into the fog! I picked my bag back up and ran after you."

Then he added, "You're fast, by the way. It was all I could do to keep track of you." He shook his head, now smiling.

But I wasn't smiling. "There was a giant beast chasing us! Then there was a whole wild pack of them!

"Did you see the beast? Did you ever see this pack?" he asked. The questions made me pause. As I thought back, I never actually saw what was chasing us. I said so. Fox nodded. "I thought so. They were lazy. They could have made you see almost anything. But since you were already frightened, they only made you hear scary noises, and your imagination did the rest."

I was having trouble accepting that there never was anything chasing me. I had been so afraid! For nothing! Not only that, I had left safety, and charged out into this strange and dangerous place. I shook my head, chagrined.

Fox went on, "I lost you a few times, but luckily you slowed down and stayed on the path. But every time I would get close to you, you would take off running again!

"The beasts were chasing us…" I supplied ineffectually.

"I suspect the demons made you think that I was the 'beasts' chasing you. You would get ahead of me and I would fall behind. Each time I caught up, you imagined that the imaginary horde was getting closer. It's quite elegant, really." He paused, stretching his neck and shoulders. He went on, "Once I realized that you were under a guise and fleeing from me, I was able to make a plan."

I waited, but he didn't seem like he planned to say any more. "And? How did you catch me?"

"Oh, that? Stealth was my primary tactic. I have been entrusted with several powerful assets by my order. My staff, Shui, is one of them." The metal running through the grains of the staff pulsed with light. "Shui was able to hide my presence from them, and by doing so, hide it from you too. Then I was able to sneak up on your 'dinner party' before you became the main course."

I was silent at first, dumbfounded. Then I started thinking. "I'm glad you did! But what were they? And will they ever find their brother? Even for demons, I wouldn't want anyone to miss their family!"

The metal running through the grain of Shui lit up and began to flash rapidly. Fox paused as if listening to something. Then he nodded, paused, and nodded again. "Once the

SoulCage has captured a demon, and removed its power, Shui is able to interrogate the demon."

"Interrogate?" I asked.

Fox smiled at me and suddenly I felt very naïve. "It means that Shui can question them and find out the truth of their history, their power, their goals... Shui is passing that information to me. And I am passing it to you." He seemed so matter-of-fact about something that was astonishing to me. "As for their lost sibling, you don't have to worry. You have a good heart, Kwan. But these are not men and women. Those were two demons of the second order. That means they were more than your basic evil. Demons are separated into four different orders. The lightning demon was of the first order. These two were of the second order."

"The higher the order, the more powerful they are?" I asked.

Fox shrugged his shoulders, "Often it works out that way, but not always. There are particularly powerful demons in each order. The best way is to think of the orders as levels of evil intelligence.

You remember the lightning demon? Fox again made the strange sound, his face contorting. It sounded like 'Mal-(grunt/snort sound)-rto'.

"That demon was powerful, but not very intelligent, so it goes in the first order. The old couple, (he made two strange sounds — 'Purkk-plahk' and 'Rrippur') was not as powerful, individually, as the lightning demon had been. But, since they had a higher level of evil intelligence, they were second order."

I was going to ask how he knew this, but he began speaking again, "Without Shui, I wouldn't know those individual demons' history or place in their hierarchy. I know what I do because Shui was able to read their power and fed me that information." Could Fox read my mind? But before I could ask, he said, "I can't read your thoughts, by the way. If you're observant, it becomes a habit figuring out where people's thoughts are headed. And because you're sensible and use logic, it becomes even easier."

He paused to check that I was understanding all of this information. "As for their 'brother', you can put your mind to rest. There is no brother. There were only two of them, from the beginning. It's a ploy to lure prey. They have clearly used that technique before."

"Is there really a city that way?" I asked, pointing down the bridge. Fox turned to look. He put his hand up to his eyes, comically exaggerating his efforts to see. I was throwing questions at him very rapidly, and he treated me with the patience usually reserved for children. In fact, I've never known him to lose his patience. He turned back to me and shrugged.

"I don't actually know, Kwan. There might be. The landscape of this realm changes, depending on which entities are strongest in an area. This is a place where the environment responds to the minds in it." he explained.

"If there weren't a city there, and they needed you to 'see' a city, they could easily have made one." He touched his index finger to his temple when he said, 'see'. "They could even have used pieces from your own memory or imagination to make the illusion seem fully realistic to you."

"Oh. And wizards?" I persisted. The existence of such people, real wizards, was unbelievably exciting to me. I was a village boy, after all. (It never occurred to me to compare my idea of a wizard to the feats Fox had demonstrated.)

Fox smiled patiently. "It is unlikely that you would meet any wizards here." He spread his hands, and smiled apologetically. "That old couple lied to you. Their goal was simple. They wanted you to lower your guard so they could feed on you. That was actually a very close call. You really did escape just in time."

It was all so strange that, even though I had seen it with my own eyes, the danger was almost unreal. I suddenly remembered a question I had wanted to ask. "What does

SoulCage mean?" Fox turned and cocked his head, looking at me. His gaze did not waver.

"How?..." He paused, working something out. "Ah, it must have been when they captured your mind... Yes, it would have to be. The same technique that let you understand them must have let you understand the language I was speaking. It is a very old language called the Sound Of Making.

"Regardless of what the language is called, I suspect their technique had the side-benefit of translating all languages, not just theirs- because they have to communicate with different types of beings to lure, trap, and eventually feed on them. I wouldn't have expected that would happen. Interesting..." He looked into the distance, considering.

He shook his head and returned to his explanation. "SoulCage is the ancient name for *this*." He held up his rosary, specifically the metallic silver ball on it. "My order calls it the Celestial Mountain Sphere, but SoulCage is shorter. Without giving you too much background information, this tiny ball is a place that can capture, and imprison powerful spirits. That is, as long as they have a body. Pure energy spirits can evade the SoulCage... So, if an evil entity concentrates its spirit enough to become a physical body, the SoulCage can pull them in and trap them '*inside* or *under* the Celestial Mountain'. When it does trap them, it extracts their power from them, and puts it at my disposal."

He let the rosary fall back to his chest. "Remember that when we want to come home, we'll need to pay for our trip here. Ragyala will be expecting spirits when he sees us next. Technically, the Ragyala was within its rights, in letting us through the Pall, but it rarely makes such exceptions." He anticipated my question and said, "The Pall is that boundary between realms, like a wall between rooms. For opening the Pall when it didn't need to let us pass, we owe a debt to the Ragyala."

I recalled what Ragyala had said. I had a dawning of comprehension as I remembered. "He said five spirits!" I exclaimed. "There are only two of us! How can he ask for five?!"

Fox explained. "You and I came over. That is two spirits we owe him. When we find your sister, there will be three of us headed back. Five in total. Shui is a special circumstance. In some ways, my staff is *alive*. In some ways, not. Ragyala did not 'charge' us for Shui to cross."

He shrugged. "It's expensive, but I couldn't see any other way. Besides, I expected we would have to dispatch the kidnapper and its minions along the way. We just need to capture their evil spirits when we dispatch them."

"This little ball is a big part of our plan." He tapped the ball. "When we are ready to leave, we will use the SoulCage to deliver payment to Ragyala. That's the main thing we need it for. But the SoulCage has the ability to unleash the power it has extracted from the spirits too. So, in that sense, it is a weapon as much as a prison."

There were more questions I had, but my sister needed help. My questions could wait. It seemed that Fox was thinking the same thing. He suggested we talk as we travel.

The scenery, while strange and exotic to me, became monotonous eventually. The bridge was old and went on until it was just a tiny point on the horizon. The sky was gray, and no sun was visible. The clouds under the bridge were constant; roiling, flashing golden white and purple. They were an exotic carpet beneath us in the beginning. But a few hours into our hiking, they seemed monotonous to me too.

Walking along the bridge, we eventually came to a much wider circular platform. The platform and bridge felt like a coin balanced on a string. I had looked over the side of the bridge several times, but had never seen any kind of supports. There were no pillars, just an unbroken sea of flashing purple clouds. And with the extra weight of the platform, this bridge seemed less and less possible.

The circular platform had a circular roof, with a large opening in the center. The effect was that the outer five feet of the platform had a ring of roof that covered it. The handrail that had kept us safely on the bridge seamlessly widened to enclose the whole circle before coming together again on the other side. The pillars that supported the hand rails rose more than twice as high, now supporting both the railing and the roof. A single, thick, gray rope, the size of my thigh ran across the top of the platform, directly perpendicular to the bridge, and angled down into the clouds from either side of the platform.

Even stranger, there were two identical wooden boxes on either side of the platform. Each box was the size of a small room and had large, rectangular, lattice-covered window openings looking out from all four sides. At the top of each box, a stone wheel was mounted on its edge. Between the wheel and each wooden box was that thick gray rope. My eyes followed the rope as it sloped down at an angle into the flashing purple clouds. The rope was a line of thick gray-green that got thinner as it pointed down to the purple sea below. I strained, trying to see past the clouds, but they extended to the horizon.

Again, I looked over the sides of the bridge at the roiling purple clouds, with their silent flashes of light inside. Fox went through his process, asking his staff to find our way. I watched again, fascinated as the staff balanced on its own. Fox stepped back from the staff. Having seen the process before, I waited to see the staff fall to knee height, and stop, hovering to point our direction for us.

The staff fell, but not like before. This time, the staff fell over completely, not halting at knee height. This time it fell all the way to the floor, slowing only the smallest amount at the end so that it did not clatter. But unlike a regular piece of wood, when the staff fell to the ground, it did not come to rest there. Instead, the thin end lifted and pointed straight up at the sky. The staff had fully inverted itself, now leaning, but upside-down.

Confused, I looked over at Fox's face. He leaned back, brow furrowed in an expression of surprise. He stared at the staff for a long moment. He reached out and picked it up, carrying it to the side of the bridge, next to the railing. Then he closed his eyes.

A moment later, he opened them, "We have to go down there. Your sister is down below these storm clouds. Shui can sense your sister's life-force." He gestured down at the silent clouds, dark and churning below us. "And apparently it's a long way down there." The wind increased ominously at his statement.

I walked over to the railing and stood next to Fox. I looked down into the purple black clouds. Flashes of silent light could be seen, illuminating them. The clouds were a flat purple carpet under the bridge, extended out on either side, all the way to the horizon. No sun was visible.

"So how do we get down?" I asked. I nervously eyed the chaos below us. He studied the purple clouds carefully. Then he looked at the thick green rope. His eyes traced the rope back up to the box. Then, he walked to the center of the platform.

Fox again asked Shui to find our way. I watched as the staff balanced again. Fox stepped back. This time the staff fell to knee height, and stopped, hovering to point at the box to Fox's left. "It appears this is our way down." Fox said. He examined the box more closely. "This room is… a box that should carry us down to the ground. There are similar devices in the mountains of T'bat. It is a form of transportation." He walked over to the small room. Reluctantly, I followed suit.

Unable to help myself, I altered my course to look down at the clouds from the side of the platform. The green rope above us slanted down and utterly disappeared into the clouds. There was no way to see where it ended up. There was no way to tell what it was like inside the clouds.

Wind blew steadily. And the illusion memory of Fox getting blown off the bridge, kept me nervous. Dread welled up in me. I looked back at Fox. Seeing my expression, he could clearly see my rising panic. He looked at me and quietly said, "Remember your sister, Kwan."

He was right. This was no time for my nerve to fail me. Cho Clei needed me. I had already been in situations I would never have imagined, and I had come through them unharmed. I had come face to face with demons and survived. I nodded and followed Fox as he stepped closer to the room.

We were standing on the edge of the large circular platform. The ring of roof above us would have made the area a pleasant pavilion. Facing us, was a carved wooden box, large enough for a few men to stand in.

The box-room was in the shape of a cube, each side a little longer than Fox was tall. The wood of the box was carved with images of dragons fighting. Even though the wood of the box was the same old wood as the bridge, the details on the dragon carvings could still be seen. I could see bits and chips of colorful paint on their scales. What I couldn't see was a way to get into the boxes.

Fox stepped directly in front of the box. Two large, exquisitely carved dragons were carved on the front panels of the cube. Fox reached out to touch one of them. When Fox touched the dragon, the front panels swung out, opening as doors into the room.

We peered into the room. It contained only two ornately carved wooden chairs. The backs of the chairs were shaped like sinuous dragons. The inside of the room was also decorated with carved dragons. Little light came in from the single lattice widow on each wall.

Fox looked back at me and nodded. He stepped in. Suddenly anxious that we might be separated, I hurried to step on right after him. The doors 'clicked' closed behind me as soon as I stepped on.

Fox and I looked at each other. There was an iron (dragon-shaped) handle on the wall, across from the chairs. A vertical track was carved into the wall below the handle. We looked out through the lattice-covered windows. It was the same view that we had seen from the platform; gray sky above, purple clouds below. The flashing inside the cloud intensified ominously. I sat down, feeling overwhelmed.

The wooden lattice work on them mercifully gave a feeling of security when I wasn't looking out of them. Fox remained standing a moment longer, then sat in the other chair. He reached out and seized the iron handle. He closed his eyes for a long moment. Shui pulsed once with a soft light. Then Fox opened his eyes and pulled the handle down. I heard the sound of a faint 'click' in response.

There was a lurch, and the room was suddenly free of the platform. My hands shot down to grip the sides of my chair. The box was slowly moving, now sliding down the green rope. We couldn't see the mechanism above the box, how it was moving along the thick line. But through the windows, I could see that we were approaching the clouds. We were not travelling fast, but I imagined that we were picking up speed.

I looked over at Fox to see if he shared any of my anxiety. It was hard to say really. He looked serious and alert, but not particularly tense. I wanted to emulate that behavior, but I was too scared. Through the window, I could see the flashing clouds rising up to greet us.

Fox leaned forward toward the window. He held Shui in his right hand. Even without leaning forward, I could see that we were still approaching the clouds.

My imagination started to fill in the terrible things that could be waiting for us inside the cloud. I imagined all sorts of terrible demons and supernatural challenges.

My nervousness grew and peaked at the moment when our box sat directly on top of the clouds. As I sat there, I could picture our position clearly in my mind; the bridge and the platform above me to my right, the green rope making a line down from the platform to the clouds, disappearing inside them. And our wooden cage being lowered down that green rope, sitting like a tiny cube on top of the huge cushion of clouds.

Chapter 9

The Descent

And without any tangible resistance, we went in. We were through the barrier into the clouds. As we entered, there was bright flash which temporarily blinded me. Instinctively, I closed my eyes. There is a part of me that would've been content to keep my eyes closed. But when I heard Fox's gasp, I blinked rapidly to open my eyes sooner.

It took a moment for my sight to return. I opened my eyes to see what our current situation was. Nothing could have prepared me for what I saw. I will try to describe my impressions, but in full honesty, I was overwhelmed.

Over the years I have learned that my first impressions tend to be of color. Because of this, the first thing I noticed was that inside the cloud, the purple had changed to a pale lavender color. The very air around me was that pale lavender color. We were able to breathe, and able to see, but the air had… color. There was also a slight tingling that I felt on my skin when we entered the purple clouds. A moment later, I realized I could even feel the tingling inside my lungs as well. Anywhere I made contact with the lavender air, I felt tingling.

The next thing that I noticed was the cause of the white and golden flashes. I had not seen a great variety of things living in my small village. I knew I was ignorant of the world. But even as an ignorant boy, I knew immediately what I was looking at was a dragon.

I had seen pictures of dragons once in a storybook father had bought me. Those dragons were long and sinuous like snakes. They had colorful scales, and long whiskers. But this dragon did not look like them.

This dragon's body looked more like a lion's, but with scales instead of fur. Powerful muscles moved beneath the scales. Its neck was long and thick. Its horned, draconian head clearly declared what it was, but its chest was bigger, its arms and legs were longer, and its wings were much bigger than the dragons that I'd seen in the book. This dragon looked more like some kind of giant lion lizard rather than a flying snake. What's more, the dragon did not have brightly colored scales. In the drawings I'd seen, the dragons always had bright red or blue or yellow scales. This dragon's scales were the color of dark burnished copper.

The dragon was bobbing in place, flapping its tremendous wings. Even inside our box, I could feel the gust of wind from the flapping wings. I imagined us rocking on the green line. The dragon was close enough that if I had thrown a stone I could've hit it. Compared to us, it was enormous. It could have grasped our entire cube in one clawed foot.

The dragon drew in a huge breath, and then blew out a tremendous burst of fire. It was a large enough blast that it could have set my whole village on fire. But the lavender cloud absorbed the fire once it got 50 feet from the dragon's mouth. The cloud turned the fire into a flash of golden light. Immediately I recognized the golden light as one of the two flashing colors in the purple clouds.

We were caught staring at the copper colored Dragon when a second dragon, just slightly smaller but similar in design, darted past the first dragon. As the smaller dragon streaked by, it lashed out with a claw, tearing a ragged gash in the side of the Dragon's chest. The copper colored Dragon had been inhaling for a second burst of fire. Before it could be released, the pressurized fire (and blood) began to spill out from the wound.

I flinched back, although I don't know if it was from the blast of heat that hit our cube or the deafening cry the copper dragon let out. I felt the air in our transport change, and I realized my medallion was using its power to lower the heat. I glanced over and Fox was also enshrouded in a bluish haze I recognized as a shield.

I must have been in shock. The dragon was so massive and so... magical, and the attack had been so sudden and savage, that I couldn't quite believe what I was seeing. I looked over at Fox and saw an expression of wonder on his face. "Fox?" I spoke, surprised that my voice had trembled. The wounded dragon stopped flapping its wings, rolled in the air and began to fall. Fire was still coming from the cut across its chest.

Before the dragon could fall 50 feet, there was a blinding flash of white light. It was so bright that I was forced to close my eyes. Then the light flashed, the tingling on my skin increased. It was a pleasant feeling, certainly noticeable. When I opened my eyes, the 'slashed' dragon was healthy and uninjured, again flapping its mighty wings. The flash of light had healed it! That was what the white flashed in the cloud had been! The dragon's injuries had been undone. Absently, I noticed that the soreness in my back and feet had vanished. I had been healed as well!

Fox finally spoke, replying without looking at me, "So this is where they've gone! Dragons Kwan!" He sounded excited like a little boy. Well, more like an enthusiastic teacher. "They have not been seen in the world of men for a long time. Many thought that they were extinct. Others thought that they had traveled to another place and were living there. It appears that the latter theory was right."

I open my mouth to speak, then realizing that I didn't have anything useful to say, closed it again. Fox went on, "This is a Dragon from far to the West of your village. It is not type that is native to 'our' part of our world. Ah, look!" It was then that I noticed the other dragons. There were hundreds of them. They flew and looped and dived.

Fox had continued speaking. He sounded like a researcher, finding a treasure. If he felt any fear, as I did, he didn't show it. "Although I suppose most dragons would have access to similar, if not the same abilities... Is it possible they have been in this place, away from the realm of men this entire time?" He spoke like he was making notes as he reasoned.

The copper dragon swiveled its huge horned head around. Then it banked in the air and dove out of our view. I assumed it was going after the dragon that had attacked it. Only when that dragon had flown off did I register just how many other dragons there were. There must have been more than hundreds. These dragons came in many shapes and sizes. Some were large and some looked tiny.

Then I realized that the tiny ones were just far away. I swallowed hard, understanding then that some of the dragons were large, and some were incredibly huge. But none of them seemed bothered by us.

Flashes of gold and white light popped and flared within the lavender cloud, dragon-fire and healing, respectively. The dragons waged unrelenting war on each other. It appeared to be a dragon melee. They were merciless as they tore into each other and then momentarily reappeared, uninjured. As I studied what I was seeing, I began to notice dragons like the ones I had seen in books.

"Are those ones native to here?" I asked Fox, gesturing to a sinuous, yellow dragon. Its body was long, like a snake and had four stubby, but muscular arms. The only thing I witnessed that could be wings were flaps, behind its ears. I didn't understand how it could fly without wings. Also, it moved like a ribbon tied to a stick. The head rapidly twisted and turned in the air and the body nimbly followed.

"That's right. These are the variety from our area. Good eye." Fox agreed. "All dragons use some form of the Gale to fly. The Western type, like that magnificent copper giant, use their wings like birds. They move the air and ride its currents. But their wings aren't big enough to lift them like birds. Dragons are too heavy. So, they use the energy of the Gale to lighten themselves. That is how they fly."

He pointed over at the yellow dragon I had been watching, "The type you recognize *only* use the GaleForce to fly. Because of that, they don't need wings… Although, I've never heard of an Eastern dragon breathing fire before. All accounts show them using some sort of the GaleForce, (which the observers called 'magic') to perform titanic feats… Maybe how they use the Gale allows them different abilities. Hmm…" Fox was positively preoccupied. He stared out at the dragons and mumbled to himself.

I sat in silent awe of the huge magical beasts flying around us. I felt tiny and completely vulnerable as the enormous titans flew around us, blowing fire and clawing at each other.

Our gondola cube continued its descent through the clouds. The dragons flew by us, sometimes quite close, but never made contact with the box. Fox and I watched as the dragons viciously fought each other, killing, dying, and reviving. Then doing it all over again. They bit and slashed at each other. Teeth, claws, and fire were all used to fight. It was a gory sight. If not for the flashing white light, healing the dragons and resetting the scene, it would have been almost impossible to watch. In retrospect, I also see I was squeamish.

We heard a sound. 'CHING! TING! ching! ching! CHING! TING! ting CHING! ching! TING!' faster and faster. Two Eastern snake-type dragons were fighting and came before our observation window. They were identical in size, about four horses long. Both dragons were the color of tarnished silver. Their bodies hung straight down from their heads. Both dragons had two arms and two legs, tipped with long and gleaming, metallic claws. Both dragons were spinning. They were each a huge spinning cylinder of claws. They were slashing at each other, clashing claws and sending off bright sparks. 'CHING! TING!' I imagined that it was like two sword fighters dueling, but with claws instead. The two dragons would turn and dart, maintaining their frenetic slashing and blocking, always perfectly mimicking the moves of the other.

"Beautiful." Fox murmured.

I couldn't help myself. "Beautiful?" I blurted out. "What's beautiful about them trying to kill each other!?"

Fox smiled kindly at me. "They're dancing Kwan, not fighting." Then I began to see it. My view widened to take in more of the spectacle around us. There were multiple pairs of dragons, gracefully swooping and dipping and twirling, touching their claws against each other. It looked like they were fighting, but they were enacting some fierce dragon dance. Sparks flew from claws as the dragons twirled and clashed. I noticed more pairs of dragons dancing. Then there were more than pairs. The dancing dragons made intricate patterns in the air as they danced. We had apparently descended through a 'fighting' area, and were now in a 'dancing' area.

Fox began speaking again, this time in low tones, almost talking to himself. "Personally, I have only ever seen one dragon. It is an Eastern dragon, like some of these. It lives in the caves below GaleTemple Mountain. After completing my training and meditations, I was led down into the caves. There, I was allowed to witness the dragon, but not speak to it."

"Speak to it? Like a person speaks?" I asked. Immediately, I chided myself. I should save my questions until Fox finishes speaking, I thought.

Fox nodded. "Yes. The head abbot of the GaleTemple spoke to the dragon, the same way we are speaking now." He glanced outside at our descent through the dragon ballroom. "They are very old creatures, Kwan. By that I mean both that they have very long lives, and also have an ancient culture. Dragons were here long, long before mankind..." Fox stopped talking, and I restrained myself from asking questions.

A new point in the dragon dance had arrived. The tarnished silver dragons had stopped striking their claws against each other. The silence left when they stopped was surprising. Now they were flying and twirling, circling their partner. Because the dragons were already close, their bodies became blurs as they revolved each other. Then the dragons seemed to grasp arms as they rotated. As they pulled in toward each other, their rotation grew faster and faster. The different dragons' shapes were indistinguishable from each other. The dragon pairs had actually merged to become one spinning cylinder of dragon. When they merged, each pair (still spinning) began to fall from the sky.

Without thinking, I stood up and pressed my face against the lattice covered window. I looked down. The dragons fell, becoming small as the distance between us grew. Then the dragons parted and flew off in different directions.

"I think we are witnessing the mating process." I felt my cheeks flush with embarrassment. I quickly sat back down. But Fox was reasoning it out to himself. "But if the consequences of the battles aren't permanent in *this* place... the mating would probably be the same... Could this cloud be a 'recreation realm' for the dragons? A pocket realm where they can find pleasure... whether that comes through battle, or more... traditional amusements?"

Our box continued on its diagonal course down to the ground. Soon the dancing dragons were above us. "There are of course different kinds of dragons, other than the Eastern and Western varieties. There are scrolls in the GaleTemple about dragons. We study them in the course of our training. There is one scroll detailing twelve different types of dragons."

"Twelve?!" I blurted out. Again, I hadn't been able to keep quiet. Nervousness must have been eating away at my discipline.

"Yes. The text was very thorough. It broke them up into several different categories: There are the Eastern and Western types we've discussed. But there are also Northern and Southern dragons too. That scroll is one of our few reliable pieces of information about dragons." Fox turned to me, smiling gently.

I realize now, as I recount this story, that Master Fox was helping to keep me calm, intentionally talking in a soothing voice. He was giving me something to focus on, aside from the terrifyingly powerful creatures playing outside. But apparently since I seemed calm enough, he began pushing me to learn.

"Take a look out there. What differences do you notice?" Fox asked me. "Shui assured me, before we got in, that we are safe in this box." Again, I blushed, feeling stupid I hadn't thought of that. Of course, he would have asked his staff! I began to relax. I was beginning to trust Shui the way Fox did.

I looked out into the lavender cloud. I realized that the cloud layer must be impossibly thick to let all of these giants soar around. For a moment, I lost myself in just watching the dragons. I forgot that I was supposed to be studying them. I couldn't help myself. It was the first time I had seen mythical beasts. I said as much to Fox.

"Don't let them hear you call them beasts. The scrolls are very clear about certain aspects of dragons' character. A few of them are what we would call 'good' or helpful. And those dragons are very good; kind, noble, brave and humble. But the vast majority of dragons disregard people. They consider humans beneath them. Maybe their disdain comes from watching our entire history... Anyway, for that majority of dragons, the reports are consistent; they are usually haughty and greedy. And they care little for men."

I retuned my attention to the outside. After a moment, Fox resumed speaking, "We are taught that there are four schools of thought about how to classify dragons. The first school classifies them by where they are found, so Eastern, Western, Northern, and Southern. The second school classifies them by their skin, so Scaled or Feathered. Then they are broken down further, into the type of scales, etc."

"And the third school?" I asked, fascinated. "Wait, scaled AND feathered?!"

"Yes, the Southern Dragons have feathers, instead of scales. As for the third school, the third school classifies them by their limbs. Notice that big red one has two arms, two legs, and two wings, so six limbs altogether. Now look at that sleek white dragon. That's a Northern dragon, by the way. Notice it only has legs and wings, so four limbs. The Eastern and Southern varieties don't have any wings at all."

Fox turned back to me, "The fourth school does the same as the third school, but with heads, instead of legs."

I was confused. "Some dragons had more than one hea-?" Before I had even finished saying head, a massive dragon rose into view. It was magnificently large and covered in horns and spikes. Then *three* more heads rose into view! The dragon's wingspan looked like it would cover my entire village. Each of its scales was as big as a man. My mouth fell open. It may have been the biggest dragon I had seen all day, or it may have been closer to us than any other, so seemed bigger. Either way, I was in awe.

The huge dragon slowly flapped its wings, rising lazily. Two of the three heads were looking up, but their eyes were closed. Only one head had its eyes open, as if seeing for all three. Sensing our presence, the third head swiveled to look at us. For the first time, I got scared. A feeling of being small and insignificant began in my stomach. The dragon's eyes were a yellow green, with huge vertical slit-pupils like a cat.

"Fox…" I began, worried. But the dragon's third head rejoined the other two and it continued its ascent. It clearly had seen us, but didn't seem to care. We were on the way down. It was on the way up. That was that.

Questions started to occur to me. "How do know all this about dragons?" I began. "And why do the differences matter with dragons?"

"How do we know these things and why do the differences matter?" Fox asked.

"Well, why did they get so specific studying dragons? Having these different schools of thought…" Fox considered my question carefully.

"We know what we do largely from the scrolls at the GaleTemple." he began. "As for the differences, the early GaleMasters believed that studying how the dragons used the Gale would help them understand it better themselves. In truth, they studied all the animals in nature.

"They believed that animals naturally understood the Gale and had much to teach us. This was the main motivation for studying dragons at first. But as time passed, those GaleMasters refined their studies, getting more methodical in their approach. That's why there are so many ways they looked at it. Was that what you were asking about?" Fox answered.

I shrugged and nodded. The tough thing about being that age was that my thoughts took a while to catch up. We descended for a long time in silence. It was difficult to tell how long we sat there. I couldn't tell time in this place without a sun in the sky.

"Look there, feathers." Fox pointed out the window. There, a massive colorful serpent flew in loops and spirals. Behind its head and on either side of its face, the dragon had long, colorful feathers. The feathers trailed its head in graceful arcs each time it turned.

With this basic education, I began to notice different types of dragons. They were all different, but they all went from being 'scary' to beautiful. Occasionally, Fox would draw my attention to something new. "There," he murmured. "Seven heads!" I was looking with interest and fascination, not fear. Fox sat back and smiled approvingly. Eventually I saw dragons in every color combination. Some were primary colors, some were metallic. I saw nearly every type of dragon that Fox could tell me about. I saw dragons breathing fire. I even saw a white dragon blowing ice. The lavender cloud made the ice as harmless as the fire had been. I even saw a silver dragon, the size of an elephant, that gave a coughing bark that shot out a ball of light. The ball of light was naturally absorbed by the flash of the cloud.

Enough time passed that I actually got accustomed to the different dragons. I learned a tremendous amount from Fox about dragons. Then he began discussing their smaller relatives, dragons the size of chickens and dogs. It was fascinating, and I felt like I was in a surreal dream. But eventually, no matter how fascinating the dream, you are ready to wake up.

We been in the transport box for hours. I had begun to wonder if we would be trapped in the box forever, when we finally emerged from the clouds. One moment, the air around me was lavender. The next moment, the dragons were above us and the air was fully clear again. We were in the cloud so long that I had gotten accustomed to the tingling sensation. But when we came out of the cloud and the tingling stopped, I could immediately feel the difference.

The scene outside our viewing window changed. As we emerged, just beneath the cloud, Fox and I both stood and looked out of the window on my left. This was the first time we could see something other than lavender air and dragons.

We could see the ground below us. Fox and I stared down the rope line. We were still high enough that I felt a little dizzy when I stood to look down. I also felt cold. Strangely, I hadn't felt cold when we were much higher up in the clouds. It was colder standing by the 'observation' window. The thick rope we were descending was fastened to some point below us. The point was near the coast of some enormous lake. I had never seen such a big body of water. I realized that I could only see one side of the lake. And we were up very high. If it was just a lake, I should be able to see the whole thing. Maybe it was the sea? I had never seen the sea.

As we got lower, I could see where we were headed. It looked like some kind of building. The building had a large square opening in the roof and the green rope disappeared into the opening. As we got closer, I noticed that there were other buildings. Together, they made up a small coastal town.

"This should be interesting." Fox said calmly pointing off to the side of our destination building. People could be seen walking around. Some were even going into the building. The temperature continued to fall as we descended.

I had mixed feelings as we approached the roof of the building. Part of me was afraid of what might be waiting for us below. It's not as though this realm had been kind to us so far. The other part of me just wanted to get out of the cube. I watched as the building grew bigger.

The building was three levels high. As they rose, each level got smaller, in steps. Fox compared it to a 'Maytek step-pyramid', whatever that was. I was anxious to get out of the box, so I didn't ask. It was a building, some kind of building, good enough.

The cube smoothly slid down the line, through the square hole in the building's roof. Below, we could see a huge brass ring, where the green rope was tied in an intricate knot. Inside the building, the cube landed on a waiting platform with a soft thud. Fox and I stood up. There were people waiting on the platform.

The doors of the cube opened and I would have jumped out, but two strange women were waiting outside, blocking the doors. I stared at them, shocked, taking in their appearances. The women had coloring I had never seen before. They both had braided, dull yellow hair and pale gray eyes. Everyone I had ever known had black hair and brown eyes.

These women wore surprised expressions like they didn't expect to see us. They looked at each other, then looked at us again. Each woman was as tall as Fox, but very thin. Their necks seemed too long as I looked at them. They both also wore black wool robes and hats. The robes were tied with thick gray belts. Their clothes were appropriate for this weather. Mine were not. I began to shiver.

Fox seemed untroubled about the women's appearance. He briskly exited the cube, passing the tall women, and pulling me along. The women stared as we walked by. They were shocked when they noticed us, but didn't seem to know what to do.

As we left the cube, they got in and sat down. The doors immediately closed and the cube lifted into the air. My eyes traced the thick green rope from its starting point on the dirty brass ring up until it disappeared into the purple clouds. As the box slowly rose, Fox and I walked down off of the platform. There were stairs down to the next floor.

We walked down the stairs as if we belonged there, but not making eye contact with any of the villagers. There were two more people walking up the stairs as we walked down. The couple, a man and woman this time, were apparently going to wait for the cube to return. It was going to be a long wait, but they seemed patient. Their clothing was similar to the first two women we saw; thick, black wool robes, gray belts, and matching hats. The hats had flaps that came down over the ears. They were tall, like the women. And their necks were abnormally long. They all looked like they were sleepwalking, eyes half-closed. When they saw us, however, their eyes shot open. Some seemed surprised to see us, some seemed shocked, but they didn't take any action aside from staring.

As we descended the stairs, we passed more of the oddly long necked people coming in. All of them showed surprise at seeing us. But no one came to talk to us. They were intent on the building, their destination. Clearly this place was some sort of transportation 'station'. I was able to look around since Fox was leading me.

The 'station' was oddly decorated. The building's walls were bare, except for one piece of art on the ground floor. When the long-necked people first entered the building, they were faced with a large sculpture of a man with a long beard, and wearing a type of crown made from an animal's skull with large antlers. His eyes gleamed, reflective metal orbs somehow set into the stone. His face wore an expression of malevolence, frozen in mid snarl. His canine teeth were long fangs. The other teeth were thin and sharp like needle thorns. It was a terrifying face. It was an evil face.

The statue was dressed in similar robes to the other people I had seen, but the belt of the statue's robe was a thick belt of gold, and his robe was sleeveless. The statue had thick arms, corded with muscle that ended in long fingers with curved claws. Below its robe, the 'man' was barefoot. But its feet were wider than a man's and the toes ended in long wicked claws. I had to look up to see its face as the statue was very tall, a head and shoulders above Fox.

Fox paused to study the sculpture. I glanced over to see his reaction. I followed his eyes to see where he was looking. First, he studied the crown. So, I looked at it closer. I realized that I couldn't identify the animal. The span of the horns was nearly as long as my arms could spread, but they didn't look like deer antlers or goat horns.

Fox's eyes travelled down the statue's arms to its clawed hands. The hands were large, out of proportion to the rest of the body. The claws were pointed, tapering to razor sharp ends. And while the statue was carved from some kind of stone, the claws and the eyes were clearly made of metal. The metal gleamed like it was new, but the statue somehow gave me the impression of being old.

Fox shook his head and said, "We should get out of here." Clearly the statue had told him more than I learned by looking at it, but I agreed. This was a nasty character I hoped never to meet.

We walked out of the building onto a road. The purple cloud above us gave the impression it was about to storm. A few other buildings were visible on the street, but looked much more humble in their construction. They were nothing like the stone building where we had landed. They looked more like tents or huts. There were more of the tall people walking around. All of them were dressed identically. It seemed like they were all sleepwalking. Eerily, no one spoke.

Before we could attract any more attention, Fox led me to the side of the building and we turned the corner. He started rummaging through his bag. A moment later, he pulled out two thick mountain robes. They seemed to be made from the hide of some animal with thick, curly, white hair. Again, I marveled at his bag. Either robe would have completely filled the bag. Holding two of them would have been impossible, for a normal bag. For a moment, I wondered just how many things he carried around in there.

We put on the thick robes. Immediately I felt better. I was not only warm, but the warmth also helped me feel more confident. The thick robe felt like a layer of protection. "Thank you! That's so much better!" But we were now two 'white spots' in a place where everyone else wore black. Somehow the fact didn't really bother me.

Fox grinned at me, "Yes, these are special robes. They are inscribed with GaleScript runes to enhance them. The runes make the robes warmer, more durable, and enhance the wearer's mood. Also," he added incidentally, "they hide our appearance from these spirits. We are not exactly 'invisible', but to these spirits, we now look like them."

"They have the magic writing in them? They're doing magic on me right now?" I held my arm up to look at it. It didn't look any different to me, but Fox nodded.

"It's not magic, as such, but yes. The runes power the robe to do more than it could otherwise. Unless a being were to focus enough attention on us, they wouldn't notice that we are different. And all we have to do is not give them reason to focus attention on us."

Relieved (and feeling inconspicuous), I felt ready to go, "Ok, where do we go now?"

For a moment, I was afraid that we would have to talk to the silent strangers, but then Fox led me further back on the side of the 'station' building. He said, "We don't need an audience for this part." Then he again sought directions from his staff. The metal inset in Shui's grain began to pulse. The staff stood on its own, and Fox stepped away.

The staff fell, and stopped to hover at knee height. I had looked around carefully as we were descending, noting the directions of landmarks. That is why I knew, as soon as the staff fell, we were headed out to sea. Although I could not see the water, Shui was pointing in the direction of the shore. Fox nodded matter-of-factly and held out his hand. Shui rose to meet it. Again, carrying his staff, Fox began walking the direction Shui indicated.

Mother had read me a story once that took place by the sea. In it, the writer gave very detailed descriptions. As a boy from a land-locked village, the story took on a vividness in my memory. Even now, as we walked, I remembered the descriptions of how the air smelled salty and how large white birds flew overhead, constantly crying. He described seeing the sunlight sparkle, reflecting off the surface of the water.

But now, as we were actually approaching the sea, I found very few similarities. There was no pleasant nautical smell. There was a smell in the air, but I could not place it. It was a smell I recognized on some level, but couldn't identify. But whatever the smell was, it was not pleasant.

The road in front of the 'station' led directly to the sea. Soon, we could see the water. In this place, there was no sunlight to reflect off the water. Instead, the purple clouds overhead just gave a sinister stormy character to the sea. Somehow, I expected to see many fishermen, but none of the tall, silent strangers carried any fishing supplies. If they didn't fish here, what did they eat? And why did they all look sleepy?

As Fox and I walked, we were both silent, looking at our surroundings. I began to notice a strange habits the long-necked people had. They did not speak. But there are times when a person can tell someone wants to speak, or that they have something to say. I was watching a pair of the long-necked people walking the opposite direction from us.

I was looking at the man and I had the distinct impression that he wanted to say something. He squinted his eyes, but did not close them. It looked like he was concentrating.

Immediately, and certainly in response, the woman walking next to him nodded once. Her arm rose and she pointed off at a building in the distance. The man nodded, and they altered their course slightly, angling away from us as they passed.

I thought about it as we walked. I was pretty certain that those people had been communicating. But they had not spoken. How could they talk without making any sound? Was it like how Fox and Shui communicated? But these people were clearly different from the people of my village. They looked different, but that was less significant to me. It was that they *felt* different. Not like regular people.

"Fox," I asked. "Are these people demons too? They look so strange. They don't talk. What's wrong with them?" He thought about his answer for a long time.

"We are in a different realm than the world you know, Kwan. It is tempting to fall back into the way you normally think about things. This place may feel more like a civilization from our world, than the forest. But this is still not *our* 'living' real world. That is the first thing to remember. Keep walking." Listening intently, I had stopped on the street. Still no one noticed.

We started walking again and Fox resumed speaking. "From what I can tell, we are still in the demons' realm, but in a different part of it. I suspect this is the same realm, just a different land's version of it.

"My best guess is that these people are spirits of the dead, that don't realize that they have died." He paused to let that sink in. "The world is a very big place Kwan. There are many different types of people. Some have coloring like these spirits; yellow hair, red hair, blue, gray, or green eyes. People from the far North, where it is very cold, often look like them. Other people, in the South, have brown or black skin. Some of the underground dwellers of Shambala have silver eyes and blue skin. The original forest dwellers even had green skin.

"I wouldn't worry about the appearance. In the first few moments, you use someone's appearance to determine if they are an obvious threat. But after you make that assessment, your attention should turn to their character. Honestly, after the first few seconds, appearance is the least useful way to judge someone.

"But as for these spirits, I think they were people from some place in the far-North of our world, who died. Now they are in a nightmare. Because they haven't accepted their fate, they came to this place after they died. They would have blocked out all memory of their deaths. They likely think this location is just a strange place they found themselves 'in their normal lives'.

"The problem is that this realm where they are being held, until they understand their deaths, is a place where evil roams free. I suspect that they are under the control of a powerful demon."

Understanding dawned in my head, "The statue!"

Fox nodded grimly, "Yes. The statue. The golden belt on its sleeveless robe was embroidered in GaleScript. It gave his title." Fox looked pensive for a second, remembering, "It said his name, which I'll spare you the sound of, and the title, which was unmistakably demonic. I think he has taken over this place and enslaved these poor spirits. Now they exist in fear, afraid to die again (which *can't actually* happen) and afraid to wake up. That demon is a nasty character, even for a demon. It's terrible." He genuinely sounded sad.

"What kind of demon will it be, Fox? Will it be more lightning, or illusions, or what?" I wanted to be as prepared as possible.

Fox was quiet for a while. We walked on in silence. "We are partners in this venture Kwan. So, I will certainly tell you the truth." I braced myself.

Fox lowered his voice, "Have you ever heard the term 'wompir'?" He looked over and saw me shake my head. "Ok, have you ever heard of an animal that drinks the blood of another?"

"Like fleas when they bite a dog?" I asked.

"Somewhat. What about the fat worms in swamp water that stick to a person's skin and suck blood. Have you ever heard of those?" I thought about it.

"I... think so. But I've never seen them. Why?" I was careful to keep walking. The road was gradually sloping down to the sea. The harbor of the small town was a single long pier ahead of us.

"The demon represented by that statue is a 'wompir'. They drink the blood of people and animals to stay alive, feeding on their life-force. In a realm like this, where nobody is alive, they feed on the spiritual energy of these beings. If they had blood, the wompir would prefer blood. Because we don't want to announce that we are alive, and thus have blood, I brought out these robes. In truth, I have other warm clothing in here," he patted his bag fondly, "but those items wouldn't hide our nature...

"This demon, being a wompir, would be able to fly and shape-shift too. That means the demon will likely be able to change its form. He may have other abilities. I don't actually know." The robe's runes must have really been helping me, because I didn't feel as worried as I probably should have been. The only things I had learned had been frightening.

The street that we were walking down turned sharply to the left and sloped downward. At the bottom of the hill, we would be at water level. Once we were down at the level of the water, we could walk the short distance to the pier.

Fox fell quiet as we walked down the hill. There were a few people walking up the hill past us, but they did not seem to notice us. Even though I felt invisible, I followed Fox's example, and tried to be as inconspicuous as possible. I kept my eyes focused on the ground in front of me. But there was apparently no reason to worry. None of the people that we passed paid any attention to us.

Once we had reached the bottom of the hill, we were in an area with one main long peer and several small docks. The small docks made it a harbor of sorts. We turned and altered our course towards the pier.

As we got closer, the wooden path out to sea looked impossibly long. It stretched out into the distance, with rowboats tied up on either side. The wood of the dock looked very old. It was discolored and rotting.

We walked onto the pier. It creaked ominously every time we took a step. I could hear the water lapping at the supports underneath us. The purple clouds above the sea were retreating back toward the coast. A strong wind was now blowing toward the shore.

Along the pier, we saw innumerable small boats tied up. As we walked, I studied the boats. All of them looked old and like they had not been used in years. Some had oars, while others were just the shell of the boat itself. Invariably, the boats were tied to metal rings on the pier.

I do remember thinking that none of the small boats looked seaworthy. And this was funny even to me, because I was not a seaman. I was just a boy from an inland village, but even I could see that the boats were in disrepair. The wood of the boats was gray and looked so old that I was surprised they were still afloat.

We had only made it about 50 paces down the long peer when we heard thumping steps behind us. We turned, then stepped to one side of the path. One of the yellow-haired, blue-eyed men hurried past us. His warm woolen coat was open and flared out behind him as he ran. His scarf fell off and fell on the pier, ahead of us. He ran frantically, clearly looking for something. We slowed down as we watched him moving ahead of us. He didn't seem to notice us at all.

The man hurried up to a rowboat that looked better than the rest. The boat was tied up to the peer like the others. The rope that held the boat looked newer and sturdier than the boat itself. Once the long-necked man reached it, he bent to the ring where the rope was tied. He untied the rope. Then the man tossed the end of the rope into the boat and stepped inside.

This boat was equipped with two oars, one on either side. The man sat down with his back to the open water, hurriedly arranged the oars, and began powerfully stroking out to sea. He was clearly heading out, directly away from "our shore". Fox and I watched him rowing out to sea. He was pulling so hard that every time he pulled the oars, the front of the boat lifted out of the water.

I had never seen someone rowing a boat, and it fascinated me. I watched as he flexed his back and arms with each stroke. He clearly was experienced in a boat. Occasionally he looked back over his shoulder as if to check his progress. The wind continued to blow, increasing its intensity.

Fox and I had both stopped to watch his effort. While he was rowing, the wind rose to meet, and then surpassed his efforts. We watched as the rower's strongest efforts could barely keep him in the same space. He rowed and he rowed, but he stopped moving away from shore. He was far enough away from us that I couldn't see his face. I had the impression that he was in panic, or despair, or something. His rowing was frantic.

The purple clouds above us flashed their golden light again. For a moment, the light was so bright that it felt like daylight back home. Then the clouds returned to the ominous purple color. My gaze was drawn upward for a moment, then returned to watch the rower.

The wind picked up, until it was a fierce tempest. It looked like it would have blown the rowing man back to shore, but he turned the boat slightly off its original course, away from the wind. Almost immediately, the wind flipped the boat over.

When the rowboat capsized, the long-necked man was dumped in the water. The boat disappeared, immediately plunging beneath the water. The man was left swimming back toward us. Fox and I stood on the pier watching the scene.

"But... Fox... Where did the boat...?" I stammered. The rowboat had dropped out of sight, sinking like it was made of iron. But all of these boats were wood. Then I saw a long tentacle emerge from the water. It waved lazily above the surface before it fell back beneath the water. The boat had been *pulled* under the surface.

Fox put a hand on my arm, and said quietly, "Don't show your reaction, but look..." He turned back to where the rowboat had been tied.

If he had not warned me beforehand, I definitely would have shouted in surprise. The boat had reappeared, dry, and tied to the pier as before. Even the knot in the rope was the same as it had been before. The boat looked like it had never been used.

Before I could think through how the boat had reappeared, there was a flurry of action in my peripheral view. My head whipped to the side to see what was happening. Two tentacles like the first one had burst from the water. One of the tentacles coiled around the swimmer and lifted him into the air. The other tentacle waved around. I had the impression that the second tentacle waving around was expressing... excitement?

The tentacle wrapped around the man waved him around for a moment, then pulled him under the water too. "Stay calm." Fox said. I realized that I was backing away from the water. I was horrified. What was that thing? What had just happened???

Fox said, "Come on." He started walking forward again, down the pier. I was frozen in my spot, unable to move forward.

"Do... do we have to go this way? This is the only way to Cho Clei?" I asked. What I had just seen somehow scared me more than any of the demons before.

Fox stopped and turned to address me, "There might be a more direct way to reach your sister, but this is the way we have to take." He gestured down the pier. "That is, if we want to bring her home."

"What do you mean?" I asked. I was confused. Of course, we wanted to bring her home! That was the whole reason we were here. But if there was a way to avoid these monsters, we should take it!

Fox explained patiently. His soothing tone helped to calm me. "Remember the price Ragyala demanded for our crossing. We will have to pay, in spirits, when we want to return to our realm." He paused. I nodded to show that I understood so far. "Shui has not forgotten that we need to acquire those spirits before we can return. So, when Shui seeks our path to Cho Clei, it is not the most direct path to her. It is the most direct path, that lets us get the spirits we need, to return. Make no mistake, Shui has been the real hero of this mission so far."

"Oh." I hadn't thought of that. I had underestimated Shui. And again, it occurred to me that I would have been lost without Fox too. Without them, I would have been dead several times over. "That makes sense." I didn't like having no other options, but the situation was clear to me. Suddenly I remembered Fox's dialogue with Ragyala. "Fox, what were you and Ragyala talking about? Light and sound... and something?"

Fox took a moment to collect his thoughts before responding. "There are a few things that are sacred to every being in the GaleSource."

"The GaleSource?" I interrupted.

Fox clarified, "It is a word we use, at the GaleTemple, to describe the entirety of all worlds, a universe, if you like. It is the collection of all timelines and realms. Our world is located in the GaleSource. All worlds are located in the GaleSource." He went on, "There are four sacred concepts to all beings, whether they know it or not.

"The first sacred concept is The Light. In this sense, The Light is a symbol for Life. It is a symbol of understanding, knowledge, truth, and conscious spirit. It is a symbol of order, as opposed to chaos. The light is a symbol for all positive things. It is sacred. Even the beings aligned with evil must respect it.

"The Sounds of Being, refers to the way the GaleSource operates. It describes the forces that determine all reality-frequency and vibration. All of the other laws we see are derived from frequency and vibration. Why things fall or float when you drop them, why the elements of creation are what they are, and many more facets of reality, all come from frequency and vibration. That is why the Sound is sacred." I didn't understand what he meant, but I stayed silent.

"The Beyond describes the Source/HighGod, and its divine realm. All of creation, and all beings come from that Source."

I interrupted, "But aren't there many gods?" I asked.

He clarified, "There are now, and have been, throughout the past, many beings we call gods. They have enormous power, compared to us. But their power is not infinite. They are 'lower-case' gods. Their life spans are much much longer than ours, but they do not live forever. They were created in the same place that we were, and their abilities come from the source as well. *All* of life comes from the Source/HighGod, from the Beyond. The realm where the Source/HighGod is, we call the Beyond, because it is 'beyond' the power of all other beings to reach it. That is why 'the Beyond' is sacred. (In truth, the Source/HighGod is everywhere. It is only most 'concentrated' in 'the Beyond'. Also, all of us can reach the Beyond, but we have to re-unify with the Source to do so.

"And last, The Primordial Fracture is sacred. The Primordial Fracture refers to the beginning time for life, as we know it... We do not know where the Source/HighGod came from, but we do know that it was alone in creation... Eventually, the Source/HighGod became bored, or wanted company, so it decided to split off pieces of itself to make more living things. Our best theories are that the Source/HighGod created life to have something to watch and participate in; somewhere between an education and entertainment.

"To make the spectacle more interesting, the Source/HighGod made us forget our origin- that we are pieces of the Source/HighGod itself. Not knowing our true nature, we feel small and alone, cut off from the Creator, the Source/HighGod. If people knew their true origin, they would rarely feel confusion and never feel fear. We would have no instinct to survive, knowing we can't die, or that we wouldn't stay dead after we died."

"What do you mean? We can't die? I've been to funerals, of course people die!" I blurted out.

It seemed that there was no end to Fox's patience. He was the ultimate teacher to me. He was always willing to pause, to review, and to re-explain things to me. Patiently, he replied, "Yes, our human lives do end. But not our spirits. After that time, we return to the Creator, pass on our experiences, lose our memories, and are reborn. The Primordial Fracture describes that initial act of the Source/HighGod splitting itself into all other life."

We walked in silence, as I absorbed all that he had just taught me. After a few minutes, he went on, "As for this place, this realm exists outside of time. (At least the way that human minds naturally understand time.) I suspect that many creatures have come from our realm to this place. For example, I suspect that these 'people' are trapped in this realm, unable to pay for their passage to the next, better realm. I think they were eventually discovered by a demon, who proceeded to feed on their spirits - the same demon the statue was depicting.

"But demons are not the only predators here. Certain creatures, which operate outside of human spirituality, appear to have arrived here too. Like that creature which sank the boat. I suspect that it is a remnant of an older time…"

I was confused, "What older time? When do you mean?"

"Well, specifically, I mean that the world has had many epochs, or long periods in its history. Over the last few million years, our world has been home to many things. There have been dragons, innumerable races, giants, huge reptiles, almost anything you can think of. But more recently, our world was flooded about two thousand years ago. Most of the creatures on land were killed off. At the GaleTemple, we have been able to piece together the sequence of events." I had paused to listen, but he gently took my elbow and led me forward once again. "Unlike the land animals, the creatures of the seas survived. Compelled by an unknown reason, many of these giant creatures moved to much deeper water, but others disappeared from our world entirely… I suspect they found a path to *this* place. I think the creature we just saw, was one of the creatures that left our world. Either way, their existence doesn't change our objective.

"Just remember your sister. Cho Clei needs us. Come, Kwan. We will take it one step at a time." Slowly, Fox resumed walking. I took a deep, shuddering, breath and followed him.

We continued to walk down the pier, between the rows of small boats. I began to notice something strange about the pier. When we first stepped onto the pier, it stretched out into the distance. The land was at our backs. But when I looked back after no more than 100 paces, the land had disappeared.

Now, the pier behind us looked identical to the pier ahead of us. It extended indefinitely in either direction. We were surrounded by the water. I felt like panicking. We had not walked far enough for the land to disappear from sight. I felt dizzy for a moment, like the entire environment around me couldn't be trusted. We continued our walk. I began repeating Fox's words to me, silently in my head, 'Cho Clei needs us. Cho Clei needs us...' over and over again.

We had been walking for some time, without seeming to make progress. As none of the long-necked people were in sight, Fox decided to consult Shui again.

I watched as Fox performed the same ritual. He placed the gnarled staff against his forehead and closed his eyes. He murmured some mysterious words, but as before, I couldn't understand their meaning. The silver metal grain running down the staff again pulsed with light.

After the brief incantation, Fox let go of the staff and stepped away from it. Shui stood there, upright and balanced. After a moment, Fox opened his eyes, looking at the staff. Shui fell until it stopped, at knee height, pointing away from us, down the pier. Fox nodded and stepped forward. He held out his right hand and Shui rose to it.

We had been looking down at Shui as it pointed out our direction. Before Fox consulted Shui and we looked down, the pier had stretched out infinitely, before us. After Shui had pointed us forward, we lifted our gaze to look up.

Miraculously, the infinite pier had become shorter. It had changed. It now ended some ten paces in front of us. Where there was infinite pier before, there was now a huge ship before us. It was not like the other little rowboats. It was twice as tall as our new house, back near my village. The huge ship had three enclosed floors. Windows were visible along the uppermost level. I craned my neck to see around the back of the ship, to see how long it was, but the back was large enough that it blocked my view.

Chapter 10

The Arkyala

The ship was made of dark reddish-brown wood, but looked much newer and better maintained than the old rowboats. New-looking, iron bands, wrapped around the ship. I studied the rear of the ship as we approached. A single long oar was mounded from the center of the top deck. The oar stretched 30 or 40 paces behind the ship, angling down into the water. It had no other sails or oars that I could see. I couldn't imagine that one oar could move such a large ship.

A wide ramp served as a walkway onto the ship. The end of the ramp rested on the end of the pier. Inside the ship, the interior was dark. Directly in front of the walkway stood an enormous cat man figure. At first, I thought that it was Ragyala. But as I got closer, I realized that the figure was the same size as Ragyala, but looked different.

Like Ragyala had been, the figure was more than twice my height. But unlike Ragyala, this giant was covered in a short fur that was so black that it absorbed light. He wore a dark gray gown down to his giant feet. The gown was tied with a silver strip of cloth at the waist. Like Ragyala, the figure's powerful shape was visible through the gray gown. It had massive shoulders and a thick neck. His gown had silver embroidery from the shoulders down the sleeves and encircled his wrists. He looked like a giant, black-furred, cat-man.

For a moment, I stood frozen in shock, just as I had with Ragyala, and could only stare at him. I noticed several similarities, like the proportions of his body were different that a normal man, just like Ragyala. His arms were longer and his hands were larger than a human's hands would have been, even considering his height. I noticed that, like Ragyala, each hand had three thick fingers on each hand. In his left hand, he held a black scepter, blunt on one end and pointed on the other, like Ragyala's.

His head was shaped like a cat's. Like Ragyala's, large, brilliant eyes looked down at us as we approached. They had vertical slit pupils like a cat. Those cat eyes shone with a glowing yellow light.

His face was impassive as he stood in front of the barge and looked calmly down at us as we approached. He stood with his feet wide apart and, like Ragyala, I had the impression of enormous power emanating from him. I wanted to look more, but the closer we got, it took too much effort to gaze directly at him. As before, it felt like there was an increasing weight on my shoulders.

As we approached him, the giant cat-man spoke. This time, the voice sounded like a chorus of men speaking. It sounded as strange and powerful as Ragyala's speech, but had a different, deeper tone. "Through your guise... We regard you... GaleMaster, Immortal, ... We regard the little one... and the spirits... with you..." Its words startled me as much as its voice had. Like Ragyala, it spoke slowly, with great rumbling volume and long pauses.

Fox dropped to one knee before the giant. I followed his example. I was trembling slightly.

Fox immediately spoke, "Great Arkyala, by the Infinite Light..." Fox reached up and touched his forehead. "By the Sounds of Being..." He touched his forehead again. "And by the Primordial Fracture..." He touched his forehead a third time. "We must ask passage... Our mission requires it."

As we kneeled before the black giant, I wanted to back away. I felt like running away again. If not for Fox kneeling next to me, I might have panicked.

The giant looked at us for a long time, his gaze passing from Fox to me. I could tell because the weight on my shoulders got heavier, then lightened, then got heavier, then lighter. Fox's staff leapt from his hand to stand unaided next to him. The metal grain running through the ironwood staff pulsed brightly. "Ah... a J'nii... Explain."

Fox stayed quiet, and didn't respond to Arkyala's command. I was amazed that Fox was daring to ignore the giant's command. Then it dawned on me that the giant Arkyala was speaking to Shui! Just as Fox had! The Arkyala listened carefully, Shui pulsed, but I could not hear any sound. Finally, the giant cat-man spoke, "Truth... The rescue... of an Innocent... We see your need... But our ferry is only for the dead... And there is still great life in you."

I sensed Fox tensing for a moment as he replied, "Great Arkyala... I request an exception...passage on your ferry...for my small group..." I did not understand, but I knew to keep quiet.

Again, time froze as Arkyala examined us. Eventually, the robed giant spoke again, "Aaah... We see... your mind... and where you wish to go... But the price... must still be paid... What... will you exchange?" Fox looked as though he expected the question.

Fox reached into his bag and went on, "I bear the blessing of the Ragyala." Fox looked up slowly, as he extracted the small glowing sphere from his shoulder bag. I followed his example and looked up as well. Arkyala's feline face was still impassive.

Fox lifted both hands to offer the blessing to Arkyala. As he did, the tiny sphere of light lifted from his hands and grew, as it floated toward Arkyala. The giant reached out with his empty hand. The massive three fingered hand/paw was held, palm out, like it was going to block the sphere or push it away. Instead, the hand absorbed the sphere. It began to shrink and disappear as soon as it touched Arkyala's hand.

Arkyala looked thoughtful for a moment, then nodded, "A blessing... from one of my brothers... Your payment... is..." Fox tensed. "...Acceptable." Arkyala finished. "Your group may ride." There was a crack of thunder as he pronounced his judgement, but this time there was no light. He didn't vanish, like Ragyala had. Arkyala was still standing there. He had not disappeared.

"By the Light... by the Sound... and the Fracture..." Fox intoned. "By the Beyond... Great Arkyala, we are grateful."

With that, the giant nodded and stepped aside, revealing the dark interior of the ship. Awkwardly, we stood back up. Arkyala, now standing to the side, watched as we walked up the ramp. Then he turned back to stand in front of the ramp again. I guessed that he was checking to see if any other passengers were coming.

"Fox?" I whispered as we walked onto the boat. "What...?" That was all I was able to say because Fox quietly interrupted me, "I will explain, but we have to find our seats first."

As we walked up the ramp, onto the barge, I was almost overwhelmed by a flurry of new sensations. The interior looked very similar to the exterior, the wood looked newer than the rowboats. The ramp led into a room that was filled with benches. Long wooden beams ran overhead in the room that we first entered. The floor was made of the same identical wood that the walls and ceiling were made of. No carvings or ornamentation were visible.

Initially I had thought that the interior of the ship was dark. But once we got inside, and my eyes adjusted, I realized that it was only dark in comparison to the gray light outside. There were no windows in that first room, but my eyes quickly adjusted. The ceiling was twice as tall as Fox was.

The benches were filled with people. But few of these people looked like the type of people that I expected. They did not look like me, like regular people. Some of them were the long-necked people that inhabited this town. Some of them, look more different than I had imagined. For example, there were several people with black skin and shaved heads. There were also people with brown skin and long, long hair.

The thing that was even more strange than the appearance of these people, was that their bodies did not appear to be fully solid. The long-necked people that I had seen outside the boat, in the village, appeared solid. I had not been able to see through them.

But without exception, every person sitting in the back of the barge, was slightly transparent. If I looked at them for longer than a moment, I began to see what was behind them. I didn't need Fox to explain to me that these people were not alive. It was clear enough that it needed no explanation.

Then I noticed that there was a door at the far end of the room, opposite the ramp. A large brass lantern, holding a single candle, hung next to the door. That lantern provided the only light for the room.

Fox and I walked through the room, not speaking to any of the spirits. I was surprised to see that only a few of them looked up as he walked by. I had the impression that most of the spirits were preoccupied and did not have attention to spare for any of the others on board, including us.

"Fox?" I asked quietly. "Where did all of these people come from? I didn't know there was a place that had so many different looking people."

We kept walking and in a moment, had reached the door at the front of the room. Only when we had passed the benches and were almost out the door did Fox respond to me. "Well Kwan, there are some massive cities in the world right now, but none of them are located near your little village. Certainly, there are cities where many different races of people live. Some have black skin, some have pink skin, or yellowish skin, or reddish-brown skin, but they all live together in the same city."- I hadn't known that. I never imagined that there were so many different types of people in the world. I didn't realize it, but my view of the world changed each time Fox made one of these unexpected statements.

"But I don't think that these people came from one of those huge cities. What you are seeing here, is people that have boarded the ferry in different places.

"You understand that the Arkyala is a being similar the Ragyala. They are guardians of the boundaries. The Arkyala's ferry is a type of transportation many different cultures have used. The Arkyala's duty is to collect eligible spirits from *several different places*, from *several different cultures*, and deliver them to their next realm. It is like a wagon that stops in different cities to pick up people, and delivers them to their destinations.

"But I'm pretty certain that none of them know the being as 'the Arkyala.' He has many names, 'Karo' , 'Damurmon', and 'Taey-li-on' are just a few of them. But the entity's actual title is Arkyala."

I was quiet absorbing this information as we passed through the next doorway. I was filled with questions, but did not ask them now. Instead, I kept quiet, walking beside Fox and stealing glances at the interior of the ferry.

We walked through the doorway into a much longer, more brightly lit room. This room had lamps on each of the walls, every 2 paces apart. There were benches in this room as well, but the 'people' in this room looked different from the last room's passengers.

In this new room, the 'people' barely looked like men. To my eyes, the first beings I saw were half-bull and half-men. Like the last group, they became somewhat transparent if you looked at them for too long. Clearly, they were no longer alive. They had muscular bodies with heavy shoulders, but were covered in faded gray-brown fur. I had been in this realm long enough to be accustomed to the faded colors. I suspected that, when they were alive, their fur had been brown.

But their heads were identical to cows. All of them had large round ears protruding from the sides of their heads. Some of them had curved horns sprouting from the sides of their foreheads, while some lacked horns. Their large black eyes were unfocused, and all were looking off into the distance. Each one sat in the same position. They all had their hands clasped in their laps, thick fingers intertwined. Their posture was uniform too. All of them sat rigidly upright, their large, bare feet flat on the deck.

After a moment, I realized that some were male, and others were female. The males wore a type of loin cloth, while the females wore an additional strip of cloth over their large breasts. The cloth was a rough, gray fabric, but I couldn't identify what kind of plant or animal it had been made of. The larger males carried wooden clubs that were much thicker, but slightly shorter than Shui. They looked so heavy that I doubted that I would have been able to swing them. (And I'm strong for my age.)

Shocked at their appearance, I stopped dead in my tracks, but Fox immediately took my elbow, shook his head, and pulled me forward with him. I looked up to see another door opposite the one we had entered. We shuffled through the long room, past the cow-people. Only when we had moved half-way through the room, did he quietly speak.

"There are many different kinds of beings, Kwan. Normally, a person would have no idea that things like them exist. But you are in a place that most people never see. Since this place exists outside of time, there is no telling how long they have been riding this ferry. They may have been from our world, ten thousand years ago."

Just when I thought I had gotten accustomed to the cow people, I noticed that there were other groups in this room. The next group I noticed was somehow more disturbing to me. I would best describe them as pig-men.

They were smaller than the cow-men, physically. Their limbs looked much thinner than the cow-men but each pig-man had an oddly round belly. The bellies seemed misplaced, a chunk of round fat on otherwise lean bodies. Each of them wore some sort of strap around their chests. The straps across their torsos were lined with pouches and small loops containing... little spikes, or... darts?

Their skin was a pale gray with patches of darker gray, that might have been pink at some time. And they were hairless. They had oversized, pointy ears, and protruding snouts. Their black eyes were small and beady, unlike the cow-people's large eyes. Some of them even had tusks.

Unlike the cow-people, I could not tell if any of them was female. I was amazed and disconcerted looking at the pig-men. I might have shown my reaction to what I was seeing, but Fox glanced over at me and patted my arm as we walked.

After the pig-men, we came to another group of 'half-men'. That was how I thought of them. They had smaller bodies, and were covered in wrinkles. It was hard to judge because they were sitting, but I estimated that they were shorter than I was. However, considering what I had seen already, their size did not shock me.

What did shock me was that I couldn't see these new creatures' eyes. They might have had eyes, but if so, they were tiny and pinched closed, folding into their wrinkles. Their faces protruded into pointy snouts, tipped with small black noses. Bunches of whiskers sprouted from either side of their faces.

The other things that most shocked me were their hands and feet. Their hands had four long fingers that ended in thick pointy claws. But these claws did not look like the claws of a predator. They seemed more suited to digging. Their hands had no thumbs either. Their feet were the same, with four long toes that ended in long, digging claws.

These were the main groups of half-men I saw in the room. But as we walked, I became aware of random unique individuals that were interspersed between the groups. There was a man-shaped creature that appeared to be made of sluggishly moving worms. There was one man who appeared to be half-monkey. His face was perhaps the most disturbing of all, because it looked so similar to a human face. His eyes were facing to the front of his face. It was then I realized that the cow-people and pig-men had their eyes to the sides of their head. There were other half-man variations, but I lowered my eyes and looked at the floor. I was unnerved and beginning to panic.

We had almost made it to the end of the room, when I spoke. I couldn't control myself any longer. "Are these... animal demons?" I hissed fearfully.

Fox kept me moving, but responded, "No Kwan, these are past spirits trying to move on from this realm."

I was confused, "So, everyone goes to the same afterlife?" I asked.

Fox shook his head, but did not stop walking. "They go to different afterlives. Just as this ferry collects spirits from different realms, it also delivers them to different destinations. You see, Kwan, except for the Source/HighGod, life is temporary, and everything in the GaleSource is on its way... somewhere. Everything, Kwan."

I spent some time walking beside Fox, thinking about what he had said. Suddenly, I found the purple sky above me once again. Gratefully, I realized that we had reached the next door, which was open. We walked through it.

This doorway opened on to an open deck in the front of the ship. The enclosed 'boat house' portion of the ship took up most of the back, but the front of the ship was a flat deck, open to the sky. A single wooden, waist-high, railing curved around the perimeter of the deck. I looked toward the back of the ship and saw the halls that we had just walked through.

As we walked out onto the deck, it took a moment for my eyes to re-adjust to the light. I looked up at the blanket of purple clouds above us. Flickers of white and golden light could be seen flashing in different areas.

"Give me your robe, Kwan." Fox said. I was surprised. That was the last thing I expected him to say.

"But it's still cold. Really?" I asked. I did not want to sound whiny, but I knew I did.

Fox reached into his bag and pulled out two different robes. These robes were made of the same thick animal fur as the white robes, but they were dyed a red-orange color. The color seemed impossibly vivid in this faded realm. Fox held the one of the new robes out to me. It was just a thick and warm looking as the one I was wearing.

"Our time for hiding is over. Now we need to let the next demon see us. This robe will keep you warm, but it will not hide our nature." Reluctantly, I took off the robe I was wearing and traded him for the new robe. I immediately felt warm, but something was missing. I don't think it was my imagination that I felt less confident and positive, as soon as the robe came off. Fox was also trading his robe for a new one from his bag. We both quickly changed clothes.

Noticing my change in demeanor, Fox said, "It is natural to feel a difference, Kwan. These robes are inscribed with runes of durability and warmth, but they will not hide us..." Fox said. Then he shook his head and a look came over his face. The look was... serious and focused. He looked fierce, and for the first time, I thought that the demon should be worried. "The time for hiding is over. Now we will announce our presence, and let the demon see us..."

There was one bench located in the center of the open deck. Fox walked to the bench and sat down. I sat beside him. He seemed ready for battle, but I didn't feel the same confidence. I saw it in him, but I wasn't feeling the same. The new reddish-orange robes kept me warm, but I still tried to sink into the garment and hide. Fox reminded me that I wore powerful protection. "Don't forget the talisman I gave you. Know that you have protection." I looked down at the medallion Fox had given me, then reached up to touch it. It was warm to the touch and vibrating slightly. Or maybe it was my imagination. It was difficult to be sure.

We sat on the bench in silence, watching the lights flicker in the purple clouds overhead. I took the opportunity to ask Fox some questions. "So Arkyala is taking us to another realm? *Farther* from home? We are travelling to those creatures' afterlife???" Only when I said it, did I realize that I was very uncomfortable with the idea.

Fox answered, "No, Kwan. We are not traveling to the same place where they are going. All of the beings that we passed through are headed to different places. The place where we're going is different from their destinations. Think of it as a stop on the Arkyala's route."

"The last time that Shui found our path, I learned where we would have to go next. It is a different place, yes, but it is not in a different realm. Think of it as a different region in *this* realm. Shui has informed me that we need to get out from the shore- out to sea, but not all the way to the next realm. We are only using Arkyala's ferry to get there."

A different question popped into my head, unbidden. "Fox, why do the Ragyala and the Arkyala call you an immortal? And GaleMaster. Are you really immortal?" Fox's expression changed slightly, seeming almost embarrassed.

He shook his head, "No Kwan, I'm not immortal. Not in the sense of living forever. Remember that no beings, not even the 'gods' live forever. At this point, that's how you should think about it. Only the Source/HighGod does that. The terms 'Immortal' and 'GaleMaster' are only titles. They show a certain level of achievement in my studies.

"I attended a… special school, high in the mountains, far from your village. You have heard me refer to it before. It is called the GaleTemple. There, I learned about many things. It really is a special place, filled with powerful masters. But, like any school, there are levels to the curriculum. Some students only learn to control the basic elements. Some learn to work with herbs and medicine to heal the body. Some focus only on meditation, or internal alchemy. Some students go even further than that. In truth, there are many different disciplines taught there.

"Some students study further and learn to manage more than those initial concepts. They go on to learn more complicated techniques. As a student rises through the ranks, they are frequently tested to make sure that they have learned well. When certain advanced tests are passed, the student receives a title. The second highest level of achievement within the 'traditional' GaleStudies is to be given the title 'GaleMaster'.

I passed those tests, and the Ragyala and Arkyala could see that, so they called me by title. When a 'GaleMaster' has learned to *fully* control their own energy, they can even control the speed at which they age. There are other abilities that come with fully controlling your own energies, but being able to slow ageing is the main goal. If a 'GaleMaster' can do that, and has passed the tests, they are granted the title 'Immortal'.

Becoming an 'Immortal' is an important goal, because it lets you gain more than one life's worth of knowledge. Most people can only achieve one life's worth of experience at a time. But if a person has more time, they can learn more. That experience adds up.

"At the GaleTemple, brothers below my rank call me 'Master Fox, the Immortal', but those are just titles. I think of myself as Fox. I have the titles, but I have not achieved true Unity yet. In my mind, I have a long way to go. My teacher, Master Eclipse, the Immortal has achieved that true greatness."

I was silent as I thought about what he said. A question occurred to me, "Fox, how old are you?"

Fox smiled kindly, but slowly shook his head. "That is one of the few questions I am not allowed to answer. It is our tradition that, after one achieves the status of 'Immortal', we don't discuss our age... I do apologize Kwan. I don't want to keep information from you, but I took an oath."

I would probably have pestered him to tell me, but my thoughts were interrupted by a loud clarion sound blasting from the back of the ship. I whipped my head around and saw the Arkyala standing on top of the top deck portion of the ship. He was holding a horn that looked like a giant tusk of some animal. He blew through the horn, then paused, then another blow, etc. He blew the horn three times, then it vanished from his hand.

"Ok, sounds like we're ready to go!" Fox said cheerfully. Before I knew it, the ship lurched forward. The Arkyala had grasped the end of the single long oar, and was moving it back and forth, from left to right. I turned back to the front of the ship and marveled at how fast we were suddenly moving.

I was amazed that one single being could propel a ship this size, with only one single oar. But that is exactly what was happening. The Arkyala did not even seem to strain with the effort of rowing the giant ship. It would have been impossible for the strongest man in the world, but the Arkyala hardly noticed. His feline face was clearly looking out to the water.

Before I thought about it, I stood and trotted to the side of the ship. I looked back toward the shore, but it was already far in the distance. It wasn't possible that we were moving *that* fast, but after a few more movements of the oar, the land had receded to a distant spot behind us. There were no other oars visible on the sides of the ship.

Remembering where we were, I quickly sat back down. Fox and I sat in silence on the deck's single bench, feeling the wind blowing into our faces. I reviewed everything Fox had told me. It was quite a lot to absorb.

Before long, I noticed that the purple clouds were being left behind us as well. The clouds stopped in a perfectly straight line. And once we passed from underneath them, I looked back and was able to see them clearly.

The purple clouds were actually in the shape of a purple cube. The line where they ended, was one bottom edge of a 'purple box'. When we were up on the bridge, we were above the box. In the town of the long-necked spirits, we were below the box. And now, on Arkyala's ferry, we were moving out from beneath the box. Another flat side of the cube went straight up, into the air. As we passed farther away from it, I could see the corners of the box too. It was so enormous that I wouldn't have expected to see the corners. But the ferry was moving impossibly fast.

I remembered another question, "Fox, is this a river?"

"Many cultures think of it as a river. But it is a small sea. But it's actually not the amount of water that is important here." I was clearly confused, so Fox continued. "The Pall, which is guarded by the Ragyala is one boundary between realms. This sea, the Fo-Sti-Xxi, is another boundary. The

Arkyala is the guardian of this boundary. There are other boundaries too, but I don't expect that we will see them."

"Other boundaries?" I asked.

Fox counted them on his fingers of his left hand. He held up his index finger, "The Pall is the boundary of fire. Without Ragyala's permission, that shimmering red curtain we passed through would have incinerated us, instantly turning us to ash." My eyes went wide as I remembered how I had just walked through it, oblivious to any danger!

He held up his second finger, "The second boundary is this river, the Fo-Sti-Xi. It is the boundary of water. The Arkyala is its guardian. According to the records we have, the water itself is the boundary. The spirits that lack the means to pay, are stuck in this place until the Grace reaches them. If they try to swim across, the water itself will stop them. It will wash them back to shore, or drown them, so that they wake back where they started. Some find the water boiling hot, or freezing cold. Sometimes, the water destroys their minds, absorbing their memories, and they forget where they were going. But however the boundary chooses to work, the water keeps them there."

Fox held up his third finger. "The third boundary is in the sky. It is the boundary of air. It has a guardian as well, like the Ragyala and the Arkyala. But that boundary is only accessible to beings that can fly. I don't actually know its title."

He held up his fourth finger. "The fourth boundary, the Ondaral, is deep underground. But that boundary is only encountered by beings like the Gartuns- those who live far beneath our feet. That gate is guarded by 'the Griyala'."

Finally, he held up his fifth finger. "The fifth boundary is located… here." Fox lifted his hand and tapped me on the forehead. "That boundary is the Zili-mayn, the 'Spirit Gate' or 'Mind Gate'. Every conscious being has the opportunity to use the Mind Gate, but in many ways, it is more difficult to access than the others. Usually, it takes years of meditation, learning to calm, and then control the mind, to access it. That is the only boundary that does not have a guardian."

"Oh. Ok, no guardian there." I thought about it. "That makes sense Fox, I guess. A giant like the Ragyala couldn't fit inside my head…"

He chuckled, "Actually, it could fit. The guardians can change their size according to their will. So, it's not really a matter of available space." He paused, as if looking for the right words. "The Mind Gate has no guardian, because you are *always* free to expand your mind. You are guaranteed that opportunity by the Primordial Fracture. When the Source/HighGod split itself to make all other life, it included the Mind Gate in every piece of new consciousness. That is, if they do the work to access that boundary."

I had gotten used to how fast Arkyala's ferry was moving. So, it was noticeable that we were slowing down. I glanced back, over my shoulder. The Arkyala was nowhere to be seen. He was gone from the top of the ship, and the long oar was unattended.

Startled to hear a voice behind me, my head whipped around. The black giant was now standing in front of us, a few paces away. Arkyala spoke, in that strange chorus of men's voices, "It appears you have a visitor…" With that, the Arkyala vanished.

Fox and I looked at each other, then around at the sea. There was no land in sight in any direction. I was about to shrug, when I noticed Shui flashing with light. Fox, looking down, took on a concerned, far-away look. His head snapped up to look out to sea. Suddenly alarmed, I followed his gaze. I did not have to wait long.

A series of eruptions from the water made my jaw drop. First one, then another, then another tentacle burst from the water. The tentacles were impossibly big, nearly as thick as the ship itself, and covered with enormous claws, spikes, and suction cups. Fox and I both shot to our feet. They looked like the tentacles of the creature that had sunk the rowboat, but were much larger. More tentacles rose from the water. They reached for the sky, and waved around angrily. I tried to count them, but the tentacles were thrashing around and hard to count. I think there were nine of them, but I wasn't sure.

Two of the tentacles were longer than the others. Those tentacles began to slap the water, making sharp 'CRACK!' sounds as they hit the surface. The tentacles were about one ship-length away from us. In the center of the mass of tentacles, at the water level, the sea was churning, a churning white whirlpool.

Our ship was slowly coasting to a stop, approaching the whirlpool and monstrous, writhing tentacles. Seeing that we were on a course to collide with the monster, I began to feel anxious. I looked over to see Fox calmly watching the spectacle.

In only a moment or two, we would reach the beast. And the closer we drifted, the more viciously the tentacles moved. They crashed back into the water, only to resurface and throw waves of water at the ship.

"It's time we go inside." Fox said. "Come with me." He walked back toward the enclosed 'building' on the back of the boat. The door ahead of us was closed, but I followed him.

He opened the door and walked inside. I expected to find the room filled with anxious spirits, as confused as I was. Instead, the room was empty. All of the benches were empty.

After I had walked into the room, Fox closed the door behind us. He took a seat on the nearest bench, and I sat down next to him. Outside we could hear the "CRACK" sounds of the tentacles still beating the water. I blurted out, "Fox what are we going to do?" but he did not seem at all concerned.

He replied, "We're going to stay right here, for the moment. Have no fear Kwan. You should understand that some things in the GaleSource are more powerful than other things. That thing, out there in the water, is a demon. That demon is trapped in this realm, the same as the others. Think of it like a prisoner, and this realm is the prison. The Arkyala is the master enforcing order in this prison. Every prison is set up so that the enforcers have more power than the inmates…"

He paused for a moment as I caught up with what he was saying. "That means the Arkyala's power is far greater than the demon's. Or rather, the power behind the Arkyala, the power behind the system that maintains this place, is stronger than anything the demon can do."

He paused again, watching to see that I understood what he was saying. "Because the Arkyala is performing a function here, he has authority. And here, in this place, his authority is sacred. No demon can disrupt the system… That means even though the demon would like to sink this ferry and kill us, it is unable to. By sacred law, this ship is inviolate. That means the demon *can't* damage this ship. In truth, nothing in this world would be able to sink this ferry. You can go to the door and see for yourself. Don't worry, you'll be safe."

My trust in Fox was such that I almost went back outside. Instead, I went to the door and opened it a tiny sliver, peering outside. We had drifted all the way to the tentacled demon. I saw one enormously thick tentacle pull back, preparing to strike the ferry.

That tentacle swung forward with enormous speed and force. As I watched it approach, time seem to slow down. I closed my eyes and braced for impact.

But instead of a tremendous crash, I heard a small and clear tone, a tiny bell being rung. Confused, I open my eyes. Each time the tentacle was about to hit the ship, a protective field, like the ones that protected us from the lightning demon, flared to life. The tentacles smashed harmlessly against the shield, bouncing off. Each time they made contact, the shimmering blue screen appeared around the ship.

And while I could hear the clear tone each time the ship's shield blocked a tentacle, I could not feel any impact. The blue shield absorbed all of the power of the demon's strikes. I turned back to Fox questioningly.

"Right now, we are at an impasse, Kwan. The demon cannot sink the ship. He cannot hurt us, as long as we stay on the ship, and he stays in the shape of that storm-beast. But, staying trapped here will not get us any closer to your sister. We will stay here until the demon changes to a different attack. The demon has already realized that he cannot sink the ship, so it will have to change tactics."

I turned back to the door and peered outside again. The tentacles had stopped moving, frozen in place. They stood stationary like a series of towers, a tree of tentacles, branching up and out, from the center whirlpool. It was an eerie scene. The boat had stopped moving, the tentacles had stopped moving, but still towered above us.

The only thing I could see that was still moving was the sky. Dark gray clouds, darker even than the purple of the dragons' cube, began to gather over our location. In just a moment, a huge storm cloud, almost black, had appeared above us. It began to rain.

In truth, I can only call it rain for the first few seconds. Quickly it became a deluge. Sheets of heavy rain fell on the ship. Soon the deck was covered in water. Fox had walked up behind me, and was peering over my shoulder. When he saw the rain making puddles on the deck, he said, "Outstanding." Personally, I could not see why he would be pleased. We were trapped out at sea, facing a terrifying demon, and now we were caught in a vicious storm.

Chapter 11

The Fourth

I thought it could not get any scarier, but it did. The tentacles, which had stopped moving, started moving again. But they were not flailing around like before. Instead, they started rotating, as if the giant creature under the water was spinning. The tentacles spun faster and faster. Soon they were a blur. The bottom of the tentacles had joined together like a single thick trunk. The colossal tentacles were spread wide, high above that. In horror, I watched as the tentacles began to form a giant tower of water in front of the ferry.

The waterspout grew to huge proportions. It became a monstrous funnel. The wide top grew to connect with the storm clouds above us. The narrow bottom of the funnel connected to the whirlpool at first. Then the bottom began to wander across the surface of the sea. The wind was a deafening howl, this close to the funnel.

I tried to peer into the waterspout, but the tentacles were no longer visible. They had disappeared, leaving only the spinning tower of water. Still, it seemed hard for me to associate this storm with a demon. The tentacles were clearly from a creature, but a storm just seemed like bad weather, a part of nature. I began to think that we were just facing a terrible storm, when I saw something I will never forget.

Two massive eyes, glowing red, opened inside the funnel. The red was disturbingly vivid, in this realm of faded colors. The demon's eyes focused on us, filled with malevolence. With that detail, it suddenly became clear to me that this was not a storm. It was still the demon's attack. The funnel didn't even need to have a mouth or any other facial features. The sinister eyes were enough.

And even if the eyes had not been enough, a low, but loud, growling sound added to the howling wind. I was so afraid that it was impossible to think. I wanted to run, but there was nowhere to run.

But something inside me turned my fear into something… different. I thought of my sister. I thought of the demons in our way. And suddenly, I could think again. The storm and the funnel cloud were steadily getting larger, but my fear had reached some limit.

I remembered the 'Celestial Mountain'. The idea suddenly occurred to me, a flash of inspiration (or so I thought). "Fox! You should use the SoulCage!"

Fox said quietly, "I can't, Kwan. Remember that the SoulCage can only capture a sprit that has a body. It has to be corporeal; to have a physical body. That tentacled 'monster' is only a function of the storm. It's complicated. Besides, Shui has told me that this demon is too powerful for the SoulCage to capture. We would need to weaken him, before we have any chance of capturing him."

"Oh." I had forgotten that part. "But isn't the storm physical?"

Fox shook his head. The storm is physical, but it isn't quite the demon itself. Think of the storm as a costume the demon is wearing. We can't capture it until he takes the costume off."

"But how do we weaken it? How can we make it take off the storm costume and become physical?" Fox smiled, seemingly pleased with my question.

"Good! You are fully tracking! Your mind is quick and able to adapt. You would make a good student at the GaleTemple. We will use the demon's weaknesses against it. What do you remember about the lightning demon?" he asked.

I thought back. "Well, um… demons are obviously dangerous… And they are proud and arrogant?" I searched my memory, but could not come up with much else.

"Good. Now I'll tell you a few more things about demons. They are greedy. And they are always hungry. Some are hungry for more power. Some are hungry for respect. Some, like this wompir, are hungry for blood. We will use that hunger against it."

With that, Fox took off his warm robe and shrugged out of his under-robe. Just like that, he was stripped to the waist. Then he strode onto the deck. Hesitating only a moment, I followed. (I kept my clothes on.) Part of me wanted to stay in the safety of the boat house. But a stronger part of me felt the need to do as much as possible to rescue Cho Clei. And also, it seemed safest staying close to Fox.

At least, that's what I told myself. But my actions fell short. Once I stepped out onto the deck, my feet were frozen in place. I watched as Fox stood in the middle of the open deck and began shouting at the storm, "Is that the best you can do?!?" His right hand was on Shui, but his left hand was held down at his side. I understood that Fox was trying to get the demon to become fully physical, but it still terrified me. "Are *YOU* afraid of *US*??? Come on, you COWARD!"

The waterspout had been a dark blue-gray at the bottom, where it connected with the sea's surface. Toward the top, the color shifted to black, that matched the clouds. But when Fox called it a coward, the entire waterspout flashed red. It was a bright red, just like the eyes had been. The rain doubled in volume, a response to Fox's taunt.

But Fox merely threw back his head and laughed, "Is that IT???" He laughed again. "Are you stupid? Man is waterproof! Is that the best you can do?" The wind increased. Soon I was leaning back against the door of the building, feeling like I might be blown off deck. Memories of the wind on the bridge came into my mind, unbidden.

But Fox did not cower. He remained standing in the center of the deck, drenched in rain, but still defiant. He didn't seem worried about being blown away. Then again, he was much heavier than I was. But whether it was his girth or his will, he was unmovable.

He continued his taunts, "You must be stupid! We are alive, you fool! You don't want drowned food! Or are you too stupid to realize it?? Don't you want to taste our hot blood!? We... are... ALIVE!!! But you're too much of a coward to claim our blood. And to think we were actually afraid of you! Ha!"

It seemed that the demon had heard enough. The tall waterspout suddenly fell back into the sea. The clouds dissipated, leaving a gray cloudless sky. Within a moment, the rain had entirely stopped.

"Ok, now we're getting somewhere." Fox said to me, over his shoulder. "Stay where you are Kwan. If this seems too intense, go back inside." I should have been able to relax somewhat since the storm had abated, but somehow the better weather made me more uneasy. It was more dangerous now, not less. I broke off from looking at the sea and glanced over at Fox. He was looking out at the sea, but glanced back to see where I was. His expression was deadly serious.

A moment later his head turned to peer at the very front of the ship. My gaze followed his. What I saw then, was so terrifying that I thought it would give me nightmares.

A black mass of mud was rising over the railing in the front of the ship. My eyes were riveted to it as it flowed up onto the ferry's front railing. It looked like a moving pile of muddy slime. Parts of the pile moved, independent of each other, like they were filled with crawling insects. The smell that filled the deck, even in 'open air' made me gag. It was worse than hot garbage or excrement. More and more of the slime flowed up onto the deck.

When the pile of black slime had fully mounted the front railing, it balanced on top, rising to a pillar taller than Fox. Red eyes opened at the top of the slime pillar, boring into us. It would have to have been looking at Fox. But even though I was not standing up next to Fox, the demon's eyes felt like they were watching me too!

The pile of stinking gore, balanced on the ferry's front railing, began to stretch upward. The red eyes rose to the top of the rising mass. It elongated into the rough shape of a man. The red eyes stayed in place as the head took shape. Horror-struck, I watched the transformation. Arms split off from the sides of the "torso."

Once it had taken the shape of a man, the details and features of the demon formed. The entire transformation only took a few moments. My breath caught in my throat as I realized that the emerging figure was the same as the statue we had seen in town. It was also the same size as the statue had been, a full head taller than Fox.

The demon had a patchy, dirty gray beard. He wore the top of some animal's skull as a crown, and horns protruded from each side. But unlike the statue, it's eyes did not gleam like metal. They remained animated with a fiendish red glow. His malevolent expression was somewhere between a snarl and a vicious smile. But the evil smile was filled with needle-like teeth and long canine fangs. The teeth were stained with… dried blood?

The demon wore sleeveless black robes with a thick gold belt. Thick muscular arms ended in long fingers with wickedly sharp, curved claws. It was barefoot, and the claws on his toes made an impatient clicking sound on the railing.

It was tall and frightening, even without the horned crown. There was a palpable air of power surrounding the demon. Even though I was scared, some part of my mind noted that it wasn't nearly as powerful as the feeling had been around the Ragyala or the Arkyala. But I could feel its powerful malice.

It stood there, unmoving, perched on the railing, a few feet above the wet deck, looking down at us. I found myself pushing backward, trying to escape the demon, but the door at my back stopped me.

Fox stood there, like a mountain, unmovable, staring up the demon. I watched Fox and saw something shiny, glimmering between the fingers of his left hand. His right hand gripped Shui, the small end of which was planted firmly on the deck. But his left hand was held down at his side. The palm of his left hand faced backward, toward me. Fox's fingers were curled around something that he was holding. I squinted to examine what was glimmering.

My eyes must have opened wide when I saw Fox 'palming' the metallic silver rosary bead. I had not seen him remove it from the necklace. The demon, being in front of Fox, couldn't see it. Being behind Fox, I could. But still Fox didn't use the SoulCage. Instead, he taunted the demon further.

"We thought you were a powerful wompir! We thought you were a hunter of weak, living things like us! Ha! The big bad demon has got no teeth! You probably don't even remember how to drink living blood! We thought you would *savor* our blood. Ha!" I cringed at his taunts, but I trusted Fox.

The wompir let out a long hiss. Its face elongated and twisted into an even more grotesque expression. Its teeth became longer. The demon's attention was firmly fixed on Fox.

Slowly, the wompir stepped down from the railing. First one bare foot, then the other, stepped onto the deck. I was afraid that the demon would speed up and seize Fox, but the wompir demon seemed to be moving slowly- on purpose. I could feel it trying to savor the experience of hunting us.

Slowly, the demon walked toward Fox. Black bile was drooling from the corners of the demon's mouth. It left black streaks down the sides of its patchy beard.

I watched as the demon slowly walked toward Fox. The sounds of its steps made a 'thump/splash' sound on the wet deck. It got closer to Fox, but he still didn't move.

When the demon was a few paces from Fox, the GaleMaster burst into action. In one quick movement, Fox dropped the silver sphere into the puddle where they were both standing. At the same time, he lifted his feet, and clung to Shui. Fox was holding onto the staff, as it stood upright, and held his weight.

Only Shui was touching the water on the deck. Fox, like a bear in a tree, clung to the staff.

In the same moment, the wompir began to flash and convulse and shake. Sparks crackled around it. I realized that Fox was using the lightning demon's power to attack the wompir. The demon's beard began to smoke, and after a moment, its robes burst into flames. As the demon burned and crackled, it shrank to Fox's size.

The crackling lightning power did not seem to affect Shui, nor Fox, as he clung to Shui. Only the demon was being electrocuted. All too quickly, the silver stone ran out of lightning power. Fox put his feet down on the deck. Immediately, the stone switched its attack. Now the demon began reeling, and shaking its still smoking head. It seemed dizzy and confused. It shrank further, until it was only my size.

Only then, did the SoulCage flare to brightness.

Again, the high-pitched, clear sound could be heard, growing louder as the rosary's light grew. That light reached out toward the hissing and screeching demon. The wompir was being pulled forward into the light of the stone. Since the stone was only a pace in front of Fox, the demon was being sucked toward us.

I watched, terrified and fascinated. The wompir's body got smaller and smaller as it was pulled into the rosary bead. The clear sound of the rosary bead grew in volume until it had surpassed the demon's wail. The demon was still powerful, and for a moment, it seemed like it might resist. But after a few tense seconds, the demon was overwhelmed by the SoulCage's power. And just like that, the demon was gone. It had disappeared, fully absorbed into the stone's light. When it did, the high-pitched clear sound abruptly cut off. We were left standing there, panting but alive.

I was bewildered. "What...?" I began. But before I could finish putting my vague confusion into a clear question, the Arkyala answered me. It was standing next to me, but I hadn't noticed its arrival.

Its chorus of male voices answered, "The GaleMaster... used the SoulCage..." That part I had understood. I had seen the SoulCage used twice before this. But I was confused about several other things.

"He used the power... of the other demons..." I suddenly remembered Fox saying that the 'Celestial Mountain' was a weapon too. He said that when a spirit was captured within the stone, that spirit's power could be used as a weapon. I had a sudden mental image of a mountain sitting on top of a supernatural prison. There was a cannon on top of that mountain, that was powered by the prisoners' supernatural forces. Fox had used the cannon?

The Arkyala had continued, pausing in its oddly unhurried speech. "... to weaken the wompir..." Fox had said that the demon was too powerful to be taken at first. So, it made sense that he would need to weaken it.

The Arkyala went on, "He lured the wompir... to stand in the water..." I looked down at the deck. The last puddles of water were quickly drying. I must have been overwhelmed, because I only remember wondering how the water was drying, even though it wasn't sunny. In fact, it was still cold. But nothing else occurred to me. I couldn't imagine why it would matter what the demon had been standing in.

An understanding flashed into my head. It wasn't that I had figured it out. The Arkyala had just *given* me a concept, straight into my mind. It wasn't like learning. It was as if layers and layers of understanding were suddenly there. The information was staggering. I just *knew* that lightning was a type of power that could travel *through* water. I *knew* that it would shock. I *knew* that it would burn. I *knew* that it could kill. Arkyala had continued speaking. In truth, there was enough time in between each of its words that I could keep up.

"Then he used... the lightning power... to shock the wompir..." I again pictured that cannon on top of the 'Celestial Mountain'. Fox had fired that cannon! And that cannon had shot lightning. That was why the demon had been jerking around and caught on fire!

And Fox had *needed* to be out of the water, or else the lightning power would have shocked him too! The Arkyala continued, "...while the J'nii protected him..." That was why Fox had been clinging to Shui, with his feet out of the water! The staff had balanced and held Fox out of the water while only the demon was getting burned!

"Then he used... the illusion power... of the next two demons... to confuse the wompir's mind..." Fox had fired the cannon a second time! This time, I imagined the cannon on top of the mountain firing a sparkling smoke that caused confusion when it hit. Finally... the wompir was weak enough... that the SoulCage... could absorb it." Two shots from the cannon had weakened the demon! Then the stone absorbed it! One more prisoner was now locked under the 'Celestial Mountain'!

The Arkyala had been looking at Fox the entire time, but speaking to me. Then he spoke to Fox, "GaleMaster... Your battle was righteous... and fortunate... We are pleased to witness it." Fox looked surprised at the Arkyala's words. "Our blessing..." When Arkyala said 'blessing', a sphere of light emerged from its chest. It pulsed and flashed brightly, changing colors. The colors were vivid and dazzling in this drab realm. The sphere of light hovered for a moment, before the black-furred giant's chest. Then it shrank down to a hand-sized ball of swirling light. It floated over to Fox. Fox reached out to catch the ball of light.

But before he could touch it, the swirling sphere of light exploded outward into millions of sparkling pieces of light. The light disappeared, twinkling out of existence.

Both Fox and I had flinched when the ball of light burst. But strangely, I felt an increase in health and positivity. The feeling was similar to wearing Fox's special 'rune-inscribed' robe. For an instant, I even thought that I smelled sweet spice buns (my favorite).

With a jolt, I realized that both Fox and I were kneeling. I had not even been aware of falling to my knees before. Still stripped to the waist, Fox bowed to the Arkyala. Then he shrugged back into his robes as he asked, "Great One, the other spirits are safe?"

I glanced up as The Arkyala nodded. "We have... moved them... to another ferry... They are there now... We are... with them there too... They will reach... their next realms..." Fox's eyebrows went up, as though he did not know that there was more than one ferry. It seemed there were limits to how much the GaleTemple knew. Or at least, Fox didn't know everything. Although, I had to admit to myself, he had always volunteered that information. "Now... we will go... the J'nii has shown us... your destination..."

The Arkyala vanished. A moment later, the ferry lurched forward again. I stood up and took a few steps away from the boat house. I looked to the back of the ship and saw the Arkyala again standing on top and easily moving the long oar. We picked up speed. The barge began to part the sea. I looked to the front of the ferry and saw waves splashing up. We were moving at a tremendous speed.

I saw that Fox had sat back down on the bench. He was reattaching the SoulCage to the other rosary beads. He was nestled in his warm robes and looking relieved. I sat back down beside him. We didn't say anything for a few long moments. I felt fantastic, but Fox was clearly contemplating something, so I tried to do likewise. Both of us seemed absorbed in replaying what had just happened, in our minds, over and over again. Or maybe that was just me.

Eventually, questions occurred to me. "Fox, why did the Arkyala say our battle had been 'righteous and fortunate'?

Fox thought carefully before answering my question. "Well...righteousness is important in the sense that it represents the same things as 'the Light".

But 'righteousness' is a term we use to describe all goodness. It means life, and love, and compassion, and constructive kindness. It implies making the wise decision even if the cost will be high. It is doing the *right* thing, instead of the *easy* thing, or the *selfish* thing."

"Do you mean 'self-righteous'?" I interrupted. I remembered Father saying that phrase before, but I couldn't remember what he had been talking about.

Fox patiently shook his head. "No. This is different from what some people call 'self-righteousness'. 'Self-righteousness' is about judging others as inferior to yourself, usually morally inferior. It is a fruit of negative judgement.

Righteousness is about positive discernment, not negative judgement. Judgement, of course, is necessary. That kind of judgement lets you distinguish good from evil. It lets you differentiate between a wise action and a foolish one. You need to be *judgmental* to use your reason. If you choose good, that is considered positive.

But the guardians use 'righteous' to mean something different. They maintain the boundaries between realms, so they experience 'existing', outside of our understanding. Beings at their level think that balance is a fundamental goal.

To them, 'righteous' means an action that promotes balance. That demon had been feeding on the spirits of those poor villagers. Our actions restored balance by capturing the demon.

We chose to come to this place to find and rescue your sister. We made the right decision even though we knew it would be dangerous. Your choice to come with me was noble, and the boundary wardens are impressed by noble actions. They never promote war, but it appears they appreciate successful battle strategy. I did not expect this, but it seems we have impressed the Arkyala.

"As for 'fortunate'... Well, many things could have gone wrong. If the demon had not let himself be provoked, the situation could have unfolded very differently. He could have focused his attack on Shui, for example. Then I wouldn't have been able to use the lightning on it. That's just one example. Many things could have gone wrong. The Arkyala was right, we *were* fortunate. It was almost too easy... but I suppose it made the battle interesting to watch."

We sat there on the bench in silence. More questions occurred to me, but I felt that keeping quiet was appropriate. Fox had bundled himself back up in his robes. He sat there, looking peaceful as the ferry flew across the sea. The gray sky above me, and the ferry moving forward had a calming effect on me. After the last encounter, I felt tired. With a moment to rest, my mind began to wander.

I felt dreamlike as we rode. I felt like the strange gray light was flickering behind the clouds. It felt like days and nights were passing in rapid succession. I felt sleepy and lightheaded. My body was warm and secure. The wind on my face made we want to close my eyes. Before I did, I remember looking over at Fox. It took way too much effort to resist powerful waves of drowsiness washing over me. Fox looked over at me with amusement.

"Sleep, Kwan." He smiled, "You will need your strength." I remember seeing him tilt his head back and open his mouth to say something, but I never heard those words. I remember seeing his face, before my eyes drifted closed. As I sank into a deep sleep, I heard, delayed, Fox's kind laughter.

***

I awoke in dim surroundings. I was lying on my back in an unfamiliar room. After a moment, I remembered past events. As my eyes cracked open, I studied a flickering candle flame in an old-fashioned silver lamp hanging on the wall above me. There were other ornate silver lamps in the room, evenly spaced along the wall every two paces. They each held a single golden flame.

I recognized the interior of the boat house. I was in the room where the half-men had been. I was lying on a wide bench near the door to the front deck. I was still wearing the basic, but warm, robe Fox had given me. On top of that, the 'rune-inscribed' robe was laying on me like a blanket.

I looked around for Fox, and almost panicked for a moment when I didn't see him. But then I noticed Shui standing, balancing next to where I was lying. Seeing the staff made me confident, both that I would be safe, and also that Fox would return. Also, I recognized the positive influence of the runes on the blanket/robe. A strong feeling of well-being had filled every place that had held fear before. My eyes closed again. Reaching panic seemed like an impossible challenge right now. I probably should have been instantly anxious, but instead, I just felt calm. and well rested.

I couldn't tell how long I had been asleep. The last thing I remembered was being on the bench, outside on the deck. I tried to go through everything that I remembered. I wanted to take advantage of this calm place in my mind, and get ready for what was next.

My mind started with what was most recent – capturing the demon at sea. I pictured the Arkyala. From there my mind went backwards to the ferry, and the long journey we had undertaken to get here. I thought back to the bargain we had made with the Ragyala. I started to count the demon spirits we had captured.

A memory of the tree exploding as the lightning demon attacked us, came into my mind. The memory had such force, that I flinched, remembering the sound the tree had made. That lightning demon was the first one we had captured.

I thought of our situation as a simple trade. The lightning demon was being traded to the Ragyala, in exchange for Cho Clei being able to come home.

Some part of me was troubled to think of trading the demon for Cho Clei. But then I reminded myself that the demons weren't alive. If they were, they wouldn't want to feed on us. And my sister was an innocent child. The demons had brought this on themselves when they had taken Cho Clei. I reasoned that it was justified, but still it troubled me. My reverie continued.

And then a progression of images started to flow through my mind. It included riding the box through a sea of dragons. I was in a wonderful place of being in between sleep and wakefulness. I could look at my recent past and think about it.

I had just been like any other boy from our village. Or, at least, that's how I felt before. But now I had seen such miraculous things that it would be hard to go back to normal life. I had seen demons. I had seen impossible supernatural creature, even dragons! But I would probably end up making dumplings my whole life. The thought made me... vaguely sad. But the positive feelings of safety, confidence, and being rested made me quickly move past that sadness. I would come back to that thought later.

Then memories of the old demons on the bridge came. That made two, then three spirits we could give to the Ragyala. That made enough spirits to pay for the trip back home. But that left the price for us getting here in the first place. With the wompir, we had four spirits to give the Ragyala. We only needed one more.

The sequence of memories continued. Flitting images of the 's'la'manda' and the 'ice hok', then the towering form of the Ragyala passed through my mind. Finally, the memories stopped on a bright and clear image of my sister. In the memory, Cho Clei was smiling and eating a shiny dumpling. She was so small, and a cold clarity came to me. We had to find her and rescue her!

Clear on what I was here to do, I sat up. Cho Clei needed us! As I sat up, I looked around. Aside from Shui and myself, the room was empty. Fox's staff, Shui, was standing upright, perfectly balanced on its end, in the middle of an aisle between benches. Flickering light reflected off of the metal grain running down the length of Shui. I swung my legs down and prepared to stand up.

Just then, Fox and the Arkyala appeared in front of me. My eyebrows went up, but I didn't jump, even though I was surprised. I was calm and deeply rested. An instant before, I was the only one in the room. Then, there were three of us.

The Arkyala looked like a black and gray mountain. The silver strip of cloth, the belt at his waist, also flashed in the lamplight, like the grain on Shui. But its black fur was so dark that it absorbed the light. Its luminous eyes stared down at me. I made eye contact with the Arkyala briefly before the power it radiated made me look away. Fox, wearing a kind expression, was also staring down at me. He extended his arm and opened his fingers. Shui tipped over, falling to the side, neatly landing in Fox's hand.

I noticed again how tall the ceiling was. The Arkyala stood tall, dwarfing Fox. But of course, the ferry would have been constructed big enough for the ferry's master. And an instant after that, the Arkyala vanished again, leaving just Fox and me.

Fox sat down next to me. He began talking in the same easy manner I had gotten used to at Fong's dumpling shop. He was relaxed and spoke in an easy tone. "You look rested! I take it you feel better?

I nodded. "I do. I really do. It feels like I just had the best night's sleep of my life." I lifted my arms high to stretch. "Where... where did you go?"

Fox pointed a single finger up at the high ceiling. "I was talking to the Arkyala. I was asking questions to find out all I could about what was ahead."

That was a smart idea, I thought. Of course, it made sense to ask questions! "Oh! What did you find out? Is our trip about to get easier?" I asked, hopefully.

Fox smiled and shook his head. "I wasn't able to get many answers from the Arkyala." He scratched his temple, looking for how to put phrase his thoughts. "The Arkyala is a powerful being. It knows much more than we do, but it still has restrictions. It can only operate within those restrictions.

"The Yalan Guardians are a part of..."

"Who?" I interrupted.

Unbothered, Fox explained, "The Yalan Guardians are wardens that keep the boundaries between realms. You have met two of the Guardians; the Ragyala and the Arkyala. There are others like the Kenyala."

"The Kenyala?! Another cat-guardian!?" I blurted out. I began to imagine a whole pack of the super-cat giants.

"We'll discuss the Kenyala later. Let's just take it one thing at a time. They are part of a hierarchy that operates in all worlds.

"We all have some purpose, some job to do. At least, everyone except the Source/HighGod. We can't really know if the Source/HighGod has a job to do, because of omnipotence. If a being is all-powerful, what would you really have to do?"

I thought about it. Fox went on, "The demons don't have a job except for working towards chaos and evil. They don't *want* to do anything constructive. But despite that, the GaleSource uses *them* to perform a job.

"Regardless of how power is used, there is always a hierarchy of power. Shui is more powerful than me. You could have guessed that much." Fox had a twinkle in his eye, as if enjoying a private joke. "Beings like the Yalan Guardians; like the Ragyala and the Arkyala, are more powerful than Shui. The Witnesses are more powerful than the Yalan Guardians…"

"Who are the Witnesses?" I interrupted again.

"The Witnesses are a category of beings who have directly seen the Source/HighGod, but retained their identities. If a being does not have enough power, seeing the Source/HighGod would immediately destroy that being."

"Destroy them?" I asked, worried.

"The power of the Source/HighGod is so overwhelming that, if they don't have enough power to resist, they will be instantly reabsorbed into the Source/HighGod." Fox explained. Then he went on, "That accomplishment alone puts The Witnesses' power in a different category. There are many other beings of different power levels, but they all fall somewhere on this scale of hierarchy. The Source/HighGod, of course, is above all. This hierarchy contributes to order in the GaleSource.

"It works the same way in the culture of men. Your father is above you. Or I'm above you, for that matter. And my master is more powerful than I am. This is one of the ways in which the GaleSource is organized.

The job of beings like the Arkyala is to keep the things here, that are supposed to *be* here. They also keep the beings *out* that are *not supposed to be* here. The Yalan Guardians are tasked with keeping beings in the realms where they belong. Unless a being has 'earned' the right to pass from one realm to another, the Yalan Guardians will stop them."

"Do you mean 'earned' like us paying for our trip?" I asked.

Fox shook his head. "We are doing something that is nearly unheard of. It is *extremely* unusual for us to come here how we did. No, I was talking about advancing through effort. If a sage meditated for many years and advanced his mind, he might be able to cross the boundaries between realms while he was still alive.

"Otherwise, in ordinary circumstances, men only cross when they die. That's what I meant. Unless a being has earned the right to cross, the Yalans will stop them.

"Once the Ragyala looked into my mind, it saw that an innocent girl had been smuggled past it. The Ragyala was... displeased to see this. That's one reason I felt confident that the Ragyala would let us pass. Its job is to stop things like this from happening, to keep evil like that out of our realm."

I listened carefully and tried to remember all of the details. It was amazing to hear such information given to me, matter-of-factly. Fox had astonishing information. I was impressed.

Fox went on, "The Arkyala is not allowed to change our plight. As humans, we have to contend with our reality, to grow and live and learn. There are challenges we face that the Arkyala is not *permitted* to make easier. The only way the Arkyala can make our plight easier is to keep the worst evil on *its* side of the boundary.

"That's why it was difficult to get much information out of the Arkyala. I had to ask for ways to help with the challenges without directly asking how to cheat the challenges. The

Arkyala knew what I was doing, of course. We treated it like a game."

"So, the Arkyala knows the future?" I asked. If that was the case, there were some questions I wanted to ask.

Again, Fox shook his head. "It doesn't work quite like that. The future is not something 'already built' that you can see ahead of time…" He seemed to be searching for the right words. "The future is a series of options. Imagine a line on the floor.

"Other lines branch off of the main line, and those lines become the main line. But the different time-lines aren't clearly visible. They depend on choices. Until a choice is made, the timeline isn't clear.

"So, the Arkyala can't use his power to take away our challenges, however much of the future is visible. But the Arkyala can tell us information, in general. As I said, I asked many questions that the /Arkyala was unwilling to answer.

"Often the Arkyala couldn't respond, and would tell me to rephrase the question. Many times, it clearly knew more than it was able to say. Still, I had to try. And while I didn't find out everything, I did get some useful information!" He smiled and rubbed his hands together.

The smile was contagious, and I felt confident and ready to face the challenge. "What did you find out?" I asked. Fox took a deep breath before proceeding.

"I found out more about our destination. We are headed to a castle in the mountains. There is a road to the castle that we will have to travel. The road will take us through a series of villages. There will be more, but that is the majority of what I found out."

I was a little disappointed. "Nothing else?" I asked, my disappointment showing.

"The Arkyala did give some other details. But because of their unique type of existence, conversing with the Yalans is always a challenge.

"The path that we will need to take to reach this castle is called the HellFire Road. We should recognize the road easily, since it will be paved with bones and lined with fire. The villages along the HellFire Road are, of course, demon villages.

The Arkyala called the castle where we are heading, a 'fortress' of 'fire and bones'. This castle is located in a set of mountains that the Arkyala described in ancient, spoken GaleScript. They are called a name that translates to 'Helpless Superstition Mountains'.
"That is where we will need to go to face the head demon, the architect of all of this. That is the place we will face Cho Clei's kidnapper, and recover her.
"But we have a few advantages this time. For one thing, the Arkyala's blessing has been sent ahead of us. It will arrive when it is most useful. Also, we do have some information, which is better than walking into trouble blindfolded.
"The last piece of information is about the actual demon itself. It is a strong demon, stronger in fact, than any we have faced so far. But it's dangerous, not because of its vast power, but because of its keen intelligence. It is unusually bright for a demon. This demon is known for being both clever *and* strong. The Arkyala warned me not to underestimate Wen-yi." Fox concluded.
"Wen-yi is the demon's name?" I asked. I began to realize that Fox would leave some parts unexplained to see if I would ask. Maybe he was seeing if I was paying attention.
"Wen-yi is what we will call this demon. Its real name is much longer and would hurt your mind to hear it spoken. So, we will just stick with Wen-yi." I had the impression that Fox was pleased that I was paying close attention.
I was going to ask Fox when we would arrive, when we heard a long, strident blast from the Arkyala's horn. I didn't have to be told that the horn signaled both arrival and departure. Fox turned towards the door and started walking. Ready for this next stage of our rescue, I followed him. When we got out onto the deck, we looked ahead at the bow. The wind was blowing full in our faces.

In the distance, we could see a massive land growing on the horizon. We approached it with incredible speed. It seemed to grow larger almost too fast. As we got closer, the details of the shore began to fill in. The land that we were approaching had a large gray area built up with blocky, right angles.

As we got closer the blocky right angles, they resolved themselves into a port. But this port was very different from the peer where we had boarded the Arkyala's ship. This was a much more substantially constructed, full harbor. There were stones carved into large blocks that made up the area where ships would apparently stop.

It was hard to tell the age of the port from such a distance, but it didn't look new. I was in the process of studying the approaching land when I noticed the landscape getting darker. The sky was rapidly turning from the light gray that it had normally been, into a darker more forbidding reddish-gray. The light of this whole realm seemed to diminish.

As we drew closer I could see several large ships at the port. Some of the ships had sails and some did not. From this distance, it was impossible to tell any more than basic observations. They were large and they were ships.

But more interesting than that, was that there was a crowd waiting for us on the dock. Toward the center of the crowd, they formed a brown and gray mass on the distant shore. At its fringes, individual figures could be seen.

For a moment I was worried, thinking the group assembled on the dock was some sort of army of demons, waiting to attack us. But Fox immediately put my concerns to rest. He put his hand on my shoulder and spoke before I could voice my concerns. "Don't worry, Kwan. The Arkyala told me that it would be picking up passengers when you and I get off. Those are the spirits waiting to get on."

As we got closer I could see that there was a city behind the port. Behind the massive stones of the port where the ships were tied up, many buildings of a sprawling city could be seen. The buildings had odd shapes. Some were rectangular some were triangular some appeared to even be domes. But they were visible from a distance so they must have been large.

The group waiting looked large too. Half of the city's population must have been assembled on the dock. I don't think I had ever seen so many people assembled together before. The group was so large that it easily surpassed the whole population of my village.

Each pass of the Arkyala's giant oar pushed the ship at impossible speeds. Fox and I stood there on the front deck, watching the land (and the city) we were fast approaching. I comforted myself thinking that we had survived everything so far. I felt different than I had at the beginning of the trip. Before I had been filled with fear. But now I felt more…capable.

As the Arkyala's ferry got closer, my eyes stayed focused on the waiting crowd. Fox had said that they were just passengers but I wanted to watch to make sure they weren't tricking us. I began to make out some features among the crowd. It looked like they had… feathers. Their heads were bigger than their bodies. I could see that even from a distance.

As we approached the port of this city, we slowed down. The Arkyala was letting us coast to slow down. I welcomed the chance to look at the buildings and stones of the port. At least we could see that the city was not deserted. Somehow that made it better than if the docks had been empty.

In truth, I didn't mind the spirits I had seen. I could feel pity for souls that had to wait who-knows-how-long to reach their next realm. And feeling pity was better than feeling fear.

As the ferry got closer, I looked at the crowd milling around on the dock. I saw that what had looked like feathers before, were just large headdresses, adorned with feathers. The feathers fanned out behind the men's heads. They looked like men, just with a dark greyish brown skin. They looked well-formed well-muscled, but were only my height.

The men with the elaborate headdresses also wore lots of jewelry. None of the jewelry was shiny or metallic though. It looked like the ornaments were made from the same type of stone as the port. Each of the men wore several stone necklaces around his neck and multiple stone bracelets on each wrist.

Aside from their headdresses and their loin cloths, the men were naked. As we got closer I realized that their faces looked birdlike. Their noses were large and stuck out like birds' beaks. And every single one of them had their eyes closed.

I looked at Fox again as we drifted closer to the dock. He again gave me a reassuring smile and nod. "As I said, there are many beings in many realms that use the Arkyala's ferry to travel. These are merely some of those beings. Either way, this is where we need to go." The dark gray clouds that filled the sky seemed to darken even further.

As the ferry drew up to the dock I could see the group that was waiting more clearly. It looked like a large group of men standing with their eyes closed, wearing loincloth's and headdresses, with vaguely birdlike faces. Each of them had heavy eyebrows and expressions of patient stoicism.

At the head of the crowd was one bird-man whose headdress was larger than the others. He looked older, and less fit than the others. His necklaces were larger than the others. And in his hand, he held a thin stick with a few feathers on top. His eyes were also closed.

The ferry pulled sideways at the last second, drifting to a gentle stop against the stone pair. Fox turned and walked back into the boathouse. I followed him. We walked through the first more brightly lit room, and then the second more dimly lit room.

From there, Fox turned and led me down a large side passage in the ferry. I hadn't even noticed the tall and wide opening when we first came in. But Fox seemed to know where he was going, so I followed him blindly into the dark passage. Almost immediately, I could see a dim light ahead of us.

I could make out a different door once we got to the end of the corridor. Before, when we had gotten on the ferry, it was through the large rear door. When we passed that large door, it had still been closed, not lowered.

This time however, a smaller door had opened on the side of the ship. I didn't see anyone open the door. But I wasn't surprised that the ship could move on its own. I was getting harder to surprise, apparently.

I looked out through the now open door and found a wooden plank that would allow us to walk from the ferry to the land. I had not seen anyone put down the plank either. It was only two or three feet to walk before we were on the dock. The ferry had docked itself very skillfully.

Fox walked across the wooden plank, and I followed. Once we had reached the other side I took a look around. This was hostile territory, but looked harmless enough. I reminded myself that we were in the demon's land. Here, that demon would have more power than other places. I had gleaned that much from what Fox had told me. In response, the red tint in the sky increased and gave the whole scene a red glow.

Chapter 12

The HellFire Road

I looked around at the dock. Aside from the huge stone blocks, there were a number of stone sculptures placed around the port. The sculptures were all in the shape of different kinds of birds.

I studied the stones I was sitting on and couldn't imagine how blocks of stone this large had ever been moved. Enormous iron chains hung from thick, waist-high pillars where the ships could be tied. The large port clearly had been built to service many ships at the same time. The port looked like it had been built for large-scale operations.

Once we exited the ship the Arkyala appeared in the doorway we had just walked through. The Arkyala raised a single black-furred hand in farewell to us, then it closed the door. The wooden plank that we had just crossed as a bridge had vanished.

A moment later, the door to the back of the ferry opened. Only then did I notice a stairway leading down from our level on the docks to the lower level of the docks. That lower level was the same height as the back door of the ferry.

The men with feather headdresses formed an orderly line, behind their leader, and began walking onto the ferry. Quickly I realized that the ferry couldn't possibly hold as many people as were waiting. But Fox assured me that the ferry would be big enough. He claimed that the ferry was like his bag. It would be as big inside as it needed to be. "If you ever get to learn about folding-space , it gets complicated very quickly."

It was much warmer here than it had been when we first boarded the ship. I took off the warm robe Fox given me and handed it back to him. He neatly folded it and put it back inside his bag. Then he took off his own robe and put it into the bag.

It struck me that the ferry had been made for the port. Or maybe the port had been made for the ferry? It couldn't have been coincidence that the dock of the ferry was exactly the height of the upper level of the port, could it?

After we had taken off our robes and gotten more comfortable, nearly the entire group of waiting bird-men had been able to board the ferry. They moved quickly and never spoke. And they never fell or tripped, despite having their eyes closed the entire time.

When all of the bird men had boarded the barge, Fox and I stood watching as the Arkyala appeared atop the barge. An enormous horn the size of its arm appeared in the air in front of the Arkyala. The horn appeared to be made from some sort of white bone. There were three, thick gold bands around the bone horn.

Fox tapped my shoulder and said, "Cover your ears." Then he covered his ears. I quickly followed his example. Shui stood on its own.

The Arkyalla pursed its lips, raised the horn to his lips and blew three long times. It would have been impossible to miss. The volume was staggering, even with my hands over my ears. My knees buckled.

The horn disappeared and the Arkyala grasped the handle of the long oar. The black giant started rowing. A small lake's worth of water rushed away from the moving oar. The ship picked up speed and quickly disappeared onto the horizon. Fox and I turned and began walking up the single avenue away from the sea.

There was a wide thoroughfare that led down to the port. The avenue must have led up to the city. It wasn't steep, but it did slant uphill. The city's buildings could be seen above and behind the avenue.

A few of the bird-men could be seen hurrying down the road, rushing to catch the ferry. I didn't have the heart to signal that the ferry had already left. They would find out in a moment anyway. There were five or ten of them hurrying down the road, but we were the only two heading up. I wondered how long they would have to wait until the Arkyala returned. I wondered if the ferry operated on a schedule. I wondered how Cho Clei was.

I stopped wondering and put my full attention on Fox. He had walked over to the side of the road. He was standing his staff upright, asking it to point our way. Shui fell to knee height, pointing straight up the road, toward the red spot in the distant mountains. Then Shui rose back up to his hand. Once the staff returned to his hand, the metal grain lit up, pulsing once.

I put my head down and walked up the road. Fox was silent, and I was absorbed in my thoughts too. We walked up the slope towards the distant mountains. I stared down at the gray stones that paved the road. My old sandals matched the pavement in that the stones looked old. But unlike my sandals, the stones were precisely assembled. Clearly, the people who had built this city had possessed skill.

The road varied in the angle of the climb, but it was always uphill. The land seemed to go gradually up into the mountains. They were not as high as I thought 'Helpless Superstition Mountains' should be. They just looked like regular mountains. They weren't towering. They didn't look particularly sinister or evil. They were just regular mountains.

The only thing that looked irregular was a tiny red light on the distance. It was slightly to our left, but almost directly ahead of us. We walked toward the mountains and the red light. The sea was directly behind us.

The road we were on forked ahead. One path led off to the right. The city was nearby, off to our right side. That path clearly led to the city. The path straight ahead of us led up toward the distant mountains.

I glanced over my shoulder to take one last look at the sea. Even if it was not the sea of my world, the sea of another realm, it was still the first time I had seen the sea. I was feeling some odd loss at having to say goodbye to it. It was a strange feeling. It was like saying goodbye to a new friend.

The land on either side of the road was hilly and covered with rocks. But as we walked on, rocky terrain gave way to ankle high grasses. We were on the stone road, but the grasses made the land seem much gentler. As we walked, the grasses on either side of the road grew longer.

But like everything in this realm, the grasses looked half-dead to begin with. As the grasses got longer, the stone road got narrower. Soon it was only wide enough for Fox and me to walk single file. Fox led and I followed.

After some time hiking, the road just ended. I had been looking down and ran into Fox's back. He was solid and unmovable, and I just bounced off, taking a few steps back, recovering my balance. He had stopped and was looking up. I did likewise.

The road that we had taken from the port had ended. The stones of the road ended in a straight line. The stones at the end were perfectly finished like all of the other stones and looked like a giant sword had precisely cut them off.

Where the stones ended, there was a dirt road. On each side of the road were metal buckets filled with something burning. The fires were lit, on both sides of the road, every twenty paces. I peered around Fox but did not pass him. If he stopped, there was probably a reason.

The sky had become a dark red black. What I saw was a line of small fires, on either side of a dirt road, that extended up into the distant hills and mountains. The dark sky made a stark contrast with the flickering light of the fires. Even though the iron braziers were only knee high, the fires in them burned brightly. But the road itself was just dirt.

Fox spoke, "On your guard, Kwan. We have reached the HellFire Road."

But I spoke, "But I thought that the road was supposed to be paved with bones." I said.

Fox only replied, "Look." Then he stepped forward onto the road, and use the toe one of his sandals to lift an object that had been sticking out of the ground. I hadn't noticed the object at first, until Fox brought it out. I was amazed to see that it was, in fact, a bone. Fox lifted another bone then another then another, proving that this was indeed the Hell-fire road.

Now that Fox had stepped onto the road, I stepped forward to stand beside him and examine the bones at my feet. The light from the braziers casting eerie shadows on Fox's face. I'm sure it must've been doing the same thing to my face. I walked over to one of the braziers and peered inside. It was burning bones.

For the first hour, I was nervous. I imagined evil in every shadow. And there were plenty of shadows considering the flickering braziers of fire. The dark sky added to the dramatic effect. After that first hour, I began to relax. You can't hold estate of super-heightened awareness for too long.

We walked between the fires along the dirt road for a long time. It was very hard to track time in that place. And even then, I was absorbed in my thoughts. I was thinking about everything that I've seen. I was thinking about my sister, why I was here. I was thinking about the existence of GaleMasters like Fox. I was thinking about the existence of creatures like the Ragyala, and the Arkyala, and demons and dragons and Gartuns and this whole world that had been hidden from me.

After walking for what seemed like hours, the braziers were spaced farther apart. First 20 paces, then 40, then 60… Until eventually they stopped lining the road. Instead, ahead of us were fields of corn. The dirt of the road was still there, but now there was corn growing out of it. Maybe 'growing' was too strong a word. The corn fields all appeared to be dead.

"Remember, we're going to encounter a series of villages. Again, be on your guard." Fox said. We approached the corn and saw that there was an alley between the rows. We walked down that alley, continuing in a roughly straight-line from where the HellFire Road had been going.

We walked through the dead field of corn. I looked back to see the braziers' lights behind us. The darkness of the sky was oppressive. Maybe this was nighttime in this realm? There were dark gray clouds passing under the black sky. They gave the impression that the inky black above us was alive.

I looked up and saw something disturbing ahead in the distance. An icy shard of fear appeared in my stomach. It appeared to be a man hung on a cross, out in the middle of the field. His clothing was old and tattered and he wore a rice-farmer's hat.

As we got closer, I could see that it was just a scarecrow. Someone had propped it up in this field of dead corn. But as soon as I identified what it was, I realized that I hadn't seen any live animals to scare away. Also, why protect dead corn? It didn't make any sense.

As we approached, two pinpoints of red light lit under the brim of the scarecrow's hat. Its face was obscured, making the glowing eyes stand out unmistakably. Those pinpoint-pupils followed us as we walked up towards the scarecrow. Fox even led us to one side of the path between the corn, then over to the other side. The scarecrow's head turned to stay locked on us.

The scarecrow was wearing farmers clothes that had been stuffed with what must have once been straw. It had decomposed to a brown mass of decaying fibers. As we got closer, I could see that the scarecrow had some kind of gourd for a head. The 'eyes' were two holes burned through into the interior of the gourd, but the lights inside those 'eyes' appeared to be floating points of flame.

We edged to the side of the path and walked past the scarecrow. We gave it a wide clearance and did not speak to it. It was utterly unnerving to see the scarecrow turn its head to watch us as we walked by. The scarecrow silently watched us. Its head was obviously turning.

We walked by. I felt a strong urge to stop and peer into the scarecrow's eyes, but Fox put a hand on my elbow and kept me moving. I suddenly felt a feeling of foreboding. I felt that something bad was going to happen to us any moment. The scarecrow was an inanimate object. It should have had no power to turn, much less, have flaming eyes. I started to get alarmed, expecting the figure to leap down off of the cross and attack. But as we crept by, it did not leap down.

We had only passed a dozen paces beyond the scarecrow when it let out a terrifying shriek. There was a roaring 'whoosh' sound and a flare of light and heat from behind us. Both Fox and I spun in alarm to stare at the scarecrow. The scarecrow had burst into flames. Its screams were the articulate screams of a living man, in a great deal of pain. I cringed inside. This place was horrible.

Fox and I hurried on past the scarecrow. I heard Fox mutter, "So much for sneaking through quietly…" The scarecrow might as well have sounded an alarm. If anything was listening, it would definitely have heard the scarecrow's scream. Whatever was waiting for us ahead now knew that we were coming. "Come on." Fox said.

We walked between the rows of corn, watching carefully for any demons. But no attack came. The red hue to the sky intensified. We did not see anything except rows and rows of dead corn. It was eerie, and I felt like talking to break the silence. But since Fox didn't feel the need to talk, I didn't speak either. He said that he wanted to sneak through quietly.

After the cornfields, we encountered fields of dead sunflowers. The flowers themselves, varied in size. But without exception, they were all dead. The leaves looked dry and crinkly.

I wandered over and reached out to touch the dry sunflower leaves. Fox cleared his throat. I turned to look over at him. He shook his head. I snatched my hand back as though the plant had bit me. I reminded myself that this whole place was dangerous, and I needed to be more cautious.

I began to think that we might have taken a wrong turn somehow. It felt like we were lost in dead farmland. We continued down the path, between rows of dead sunflowers. Fox leaned in, "Whatever comes next. Don't stop moving.

The Arkyala mentioned 'motion' several times. I think that itself is a clue." Not long after that, the end of the field came into sight.

I saw a pulse of light out of the corner of my eye. It was so dark in this place that Shui's light was a clear beacon. I looked and saw that the metal grain of Shui had flashed once. I knew by this point, that happened when Shui was giving a warning. Otherwise, Fox seemed just to 'think' to his staff, and then would receive a silent response. Or maybe that just how Shui was warning me.

Fox spoke again. "The first demon village is ahead of us." I looked up to see the familiar dirt road, lined with the iron braziers. The simple metal buckets and their bright fires were a welcome sight. They looked the same as before, but the road was narrower than it had been. I looked at it, and judged I could sprint from one side to the other in only a few seconds.

There were no bones visible. The road was just dirt. And though it was still at a slight incline, the road felt flat enough. But knowing that there were bones *under* the dirt was really disturbing. If I let my mind wander, I could imagine feeling skeletal lumps underfoot. The knee-high fire braziers were spaced every 20 paces.

I looked ahead up the road. The path sloped gently, but always uphill. We were heading into the mountains. In the distance, but within sight, I could see a collection of small buildings. The cluster of houses I could just barely see in the distance must've been the first village. The Hell-Fire Road was the village's main street.

As we got closer the houses became larger and I could look at them better. They were all a brown gray that was somehow more pale and regular than I would have expected, even in this place. It's not that the wood was dry, instead it was like the wood was not fully there. If I focused on one of the houses, it seemed to shake for a moment, the image vibrating for a moment before steadying. It looked as though the house was somehow not quite real.

The houses appeared to be very simple and each was only one floor tall. The front doors of each of the houses faced the Hell-Fire Road. The windows of each of the houses was completely black. Some of the windows were only square holes cut into the walls. The waxed paper in the few windows that still had it, was torn and charred. The roofs were made of old and cracked, burnt tiles.

I had the impression of being in a deserted farm community. It seemed clear that this is where the farmers would live, if someone attended the fields of dead corn. The total population of the village couldn't have been more than a few dozen.

As the approached the "village", I began to get an evil feeling. There was something "wrong" about this deserted farm village. It looked like a place for humans. It looked like the kind of place where poor farming families would have lived. I had seen enough strange things on this trip that I should have been comforted by familiar things. But instead, I got a terrible and alien feeling from this "human looking" village.

This was an evil place and there was some malevolent presence here that was eagerly, and hungrily awaiting us. I began to get the feeling that the wooden houses were only shells and that there were pieces of something conscious and hateful inside each of them. Maybe… it was the same evil thing in all of the houses? I briefly pictured each house as an evil shoe, worn by a single grotesque demon with two dozen feet. I was clear that this 'poor, deserted, human, farming village' was not what it appeared to be. It was a place of unspeakable evil.

The village looked abandoned. But I felt that something clearly was here. The village may have looked dead, but this place was very much alive with evil. I knew that we needed to pass through the village. I knew that we needed to keep moving and not stop. That suited me just fine. We had not even entered the village yet, but the tangible feeling of dread that I got from it, made me want to balk. The rising panic was like the feeling of being chased by the imaginary demons in the fog.

The iron braziers stopped lining the road as we entered the village. Where the houses started, the fire buckets stopped. It was like there was a line that we crossed as we entered the village, and when we crossed it, the evil in the village woke up.

I began to feel strange, somewhat nauseous as we walked. Fox kept the same steady pace. I marched along resolutely, staying next to him, on his left side. We walked down the center of the road, trying not to be any closer to the houses than necessary.

A series of impressions began to occur to me. One impression was that the houses were breathing. I imagined that the wood in the walls of the shacks was bending, flexing inward and outward as though breathing. And then I imagined I could hear the breathing. The sound was a low and rumbling wheeze that seemed to control the wind. Hot, fetid gusts of wind began to blow.

At the same time, I began to feel lightheaded and dizzy and imagined I heard a persistent, sinister whispering. What was most disturbing was that the whispering was not in my ear, it was in my mind. It felt like the whispering was almost a buzzing, like an insect. The buzzing was too fast to understand and needed to slow down. I didn't understand what the whispering was saying but it wouldn't slow. I slowed my pace walking so that I could better concentrate. Maybe if I slowed down, the buzzing would slow down? I would just pause for a moment and be able to understand, then I would start moving again, I thought.

And I probably would have stopped too if it weren't for Fox grabbing my forearm and pulling me forward. This time there was an audible sound. There was a low and sinister growl that seem to come from all of the houses at once. We were surrounded by the menacing vibration. There must have been more than 20 houses along the street, but it seemed like a single evil presence connected all of them. It was that presence that was attacking us.

Again, the evil presence urged me to stop. Not releasing my arm, Fox continued to pull me forward. He hissed, "Keep moving!" The growl coming from the houses grew in volume and intensity. The strange whispering sound continued in my mind, but louder. Fox leaned in again and said, "I'll guide you. Just study your amulet. Trace the patterns it makes with your mind."

As the attack came, I had been looking down at the ground in front of me. Bewildered, I glanced up. We were only a quarter of the way down the street. We had made it this far through the farm village, but had not actually seen a single demon.

But despite not being able to see the attacker, I felt my mind shaking in response, actively resisting. Somehow, I felt that this place was more dangerous than any I had seen so far. The sinister whispering took on a rhythmic, chanting cadence. It felt like there was an itching, buzzing behind my eyes. If not for Fox pulling my right arm forward, I would certainly have stopped.

I put my left hand to my chest and squeezed the amulet that Fox had given me. I pulled it out and looked down at it, struggling to focus my vision amid the buzzing and whispering. I began to trace the patterns made on the amulet.

Almost immediately, it calmed my mind to see the perfection and regularity of the geometric shapes. The triangles, circles, squares and stars all helped to re-establish order in my mind. In that moment, I understood, on a visceral level, that order provided a shield against chaos. The order that was established in my mind by studying the amulet made an unbreakable wall, against which the waves of chaos broke.

While I was studying the pattern, I could not hear the sinister whispering in my mind. But when the actual houses started to make noise, my ears could not ignore it. The wood of the houses, not in good shape to begin with, began to shake and rattle. It was as though tremendous winds were trying to take the houses apart. The doors rattled in their frames. The roof of each house seemed like it wanted to blow off. The roofs clapped loudly on top of the supporting walls. I could hear the noise, and some part of my mind could visualize what was happening, but I kept my eyes locked on the medallion.

Fox had not released my arm since he had grabbed it. Now, his grip tightened, and he said, "Keep moving! Don't panic, and don't run. But. Keep. Moving." Still studying the medallion on my chest, I nodded and kept walking. It took all of my restraint not to panic and start running with the very buildings around me shaking and moaning.

Chin resting down on my chest, I studied the medallion's patterns and let myself be led up the terrifying village street. I didn't realize it, but I was sweating and getting shaky as we walked. All I knew was that I had to keep walking. I remember putting one foot in front of the other and then… nothing. I had kept walking, but remembered nothing else.

I was in a daze, later, when Fox told me that we had made it through the village. We stood on the Hell-Fire Road. Fox had his hands on my shoulders and was peering carefully into my eyes. The demon farm village was still visible to my right down the road. The evenly spaced metal braziers were the only illumination again. As he studied me, I studied Fox's features in the flickering light from the braziers. His features showed genuine concern.

Then a stale-smelling wind blew down the street. It felt as though it would rain, even though I somehow knew that rain never came to this place. I was reminded of the weather on the day that we had left, so long ago. It seemed like my village was so far away. There was a series of lightning bolts that struck one spot on the mountain. Its brightness was such that both Fox and I looked up at the light. A moment later, the sound of thunder came rolling back to us.

Satisfied that I was healthy enough to continue, Fox turned and continued walking, albeit more slowly, up the Hell-Fire Road. Still shaken, I followed. At least now, I had the feeling that we were on the right path. Clearly this was the Hell-Fire Road and clearly, that had been a demon village.

It took me several minutes of walking before my head fully cleared. There were lingering feelings of confusion and fear, but under all of it, I remembered that I was there for a single reason. I had a duty… a purpose. My little sister needed me.

I had the feeling that comes after something dangerous passes. I knew, with a certainty in my gut, that something lethal had almost taken us in that village. If we had stopped, I was sure we would have died.

But Father had been clear- family does not run from danger in times of trouble. My courage felt weakened because I knew we had barely escaped. But we didn't have the option to fail. And even though the first village had shaken me, I told myself I would never give up.

The night had taken on the appearance of the end of dusk. The sky was dark, but not completely black. The red haze in the sky was more pronounced, the higher we got in the mountains. It was odd how vividly colors stood out in this realm of diminished richness. Here, the colors were pale and much less intensely saturated. Roughly one hundred paces from the sides of the Hell-Fire Road, trees silently stood.

Fox and I trudged on. The road ahead of us was a straight path leading uphill, into the distant mountains. The braziers of fire stood, knee-high on either side of the path. There were the distant trees, and dark shadows on either side of the road. The only sounds I could hear were the rhythmic, crunching 'krshh…krshh' sound of our footsteps on the road.

We walked on in silence. I, at least, was waiting for some new terrible thing to present itself. Fox didn't show any emotions. If anything, he seemed serious, but positive. We were getting closer to our goal, and it clearly made Fox more energetic, more resolute.

The distant trees on the side of the path gave way to a slope on our left side. Going straight on the Hell-Fire Road already had us walking up a steady incline. If we turned left and stepped off the road, we would have to walk up a much steeper incline. What had seemed like one mountain from a distance, was now a range of mountains. The slope on our left led up to a ridge that ran parallel to the Hell-Fire Road. To our right, beyond the light cast by the braziers, the trees were larger than before.

We walked long enough that I had time to catch my breath and regain my nerve. I had put the last encounter in perspective. I tried to figure out what scared me so much about the last village. This last experience had been different from the other demons. It had been... personal. It had come inside my mind.

Even though the demon couple had used illusions to cloud my mind, they had only taken over my perceptions. My thoughts and actions had still been under my control. In this last village, the demonic force had almost taken over my actions, my very willpower. I vowed to keep a calmer and stronger mind next time.

As we trudged uphill to the next village, my imagination took hold, thinking about what type of village would be waiting for us next. I had vowed to keep my mind stronger next time, but what would next time look like? If only I had some information about what was coming next, I felt like I could prepare. I could get my mind ready.

I had my head down and was walking. My eyes were cast downward and I was only looking at the ground in front of my feet. I was listening to the sound of my breathing, my footsteps, and Fox's footsteps.

Fox reached out and tapped my shoulder. I looked over at him, but he was looking up the road, up the hill in front of us. I followed his gaze and watched as the second demon village came into view.

What was most puzzling about when I first saw was it scale. I realized that we were closer to it than I first thought. What confused me was that the buildings were so small. In the last village because the buildings were normal, man-sized structures, we were able to spot them from a distance.

The buildings the upcoming Village, however, were different. They were half the size of the buildings in the last village. My mind somehow had trouble accepting the idea of how big the inhabitants had to be. They would have to be half of my height. Was it a village of demon children?

As we got closer to the village I noticed that the size was not the only difference. The style of the buildings was very different from anything that I'd seen before. But just like the other village, the small buildings lined the Hell-Fire Road. In each village, the Hell-Fire Road was the 'main street' of that village.

As we got closer, I could see the buildings more clearly. They were round, with circular walls that came up to chest height. The roofs of the little huts were oddly shaped domes with points, like the top half of onions.

There were dozens of the small huts on either side of the path. Again, the braziers stopped at a line where the huts began. Before we crossed that line, Fox leaned in to me and whispered, "We have to use stealth as we pass through this village. Again, we have to stay in motion. If we keep moving, our chances of survival are much better. Remember, move quietly and touch nothing."

I glanced up at the huts. They looked like they were made of some sort of gray grass or thatching. The walls and the roofs were made of the same grass, seamlessly woven from one into another. It looked like the round walls had grown their grassy roofs. There were lights visible in the doors of some of the huts. But there were no beings visible. I nodded at Fox and we crossed the line.

I felt nervous after the farm village, but knew that I needed to keep calm and move with stealth. Fox's instructions were clear, but my fear was much closer to the surface than I hoped it would be. I had pictured myself 'brave' in the second village, but I didn't feel brave now.

If we stayed on the road it would be a clear path through the village. While the small huts did have lights on and some of them, we didn't see any figures. This probably meant the odds were good that we can make it through undetected.

I didn't really have anything to carry, but I noticed Fox's hand on his bag, making sure that nothing inside it made any noise. I thought about how to move more stealthily. I tried to roll my feet as I walked bent my knees. I realize that it was a comical tiptoe crouch that I had fallen into. It wasn't stealthy but Fox didn't correct me or make any kind of suggestions. So, I continued my crouching 'speed tip-toe'. Fox just walked quickly, never seeming to make noise unless he intended to. As I listened carefully, I could hear my soft footsteps on the dirt of the road. I couldn't hear Fox's steps at all.

As we made our way through the town, the first few huts now behind us, we began to see pottery, (mostly large cauldrons and large pots) that were stacked in piles on either side of the path. as we approached the stacks closer we noticed that they were piled in a haphazard way. The way between the pottery piles was twisting and convoluted. We didn't really have any choice about making our way through the village, so we pushed on. Stealthy as we could be while continuing to stay in motion. We had made it through 10 paces where the pottery was stacked piles on either side of us. But up ahead of us, the stacks grew closer and closer together.

We were passing through a particularly narrow spot on the road, between pottery piles in front of the tiny huts. Some doorways were lit with a dim light. Other doorways were dark. We had not seen anyone or anything so far.

I was trying to move carefully, but for a split-second my concentration wavered, and I looked to the side. There I saw something coming out of the front door of the little house. Its appearance was so shocking to me, that I jerked back, stumbling off balance, and crashed into the pile of carelessly stacked pottery. The sound was horrible. Frozen in place, sprawled on my backside amidst the broken pottery, I had stopped. It was the least stealthy way possible to cross the village. And I had broken the one main rule - don't stop. I felt that the tide of our good fortune was about to change. And it was my fault.

Immediately, I felt terrible for destroying whatever stealth we had. But the features of the little figure were an overwhelming surprise to me. It was short, and I estimated that it would probably only stand a little above my belt. But it's size wasn't what bothered me.

Its proportions were all wrong. Its arms were longer than they should have been. Its legs were shorter than they should have been. Its skin was a chalky white, as was its rope-like hair. And its head was much larger than it should have been. That was clearly the most disturbing part.

What's more, the face did not look human. The large head wore a face that looked like a large wooden mask. It looked like the mask had been carved from some sort of wood and then painted white. The eyes were large, bulging ovals, and seemed to be closed. When the eyes were closed, the black painted eyelids made a vertical line across the wide black eyes.

The little figure's nose was narrow and pointed. The lips were thick and full, making the mouth much wider than it should normally have been. This odd face was placed on a head that was one third the size of its body. The strange mass of white, rope-like hair framed that huge face. It appeared that there were other marks carved into the face as well. The forehead was inscribed with symbols, as were the cheeks and the chin.

When I jerked back in surprise and knocked over all the pottery, its head snapped up to look at me. Its eyes opened in surprise. When it did, I saw that the orbs underneath were black and red. Where there would have been whites in the eyes of a person, these eyes had a glowing red.

When the thing saw me, it opened its mouth to reveal a mouthful of irregular, but sharp, pointy teeth. It squeezed out a hissing squeal sound and raised a long arm to point at me.

Almost instantly several things happened. Fox thrust out his hand and urged me to get up. My eyes, however, were fixed on the sequence of doorways lighting up as the other villagers heard the strange call. Strange pygmy figures started coming out of all of the houses. All of them had large, mask-faces.

Each of the masks was different, but all of them had glowing red instead of whites in their eyes.

The first pygmy demon, who had first spotted me, now let out different sound. Instead of a squeal-hissing this time, the squealing was combined with snarling. The little thing sounded angry. It put its head down and charged.

It moved much faster than I thought his little legs could carry. Its eyes were focused on Fox. I felt certain that it would run up and sink its sharp teeth into Fox's leg.

Instead, at the last second, the pygmy demon swerved to come towards me. With an athleticism I did not expect, Fox kicked his leg up and sent the pygmy demon flying.

I scrambled to my feet, barely cutting myself on pottery shards in the process. But by the time that I had looked around to get my bearings, two other pygmy demons were on us. One of the demons was clearly staring at Fox, aiming for him as it ran up. The other demon was clearly staring at me.

I stumbled back, but without a weapon or any formal training, I didn't know what I would do. Quickly, I bent down and picked up a shard of broken pottery. I guess I planned to stab the little pygmy when it came into range.

But, to my surprise, the attacker swerved at the last moment and darted towards Fox. The one that had been coming for Fox swerved and came towards me. It would have gotten me, had it not been for another defensive kick from Fox.

While Fox was quick enough to kick the demon that was heading for me, the other one would get him before he could kick it. I was in the process of shouting warning to Fox, when he thrust out Shui in front of him. The little pygmy leapt for the staff, instinctively biting its end.

The diminutive demon had jumped into the air to bite the staff. Also, the end of Fox's staff, was as big as the pygmy mask's mouth could stretch. This demons mask was different from the first one. It had a large bulbous nose protruding from it. It also had fat wrinkles carved into the face. I couldn't tell if the wrinkles were supposed to make the face look like it was threatening, or grimacing.

The angry pygmy demon had its mouth clamped around the fat end of Fox's staff. It was trying to gnaw on Shui, but the ironwood was too hard. Fox held the staff, suspending the demon in the air. Its long little arms and short little legs flailed around. It was stuck, the legs couldn't reach the ground, and the arms couldn't pry the demon's face off of Shui, it wouldn't let go, and it couldn't bite through the ironwood.

Fox braced himself and turned slightly. He was pointing Shui, and thus the demon, at a trio of oncoming demons. The metal grain running through the ironwood staff, flared brightly. Then the pygmy demon, biting the staff, was violently shot off of the end. Part of the head burst apart when Shui discharged the blast, but the body of the demon flew backward. Flying at tremendous speed, the body crashed into the three demons charging in behind it.

Fox grunted, "They don't look where they are attacking. The eyes look to the side of their target. Devious, really." He spared a glance back at me, again checking to see that I was unhurt. We both stood there, panting. A pot that had been precariously balanced, fell and broke. I jumped at the sound. Fox flinched. "You've got to wa…" But he didn't finish his sentence. The sounds of our first 'skirmish' had raised the alarm.

All of the little hut houses' doors were suddenly filled with tiny angry figures. Glowing red and black eyes peered out at us. They instantly understood that we did not belong there. Alarm immediately became anger.

Before the demon horde began their hiss-squeal battle cry, Fox roared, "Run!" He grabbed the tunic at my shoulder and shoved me forward. I didn't need any urging. My sense of self-preservation, striving to survive, gave me speed I never had before.

The pygmy demons began screaming and ran after us. The sound of them screeching for our blood was tremendous motivation. Feeling like their sharp little teeth were about to ravage the backs of my legs, I ran. My legs pumped faster than they ever had before.

Luckily for us, the horde stopped to investigate the fallen demons. This gave us the crucial time we needed to gain a lead over our pursuers. There were squeals that sounded like outrage, and a chorus of hisses behind us. I did not look back. We ran at top speed. I tried to make sure I didn't trip. In my peripheral vision, I could see Fox reaching into his bag.

We had passed the area where the little onion-domed huts ended. I hoped that the little demons should have fallen back and given up the chase. Instead, they kept coming. I could hear them. And it sounded like they were getting closer. Fox was digging around inside his bag as he sprinted beside me.

We ran as fast as we could, but I knew that I couldn't keep up this pace forever. Fox clapped his hand to my forehead, putting a metal ring on my brow. Not slowing down, I looked askance at him. He was wearing a wire ring on his broad brow too. Apparently, these things were what he had been searching for in his bag.

The circlet was actually wider than a wire, more like a golden finger ring that had been blown up to the size of a crown. A single, opaque, beige stone was mounted on the golden loop. I reached up and felt a similar stone on my forehead. I was out of breath, panting hard. I began to panic as I realized I was slowing down.

A moment later, Fox put a hand on my shoulder and guided me off to the right of the Hell-Fire Road. He slowed us to a trot, then stopped a moment later. My heart was pounding, the sound thundering in my ears. I gasped for air. Why were we stopping?! But Fox put his hand up in a sign for patience, so I tried my best to calm down.

A moment after that, our pursuers had arrived. An army of furious, masked pygmy demons came running up the road. Their white-painted limbs were pink in the red hue from the sky. The pink limbs waved furiously as they thundered up the path. I might have cried out, but Fox put a hand over my mouth. I couldn't understand why were still out on the path. Shouldn't we be hiding?

A moment later, the entire village was running by, wildly screaming. There were more of them than I had expected. I estimated more than one hundred of the pygmy demons that ran by. It was a river of white limbs, red eyes, and large masks, screaming and hissing as it flowed uphill. Somehow, though, they didn't see us.

Each of their masks was different, but there were certain similarities among all of them. All of them had the same black and white color scheme. All of them had big and wide lips. All of them had the red and black eyes. The size of the eyes varied, but they all glowed with the same unnatural evil. Some masks had noses, while others had no noses at all. Some had small horns, white rope hair or badly-stitched scars, some only had eyes and lips. Some faces were rectangles, while others were ovals with pointy chins. I was trembling as they ran by. My chest was heaving, but I didn't move otherwise. It was impossibly strange watching the demons run right past us. They were so close that I could have touched them.

All of their bodies were white in the reflected light of the braziers. They looked like they had gone swimming in white paint and then it had dried on them. The paint seemed to crack and flake off where joints moved. Their arms were long and many of them ran with their arms hanging down at their sides. Their fingertips reached almost to their knees. They were all barefoot. I couldn't distinguish if they were both male and female, or just one gender. Each pygmy demon wore a short, woven skirt around its waist. That was the only clothing they wore.

Despite the fact that they didn't have any weapons, they terrified me. They were small but they projected menace. The little demons didn't have to carry weapons for me to know they were dangerous.

It just didn't make sense that they wouldn't notice us. I looked down into my side and saw that I was standing close to one of the iron braziers. I saw what was inside the metal pot. The metal pot was a knee-high bucket, large enough to place your foot inside. And inside, the brazier was full of bones.

Realizing that I was standing right next to the brazier, I tried to inch away. Fox put his hand on my shoulder and squeezed, urging me to stay still. I felt like the bone fire next to me must have lit me up like a beacon. But still, somehow, the pygmy demons did not see us.

After a moment or two, the furious horde had run past. It had taken a moment or two before we were sure that the last, slowest demons had passed us. I prepared to take a step forward, but Fox instead urged me to stay still.

After a moment, he spoke. "That was close." he said simply. "Don't move yet. They have passed us, right now they are ahead of us in the direction we need to go. If we leave now, there is a good chance that we will run into them later. We might not. I'm not entirely certain how this realm works, but I think that we should wait."

Still panting, I could only nod to agree. If Fox thought that it was better for us to stay here, then we would stay. It was that simple for me. He went on speaking while I caught my breath. "We will stay here and wait for them to return. I imagine that they will soon figure out that we escaped them. Then, they will return home to their village. After they do, we will be able to continue on our journey."

"You must be wondering how we escaped." Fox said quietly. "The circlet that I put onto your forehead, while we were running, is a very special tool. Even the wisest GaleMasters only have theories as to how they work. But the idea is simple. The circlet you are wearing, and the one I'm wearing, render us invisible."

My face must have shown an incredulous expression. Fox reassured me, "It's true. What you're wearing is a very special artifact. It was one of a number of devices left behind from an ancient time. For this wandering, I was entrusted with two of them.

He paused and loudly cleared his throat. I winced at the noise that it made. If there were demons still around, they would definitely hear us! But Fox did not seem worried. He went on, "You remember the rune inscribed robes that we wore, when we first came down through the Dragon cloud?" I nodded. How could I forget?

Fox continued, "Those robes used a very specific kind of power. They had the ability to make us look like whoever saw us. If a giant saw us and we were wearing those robes, we would look like giants. But we wouldn't actually become giants, of course. It's a weak form of illusion, somewhat like a mirror.

"The runes on those robes also had the added benefit of making us feel better. Well, these circlets won't make us feel more confident or positive. What they will do is hide us-completely. They will hide our appearance and show only what is behind us. They will also mask our sound so that noises like a sneeze, for example, are inaudible to anyone who is not wearing a circlet. It will also mask our scent, if we were hiding from some type of creature that hunted by smell.

"Unless we were to knock something over, or take something, the demons would neither see nor hear nor smell us. Of course, if we moved something or took it, the demons would notice its movement or its absence. But still, they wouldn't be able to see *us*. It is a much stronger form of illusion than the robes.

"Of course, a strong enough being would be able to see through the circlet's illusion. but luckily for us, I don't think a strong enough being would lower itself to live in a village. Remember that demons are haughty and arrogant. Any demon with the strength to live on its own and fend for itself, would feel obliged to do so." Fox seemed to go into one of his contemplative moods. I could tell because his tone of voice changed when he was considering abstract ideas. "Although, I suppose a large amount of antisocial behavior is normal for a demon. In demon circles, only the weak ones seek community… because the strong demons wouldn't *need* community."

Finally, I had my breath back enough to speak. And since I knew that I would not be overheard, I felt free to ask questions as long as I didn't move.

"If you had invisibility crowns, why didn't we wear them before this? Wouldn't it have been safer to walk around invisible?" I asked.

Fox said? "Everything in the GaleSource works with balance, Kwan. Everything has its price. To use an ability like the circlets provide, takes a lot of power. That power does not come from this stone." Fox lifted a finger to touch the beige stone at his forehead. "The invisibility the circles give you, are powered by *your* life's energy. If you'll think back, your running speed slowed down as soon as I put the circlet on your head. That's because a portion of your energy was siphoned off from running to make you invisible. if we had worn them the entire time, we would have been exhausted for this whole adventure. And when people are tired, they make mistakes. I thought they would hurt our chances until we needed them. I wonder if I miscalculated how much energy you had."

This was one time when I wasn't really listening. It was unlike me, as far as time with Fox went. But I was distracted by our position and I tuned out what Fox was saying. I forced myself to focus. I had other questions. But first, I felt the need to apologize. "I'm really sorry Fox. I didn't mean to give us a way back there. The... The demon really surprised and scared me. But it's no excuse!"

Fox looked at me for a long moment. Then he quietly said, "You did not offer it as an excuse. It was a clear explanation. What happened back there was understandable. I have gone through years of training up at the Gale Temple to learn how to deal with the things that we find here. You have had *none* of that training. To be honest with you, I have been impressed with your abilities and behavior so far. You have shown that you can think, even under pressure. So don't start whipping yourself. Accidents happen."

I nodded gratefully, although I knew that Fox would probably say something like that. He was not the kind to try to make me feel bad. He seemed to only want for me to learn. So I asked another question, to learn. "How did Shui shoot off that demon when it bit him?"

Fox smiled at me, as if sharing inside joke. "I too think of Shui as a him. To me, his tone is clearly that of a masculine warrior. But the master entrusted with Shui before me, was Mistress Dew the Immortal. And I read in her records that she thought of Shui as female. Maybe any companion who travels with Shui feels that way." Again, Fox took on the contemplative tone, as if striving to be thorough in his explanation. "But to be honest with you, as I understand it, Shui is a powerful spirit from a time before modern men.

"There was a time long, long ago when many different types of powerful beings existed alongside men. Old and powerful beings have many abilities. Shui can do more than you've seen…" Fox did not have a chance to say any more.

He paused, hearing noises from up the road. We stood still and watched the stream of pygmy demons returning home. The demons were walking as they marched home, not running. They had a completely different temperament on the way back. It wasn't that they seemed upset, or dejected. Rather, they all seemed like they were communing with some force. The eyes of each and every mask were closed. They walked in silence, long arms swinging at their sides.

It took longer for all of them to walk back past us. I thought that all of them had passed, and was preparing to move. But Shui pulsed once, and I paused. A moment later, the last pygmy demon sauntered down the road. Shui had saved my life again.

When Shui signaled that the way was clear, we returned to our uphill trek. We had survived the second demon village. If I weren't numb from the terror of dealing with the little demons, I might have taken a moment to be impressed we had come this far.

As though sensing our fatigue, the slope of the road angled up sharply. The Hell-Fire Road was taking us up into the mountains. I didn't say anything, but as I looked ahead, I had doubts. The slope angled up so sharply, that it would be more mountain climbing than hiking. It quickly became closer to vertical than horizontal. How would we get up this incline without ropes or special equipment? Would we scramble up like goats? But Fox didn't seem troubled, so I set the question aside.

Fox never seemed to get tired, but he slowed a little, out of consideration for me. If I weren't young and strong, I don't know how I would have kept up. The third village was upon us almost before we realized. I was sure that we had only been walking for a short time, but we were already approaching a line where the bone-burning braziers stopped.

I turned and looked over my shoulder on an impulse. I was surprised to see that we were much higher up the mountain than I thought we were. There were lights on, down in the port city by the coast, and I could see them, distant and twinkling in the distance, below us. We had not been climbing for long enough to reach this high. It looked like we had already climbed halfway up the mountain. And we couldn't have been walking more than seven or eight hours.

Up the mountain, far above us, I could see a thin line of light. I assumed it was the continuation of the Hell-Fire Road. But did we have to climb up the mountain in the dark?

I reached up, instinctively touching the circlet on my forehead. If not for that talisman I don't know if I would be able to make it through the next village. As we crept closer, I leaned in to Fox and whispered, "are you sure that we are invisible to others?" I asked.

Fox replied in a normal voice, "I'm sure. You don't really need to whisper. The circlets hide our voices as well as our scents, remember? Only I can hear you." I felt reassured, and straightened my back a little as we walked towards the village. I looked ahead and saw that we were almost at the end of the iron braziers, but there was no way forward. The road stopped in a dead end!

It just didn't make sense. We had come so far only to have the way just stop? As we got closer, I could see- what looked like a mystery was just a trick of shadow and angle.

Chapter 13

Into the Mountain

We weren't stopped. A tall, gaping opening in the mountain was ahead of us, the only path forward. There was a door that was exactly the same width as the path, a black semi-circle. The Hell-Fire Road went… underground?! Through the door, we could see that the road continued- down into the unknown, *into* the belly of the mountain. I knew with dreadful certainty that we would need to go into that unknown. It had been hard enough just to climb the outside of the mountain. Now we had to go into it.

The iron braziers continued inside the mountain. The path continued, but went slightly downhill. That was why we couldn't see the fire pots until we got closer. We had been looking up- up the trail and up the mountain. To see the braziers, you had to be at the opening of the cave, looking slightly down.

We paused at the opening to the cave. Because I saw that the braziers continued, I reasoned that we weren't really at the village yet. Or, I worried, maybe this 'village' was much larger than the other two, maybe it followed a different pattern.

Either way, we needed to enter the doorway into the mountain. Cho Clei was somewhere on the other side, and I would do whatever I needed to help her. Fox took a deep breath and let it out slowly. Then he stepped into the cave. Copying his deep breath, I steeled myself, and followed him inside.

Like the last village, we could not see any demons at first. I had expected a demon crouching just inside the opening, waiting to pounce us. There was no demon.

This time, I didn't allow our initial good fortune let me relax. I knew that there would be demons inside, if not here at the opening. My guard was up.

Fox said, "All we have to do is get through this next village. We shouldn't engage with any of the demons. In fact, we should remember why we are here. We must stay focused on getting through to your sister."

I nodded to myself, relieved. Just walk through. Just walk through. I repeated the phrase to myself. The task seemed easy enough. I vowed that this time I would be more careful and not give us away. My courage would hold. I swore it.

Fox took the lead as we made our way underground. He walked a half-step ahead of me. While there was fire light coming from the braziers inside the mountain, Shui, Fox's staff, also shone silvery light from its metal grain.

We walked along the path. I tried not to show it, but I don't think I've ever been more afraid for my life. And because of that, I set myself to studying the environment. The path that we were walking on sloped downward like a long ramp into the mountain.

The HellFire Road was now a rocky tunnel. I thought back to the tunnel opening to the inner world. I remember back to first coming into this realm. I remembered seeing the cave opening to giant figures on either side of the opening. I remembered how they had been bigger than Ragyala and had the faces of lizards. Fox had told me about the groups of beings that live deep under the ground.

"Fox? Is this one of the Gartun tunnels? Is this leading us down to the underground realms?"

As always, foxing to consider before he replied. "No, I don't think so. The Gartun tunnels almost always have sentries. There is also a system of identifying marks that they use. This tunnel has none of those marks."

I realize that I had been looking forward to maybe seeing this underground realm. Instead I shuffled on next to, but slightly behind Fox. The bones burned in the iron pots on either side of the path and Fox's staff let off a soft glowing light.

We walked down the rock path and I noticed that the dirt had disappeared. Somehow, I felt relieved to notice that there were no more bones beneath my feet. I said as much to Fox. A look crossed his face that I could only identify as… Pity.

"Oh Kwan. You thought that we were walking on bones this whole time?" I nodded. He continued, "No, the bones were only at the beginning of the road. I tested a few times along the way. I think that those bones at the beginning -like a road sign to let us know where we were, and where we were going. I'm sorry you were working under that idea. It must've made this hard time even harder. Well, at least you know the truth now. Often that's the best life will do for us, and we have to live and learn.

The surface of the tunnel overhead was the same roughhewn rock that were walking on. It was neither polished nor smooth, but it was even enough that we didn't have to pick our way down and worry about falling rocks.

We were walking along the downward sloping path for quite a long time. I started off the journey anxious, worrying about what we would find. And as we walked down that long hill through the tunnel, my anxiety grew. They got higher and higher until some sort of release valve went off inside of me. I found myself getting less and less anxious somehow. In retrospect, I had gotten complacent.

I found myself given over to reverie, remembering my journey to get this far. It was astonishing to me that a boy from my farm village was now on this mystical adventure. It was clear that my life had changed. What I didn't know was how much more it was going to change.

It began to get colder as we descended into the mountain. Fox paused for a moment and took out warm but thinner robes for us to put on. It surprised me how many clothes he kept in that bag. It was as though he traveled around prepared for every kind of weather, *and* to keep a guest comfortable in any kind of situation. It was an impressive bag, and I wondered what else he kept in there.

We put on the robes, and they were warm, but they did not have any runes to enhance their utility. Still, they were warmer than nothing. I was grateful for this little thing. I realized that all of these small actions on Fox's part made a big difference for me on this rescue mission.

I had my head down and was walking, looking at the shadows on the rocky path. I was studying the way that there was a myriad of shadows on the ground. Imperfections in the smoothness of the path, flickering light from all of the braziers, and the soft glow from Shui, made the shadows dance hypnotically at my feet.

I had been walking and ran into Fox's arm, surprised. He had slowed and put his arm out bar my path, so that I did not pass him. My head snapped up to look down the path. It appeared that there was someone waiting in the distance.

The figure of a man waited at the side of the path up ahead of us. Fox had not stopped, apparently still obeying the Arkyala's advice to keep moving. But he had slowed down. We were continuing to walk towards the figure, but were approaching cautiously.

A moment later Fox seemed to relax. He turned to me and said, "Don't worry. Shui has told me that it's not alive. It is… a statue." We continued walking but still at a slower pace.

As we got closer, I was astonished to see the figure. It was the carving of a girl. No, it was the carving of a woman, in her 20s. She was very beautiful, and the carving showed skillful artistry. I have not been exposed very much art, being a boy from a rural village. But even my uneducated eye could see the tremendous amount of skill that went into producing something like this. Not only was the figure exquisitely carved, but the clothing was too. The clothing was carved with such skill that the folds in cloth even look natural. The statue was shaped like a beautiful girl walking, carrying a basket. Fruit was spilling out of the basket. She clearly was human.

Our pace slowed to a crawl when we got very close to the statue. It was carved with such exquisite skill that the statue conveyed and innocence and hopefulness to the woman. I marveled that something as simple as a carving could bring out such emotions and thoughts in me. Quite simply, it was beautiful. Its craftsmanship was astonishing.

This terrible place was conditioning me. Part of me expected the statue would break into hellish screaming. But it didn't. It stood there silent, looking demure, frozen in time. We kept moving and walked past that statue. A few minutes later we came to another statue.

This time it was the statue of a man. He wore a style of armor I had never imagined before. The armor had no curves, only sharp angles. A pointy, angular helmet lay on the ground beside him. He looked like a strong warrior, but his armor was battered. He wore a sword and was in the process of drawing it. His face wore an expression of fear mingled with desperation. It made me very uncomfortable to look at that face. The hair framing the face was frozen in place, blowing in the nonexistent wind. Again the statue was exquisitely carved. I doubted that the best sculptor alive could do a better job.

Then we came across another statue, then another. Before we knew what was happening, the path led us to a point where we were surrounded by statues. There were statues of men, women, and children. Each of them was vividly lifelike. And each of them was staring at us. It was so unnerving that I almost balked.

Actually, the statues were staring at the path we were traveling on. Clearly, whoever placed the statues had clearly done it intentionally. The effect was disturbing. Both Fox and I increased our pace to pass through the area quickly.

The sculptor had skillfully conveyed a delicate and subtle sense about each subject. The HellFire Road apparently ran through an impressive garden of statues.

I realized that the small tunnel we had been going through had opened up into a large cavern. The path that we were on was still the same size, but instead of rock walls around us, there was now a large enclosed space. There were no stars in the sky. But then again, I couldn't recall having seen any stars since we had crossed over to this realm.

Also, I noticed that there were trees in the distance behind the sculptures. I stared at them dumbfounded, not quite able to process what I was seeing. How could trees grow underground? There was no light. Trees needed sunlight to grow, didn't they? I began to notice not only that there were trees, but that some of the trees had been cut down. For some, there were only stumps remaining.

As we wandered through the garden of sculptures, Fox made sure that we kept moving. Still, though I knew that we were on heightened alert, it was a nice place. Sure, it wasn't nice being underground, I supposed. And it wasn't nice being surrounded by buckets of burning bones. But the statues themselves were so beautiful that I couldn't ignore how nice it was to be around them.

It was then that I realized I had been feeling tired. And being around the beauty of these sculptures made me feel a little better. We continued our wandering, and I couldn't help but admire the sculptor's work.

But we never did stop. Fox and I made it a point to keep moving. The statues were beautiful, but we could not linger. I remembered my sister and stayed focused.

Eventually we left the statue garden behind. The path continued, but the iron braziers stopped at a point ahead of us. Just beyond that we saw a shantytown of leaning wooden buildings against the red sky. It was completely hidden behind perimeter walls. Black clouds passed by overhead. A dark alley between two buildings stood as an entrance, directly ahead of us.

Off to our left, we heard the unmistakable sound of a tree being felled. We turned to peer in the direction of the sound. Was it possible that there were demon... loggers? It didn't make sense, but I remembered that sound. I had cut down trees for Fong... recently. That seemed so long ago now. If there were loggers, they were out of our sight.

Maybe it was demons cutting down trees. Maybe it was something else. At this point, nothing would surprise me. But since we couldn't see anything, we kept walking to the third village.

The third village was larger than the other two had been. Its buildings took up three times as much space as the farm village. It was much larger than the pygmy village, of course, too. But its size was not the most intimidating part.

It was more frightening that we couldn't see anything inside the village. Who knows what might be happening inside those walls? In the other villages, at least we could see down the Hell-Fire Road. Our path through those villages, between the buildings, had been clear. This village was different. We were going in blind. It felt somehow much worse.

As we got closer I saw that the "buildings" were very poorly made. Some of them were leaning as though they had given up, or been kicked. They were made of wood, but seemed like the sloppiest kind of construction. Was it possible that the demons had to cut down the wood to make their houses?

For the first time, I heard the sound of an animal. It was clearly the bark of a big dog. Three barks, actually. Then a snarling sound. I began to get tense. "Remember, they cannot see us." Fox said. I nodded, following.

Fox and I walked towards the opening between the rows of buildings. Despite my feeling of foreboding, I walked on. I suppose my trust in Fox was even bigger than my fear of the situation. More importantly, it was what I had to do to help my little sister. Still, I had the feeling of going into a lethal animal's den. I clamped my jaw shut and we marched in.

As we crossed the threshold into the alley, I almost stopped. It was the first time I had seen this new kind of demon. It looked like some kind of upright animal. The demon had a fat belly and fat haunches. It was covered in spiky, matted hair.

The demon had a vaguely recognizable face. It had a small snout that ended in a small nose. It had long front buck teeth that extended down past its bottom lip. It also had whiskers on either side of its small nose. Large furrowed eyebrows angled down toward the nose, making it look angry.

It looked like it had been dipped in grease and had pulled itself out and shaken 'most' of the grease off. The greasy hair stuck out, spiky, and in patches, covering most of its chest and legs. Bald patches made it look somehow diseased. The bald calf muscles bulged, and the animal demon's feet seemed abnormally long. It walked on the ball of its foot, like a wolf.

It was carrying a tray full of wood from a place on one side of the alley to another on the opposite side. I nearly stopped, partly because the demon's appearance was so shocking, and partly because it surprised me. After waiting so long to see them, my guard had fallen by the time we did actually encounter a demon.

After noticing what the demon was carrying, I noticed that there was wood stacked everywhere. Baskets. There was wood in wooden trays. There was wood stacked in piles next to the wooden walls. What must have been wood harvested from the dead trees, was everywhere throughout this place.

Fox kept us moving, reaching back and taking my forearm, pulling me through. "Remember to watch your step." Fox said. I panicked and felt my eyes widen in alarm. They would hear us! Addressing my thought before I could say anything, Fox reminded, "And remember, they can't hear us." He spoke in a normal voice. He wasn't even whispering.

We progressed further into the alleyway, and I felt the walls closing around us. There was the feeling that we were almost immediately trapped. There were no braziers of fire inside the underground village, but there were torches that burned, hung on the walls outside each building. While they continued to burn, and provide light, they did not seem to make any smoke. They reminded me of the flame inside the lanterns on the Arkyala's ferry.

I thought that I was braced after seeing the first demon, but I was unprepared when we came upon a trio of the beaver-rat demons. All of them had beady eyes and long, wiry arms and chests. All of them had wicked looking teeth in the front. One of them snarled at the other two, opening its mouth in the process. I could see their mouths filled with black, pointed teeth. Aside from the two front buck teeth, the rest of the teeth were different sized spikes. What was really shocking was their "hands".

Where they should have had hands, each of the demons had metal attachments on their arms. Two of the demons had long saw blades. The saw blades were serrated and almost as long as my arm. The third demon had a large axe blade attached to each of its forearms.

It took me some time in our wandering through that alley before I came to trust the power of the circlet that I was wearing. None of the demons that we passed gave any sign that they were aware of us. None of them noticed us at all.

We heard barking up ahead of us. Part of me looked forward to seeing an actual dog after having been in this strange, cruel place for so long. I was shocked as we saw the first "dog". What we saw can only roughly be described as a dog, without skin.

The thing looked instead more like a small, muscular, cross between a bull and dog. Without skin, all of the corded, gray, muscle fibers could be seen. It had horns that stuck out a short distance on either side of its forehead. It barked several more times. The sound was between a cough and a snarl.

I worried that the demon dogs would be more aware of us than their masters. I knew that a dog's senses were sharper than a man's. It might be the same for demons and demon dogs. But as we progressed, it became clear that the 'dogs' couldn't see or smell us either. We walked past several of them but they did not respond.

We noticed many variations on that original demon as we wandered through the alley. All of them looked dirty and had greasy fur. The pattern of bald patches on their bodies varied, but they all had patches. For the most part, their bodies were similar until it came to their hands. Each of them had buck teeth and big, powerful hands. All of them had long fingers.

They all had the same yellow, crinkly, parchment like skin under their greasy fur.

Some of them had blade-like attachments on their fingers. Some were like knives some were smaller, intricately-shaped tools. Then I noticed what they were doing. Many of the demons in this village, from what I could see, were involved in carving wood. Some of them seem to gather the wood. Others moved the wood around. And others still carved the wood. Was it possible that they were art-loving demons?

Suddenly, I connected that these demons were the artists who made the sculptures in the garden. It felt strange thinking that these evil things, in this evil place, would be able to create such beauty as the statues. The long saw-armed and axe-armed demons were the lumberjacks. The demons with the blade-tipped fingers were the artists.

I also began to notice that the demons ate. I couldn't make out what they were eating at first but there was a crunchy chewing sound. As I focused on it the sound of chewing around me was very loud.

Then I became aware of the sounds of soft crying punctuated by sharp screams. I realized that I was clenching my fists as we walked through the alley. There were other alleys that I could see branching off of this first one. But each of the alleys looked almost identical to this one. They each were filled with greasy-haired demons sitting in front of each building carving pieces of wood. The ground in front of each of the places was littered with wood shavings.

As we moved through the 'village', I became aware of two things. One thing was that the sounds of screaming and crying were coming from the demons themselves. We walked past more than one building that contained a chorus of demons pretending to sound like screaming humans. It was like walking past a nightmare singing class. I didn't understand what I was hearing. I just knew that it was unnerving, and hurt my ears, and that I wanted to be away from it.

On the way ahead of us, was a particularly old looking rat-beaver demon. His greasy hair was being a lighter, thinner gray than the others. In front of his house he had several exquisite carvings. Each one was absolutely realistic and life-like. In fact, the carvings were so realistic that we slowed to inspect them as we passed.

The old demon was working on carving a baby. The carving looked exactly like a human newborn. Its little face was frozen in an expression of mid-cry. The swaddling blankets around the baby were carved with such precision that they looked soft. Each of its fat little fingers had been carved with perfect realism. It looked as though an actual baby had been turned into wood. The baby had even poked its fat little toes out from the blanket.

There was a wheezing-snarling sound from the old demon. He was apparently upset. I looked at what he was doing, and he seemed furious at a mistake with his carving. From what I could see, the mistake was that one of the folds on the fat baby's ankle had a little nick on it. It was a tiny issue, but it did mar the perfection of the carving. The frustrated old demon used the long blades on his fingertips to slash across the baby statue. Then, he threw the carving out into the street.

Coincidentally, at that same moment, the 'choir' of demons was practicing the sound of a baby screaming. The sound of the 'baby screams', along with the visual image of a baby being thrown into the street, provoked a spontaneous rush of demons into the street. Some of the demons appeared to be children themselves, but then I realized that they were just smaller sized demons. They only looked like children, but their viciousness made them the equal of any of the adults. They pounced on the wooden baby carving, tearing it apart. There were seven or eight of the demons, 'adults' and 'children'. They slashed at each other in their attempts to get a piece of the 'baby'. I watched one in particular tear off the 'baby's' head and bite down on it. Its jaws snapped, crunching the wood and splintering it between its teeth.

I could see large splinters of wood that must've been cutting the insides of the demons' mouths, but they did not seem to mind. Rather than their mouths filling with blood from their self-inflicted injuries, their mouths filled with black smoke. As far as I could tell, instead of bleeding, clouds of foul-smelling, black smoke began billowing from their mouths. They gleefully tore into the carving. Only after the wood had been devoured did the demons straighten up, with black smoke still issuing from their mouths, and wander back to their own carving stations.

"It seems we may have figured out what these demons do." Fox said. "I'll have to write about this in my next scroll. I had never heard of demons eating wood before. I imagine this is a behavior that comes out of being denied any other food source." Fox said.

I was amazed that Fox could be analytical facing something like this. I had to admit it did seem strange. I stared at the old demon's fingertips.

The demon's fingers were made of demon 'flesh', but the tips of the fingers seemed to morph into hard and sharp carving tools. I couldn't tell if the tools were made of metal or some kind of bone, but they had cut the wood like it was soft. It looked like the tools were part of the fingers, and the flesh had flowed into hard 'tool' shapes. The claw-tools looked metallic at first, but then I peered more closely. The carving claw-tools gleamed like a white metal, but, on closer inspection, they looked more like a polished bone material.

I don't know if the demons had mutilated themselves to but those carving attachments on them or if they could naturally shift into those forms. Either way, I guessed it made sense for them to adapt.

Fox reasoned on, "But since they can't effectively be killed in this realm...they couldn't starve, but they feel hunger?" He drifted off, musing. "It really is fascinating." We made our way past the demons crowding this section of the street. I was careful where I placed my feet, moving with precision and care.

When we had passed them, we came to an area where demons were... receiving acting lessons? We walked by many doorways where demons were inside, pretending to run, pretending to fall, and pretending to be overwhelmed by attackers. Some were practicing scrambling backwards in a panic. Some of the demons were trying on 'human looking' clothes. But the clothes looked strange. It appears that the clothes were made of carved wood too. The wood was shaved into thin panels and mimicked a woven pattern. The demon's large joints, like the waist, knees and elbows rested in specially carved pieces that connected to the other parts. The end result was clothing that did not appear to move smoothly. The demons' clothes looked like some kind of wooden plate armor when they moved.

"It appears the smaller demons are favored for the 'victim' role." Fox observed quietly.

"Victim?" I asked, alarmed. I had almost stopped moving.

"A working theory. Come on, keep moving." He replied. The street of the village opened up into another wide clearing. There were no iron braziers, so I knew that we were still in the village. The clearing was a wide field. It was strange to see such a large open space underground. I knew that we were still under the mountain and it shocked me to see such a huge open cavern. I could not even see the roof of the cave high above us. The clearing was circular, and there were a dozen demons waiting in the center.

We skirted their group and stayed outside of their pack. But we did come close enough to take a closer look at what they were doing. What we saw, I will never forget.

One of the larger demons of the group threw back his head and sounded a long and deep, guttural yell. The sound was chilling. But even more surprising, the demons gathered in the clearing, all took off running. Within a few seconds they were gone. The demons moved very quickly. I realized that if the pygmy demons had been able to move this fast, we would definitely have died. The simple truth of the idea was appalling and undeniable.

I watched as they ran away. They moved so quickly that I could barely track them with my eyes. Within a moment, they had all vanished. At the limits of my sight, I could see the trees surrounding this clearing. The had apparently hidden in the woods.

Fox and I kept moving, but slowed our pace to watch what was going on. We shuffled through the open space, watching to see what would unfold. We did not have to wait long.

A moment later, a lone figure appeared at the opposite end of the clearing. The figure was small, and walked the way a person did when they were exhausted. Its shoulders were slumped with fatigue and the feet barely came off the ground as it walked. The figure was wrapped in oddly stiff robes as it shuffled towards us. It was holding something.

Fox's staff flared once. In response, Fox altered our course so that we were going more towards the outside of the clearing, rather than straight ahead. I did not question the change in course. "Shui could see that the way we were headed was going to put us in danger. This path is safer." Fox said. "Remember, keep moving." He said.

The girl, (because I had the distinct impression that it was a girl) walked towards us. I could faintly hear a whimpering coming from her. As the girl walked towards us, I realized that the sound was coming from what she was holding. It was a baby. Or at least that's the way that it sounded.

I felt myself drawn in to what I was seeing. Or at least I suspected what was happening.

The girl drew closer. The 'cloak' she was wearing shifted awkwardly as she hobbled down the road. Then, like a nightmare, the demons call sounded again. This time it came from the distant woods.

The girl's head whipped around looking for the source of the sound. The girl took off running, clutching the baby to her. She was impossibly slow compared to the speedy demons. The horde of rushed in from several different sides. They sprinted across the open ground between the distant trees and the girl. Some of them ran on all fours. The demons snarled, the 'girl' panted, and the baby cried.

When they got close, the demons leaped into the air, pouncing on the girl and tackling her. The baby went flying. As one ravenous group, the beaver-rat demons changed targets, pouncing on the baby. I lost track of what was happening in the flurry of limbs and snarling. I heard the baby crying and screaming amidst the snarls. I would have stopped to watch the savage carnage, but Fox pulling me forward saved me.

It was horrible and I wanted to look away. But I couldn't. Just when I thought that I could not take anymore, a figure could be seen leaping over the others. It was a dynamic leap. The figure's wooden clothes were thrown off as it hurtled through the air. The figure barreled into the center of the group, joining the feeding frenzy. In the moment, she held up the wooden 'baby's' arm triumphantly, before greedily stuffing it into her mouth.

It took me a second to realize that that figure been the 'girl'. She had apparently played her part, and was now devouring the carved 'baby' with the others. I could hear 'her' making a dwindling sound of a baby shrieking, despite all of the snarling and snapping of jaws. She had been making the baby sound all along!

Demons attacked not only the baby, but also each other. They tore into each other with savage, blade-tipped fingers. Teeth flashed as some demons bit each other. As before, instead of bleeding their wounds began to issue a foul black smoke instead of blood.

The big demon that had sounded the initial horn seemed to be enjoying beating the others. The baby had not last very long as a diversion. Once it had been chewed up, there was still too much violent energy for them to just quit. The biggest demon was taking advantage of this time. I watched as he picked up a rock and swung it viciously into the face of the demon next to him. The first demon roared in delight, while the second one roared in... pain or... something else.

The demons face split open, displaying the cracked skull beneath. I watched, transfixed, as smoke hissed out from the broken face. One strange thing I noticed was that the demon's teeth were part of its skull. Seeing this reminded me of a beaver skeleton I had found in the woods once when I was younger. Was it possible that these were... beaver demons?

"They pretend to be humans screaming to enhance their excitement. Fascinating... It's tough to watch, but fascinating." Fox said. We kept moving. Fox continued his musing as we walked. "One demon plays the victim. It appears that this is a 'victim' trained to act as a vulnerable human. It is a type of interactive performance.

"But then I would have to wonder how the victim demon was chosen. Was it because of their small size? Or would it be based on the ability to make two voices? Or are they selected like a civic obligation? Does every demon in the village have to do it at some point?"

We walked on, and I expected that the cavern would again close up to become a narrow tunnel. I expected that the demon road would stay narrow. Fortunately, I was disappointed. The cavern, as I thought of the chamber we were in, got bigger and bigger. Soon it felt like the whole mountain was hollow and we were walking through that giant central space. The roof was so high above us that it might as well have been the sky. The only difference was that the roof didn't have the red tint of the sky 'outside' of the mountain.

I was doing my best to think through everything that it happened to us so far. But I still had some questions. "Fox? Why did those demons put off smoke when they got hurt?" I asked.

"Not every demon is the same, but beings like those are created of fire. Well, it's more than fire. But for the purpose of this discussion, the understanding works well enough. It is fire, and a form of evil, that provides their life force. It is not a living spirit, pumping living blood through a living body. So when they are cut or injured, there is no blood to come out. Instead, their internal fire, and rot, begins to escape. This comes out in the form of black smoke, or a tar-smoke. If we had stayed around a little longer, we would have seen that the smoke healed their injuries. In this place, beings like that cannot die." He said.

Then, as an afterthought, Fox continued. "Did you notice that the wood they use splinters very easily?" I nodded and he went on. "I can't be sure, but I think I know how they use this. You saw the smoke from all of the injuries once the frenzy began. And while they cannot die, they can feel pain. I suspect that for beings like those, pain is better than an absence of sensation. I think that they choose to fill their mouths with splinters, because the pain enhances their experience. The pain makes their existence richer, more real, adding to the experience just like the screaming. It adds another dimension to their fantasy hunt."

From our place on the road, inside the mountain, I couldn't tell if we were going the right way. But I supposed that Fox, keeping in touch with his staff, would let me know. So we kept walking, but I started to feel ill. I was feeling lightheaded and tired, and my body seemed heavier than normal.

The monotony of lifting my heavy feet and putting them in front of each other over and over again made my mind start to go numb. I felt many things, but fatigue was at the top of the list. For the first time, it occurred to me that I was sleepy.

Being sleepy made me think back to when I had slept on the ferry. There was something that I have been wondering about since then, but had not asked. "Fox, I have a question about when we were on the ferry." He did not say anything, but only kept walking, and waited for me to go on. "When I fell asleep back on the ferry, was that some kind of spell? Did the Arkyala knock me out?"

Fox looked at me with surprise. "I did not expect your mind to go in that direction. But no, the Arkyala did not 'knock you out'. It did give you one impression, however. You might not have realized it at the time, the Arkyala let you know that you were in a safe place. It let you know that harm would not come to you. You slept on your own. And honestly, you needed it. Didn't you feel much better afterwards?" I thought back. I certainly had felt better, but I thought that was because of Fox's rune-inscribed robe, not the power of restful sleep.

"We have been through a lot, Kwan. You, more than me. You were the one who had to deal with the demon couple's illusion. You have seen things already that would break a less adaptive mind. And you have not even had the training to prepare you for what we've encountered. It is a credit to your potential and capabilities the way you have handled yourself in this realm."

I would be lying if I said that I was not proud to hear a compliment from Fox. When he recognized me, I felt like I was being recognized by a respected teacher.

We walked on, endlessly. The Hell-Fire Road seemed to go on forever. Was this mountain like Fox's bag? It didn't seem like any mountain could contain the vast distance we had traveled. In my mind, I pictured the giant hollow within the mountain shell. Fox and I were ants crawling through that enormous expanse.

Ants? Fox and I were not ants, I thought. I shook my head to clear it, but that was a mistake. I felt worse and worse. There was definitely something wrong with me. My head was aching, but I marched on. Until Fox called a stop, I was trying different techniques to keep myself awake.

At first, as I started to really feel unwell, I thought about Cho Clei. What was she doing? What kind of shape was she in? How had she been during this time? Fox had given me the impression that she was frozen in time, and for her sake I hope he was right.

For a few agonizing moments, my mind turned to the worst-case scenario; horrible visions, and nightmares. I imagined my little sister being hurt and it made me nauseous. That anger kept me awake and moving, able to ignore how weak I felt.

I also thought about Father and Mother. With them also, I hoped that Fox had been right. He had said that our time in this realm was 'outside' the rules of *our* world's time. He said that we would be able to return soon after we left. Certainly, it had been difficult to judge time in this realm. I had planned to keep track of how long we had been here, but the constant events around us made it easy to forget that plan. Now I could only guess how long we had been here, definitely days, maybe even… weeks? If time in this place ended up being the same as time at home, then both my sister and I would have been gone… for weeks. My parents would have had both of their children vanish.

I desperately hoped that Fox was right. If he wasn't, my parents would be inconsolable. I supposed the loss of both of their children within the span of a few days would overwhelm any parent. The last thing that I wanted was to worry Father or Mother. I would not disrespect my parents that way. I was doing what was necessary to look out for my family. The only reason that I was 'gone', was to bring my sister back. When I was little father had told me that Cho Clei was my responsibility. Now, I really felt that responsibility.

And now she was by herself in this strange dark place, at the mercy of a demon! I had seen demons up close and was terrified to think of what situation my sister could be in. I had to think of something else. Worrying about her was making my head ache. And my legs were trembling, I think. Because we were in the habit of not stopping, I kept walking, using my legs, so it was hard to tell what condition they were in.

Fox pulled up and said we could stop moving now. I was sure he was going to say we could rest. Instead, he said, "You don't look good Kwan…" He leaned in and peered at me. "Uh-oh, I think I have made a miscal-." Aside from a feeling of falling into darkness, that was all I could remember.

***

I woke up, it again took me several seconds before I could remember where I was. I looked around and saw Fox sitting nearby, looking at me. I was lying there with the rune-inscribed robe draped over me like a blanket.

In a rush, a flood of memories came back to me. I suddenly realized that we were still in the demon realm. Somehow, when I was unconscious, I had somewhat relaxed and forgotten that.

I sat up and looked around. The Hell-Fire Road was visible 20 or 30 paces distant. A few feet away from me, Fox was sitting with his legs crossed. He was staring at me and looked very serious. His staff, Shui, stood upright, balanced next to him. "Kwan, I owe you an apology." I was confused, what was he talking about? "I imagined that you had more energy than you did. And I did not emphasize *how* the circlets operate. I realize only now that the stress of being in this place has been draining your energy faster than I thought.

"I told you how the circlets work while we were waiting for the second village's demons to return home. But I could see at the time that you were distracted and had stopped listening. I could have made a bigger deal trying to make you aware of the cost of invisibility."

Fox went on, "The circlets perform a tremendously powerful function, rendering us fully undetectable. But, they are powered by our own energy. Because we are the power source for them, the longer we wear them and the longer we are invisible, the more tired *we* become."

Fox grimaced as he confessed. His eyes never wavered though. "At the time I thought, 'He is getting this powerful tool from me, so I have the responsibility to keep him safe.' So, I calculated how much energy you could 'spend' on powering your circlet. But I underestimated one key factor.

"I imagined that you had more energy as we travelled. I didn't realize that the stress was taking so heavy an energetic toll on you. It is, of course, completely natural and I should have foreseen this. *That* is why I owe you an apology. I should have had you take the circlet off sooner. In fact, we only really needed to wear it when passing through the actual villages."

I extracted my arm from underneath the warm robe reached up to my four head. Sure enough, the circlet was gone. Suddenly insecure, I looked around warily. I suddenly felt naked knowing that I was visible. It was surprising how quickly I had begun to rely on the feeling of being undetectable. Over the course of a few minutes, I setup and prepared myself to continue traveling. I did feel better. The subtraction of the circlet, combined with the addition of the rune inscribed robe let my energy return to full. It had not taken long, because I was young, so I naturally had a lot of energy.

I asked Fox how long I had been unconscious, and he told me it had not been very long. Again, he reassured me that time was very subjective in this place. I didn't understand so he explained it further. Somehow, I was just as confused after the explanation as before.

For example, he told me that the time I experienced was longer for me, because I needed it to heal properly. And the time while he was watching over me was shorter for him. This realm defied objective measurement, and time was one area where it was particularly flexible.

I felt reassured that I had not slowed us down too much. I understood that I had passed out because the circlet drained my energy. But I also understood that meant I hadn't been strong enough to 'pay' for the invisibility. I felt uncomfortable, bordering on shame. It was like worrying that I had disappointed Father. I needed to become stronger if I was going to save Cho Clei.

I got up and Fox and I were back on our march to the fortress castle of 'fire and bones'. As we walked the ceiling of the giant cavern seemed to get lower. At first it was just a feeling. But after a few more hours of uneventful hiking, we could see the top of the cave and we were again in a tunnel.

The tunnel out was much longer than the tunnel in. We went through an area where the tunnel was narrow enough that I had to walk behind Fox, single file. I worried that it would get smaller, but fortunately, it didn't. The narrow portion only slowed us down.

Eventually, the tunnel widened again. I expected another huge cavern, but we had reached the other side of the underground Hell-Fire Road. The last cavern was so large that, for a moment, I wasn't certain if we were outside or not. I wasn't sure until I looked up.

The tunnel opened up to expose a red-hued, mountain sky. A point on the mountain glowed bright red above and ahead of us. That must have been our destination, but it was larger than it had been... I could just barely make out a castle's shape in the middle of that red spot. It looked like there was a large area of fire up on the mountain, surrounding the castle.

Without a word, Fox and I followed the path out of the mountain. The iron braziers were a constant as we made the transition. As we stepped out under the red sky, I felt relieved. We were still on a mountain path, but now it felt different. Even in this gray and dead place, with its faded colors, finding an exit from that subterranean hell was rejuvenating. I had not realized how much it was weighing on me being down there. It had been terrifying. But now, in new surroundings, I was more optimistic.

Our pace naturally sped up as we were, once again, *outside* of the mountain. We were still in the mountain range, and we were walking up to the peak of the biggest mountain in that range. But not having a city's worth of rock above my head improved my morale.

When we first walked out of the mountain tunnel, I found the red sky reassuring. Or at least, better than being enclosed. It would have been nice to see stars, but the dark clouds and red sky were better than rock overhead.

As we walked, Fox nodded and put his staff on his back. Then he pulled his long flute from his bag. "Aren't you afraid the demons will hear us?" I asked. I had a brief memory flash into my head. It was the memory of the pack of beaver-rat demons racing in to devour the wooden 'baby'. They had been so fast, flooding out of the woods and closing in from all directions. They had been sprinting low, like a pack of wolves, teeth bared.

But Fox smiled and shook his head, "Shui has checked and found that we are 'in between' dangers. There is nothing dangerous too close to us. A little music might help us!"

"How close to us is too close?" I asked, worriedly. But Fox only winked and started playing. He played as we walked. This time the melody was upbeat and easy to repeat in my head as we walked. Soon, I felt very good as we marched on. I felt energetic and much more cheerful than I had before. I could say it now, but before I was feeling more stressful than I would have admitted.

As Fox played and we walked, the terrain changed. At first, we were walking up a rocky slope toward the red spot up on the mountain. There we would find the demon that kidnapped my sister. But then the rocky incline flattened out, becoming a wide plain covered in grassy weeds.

I would have called it a grassy meadow if it had been green and sunny. But the red-hued, dark sky was clearly more like night than day. And a sinister night, too. The dead, gray field we were crossing went to the horizon, before rising sharply, becoming the last incline to the peak.

The last incline??? I had to look again, our position just then dawning on me. Somehow, we were much closer to our destination. That was why the red spot had looked larger! I felt slow for not realizing it before. Somehow, we went *down* into the mountain, and came out *high above* where we went in.

I wanted to ask Fox how this was possible, but he seemed happy playing his flute and I didn't want to interrupt him. His playing really was good. It was a rejuvenating, alive and beautiful in this dark place.

Chapter 14

The Shomyira

Despite our brisk pace hiking across the field, Fox had no trouble playing the flute. I was managing our pace without getting *out* of breath, but I certainly didn't have enough wind left over to play a flute. Apparently, he was very fit under that fat belly, and had amazing breath control.

As we crossed the great field of weeds, I spotted a point of yellow light flickering in the distance ahead of us. "Fox!" I said, pointing across the field to the light. He nodded and kept walking and playing. Fox seemed relaxed, but I had serious misgivings. We continued walking, steadily getting closer to the light.

As we got closer, we could see that the light was coming from a small camp fire. The silhouette of a single figure could be seen sitting next to that fire. My wariness increased. Who was this figure? The little fire was directly in our path. It was impossible for us to miss it.

When we got close enough to see the figure clearly, I relaxed a little. The figure was my height, which was somehow reassuring. Also, the figure gave the impression of being a female, even though she was wearing a hooded cloak that hid her face in shadow. The cloak was made from a shimmering, silver material. The silver cloak flashed occasionally as we got closer to her, reflecting the yellow firelight. I also felt confident the figure was female because of her narrow shoulders.

We approached. Fox played his flute, I followed. Soon I could see that it was indeed a female shape wrapped in a silver cloak. The cloak itself had a hypnotic quality. In this world where everything was gray, the cloak was silver. It flashed a golden color in the yellow firelight. The woman wore the cloak's hood up, and it was deep enough to completely mask her features. She was kneeling, waiting for us. Her posture was erect, her hands clasped in front of her. Fox stopped his playing. I heard the fire hissing and popping as we stepped close.

I waited for Fox to speak. He was apparently waiting for her to speak. She studied us for a long moment. While I couldn't see her face, her hood was turned toward us. I could feel the gaze studying me. Then she said, "This one has been waiting for you, GaleMaster."

Fox put his flute away, never taking his eyes off of the woman. "Show yourself." Fox replied. Then, as a deliberate afterthought, "Please." He took Shui from the satchel's loop, behind his back. Fox held the staff in both hands, vertically. The small end was planted in the sand. "Who, or what are you?" Fox asked. It was quiet, except for the sounds of the fire.

The woman raised her hands from her lap. I noticed that her hands were wearing gloves the same color as her cloak. She took the hood and pushed it back, over her head. I nearly gasped in surprise. She might have been female, but she wasn't a human woman. Her face was that of a silver snake.

The snake face was roughly the same size as a human face (maybe a little wider), but the similarity ended there. The face projected outward, tapering to end in a squared, silver, snout. Her head was smooth, with no ears and no hair at all. She didn't even have eyebrows. Her eyes were silver with vertical, black pupils, like a cat. Similar to a snake, her eyes were positioned on the sides of her head. Her skin was the same color as her cloak... Then I realized that her skin *was* the cloak. Her exposed hand and face skin had faint outlines that looked like scales.

Her mouth was a black line that wrapped from one side of her face to the other. When she spoke, the whole face parted, "This one iss The Shomyira. We come on an errand, GaleMasster." She placed a faint emphasis on the 's' sounds.

Fox's demeanor changed, from suspicious to… something I couldn't recognize. It was like an explorer finding something new. "You are of the Yira? I have never met one of your kind before." The snake woman simply nodded. Then Fox bowed at the waist, but stayed standing. He said, "Respect to the Yira." Fox bowed two more times. The snake woman looked pleased. "Why have you sought us out?"

Her eyes blinked, the eyelids sliding sideways across her eyes. She appeared to think about the question. "The Shomyira has come... because the Yira follow the Yala this sscycle."

Fox smiled, "I asked the wrong question. Excuse me, Shomyira." He bowed again. "What is your errand?"

"Ah... the purpose for finding you was ssimple. We are a messsenger, performing a delivery." She looked back and forth between us. "We come to deliver the blesssing of the Arkyala to you."

The fox seemed surprised to hear this. He straightened up and looked over at me. His eyebrows were up, and an expression of surprise. Although, to be honest, there was nothing in this entire realm that had failed to surprise me. He spoke, "We are very grateful that the Arkyala has sent you. I was only surprised, because I did not expect the blessing to take this form." He paused and glanced over at me. "If The Shomyira does not mind, I will explain a few things to my young companion. A small bit of background information will help him to understand what is happening now."

The Shomyira seemed to see the wisdom of his approach, and nodded her agreement. Fox turned to me. "Beings like the Ragyala and the Arkyala belong to a group, called the Yalans. Another group of beings were qualified to guard the boundaries between realms. This group is the Yirans. They take turns guarding the boundaries. And whichever side is in command, while they are 'serving', Yalan or Yiran, have their already-tremendous power enhanced." He paused and turned back to the silver snake woman. "Is that an accurate way to describe it?" Fox asked.

The Shomyira seemed to think about the question very carefully. "Your description is adequate. During this celestial cycle, we follow the Yala. During the next celestial cycle, the Yala will follow usss. Thiss is the way it has been since the beginning."

Fox went on with his explanation. "When the Yalans serve as the guardians, the Yirans are their elite helpers. Likewise, when the Yirans serve, the Yalans are their elite helpers. They are elite, because they not only possess their own power, but also their own judgement."

The explanation seemed clear so far. I nodded to show that I was following. I felt hesitant to talk, recognizing that I was out of my depth. Fox continued, "If you'll recall, when we first crossed over into this realm, the Ragyala blessed us." I nodded, remembering. "That blessing was similar to a gold coin. It was similar to money in that it could be spent in different situations. The guardians of the boundary between realms have the power to grant these kinds of blessings.

"But there are other kinds of blessings that they can give as well. It appears that The Shomyira is one of those blessings. And Kwan, an enhanced Yalan blessing is a special gift. We are fortunate." This time, it was the Yiran who nodded. She seemed pleased at how well we grasped the situation.

"When the Arkyala blessed you, he enhanced the blesssing, asssigning it to Shomyira to fulfil. So, I have some flexibility about the *forms*. I can choose what *form* of help to give you..." She blinked, and again the eyelid slid across they eye from the side.

Fox spoke softly, "And what form of help did you decide would be most useful?" He asked. "Will you travel with us, as an ally and guide in this place?" The Yalan stared at Fox for a long time before speaking.

"There are ssome limitss as to how much I can help you. But if I had been in the possition of the Arkyala, I also would have rewarded your effortsss, Sso I would like to help you as much as I can. But accompanying you is not a possssibility." I looked over at Fox. He seemed disappointed, but not surprised.

"In truth, you need more than one form of assistance. Generally, the most usseful thing a being can have is information. I will be giving you advance information about what lies ahead." The Shomyira said. As she finished speaking, a flurry of lightning bolts struck the red spot up on the mountain. Fox and I both snapped our gazes up to the lightning.

Immediately, our attention returned to Shomyira. "The besst way would be you lissstening to everything I'm going to tell you. Ssome thought has been given to how thiss will be arranged. If you have any questionss at the end, you can ask to have them clarified, but that may not be posssible. I would ssuggest that you let me finish all of the information first, before asking questionsss." Fox and I both nodded.

The Shomyira continued, "You have done a very good job in making it thiss far. It was a combination of sskill and luck that enabled you to sssurvive the demonic villagess. I will warn you that there is ssome force asssisting you in your journey through thiss realm, but it iss well-hidden. It has been following you since you entered this realm.

"After you continue passt this meeting, you will eventually (in the next few days) reach a labyrinth." Lightning struck as the snake woman pronounced the word 'labyrinth'. "This labyrinth iss, in many wayss, a stone death-trap. There are numerouss beingss inside the labyrinth. Some are mindless beasts, some are cunning, but all of them will be trying to stop you. Even the walls and plants can be hostile. In addition there are many mechanical trickss and boobytrapss from when the maze wasss created.

As I listened to her, my ears were becoming accustomed to her snake-like speech. Her overemphasis of the 's' sounds was less and less noticeable to me.

"There is one threat that iss bigger than any of the otherss. It'ss lair is at the center of the maze. This is a single being, a monstrouss half-demon and half-animal. That creature iss called the Kaitaur." There was a flash of lightning as she said the name. "It is extremely dangerous. It is also completely dead."

"Dead?!?" I blurted out. I was surprised and had forgotten that I agreed to keep quiet until the end. The Shomyira did not seem surprised or upset at my outburst. She seemed calm, more than anything else.

She answered, "Yes, the Kaitaur is… a shell. It is a shell constructed by a demon necromancer. The demon buildsss… twisted thingss. Insside, it is filled with a *dark* energy." I looked over at Fox. He looked serious, eyes narrowed as we listened. "The energy is made up of hatred for life, combined with a residual instinct from the animal spiritss that were used to create it. Itss lack of living intelligence makes the Kaitaur much more difficult to deal with. As a threat, it cannot be reassoned with, and hass enough power to destroy you both." I found myself looking into the small fire as The Shomyira spoke.

"The demonic portion of the Kaitaur will be recognizable to you. The animal portion is a combination of attributes from animals in your living world. As a result, the Kaitaur is strong, has an abundance of mindless motivation, innate weaponry, and a beast's instinct to kill. Relative to you, the Kaitaur is extremely strong. It'sss bone clawsss are poisonouss to life- they will easily kill."

I was inclined to ask a question about this terrifying sounding creature, but since Fox was quiet, I decided to emulate his example.

The Shomyira went on, "We are restricted in how much we can tell you about how to pass this creature. It is a grave and legitimate challenge upon your path to save the innocent."

Fox held up his hand to stop her. He asked, "Is there nothing else that you can tell us about how to beat this creature?" The Shomyira looked up at him and seemed to abruptly change the subject.

She said, "We could not help but admire the sssound of your flute as you first approached. The GaleTemple understands some of the power of sound. In many situations, musical talent can be as powerful as martial talent." This was not what either of us expected. "Music has different effects on many different creatures. Some creatures can see music. Others are blinded by it. Some can be confused by music, and some seek sleep." When Fox asked for a way to beat the Kaitaur, my hopes soared that it might be easier than it first appeared. But The Shomyira was apparently changing the subject. I remember thinking, who cared about music?! But I wouldn't dream of being disrespectful like that. It was disappointing though. We didn't find out how to beat the Kaitaur, but there was no harm in asking.

"One particular danger of the labyrinth is that creatures work together. They develop relationships that benefit both of them. The Kaitaur has developed just such a relationship with smaller creatures that also live in the labyrinth. These little creatures serve the Kaitaur. It is not entirely clear how each benefits from the relationship, but their alliance existss. So, you will need to defend against them while you confront the Kaitaur.

"There are other dangers in the labyrinth, both traps and creatures, but you will have to manage them as you find them." She stopped speaking and looked back and forth between us. Fox took this opportunity to ask a question.

"What can you tell us about the demon necromancer that created the Kaitaur?" he asked. The snake-woman made an almost imperceptible smile as he did. It was the smallest twitch at the corner of her mouth. It was… pleasure at having the right questions asked.

The Shomyira said, "This demon necromancer is remarkably powerful, by the standards of this realm. It is uncommon for a demon to be intelligent enough to create a plan, much less to create an entire lesser demon. But it appears that this demon has been creating other servants.

"The Kaitaur is one of thosse servants and a perfect example of the demon's work. It is able to work with both the corpses and spirits of deceased beings that end up in this realm. It is posssible that you will recognize aspects of the Kaitaur, since an animal from your realm was used to construct it."

"Your besst option with many dangerss here, is to use the 'ShadowLoops'. When she spoke the word, it sounded strange to my ears. It was similar to when the demon couple had clouded my mind with illusions. After that, I had been able to understand the word 'SoulCage' even though it had not been spoken in a human language.

When The Shomyira spoke the word, an image appeared in my mind. It was an overlay of two separate concepts in my mind. The first was the concept of shade or shadow, something that hides other things. The second was the concept of a loop, or a ring. A moment later, an image of the circlets came into my mind. Apparently, the circlets that we wore to become visible- were the 'ShadowLoops'.

But the ShadowLoop drained too much of my energy for me to use it. So, I would be visible inside, even when Fox was invisible. I felt a hollow pit form in my stomach. But even as panic grew within me, I did not speak. Instead, I tried to think brave thoughts. If it was going to be extra dangerous for me, it didn't matter. I would take any risk to bring back Cho Clei. I felt Fox's gaze on me.

But before my panic could progress any further, Fox spoke, "The Shomyira, that proposes a problem for us." He gestured to me, without taking his eyes off of her. "My companion is physically quite large, but he is still young. The 'ShadowLoops' draw more energy from him than he can sustainably create. With training, he could certainly learn how to rapidly replenish that energy. But the last time he wore one, they robbed him of his strength, incapacitating him."

I wanted to hang my head, feeling shame rise. I was the one that wasn't strong enough. I was just a liability to Fox. I would have pursued that thought further, but Fox turned and put a hand on my shoulder.

He turned back and continued to speak to The Shomyira, "I would not use the protection of a 'ShadowLoop' if my companion cannot." I felt a wave a relief wash through me.

"We came to this realm together, and he is my responsibility. You know our mission; to bring back his sister." Fox gestured to me. "But, as far as I am able, I plan to keep him safe as well. If he can't use a 'ShadowLoop', I won't either." Then after another moment, "But thank you for delivering the Arkyala's blessing."

The Shomyira did not seem surprised. Her serpentine face did not change its expression at first. Then, her mouth widened into a smile. "The ethics of the GaleTemple are known among both the Yala and the Yira. The worthiness of your mission was assumed, and now you have left no doubt about your loyal character." The Shomyira raised her right arm and held out her hand. "The blessing has not been delivered yet." She waited.

Fox looked at her blankly. He glanced over at me, but I had no idea what she wanted. She spoke, surprising us both. "Give us the 'ShadowLoops'." Fox seemed taken aback.

"But… they are not mine to give." He said simply. "They have been loaned to me by the GaleTemple."

The Shomyira's smile grew a little wider. "You mistake our meaning, GaleMaster. We do not ask to keep them."

I looked over at Fox. He looked puzzled. "Then, why do you want them?"

This time, it was The Shomyira who looked surprised. "We came to give you the Arkyala's blessing. As we mentioned, we have flexibility in the form of the blessing. There is one piece of assistance we can offer you…" The Shomyira held her hand out placidly. A long moment later, when Fox still hadn't moved, she said, "Please."

A moment after that, Fox reached into his bag and pulled out the two circlets. He took a step forward and handed them to The Shomyira. She took the two circuits and held them in both hands. After examining them carefully, she began to speak the first few lines of an incantation and the circlet's glowed in response. The small stone that was located at the forehead position on each circlet was pulsating with light that changed colors. After 10 long breaths, both stones stabilized as shiny black beads. An occasional current of electricity like a spark ran over each stone every few seconds.

She looked up and offered the circlets back to Fox. He took the circuits back uncertainly and looked back at her questioningly. Clearly, he was as puzzled as I was. "What… what did you do to them?"

The Shomyira explained, "Devices like the shadow loops have a few different activation modes. They are largely concerned with how each 'ShadowLoop' gets its power to act. In one mode, beings with ample power who would not notice a drain on their energy, become the power source for the circlet.

"In another mode, when different pathways are activated, the 'ShadowLoops' have an ability to power themselves. Or, to be more accurate, they draw their power from the emptiness between realms.

"As you know, GaleMaster, empty space holds limitless energy…" Shomyira was saying.

I was trying to follow what Shomyira was saying, but I didn't understand. Forgetting myself again, I blurted out, "Limitless energy from the air??!"

The Shomyira turned to me. "Not from the air you breathe. The empty space between the air." I still didn't understand, but I realized that I should be quiet and listen. "The 'ShadowLoops' have the ability to draw their power from that emptiness. That mode has now been activated."

"So…" Fox began.

The Shomyira nodded, "Now the two of you will be able to wear the 'ShadowLoops' when you need them. They will no longer be a drain to your energy. *This*, is the Arkyala's blessing." She made a gesture, pressing her palms together.

Fox bowed. Relief immediately following comprehension, I bowed as well. "Our gratitude is profound. We thank the Yala and the Yira for this valuable gift." He straightened up, and I immediately did the same. "But, how is this done? In the

GaleTemple, little is actually known about the 'ShadowLoops'. How did you switch the modes?

The Shomyira had no hair at all, not even eyebrows. But the area over her eye, where an eyebrow would have been, arched in a very human expression. She answered, "The beings that made the 'ShadowLoops' lived a very long time ago, by the standards of man. But the Yira and the Yala were before them. I remember meeting two of them, here, in this realm."

"Here?!" I blurted out again, immediately embarrassed. Fox was thinking and didn't seem to mind my questions. He had that faraway look in his eyes again.

"Yes. Many beings who do not 'belong' in this place still manage to come here. The Yira and the Yala have interacted with members of their world, because every advanced society learns to travel the realms eventually.

"They considered themselves natural scientists, and did have an advanced understanding of spirit and the natural laws. They were able to advance far, because they had more time than other groups. In other words, they were an old civilization, lasting much longer than most. They studied the energy of vibrations and the mind. That, combined with a natural talent for creating, let them invent and build devices. And the longer they studied, the more they learned. Their creations became more powerful and more sophisticated. The ShadowLoop is perhaps the least powerful of the things they developed, but it should give you some idea of their level of skill.

"Both the Yira and the Yala have access to insights which are beyond that race's knowledge. Because our understanding surpasses theirs, nothing they ever created was a mystery to *us*. Both understanding their devices and modifying them is not challenging for us. That is how it was possible for us to change the mode of your ShadowLoops."

Fox looked down at the ShadowLoops in his hand. He looked impressed to me. He looked up at me and smiled. Deeper relief than before flooded through me as I knew that we would be invisible, like before. It had been reassuring to think that Fox would not have let me be in danger alone. But both of us being invisible gave me much more confidence in our chances.

The Shomyira began again, "You confess the GaleTemple knows little of the ShadowLoops." It was not a question, it was a statement. Fox nodded anyway. "We offer a few other insights to you. You may already know them, but we feel obliged to warn you." Fox didn't need to tell me- I knew to pay attention.

"First, know that the Shadow has its limits," she began. It took me a moment before I realized that invisibility was what Shomyira called 'the Shadow'. It made perfect sense when I thought about it. "You may know of situations where some forces will cancel out other forces?" Fox nodded. I just watched and listened.

"The same will happen when your music encounters the Shadow. Understand that when you play music, the ShadowLoops will not work, and you will be visible to the demons. Music is powerful vibration, and will break the action of the circlets. So be very clear, if you make music, you will be visible."

Fox seemed alarmed or that he was bracing himself after receiving bad news, "I... see." He apparently 'saw', but I couldn't see. I didn't understand why it was important. If music broke the ShadowLoops, then don't play music.

The Shomyira continued, "Another limit of the Shadow is that some beings can see through it. For example, even wearing the ShadowLoops, the Yala and the Yira can still perceive you." Fox nodded. He had apparently already known that. I hadn't. What other beings could see us, even when we were 'invisible'? Seemingly in answer to my question, she responded, "Or, the spirit you call Shui, in this staff, can see through the Shadow." The Shomyira gestured to Fox's staff. I suppose that didn't surprise me. From what I had seen, the staff was full of abilities. "You will be able to hide your presence from the lesser demons of the labyrinth, but the Kaitaur will still be able to sense you, even hidden by the

Shadow. It won't be able to 'see' you, but it has other senses that will be able to detect you well enough to hunt you.

"Winged ones and the Trickster will be able to see through the shadow as well." The Yira said.

This time it was Fox who spoke. "Winged ones... ok. And who is the Trickster?" I looked back and forth between them.

"The Trickster is the last danger I can warn you about. If you run into the Trickster, beware him. He will not harm you, but he will try to get you to harm yourself." The Shomyira did not seem particularly bothered by that, but it deeply disturbed me. It would get *me* to harm *myself*???

Fox asked, "Is this Trickster the one that has been watching us since we got here?"

But the Yira only shook her snake-like head. "The Trickster would not be helpful, but whatever has been following you in this realm is... asssisssting you. It has warded off scertain threats along your journey. It has been... pressserving you." Then The Shomyira bowed.

"We have conveyed the Arkyala's blessing, and told you all that we can. Remember what you have been told." The Shomyira stopped speaking. Fox and I stood there staring at the Yira. The Shomyira sat there looking up at us.

I was going to ask something when The Shomyira disappeared. I don't remember what I was going to ask, but one instant, I was about to speak, the next instant, she was gone. The Shomyira had just vanished, leaving us standing next to the fire. We stood there, facing the fire, and the spot the Yira had just occupied. I had seen giant cat-men and lightning demons, but seeing something just 'blink' out of existence was unnerving.

I stood there dumbly, but Fox reached into his bag. He said, "They aren't much for saying good bye, are they?" He winked at me. "Oh well, we certainly shouldn't waste a fire! Have a seat. Let's have a cup of tea." With a wide smile, he pulled the teapot from his bag.

***

After two cups of tea (which my body didn't need) and a rest (which my mind did), I felt refreshed and ready to go. Fox had patiently answered the questions that had occurred to me. I had learned a tremendous amount about a subject most people never knew existed.

I learned inconsequential things, like the fact the Yalans looked like human-felines, while the Yira look like human-serpents. I learned about the hierarchies that administrate the GaleSource.

With the tea finished and our plans clear, Fox packed up. He handed me the ShadowLoop circlet as we prepared to leave. I have to admit that I felt relieved to get it back. It represented tangible security in a place where everything was threatening. I wanted to put it on immediately, but I wasn't sure if I should. I looked askance at Fox. "Can I... can I put this back on?"

Fox did not have to consider long. He nodded quickly and as I put my ShadowLoop on, he put his on too. "Before, I would have had us wait until we were closer to danger before putting them on, because I knew that the ShadowLoops would drain our energy. But now, since The Shomyira has changed that, we can wear them all the time. Truly, it really is an invaluable gift."

I felt a sense of relief as soon as I put the circlet over my forehead. I imagined that Fox also felt the same way. There was a heady feeling that came knowing that you were invisible. The feeling started as security but quickly turned into bold confidence. It was enjoyable.

And with that, now invisible to any watching demons, we continued our march into the mountains. Since we knew that the labyrinth waiting ahead of us, we kept straining to see when it would present itself.

I wouldn't have imagined before that rescuing my little sister would involve so much hiking. I wondered if, after this was all through, if we could rescue my sister and bring her home, would my legs be more muscular? It felt like we hiked up the rocky trail for hours and hours.

One thing about me was that I like to have advanced information if possible. I like to be able to know what is coming. And, ideally, I would have a plan about what to do. "Fox, what are we going to do? What is our plan going to be?" Fox did not stop hiking, but he did look over and speak as we walked.

"Well Kwan, we will try to do as The Shomyira recommended. when we get to the labyrinth, hopefully our newly enhanced shadow loops can hide us as we sneak through. We will rely on my staff to guide us through the maze. Shui should be able to tell us which directions will lead us best avoid trouble. When we get to the Kaitaur is where things get challenging. Ideally, we would be able to use the shadow loops to stay invisible and sneak past the Kaitaur. But since it will be able to detect us, regardless of the ShadowLoops, that poses a different problem." Fox said.

I nodded emphatically. "I know! I was following what The Shomyira was saying. I hoped that she would tell us how to get around the Kaitaur, but she wasn't very helpful." I tried to keep the disappointment out of my voice but I knew that was probably apparent to Fox.

"What do you mean?" Fox asked.

"Well, she didn't tell us how to beat the monster. I was hoping that she would give us a clue to help us get through the danger." I said.

Fox turned and explained patiently to me as we walked, "The Shomyira did give us a clue. It won't necessarily be easy, but The Shomyira did point the way for us."

I was confused, "She did? You asked her, and she changed the subject! We wanted help, and she just started talking about music. I guess she didn't want to come out and say no to us, so it was easier to change the subject.'

Fox threw back his head and gave a booming laugh. It was so loud that it startled me. I looked around, panicked that a demon might have heard him, but then I remembered the

ShadowLoops. Even if a demon was standing next to him, it would not be able to hear him. "When the Yira talked about music, she wasn't changing the subject. She was pointing us toward a solution. We just have to read between the brushstrokes. She was letting us know that music could subdue the Kaitaur, and let us pass it. Think back to what Shomyira told us."

I tried to remember everything Shomyira had said, but it was already clear to me that Fox's mind was trained to a much higher level than my own. It had not been that long since we were sitting before Shomyira, but already the details felt fuzzy.

But for Fox, the events were clear. "She mentioned that she admired the sound of my flute. Then she pointed out that music could be as powerful as the martial arts."

I did remember that. I said as much. Fox went on, "Then the Yira talked about how music can affect different creatures in different ways, blinding them, confusing and weakening them, even putting them to sleep."

Comprehension started to dawn on me. "So playing music is the key?!" I had completely missed it.

Fox agreed, clapping me on the back. "That was my understanding. But I wanted to check to make sure that I was right. So I asked Shui if it could add anything." I clapped my hand to my forehead. Of course! I had forgotten about Shui. "Shui has knowledge of beings like the Kaitaur. Apparently, golems like it have been made before. And all of them have the same weakness. Music…"

"Music? Why?" I asked.

"Shui believes it is because the process used to create beings like the Kaitaur, always leaves out the key component that makes them 'alive'. While parts of demon spirits animate the Kaitur and make it move around, it does not have an immortal spirit- at the GaleTemple we call that the 'soul'. The ability to process music is somehow linked to this 'soul'. Simply put, creatures without a soul, cannot deal with hearing music. It overwhelms them. For a creature like the Kaitaur, we will hope the music would blind it, then put it to sleep." Fox explained.

"You remember me talking about the hierarchies of powerful beings, with the Source/HighGod at the top." I did. He went on. "The highest levels of power are occupied beings with souls. In fact, the most powerful demons even have a type of souls. They aren't quite like our souls, but their 'souls' have similar value in *some* key ways... But we don't have to worry about that, since the Kaitaur is not one of those demons. It *is* dangerous, certainly. But its power will never approach the levels of his master. Even though none of the demons are alive, we can only collect demons with a certain level of spirit. Otherwise the SoulCage won't bother..." Fox concluded.

"Oh! So we are in good shape! We will be invisible, sneak in, you'll play music to put the Kaitaur to sleep, then we'll sneak out on the other side!" I had another moment of gratitude that Fox was here. Without his training and power, I had no chance of dealing with this realm on my own. There were so many things I would have missed, or misunderstood. And there were an even greater number of things that would have killed me. "That sounds simple enough!" I said.

"Well, not quite. Think back to the other warnings Shomyira gave us. It looks like music will let us overcome the Kaitaur. But music will also overcome the ShadowLoops' power, so we will be visible. And while we are visible, the Kaitaur's helpers will be able to see us and attack us. I doubt it will be simple, Kwan." His tone was kind, but everywhere my mind turned, I saw I was out of my depth.

We both fell into silence as we hiked up the mountain. The glowing red spot (and the fortress at its center) grew clearer as we got closer. For the first time, I could see the castle. From this distance, it looked tiny, perched high up on the mountain. The sky had a red hue. Combined with the red glow surrounding the castle, it felt like we were approaching fire. I even imagined it was getting hotter, the closer we got to the castle. I was so busy looking up, trying to make out the castle's detail that I ran into Fox's outstretched arm. Startled, I looked up to see why he had blocked my path. Ahead of us, the

HellFire Road split into two different paths. Both choices pointed up toward the castle, so both choices looked reasonable.

Fox spoke to Shui and the staff balanced on its own. I had seen the process several times before, and knew what to expect as Fox asked for direction. Like before, the staff fell. Like before, the staff stopped at knee height. It was pointing to the path on the left. But unlike before, Shui jumped over to point at the path on the right. A moment later, the staff jumped back again. The metal grain running through the ironwood flashed brightly and seemed to leap up into Fox's hand.

"Don't move, and stay calm Kwan. Act casual. Shui is unable to determine the way. Something strange is going on. And, we are… being watched." Fox kept his voice deliberately low.

"But, but, we're invisible!" I whispered back insistently. No one should be able to see us! Shui flashed again, brightly enough that I blinked. Apparently, this time, it had flashed in warning, because when I opened my eyes, a figure was dancing before us.

It took me a few hard moments of staring at the figure to make sure of what I was seeing. Facing us, ahead on the path, was me. Or rather, it was an imperfect copy of me. He was wearing the same clothing that I was. But his clothes were all a uniform clay gray color. It was like I was looking in an old dirty mirror.

Perhaps strangest of all, he seemed happy. A wide smile stretched his (my) face. The smile was wider than I could have made my smile. It was like the mouth was made of dumpling dough that had been stretched too wide. The eyes, however, were not smiling.

I would have said that the figure was standing there, but it was doing a hypnotic swaying back and forth, moving its arms around in a way that I could only describe as dancing. I hadn't danced often in life, but it certainly was not the way I dance. It was unnatural. His movements were flowing like he was underwater. His limbs looked like the bones were noodles.

It was somehow more off-putting than I can describe. Seeing my face stupidly grinning back at me and dancing in place made me want to back away as much as any of the demons we had encountered so far.

"I would surmise that this is the Trickster. Let me speak for us…" Fox said to me in a low voice. Oh! That made sense. Shomyira had warned us that the Trickster would be able to see us, even if we were wearing the ShadowLoops. And she warned us to beware of him. I was instantly on my guard.

He called out to the figure in a language I didn't speak, "You must be the Trickster!" The figure was still staring at me. Somehow, I had understood what Fox had said! It must have been an ability left over from the old demon couple on the bridge! The possibility that occurred to me was intoxicating… Maybe I could understand *any* language now!

"Fox!" I hissed, trying to contain my excitement. "I can understand what you're saying!" I trailed off, as the figure before us paused in his dancing and bowed in agreement. His eyes were locked on me the entire time. Then he went back to dancing. Apparently, he was admitting he was the Trickster. That was disappointing. Somehow admitting his identity didn't seem very tricky to me.

Fox looked over at me, eyes wide, then narrowing in calculation. He looked back at the Trickster. "Are you here to attack us?" he called. The Trickster, still dancing, still wearing the same dopey smile, slid his gaze over to Fox. The Trickster shook his head slowly.

The Trickster then opened its too-wide mouth and spoke in the same language Fox had used. "Not here to hurt you, *fren*! Came to help! Yooouuuu understann'?" Again, I understood! I was tempted to confirm this to Fox, but I thought it best to stay quiet. Not only did I understand the meaning of the Trickster's words, I could hear that it was difficult to say the word 'friend'. It clearly was a concept that was foreign to him. I remembered what Shomyira had told us. 'Do not trust the Trickster. He is not your friend.'

Fox nodded and seemed very sincere, "What help can you offer us, friend Trickster?" I didn't understand how Fox could be so nonchalant. This figure before us was the same Trickster that Shomyira had warned us about. He was not our friend, no matter what he said. Surely Fox remembered that, I hoped.

The Trickster spoke, but continued his dancing the entire time. "Offer? Offer directions, of course. Yooouuuu understann'?" He gestured toward the split in the path, behind him. It was the oddest sensation. My ears were hearing a harsh and confusing alien tongue. But my mind was understanding, like the meaning was just absorbed.

Fox did not move. He asked, "So what would be your advice?" The Trickster looked at Fox, never breaking eye contact, still dancing. He cocked his head to the side, considering. The trickster turned, in his dancing, and looked up the path.

His/my face turned back and said, "The right path is death, *friend*." He looked away from Fox and focused his grin back on me. "So, don't take that way. Yooouuuu understann'?" The Trickster kept dancing.

"So, you recommend we take the left path?" Fox asked. He still hadn't moved. His staff stood in front of him, firmly planted in the ground. The trickster stopped his dancing finally, and bowed, signaling his assent.

I began to see several different things. I began to see that Fox was not going to rush anywhere, now that he knew we had a challenge in front of us. That challenge was a puzzle, where the trickster was pitted against us. We had to pick the correct path. He would try to trick us. But Fox understood this 'right path/wrong path riddle' game. I resolved to just sit back and watch.

Fox spoke to the Trickster, "We have been warned against you, Trickster. We know that you would confuse us into causing our own deaths." The Trickster's face, my face, looked offended and hurt. Fox went on "So if you recommend the left path, and we know that you will mislead us, then you're actually recommending the right path."

"That would be logical, wouldn't it?" Fox asked. The smile disappeared. The Trickster looked like he had been caught in mischief. Maybe it was easier for me to read nuance in the Trickster's face because it was my own.

Fox continued his reasoning. "Do you care to admit we are right? Is it true that the left path is certain death?" With a guilty look, the Trickster nodded, and hung his head in apparent shame.

"You are clever. Yooouuuu understann!" The Trickster said, looking up. He winked at me. "What you say is true. You have beaten me! Well played! The left leads to death." Then he resumed his dancing, as though music had started playing again. (But I couldn't hear any music.) Instantly, the contrite expression was wiped from his face, and replaced with the dopey grin.

Fox did not move, so neither did I. Instead, Fox reasoned on, "But, as we have already established, you are the Trickster, and not to be trusted." The Trickster's (my) face looked hurt and offended again.

"So far, you recommended a path that would have sent us to certain death, had we chosen it." The Trickster's (my) face looked mischievous and guilty.

"When caught in your deceit, you recommend the other path." The Trickster was still dancing, but looked more wary now.

"But we clearly can't trust that path, since you are still the Trickster." The Trickster's (my) face looked hurt again.

"So, we know we shouldn't pick the path on the right, because we can't trust your assistance. And we also know we shouldn't pick the path on the left, for the same reasons." I looked at the insulted and pouting expression the Trickster made with my face. His dancing even slowed like it was harder to dance through the insult.

Fox reached a hand up to his rosary as he continued to speak. "We need to know which way to go to reach the 'fortress of fire and bones'. We can never trust your advice while you are free to lie to us. We would need some way to *force* you to tell the truth. That's a big challenge for a being like you- forcing you to do *anything*." His/my face looked smug, then thoughtful and glum, sympathizing with our problem. Then the trickster shrugged and resumed his languorous dancing. His smile returned, even wider.

Fox went on, "Luckily, I am not entirely unprepared for this journey. I have several useful and valuable items I carry from the GaleTemple." The Trickster slowed its already slow dancing and cocked its head (my head) to the side. His (my) face looked suddenly wary, confused.

"One of the items I carry is able to get the information we need..." As Fox said this, the Trickster took a step back, eyes growing wide. Fox pulled the SoulStone from his rosary. "*This* is able to capture entities like you and *force* them to tell the truth..." Before Fox had finished his statement, the Trickster disappeared and the whole realm seemed to shift around us. The HellFire Road was suddenly gone. Everything around me was gone, except for a heavy mist that filled the air. I was disoriented, and shook my head to clear it.

I stood there in the mist wondering what to do next, when I heard Fox's voice next to me. "Don't move," he said. I didn't. I just stood there waiting. I felt dizzy, like I was spinning. Even though my eyes were open, all I could see was mist. I held up my hand in front of my face. I could see it, and when I looked down, I could see my body. But I couldn't see anything beyond that.

For a moment, I had an impulse to lurch forward, losing my balance. But Fox said, "Steady..." just in time for me to regain my balance. A moment later, the mist cleared.

***

My vision swam before my eyes. I would certainly have fallen, had Fox not grabbed my shoulder and pulled me back.

Disoriented, I tried to make sense of what I was seeing. Everything around me looked different.

Before, there had been the HellFire Road ahead of us, splitting into two paths, but both heading up higher onto the mountain. The demon fortress had been a spot of red above and ahead of us.

But now, Fox and I stood on the edge of a cliff. The road we thought we were on was not there. If we had taken one or two more steps, we would have fallen off that cliff. It was not as high as the bridge had been, but the fall would definitely have killed us.

If I had stumbled forward, if I had lost my balance through dizziness, I would have died. Fox had saved me again. I looked down and saw that a broad plateau stretched out below us. The land extended from the bottom of the cliff into the distance. The grounds of the plateau had walls of stone and walls of foliage arranged in a maze. From this vantage point, I could survey the enormous maze, seeing openings and 'dead ends'. Trees were even visible within the maze, it was so large. This must be the labyrinth! Beyond it, level to where we were, was the demon's fortress! Only the gulf of the labyrinth stood between us and Cho Clei.

I didn't understand what was happening, and how we were in this place. How had the castle fortress jumped closer to us again? "I... I don't understand..." I said ineffectually.

Fox spoke simply, "You saved us." My expression must have shown my confusion and skepticism. I had nearly walked off a cliff! Fox went on, "You understood their language when I spoke to it." He looked at me expectantly, but I still hadn't grasped his reasoning.

He continued, "When you were placed under the demon couple's illusion, you were able to understand their language. While it is *possible* you could retain the gift of languages, it isn't the kind of ability I would expect to stick with you, not long term." he said kindly. I tried not to look disappointed.

I had secretly been hoping that I would be able to understand all languages forever. Fox went on, "Because you could understand the Trickster's language, I could deduce that we were in an illusion, at least with *reasonable* confidence. It is possible you understand all languages, and we should perform a small test of this later, but it was unlikely. So, you understanding the Trickster suggested our senses were being clouded. It was not conclusive, but it seemed likely enough. And when the Trickster revealed itself, I only had to confirm my suspicions and break the illusion."

"Did you know he was going to walk us off a cliff?" I asked.

Fox shrugged. "It seemed likely. That, or something like it. It only made sense, considering what Shomyira had said. 'It wouldn't harm us, but it would try to get us to harm ourselves.'" He quoted.

Fox pointed at the drop-off in front of us. The HellFire Road stopped at the edge of the cliff and appeared to just end. I crept up, slowly and carefully, toward the edge. On closer inspection, I could see that the drop-off was not perfectly vertical. There was a slight slope to the drop-off that provided just enough space for narrow stairs set into the cliff face. They descended all the way to the bottom. Far below, dotted lights on either side of a line, must have been the continuation of the HellFire Road. It led all the way to what must have been the labyrinth's entrance. The dotted lights must have been the braziers on either side of the road.

Chapter 15

Labyrinth

Without preamble, Fox stepped up to the edge. He adjusted his shoulder bag and started down the long staircase. After a moment, his head was not visible from above. I looked over the edge. seeing the labyrinth below, so close, waiting, made the whole challenge feel more real. Terror spiked within me and I began to imagine the fearsome Kaitaur.

A moment later, Fox's head reappeared. He winked and said, "You're wearing your ShadowLoop. Always avoid being prematurely scared, in life. We have a mission. We have a plan. With courage and a little luck, we will get your sister back. Come on." He winked and disappeared again. With a deep breath, I followed.

***

It quickly became monotonous walking down the stairs behind Fox. The stone stairs were carved into the cliff face, and had no side rail to hold. My natural tendency was to lean away from the drop off. As we walked down, height of our descent was much longer than it had been before.

I looked over as we walked down and surveyed the labyrinth below us. The closest thing my mind could imagine to what I was saying, was a spider's web. This is to say that the labyrinth was vast and intricate, with long avenues and precisely branching off shoots.

I looked over at the castle in the distance. As we descended the steps the castle once again was rising to be above us. From this height I couldn't see much detail, and certainly not any creatures inside the labyrinth.

It appeared that the labyrinth/plateau/forest encircled the castle. It looked like the labyrinth was surrounding the castle like a moat.

Some parts of the labyrinth I could see, and other parts were completely obscured. It appeared that there were buildings inside the sprawling maze. There were places where one or more trees were collected. Their spreading branches obscured what was below them. Still, I tried to remember what I was seeing. I can only assume that Fox was doing the same thing.

After descending about 200 paces, we reached a platform. On the platform we were able to turn around, and the stairs continued, now descending the opposite direction. From this vantage point I could see that the stairs made a zigzag pattern below us, doubling back on itself, all the way down to the ground.

After the first 50 paces, I began to notice that there were pictures and messages carved into the stone of the cliff face. In the beginning, I thought it was just something to keep me entertained as we walked down.

After a while of walking down the steps, looking at and touching the carvings, I began to understand that these pictures were telling a story. Each carving was a scene from a story about the same specific demon.

After a number of steps, the meaning of the carved scenes was clear. This demon was horrible, violently crushing a string of other demons. Carving after carving showed the demon slaying demon after demon. It was often written in that strange language that only Fox could read. But most of the time, the pictures were self-explanatory.

The message was simple. This demon was scary and facing it was a guaranteed death. But the way the message was received was not simple. When I looked at the pictures carved into the cliff face, they were just vivid pictures, and I had to figure out what was happening in each one. But if I reached out to touch the image, an *understanding* came into my mind. It was a combination of the image, combined with complete and instant comprehension of the scene. I *knew* what the images were showing. For example, the picture I had just examined was a mystery to me. But when I touched it, I knew that this "'Prince of Evil' used its phenomenal cleverness and power to kill one of the 'Lowest 7'". The information was clear in my mind, like I was in the actual process of learning. I didn't know what the 'Lowest 7' was, but it was still much more information than I could guess from the picture. However, when I took my hand off of the image, the knowing in my mind changed. The image was just an image, once again. What I had learned remained, but it changed into remembering. Eventually, the images became more vicious and the *understanding* became so dark that I stopped touching the images. I had learned enough.

I began to notice that it was getting hotter as we descended the stairway. But it was different from the type of heat at home. This was not like a hot day. This was the kind of heat that reminded me of cooking in Fong's kitchen. It was a dry heat. There was a smell in the air, like wood burning, but there was no smoke.

I was glad that my clothing was thin so that I could stay cool on our descent. I only wish that I had some sort of way to document what I was seeing. I was sure that a map would be priceless later.

There were areas that were enclosed, with walls of stone, like rooms. And then there were other areas where the rooms and the walls were only made of plant matter. Trees? Vines? I couldn't tell what kind of plants or trees they were, but the difference between the precisely cut stone in the organic plants was clear.

As we plodded down the steps, I kept my right hand touching the cliff face as I looked out onto the labyrinth. I started to have ideas about how we would approach it. For one thing, the walls did not look that high. I imagined that it would not be a difficult challenge for me to climb over them. The more I thought about the idea the more confident I became. I was a fit boy, after all.

Another idea was that if the walls were just plants, we should be able to cut through them. I imagine that Fox had a saw, or an axe or sword... something, some way to cut through the trees. (Probably tucked away in his shoulder bag!) But then, the more I studied the labyrinth, I realized that it wasn't realistic to cut through all of the walls. The valley in between us and the castle was enormous.

I couldn't see in very great detail at first. But as we descended, I began to see more and more. The edge of the labyrinth was a straight stone wall that ran parallel to the cliff face. The scale of what we faced was astonishing. It felt like looking across a whole countryside. I couldn't imagine how we would cross it, not before Cho Clei was an old woman.

Three large black birds could be seen gliding in looping circles above the labyrinth. It was difficult to tell their size, but the fact that they were far away and still recognizable as birds suggested that they weren't small. Aside from the red-tinted clouds, the birds were the only things I could see in the sky.

As we walked, I fell into a trance-like state of mind. My hands again brushed each of the carvings in the stone face as I plodded down the endless steps. I must have been aware of them, because my mind was filled with dark images, that told more of the story. This demon was special in its unusual intelligence and was to be feared, not respected. I suppose it could have been daydreams born of fatigue. But at the time, I did not question any of it. I only report that it happened.

I would occasionally look up from my trance and get a vague impression of the labyrinth stretching out below me, and the castle above me. The more I looked at the castle, the more I had the impression that the red glow around it was from things burning. Was it possible that the whole castle was on fire?

Each few hundred paces that we descended led us to another platform. There we would turn around and to send a few more hundred paces. Then we would repeat the process.

My trance and its visions made it difficult to tell just how long we were walking down the steps. It also didn't help that the light in this realm did not reflect time passing. It felt like we could've been walking down those steps for days.

In between the dark scenes depicting the demon's exploits, my mind wandered. I wondered who built the steps. I wondered who made all of the carvings that I had examined all the way down. When we were a few minutes from the bottom, we heard a sound that made a shiver run down my spine. The terrifying sound was somewhere between a bellowed scream and a shrieking roar. Both Fox and I stopped in our tracks. Our heads had been alternating between looking down at the steps (so that we didn't fall) and looking out at the maze. When we heard the sound, both of our heads looked to the side. The sound was long and loud, and conveyed deep rage and fury.

We stared out over the labyrinth, but could not see any creatures. From this vantage point, I could see that the walls of the maze followed the contours of the ground. The plateau was not flat after all. It had only appeared that way from above. The ground sloped upward toward the red castle in its center, and the walls went up with it. The effect looked like the labyrinth had once been flat, but the ground under it had been pushed up. It looked like the fiery castle had burst forth from the mountain and risen to its current position. In the process, it had lifted the labyrinth.

At least it looked that way to me. Maybe the castle had brought the labyrinth when it erupted? It struck me how little I knew. I wanted to know as much as Fox! Either way, the bellowing sound did not repeat itself, and we continue our descent.

When we finally reached the bottom, we could see that the labyrinth was only a short walk from the base of the cliff. It appeared that there was a wide door opening in the labyrinth wall, directly facing the last few stairs. The HellFire Road continued the short distance to the labyrinth's entrance, lined with braziers of burning bones.

I felt a vague sense of stupor. We took a moment to stretch our bodies and clear our minds after the long stone stairs. It was certainly warmer down here than it had been before and I took the chance to readjust my clothing. In comparison to Fox's garments, my clothes were very simple. I hadn't realized it before, but compared to his, I have the clothes of a peasant. It didn't bother me though. In fact, I felt grateful that my clothes were light and cool in this dry heat.

As Fox stretched, he looked me up and down. "How do you feel? I know that this trip has not been easy on you. Not physically or mentally... And this is going to become harder before it gets easier. We need to be on guard. And even though it may be hard to believe, we are entering a rougher area than we have been through before."

"Harder than it has been?" I asked incredulously.

He nodded and smiled sympathetically. "The important things to remember here are first, we are invisible. The beings that we should encounter, aside from the Kaitaur, should not be able to see us. Like before, you and I will be able to speak to each other. Like before, we will try to avoid touching or moving anything." I nodded once.

"When we get to the Kaitaur, I will play my flute. I expect that the music will paralyze it so that it can't move, and we can pass through." When Fox said 'Kaitaur', there was a flash of red lightning across the red hued sky. The craggy peaks of the Superstition Mountains loomed large above and around us. "Courage, Kwan, we will rescue your sister. Have faith that we will be able to overcome any challenge we encounter." I nodded again. "Let's go." He said as he turned and walked the small distance from the bottom of the stairs toward the labyrinth.

We had seen the outer wall of the labyrinth as we were descending the steps. I had imagined that those 'little lines' from above would not be serious obstacles. But as we stood before the labyrinth, I saw how mistaken I was.

The walls of the labyrinth were three times my height and extended off into the distance on either side of us. They were made of a gray stone that had leaves and thorny vines growing on it. The vines had stained the stone a green color. I knew from above, that they eventually angled in, to surround the castle, but from here on the ground and looking sideways, the walls looked straight. They went on to the horizon. There was something strange about how proportions worked in this realm. When we were climbing down the steps, I could see that the wall angled in to surround the castle. But here on the ground, the scene looked different, bigger than it had before. The 'door' opening showed us how thick the walls were. Unless it was hollow, the wall looked as thick as my arm was long.

Also, the stone walls were polished to such smoothness, that I doubted I would be able to climb them. I almost laughed at how wrong my estimates had been. A giant wouldn't have been able to climb these walls!

I studied the walls and looked to each side. The labyrinth took up the space of 500 villages. An idea had occurred to me. "Fox, this labyrinth is huge, bigger than a city." I said. He waited for me to go on. "I was wondering if we would even see the Kaitaur. This place is so big, the monster could be far away from here! Maybe we could make it through without meeting the monster!"

Fox thought about it for a minute, then shrugged. "It's definitely possible, but I wouldn't count on it."

We stood before of the opening to the labyrinth and tried to peer inside. There had not been anymore shriek-roaring, so we were more relaxed. Fox tapped my arm and drew my attention up to a metal plate hanging over the door. There was writing on it, a long inscription. Fox read it carefully, several times.

"It is a warning. Once we enter, we are committed. That means we are gambling our lives, Kwan. It... warns of the Kaitaur and describes its ferocity in extravagant terms. Then it goes on to warn about the master of the castle, the master of the Kaitaur. This is the demon we came to find. This is the demon that took Cho Clei. According to this sign, we face the arch-demon Wen-Yi." Fox explained.

"What is an arch-demon?" I asked. I only knew that it sounded scary.

Fox nodded approvingly. "Good. At the GaleTemple, we are taught certain rules for living. The first one is: Ask, don't guess. If you have a resource for more information. That's the first step to understanding. To answer your question, an arch-demon would be the highest level of demon. But you already figured that. What you were really asking, as I understand it, was two questions: Are we facing an arch-demon and if so, is there more reason to fear this Wen-Yi?" I thought about that for a moment. It made sense. Those were the two questions on my mind. It was amazing to me that Fox could see the ideas behind and beneath the words. Then he answered my questions. "We are taught that there are seven arch-demons, the 'Lowest 7', and each one is exceedingly powerful. We are even taught their names. Wen-Yi is not one of the arch-demons' names. If you remember, demons are arrogant and vain. To expect honesty from any demon is a mistake. They will lie to impress and frighten you. I do think it's likely this demon is really named Wen-Yi and that it *is* powerful. But it's also *very* likely that this demon is exaggerating its power. So, for your first question, I doubt he is an arch-demon. For the second question, it seems better to talk in terms of caution, not fear. So, we do need to be as cautious as possible regardless of the demon's rank. You should be at maximum caution when dealing with any normal demon. So should you fear this demon more? No. Because it's not an arch-demon. And because you should *already* be at maximum caution." Fox always had a gift in how he could explain things in a way I could understand.

We looked inside to see the 'lanes' that made up the labyrinth's streets. The lanes were wide enough that three men could have walked abreast with their arms out. The high walls and the wide lanes gave the impression that we were in a giant's lair.

The wall facing us was made of stone, but sections of tall bushes and trees were visible too. The foliage always grew to the top of the wall, and no higher. The plants were too dense for us to get through the walls and covered in wicked thorns the size of my thumb. Maybe I could climb to the top without getting cut up too badly?

The metal grain in Fox's staff flashed again. "Shui has determined that the thorns are coated in a poison. Trying to climb these hedges would be a death sentence," He said. "I thought about trying to get a better view of the maze too." Fox confessed.

Without further comment, he walked calmly into the labyrinth. Less calmly, I followed. Part of me expected that we would be attacked as soon as we entered the labyrinth, just like when we entered the mountain to go underground. But just like then, nothing attacked us when we walked in.

We walked in through the wide door opening in the wall and paused a few steps later. Both of us had the same idea, to stop and look around carefully before we went any further. We looked to either side of us.

From this vantage point, inside the maze, we could see a long way in either direction. We were standing on a long alley, the outermost path of the labyrinth.

There were halls that branched off of the path we were on. Fox asked Shui for guidance whenever we reached a point where the path branched off. Each time, Shui was able to take the worry out of navigation. Fox explained, "There have been constructions like these for thousands of years. They are traps. Several records at the GaleTemple describe these mazes. There have been detailed studies from great masters about the mazes.

"For example, some mazes had only one correct path to get through them, while other mazes had more than one way to pass. Some contained 'monsters', and were intended to trap the visitors and funnel them toward the danger. Other labyrinths had no way through. In them, every path leads to a dead end. Those mazes were designed to get a person lost so that they starve to death." Fox explained.

"That's horrible!" I exclaimed. Somehow, I had never given much thought to starving. As I thought about being lost and starving now, it was appalling.

"I agree. In mankind's history, our willingness to hurt each other knows almost no limit." Fox paused and looked disapprovingly down the path again. Speaking so quietly that he must have been talking to himself, he murmured, "It is a rough school we are born into…" Then, he returned his attention to me.

"Kwan, it's important to understand where the threat comes from in a given situation. For example, what is threatening us now?" He waited patiently as I thought about it.

"Well… the demons in here are the threat. The Kaitaur!" I exclaimed.

"The demons in this place, and specifically the Kaitaur, are very dangerous. But you don't see them now, do you?" I shook my head. Fortunately, we had not seen any threatening demons yet. "That was the initial idea behind the labyrinth. The goal of this place is to get us lost, exhausted and confused so that the Kaitaur will have an easy time defeating us. So, the first threat in this place is disorientation." I hadn't thought of it like that, but it made sense.

"Because Shui is able to tell us the correct turns at each path, we have a tremendous advantage over the labyrinth."

"But how do we know this isn't one of the dead-end mazes?" I interrupted.

"That was the first question I asked Shui. It is not. There is a path for us to get through this labyrinth. So don't worry. Also, remember that we don't need to eat in this realm. So you know that you *cannot* starve in *this* place."

We walked slowly at first, very cautiously. I noted that there were multiple bushes along the path. They all looked dead, but were somehow overgrown with lifeless, gray leaves. Could dead plants grow new, dead, leaves? I could also see many dead weeds down the path, at the base of the walls.

At each hall that branched off of our current path, Fox asked Shui for guidance. Each time, Shui was able to show us the right direction. And each time Shui steered us to the correct path, I felt more and more grateful that we weren't at the mercy of this place. It would have been impossible for me to tell the right way on my own.

It had been reassuring at first when we had passed into the labyrinth. Even though we couldn't scale the walls, it was nice to think that the 'outside' was only one wall away. But soon we had turned in toward the castle, and after only a few more turns, I was thoroughly lost.

At some junctures, we turned down the new paths. Sometimes we ignored the turns and continued on our way. We even passed one doorway with steps leading down under the labyrinth.

When we reached it, Fox spoke to Shui and the staff balanced on its own, as usual. Before it fell, I found myself dreading the thought of going underground again. Apparently, our time passing through the three demon villages had stuck with me. A wave of relief passed over me as Shui pointed to us continuing on our path and not going underground. Whatever danger the Kaitaur was bringing us, I imagined something worse was waiting down the stairs.

Soon the labyrinth had become an endless series of left and right turns. We fell into silence as we walked. Eventually I got lost in my thoughts and I assumed that Fox was doing the same. We would have been taken by surprise, had it not been for Shui flashing. The staff flared to light insistently, drawing our attention.

We had just taken a turn into a new pathway of the labyrinth. The way in front of us initially was clear. But when Fox's staff flashed, we both stopped and peered ahead. Fox seemed curious. Whereas I was just scared. We didn't have to wait long.

There was apparently an intersection 50 paces ahead of us. Our path continued straight ahead, but the crossing hallway branched off to the right and left, perpendicular to us. We knew that the opening was there before we could see it, because a giant snake slithered into view.

I had seen snakes before. They were common enough in the countryside. And I lived in a rural village, where wildlife was plentiful. I don't think I'd ever really seen a big snake before, but I understood that they could grow as big as a man's leg and 20 paces long. This snake was roughly the thickness of a cow. It was travelling the labyrinth path that crossed ours.

The giant snake's head was actually quite pretty, having a pattern of dull gray and black scales. Its eyes were dead as it patrolled the halls. I wondered if this snake was another monster that Shomyira had not told us about. From the dead look in the snake's eye, I imagined it was not conscious of anything. But when the slithering body paused and the snake's head whipped over to look at us, I gasped in fear. I was tempted to turn and run.

Fox grasped my arm and said, "Don't move. It can't see us! Or hear us. So, stay calm. Look!" We both stood there, frozen in place. A moment later, the giant snake's head turned back. It continued slithering down its original path. It seemed like the body was slithering before us, crossing our path, much longer than its body could have been. "I believe the snake was a sentry, checking to see that the labyrinth is clear."

It made sense. This labyrinth was too large for the Kaitaur to fill. I thought of the snake like a security guard who checks to make sure that a building is empty. At least we had gotten that out of the way. Now we should be able to continue unobserved. I said as much, "At least we got past the sentry. Now we won't have to worry about that."

Fox shook his head, "Kwan, this place is too big for one sentry to watch. It is possible will see more giant snakes. Or, we could meet that particular snake again. The labyrinth will certainly have paths that could bring the snake back to us. Or other sentries could appear in other forms, maybe not snakes. The important thing to remember is that they *can't see us.* Either way, keep your guard up." We walked on, albeit a bit slower. I also noticed myself trying to walk more quietly, even though I knew that the circlets hid our footsteps.

"It's fortunate that this labyrinth has stones that pave the paths. If It were especially dusty or grassy, our footsteps could be visible as we crushed the grass or disturbed the dust." Fox mused.

After another never-ending series of disorienting, but unremarkable turns, we reached a long path with small rooms branching off of it. The rooms gave me the clear impression that they were actively used, or lived in. Each of the rooms seemed dark since they had ceilings in these rooms which blocked out the red sky.

The first room we passed contained a series of puzzling items. It was filled with strange furniture. There were crude wooden planks the length of my shin. Each of these planks was elevated off the ground by four short posts. Stacks of the planks stood, one atop the next, up to the height of the walls. They almost looked like dozens of tiny bunk beds. Maybe they were display stands for dozens of small items? We kept moving, and were on to the next room before I could work out the puzzle. We passed more and more of the display stand rooms.

After those display stand rooms, the next rooms were lined with rows of shelves, and each of the rooms contained a... ladder? It looked like a ladder because it had two long, parallel poles connected by short cross pieces. But the cross pieces were too narrow for a man and spaced together too closely. It was also narrower and lighter than a man's ladder would need to be.

The shelves were evenly spaced every few feet going up the stone walls. They looked like they had been carelessly made. I had the (honest, but guilty) thought that the shelves looked like something Fong might have made. The wood of the shelves was warped and uneven. I wouldn't have usually thought about carpentry. I didn't normally notice woodworking. Maybe it was my recent experience with the demon wood carvers that made me notice the crudeness of the shelving? The shelves were bare, and I couldn't imagine what they might normally hold.

We walked past empty room after empty room. There was nobody in any of the rooms, only the strange wooden constructions. I had stopped counting after the 20th room. They were all empty. So, when we walked by a room that was finally occupied, I almost didn't register what I was seeing.

The stone room kept the sound from escaping into the hallway. Otherwise, we would have heard the sounds of bones scraping on whetstones. Inside, a little demon was sharpening the tip of a disproportionately large spear. The demon was small enough that he only came up to my knee. I recalled the masked pygmy demons that had chased us and compared their size to the new demon. The pygmy demons were like giants compared to this new small demon. Then I noticed that there were more of the little demons sharpening more little spears in the room.

I could instantly place what was most disturbing to me about these new demons. None of them was taller than my knee. They were the size of dolls or babies. Or rather, they were the size of little kids when they first learn to walk. But, unlike toddlers, they did not move with any uncertainty. They moved like little men, not graceful, but not toddling either. The similarity was more to vicious, dirty little men than anything else. Their legs and arms were roughly the size of a small toddler, but had wiry, defined muscles. It was obvious those limbs contained strength. Their skin ranged from a greenish yellow color to gray. From the doorway, we could smell a pungent stink coming from them.

When we first saw the little demons, they were sharpening white bone blades. (The non-sharpened end identified the material.) Because they were doing a manual activity, I was able to see their hands. The hands each had wiry little fingers with long, dirty fingernails. The skin itself seem to be caked with grime.

The demons' bodies were so small that I could not help but think of them as demon babies that all needed their diaper-cloths changed. But their heads were larger than a child's head would be. And, as I remembered from Mother, babies' heads are larger (proportionally) than adults' heads are. Still, these little demons had larger heads (and necks to support them) than I expected. For better or for worse, I kept coming up with simple village terms to think in... These demons had heads the size of large cabbages.

The little demons did not appear to be wearing masks. Their exposed faces, though dirty, had vicious, but relatively human features. They had eyes, noses and ears. The eyes were larger and rounded on some, and small and beady on others. But all of them had a small, red points of light where pupils should be. Some of them had longer hair than others. The ones with longer hair might be female? Or, I reasoned, they might not have had genders. It was hard to tell. (Again, fear made me analytical.)

Some of them had patches of mottled skin on their faces or arms or legs. Some had pointy or flat noses, but otherwise just looked like exaggerated versions of human faces. Others' faces looked more like they were a combination of animals and children. Some had whiskered faces that reminded me of rodents. Aside from their uniform height, all of them looked different from each other. And all of them looked feral.

They wore a pitiful collection of clothing. Some wore flimsy cotton shifts that were falling apart while just barely covering their little limbs. Some just wore loin cloths, exposing saggy skin on their little bodies. Some had helmets, but no other armor could be seen. All of them had gray hair. Their hair looked like it could have been white, but was so dirty that it appeared gray.

They were making chattering noises to each other. At first, I only recognized it as sound. But the longer I listened to the demons chatter, the more I felt like I could understand them. I looked at their mouths when they spoke. Surprisingly, very few of them even had teeth. I spotted several that only had a single tooth. Some had wrinkles on their yellow skin, whereas others had tufting patches of fur on their arms or legs.

I tried to stifle my reaction, but a sound escaped my lips. Fox put his hand on my arm, and urged me forward before I made a bigger reaction. We continued moving forward, but I noticed that I started to hunch my back to crouch a little lower. My posture reflected that we were 'sneaking'. As we walked I felt grateful again for the invisibility the circlet granted me.

We passed several rooms full of the little demons sharpening their bone spear tips. Some appeared to be sharpening smaller bone blades too- bone knives? We made it a point to continue walking past each room and did not stop. It took some discipline to keep moving because, even though I was scared, I was curious about the industrious little demons. It had first struck me as odd that the village of wood carving demons put themselves to *work*. They stayed busy and kept carving. These little demons were also *working*. Did they decide to do this, or did they have a master directing them? I realized with a jolt, that we were in an area of the labyrinth that we weren't supposed to see. Somehow, we had reached the secret workshops of the little demon sentries. We were now 'behind the scenes' of the rest of the maze.

At one point a small group of the demons emerged from a room ahead and ran down the path toward us. Fox and I put our backs to the wall, making space as the six little demons ran by. It would have ruined our plan to have one of them bounce off of us while we were invisible. They were small, but looked fierce. Despite their little legs, the demons were surprisingly quick when they were in motion. I mentally compared them to a troop of tiny warriors running on patrol. Strangely, they were quiet as they ran. Their synchronized footfalls could be heard, but they were not chattering in their strange language.

Each of them wore a grim expression on its face. Their spears were taller than they were. As they ran, they kept the spears upright. Between the expressions on their little faces, their glowing red pupils, and the bone spears, they were very intimidating.

They passed and we resumed walking. Fox said, "Quite organized for demons… Interesting…" But he did not say any more. Still we continued down the long hallway. We passed another dozen rooms of the little demons sharpening their spear tips. (Some of them were doing other jobs- such as retying the bone spear-tips to their wooden shafts. But they were all working on maintaining weapons.)

So far, once we found the area of the tiny demons, we had come across room after room with puzzling wooden constructions. Then we had moved past numerous chambers with shelving, then sharpening stations. Next, we reached a series of rooms I can only describe as cages. There were bars on the only doors to the rooms. There were dozens of these cage rooms, but all of them were empty.

After these rooms, we came to an open area. It was large enough that it even contained a few trees. It seemed to be a clearing within the larger maze itself. About thirty small demons could be seen standing in a group. All of the little demons were listening to one of their number who was addressing them, standing atop a small stone cube. The demon did not have any insignia that I could see to distinguish it from the others. But from the way that they were listening to that demon, it was clearly their leader. I stepped behind a nearby tree, trying to be inconspicuous as we observed. Fox stood near the tree, more confident in our invisibility.

Off to the side, two giant effigies had been constructed out of wood scraps, dirt, and pieces of bone. The effigies were poorly crafted, but good enough to show that they were intended to look like *us!* One was taller, with a big belly, and holding a long stick, obviously Fox. The other, clearly representing me, was smaller, leaner and crouched timidly. I felt my mouth drop open, offended- I didn't look like that, did I?

He was finishing a speech, barking out words in their strange language to the assembled audience. It was clear that the demon was giving the others some kind of instruction. Every few words, he would jab a finger out to point at the effigies of us. Fox translated. "…by surprise. But we do not know when." I looked over, confused, but Fox was listening intently, and did not explain. When the little demon spoke, Fox spoke. When the demon fell silent, Fox did too.

The demon spoke. I waited. "For the final time, you know what to do." Fox translated the demon's words. "Go!" Each of the little demons scattered, faster than I would have imagined possible. It was vaguely reminiscent of the wood carving demons. While these tiny demons were small, it would have been a mistake to underestimate them. Their little legs pumped furiously as they scattered. A moment later they had cleared the open area without leaving any trace behind.

We stood in the clearing, surrounded by walls with the red-tinted sky overhead. Their instructor remained where he was. All three of us waited, and watched. For a moment, the clearing was quiet and still.

Without warning, the leader demon bellowed into the air. I jumped, startled at the unexpected noise. Fox translated, "Intruders!" The leader demon continued, this time shouting out a terse speech. Again, Fox translated. "The Living are there! Go! Remember what you practiced!"

Suddenly a flurry of small demons rushed out of nowhere, closing in on the effigies. When I got close, they took up stances in a ring around the crude likenesses of us. Then they brandished their spears, jabbing them toward our effigies in the air. But, curiously, the demons did not stab them. What were they doing? Maybe they got pleasure from frightening their prey before they killed it.

The little demons snarled and yelled, clearly trying to seem intimidating. They made distorted, grotesque faces. The leader demon yelled again. Fox translated, "More!" The little demons yelled even louder. They jumped up and down, working themselves into a frenzy, but still not actually attacking the mock 'Fox and Kwan'.

We stood entranced, watching what they had planned for *us*. The demon leader yelled, followed immediately by Fox's translation. "Now!" The little demons threw down their spears and jumped on the effigies of us. They tackled the 'figures' of us to the ground. Then a demon I had not noticed before, ran up with a length of cut vines. They tied up the sloppy piles of bone and dirt as best they could. After they tied up the effigies, they dragged them a few feet. Then they stopped to turn back and look at their leader. While it didn't seem able to look happy, the demon nodded and spoke to the group. Fox translated, "Better. We don't know when they'll be coming, so be prepared." One of the 'victorious' little demons threw back his head, gave a high-pitched snarl. The demon started chewing, but quickly began coughing and most of the dirt fell out of its mouth. The other demons made grunting noises. Were they laughing?

The demons turned back and headed towards the hall that we had just come out of. "Come on. We should keep moving." Fox said. We resumed walking. Then, some thought must have occurred to Fox. Surprising me, he turned and rushed over to the leader demon. He reached out his hand and waved it around in front of the demon's face. He even snapped his fingers a few times! Fox's hand was nearly the size of the demon's whole body.

I jerked back, thinking that Fox had lost his mind. But the little demon did not react to Fox's hand. He was still staring at the other little demons as they left. It could see straight through Fox's hand. Then Fox turned and trotted back over to where I was. Together we kept walking. I wanted to yell and ask him what he had been doing. But I was more focused on getting away quickly than asking questions.

My panic must have been clear, but he ignored it. Instead, Fox began calmly speaking as we walked away from the little demons. He seemed to be talking more to himself than to me. "It appears the mystery gets a little deeper…" He said.

His comment took me by surprise. The unexpected statement pushed the panic out of my confusion. "What? What do you mean?" I asked. I knew that I was young and out of my depth, but I felt like I was confused so often. Fortunately, Fox was patient and always willing to explain.

"Let me ask you a question. What did you make of what we just saw?" Fox asked. I thought back and tried to be as reasonable as possible.

"There were rooms filled with little wooden racks. I'm not sure about those."

"Beds. Although creatures like these more 'turn off' than sleep." Fox interrupted. Oh. Little beds... racks of little beds... That made sense.

I went on, "Then they had rooms of shelves..."

"Weapon storage, most likely. Those bone spears must live somewhere." I nodded eagerly. I had figured that was likely once I saw them sharpening their spears.

I continued, "Then areas for sharpening those weapons, and finally, training space. Fox, it looks like those little demons are planning to ambush *us!*" I said.

Fox agreed, nodding. "Anything else?" He asked. I couldn't really think of anything else so I shook my head. He went on. "I agree with you. We saw them practicing an ambush. It seems likely that those two targets were meant to represent you and me. Not flattering likenesses, I admit, but overwhelmingly likely. But there are a few problems with that." He said.

I was trying to think like him, but I still couldn't quite get it. Fox went on, "Did you notice when I ran over to wave my hand in front of the demon's face?" Fox asked. I nodded emphatically. "What did you think I was doing?" I couldn't imagine.

"I waved my hand directly in front of its face." Fox answered. "And if the demon saw me, it would have reacted. They were looking for us, after all." I nodded, following so far. "But the demon couldn't see us. So, I was able to find out that we are still invisible. But that creates more questions than answers... Like *how* do the little demons know that we are here? How do they know that we are coming through the Labyrinth? Even in a realm like this, there must be several ways to reach the demon's castle. How did they know we wouldn't take one of those other ways? Somehow, they know that we are here, even though we are invisible. They can't see us, but they are *expecting* us. I can only reach one conclusion.

They have been *warned* that we were coming. The questions keep growing. Who warned them? Who organized them? And why do these demons want to capture us, and not immediately kill us? Where do they want to take us? Also, who do they put in those jail cells? There are more questions, but that's probably enough to consider for now."

Of course! When Fox explained, it seemed so clear. I had a question occur to me so I added it to Fox's list. "And why did that little demon eat dirt?"

He seemed surprised at my question and responded, "I think I can answer that one. Kwan, hunger is a universal condition. But these creatures are not alive. It appears one condition of their existence is that they can't eat. At least not food. I doubt they have any systems to even digest food. But they apparently *want* to eat. Hence the dirt."

"Even the Ragyala eats?" I asked.

Fox cocked his head to the side, considering the question, "With higher beings, their 'food' is direct connection to the GaleSource. The scrolls in the GaleTemple libraries tell us that much."

I was going to ask him another question, but the room coming into view ended my question before it began. Fox and I stopped to watch.

The room was like others that we had seen before we entered the clearing. The room itself was not remarkable. It was the action going on inside the room that was remarkable. There were eight or nine of the little demons viciously beating a figure on the floor. They were kicking the figure and hitting it with the shafts of their spears.

All I could see was flashes of a battered mask through their furiously kicking feet. After a second I identified the mask. It was one of the pygmy demons from the village we had passed through! I somehow didn't imagine these demons had contact with each other.

Imagining that they knew each other and were enemies, was astonishing. We watched as the pack of little demons beat the larger little demon into submission. Since the pygmy was twice the size of any of the smaller demons, they were fighting dirty. The fight was ten against one, so they clearly didn't worry about fairness. The little demons swarmed on the pygmy, punching and kicking it while it was down.

Another little demon appeared with a length of vines, and they began tying up the pygmy 'giant'. The mouth of the mask opened to bellow indignantly. For the first time, I realized the mask was the demon's actual face, not something worn on top of it.

We didn't stick around to see what they planned to do with the pygmy. Instead we kept walking, albeit a little faster. Having just seen a demonstration of their viciousness, we were wary. "And now we have more questions..." Fox said. "What are they planning to do with that pygmy demon? Does it have anything to do with us?"

We hurried on past the little demons, anxious to get away. There were a series of sharps turns we apparently had to follow to reach the next section of the labyrinth. It was a long hallway that twisted and turned, but had no doors. The options and choices fell away here. These turns were the only way through this section where the little demons lived and worked. I put my head down and plodded along behind Fox.

From what we could see, there was only one way to pass through this section. We had to follow this single hallway. Until then, we lacked choices and options so we didn't need to consult Shui.

The way out of this section had us pass through a narrow gate before we could reach the next area. This gate was at a high point and the terrain sloped down from there. The ground did not level out and incline again until several miles away. In the distance, we could see the Bone Castle.

Walking head down, I nearly bumped into Fox again. He had stopped abruptly. I heard him speak quietly to himself. "Uh-oh. One way through, a 'bottleneck', and it looks like there are sentries..." I looked up. The gate we needed to pass through was just a point where the hallway narrowed, and we needed to pass single-file. There, above the narrow point where we needed to pass, were two red-black bird statues standing on the opposite walls facing each other. The statues were black, but their feathers were polished so that they reflected the red clouds above. Their beaks pointed towards the spot we would need to walk through.

Even though we knew we were invisible, we tried to be especially stealthy as we passed. I rolled my feet from heels to toes, trying not to raise any dust as I passed. I was fully creeping. I could feel that my back was hunched. I was even squinting my eyes, as though I could make my sight quieter. It was silly, and I knew it, but I couldn't help it.

Fox had slowed somewhat to move carefully, but he never seemed to make any noise when he walked. In comparison, my steps were loud and clumsy. As we approached the narrow gauntlet between the birds, the tension grew.

The birds also appeared bigger when seen up close. As we got close, I saw that the birds were nearly as tall as I was. Their beaks were polished black knives as long as my forearm. Perched atop the walls, their black talons were curled over the side.

Every step we took, I felt the tension rise. My eyes were locked on the statues' heads. We crept toward them. There were two bird statutes, one on each wall, facing each other. Both of their heads were pointed down to look directly at the path. Then, in unison, both birds turned their heads to look at us.

We were close enough that Fox could have reached out with his staff and touched one of the statues. My heart leaped into my throat and a strangled cry escaped my lips. Once their heads turned the spell seemed to be broken. They moved their entire bodies. Their talons clicked on the top of the stone wall. Their bodies turned to fully orient on us.

"No good." Fox said. "It looks like we've been spotted. The winged ones…"

With a jolt, I realized that these were two of the birds that we had seen circling above the labyrinth when we descended the steps down the cliff face. When I saw them before, I thought that they were probably big birds, but I had no idea just how big they were.

When the birds turned to us, my first thought was that they were going to attack. Looking at their beaks, the thought was terrifying. But these were sentries, as Fox had said. It looked like they just did the spying and left attacking to… the Kaitaur? (or maybe those vicious little demons).

The black birds launched themselves into the sky and wheeled to head to the distant castle. We watched them fly away. Fox wasted no time, "We've been spotted, and I don't know what they're going to do. Two things are clear: First, we should get as far away from here, as fast as possible, before they respond. And two, we should avoid those birds because they can take away the surprise invisibility gives us." I was consistently impressed with Fox's ability to think so clearly.

"Come on, Kwan. We don't have any time to lose." With that, Fox took off running. Refreshed by my terror, I followed. We sprinted down the long corridor.

Chapter 16

Shogatt

When fatigue made us drop back to a walk, we were still in that long corridor. There were no doors branching off of it. We walked long enough that it looked the same in front of us as behind us. It was an uninterrupted channel we were in. Gray stone walls hemmed us in on either side. The sky was now a brighter red above us. It made a disturbing 'never-ending' perspective that I associated with this realm. The path seemed to go on infinitely. I knew that couldn't be, but that's how it looked.

I switched between looking forward and looking back. I had been looking over my shoulder, checking to see if the view behind us was really identical to the way we were heading. They certainly looked identical, at first. But then I saw motion far off behind us.

The movement was tiny at first, being so far in the distance. "Fox…" I pointed behind us in the distance. We both watched, trying to identify what was approaching. Soon we could hear a faint clapping sound. We stood and listened, squinting our eyes to get more detail. It looked like a series of larger and larger squares was chasing us. Shui flashed, but I still couldn't identify the threat. Fox listened to his staff. "The walls?" Then to me, "Run!" Fox said.

I had been conditioned by this place to run first and ask questions later. Fox and I took off running. He yelled an explanation to me as we ran. "It looks like a trap! The walls are moving behind us! The maze is… changing." We ran hard again and soon had no breath to talk.

I spared a glance back over my shoulder and saw that a series of stone walls was snapping into place, cutting our long hall into a series of enclosed boxes. The new walls seemed to be bursting out from the sides of the long hall, intersecting it. Each time the enclosing walls stopped moving, they hit the adjacent wall with an audible boom. Fox and I ran, but the booms were getting closer, louder. I could barely hear him over the sound of my thundering heartbeat in my ears and the rhythmic booming chasing us. "Trying to trap us…"

My heart was pounding in my ears. My breaths came in gasps. The sound of the walls slamming closed behind me got so loud that I thought they would crush me. Then Fox, slightly ahead of me and to my left, threw out his arm to stop me. I skidded to a stop as a wall slammed into place in front of us. The wall moved so fast, erupting out from our right that when it connected with the left wall, the BOOM was deafening. My ears rang.

A series of realizations hit me in rapid succession. The wall behind me had closed and I hadn't heard it. Actually, I had heard it, but in my frantic sprint, I couldn't tell that the closing walls had caught up to us. I thought the slamming walls were farther behind me. I had been dangerously unaware.

Then I realized that Fox had stopped short just to help me. He had *slowed* his pace to stop me. The wall might not have hit us, it might have separated us, it might just have hit me. Fox had made sure that we would be on the same side when we got trapped. Actions like this showed his foresight and thoughtful character. Again, I felt grateful. Which brought me to the last thought; we were trapped.

I looked around at the four walls that enclosed us as I caught my breath. I studied the wall that had almost separated us. The sound of more walls 'closing' could be heard on the other side of the wall.

The sounds faded off into the distance as a series of diminishing booms.

After a moment, I concentrated through the surprise and examined the new wall. The wall facing me was covered by a series of different sized, mouth-shaped holes. They were clearly mouths, having lips and fangs that were carved in relief, raised from the surface of the wall. And each of these mouths was frozen in mid-scream. Or maybe they were laughing. It was difficult to tell. A shiver ran down my spine.

Fox was looking around at the wall behind us. I was going to ask Fox what we were going to do. I don't remember if I said anything before the first stream of water shot out of the hole right in front of my face. It wasn't an incredibly strong stream of water, but I stumbled in surprise, falling back. Even though it was only the diameter of my finger, the stream of water caught me across my eyes and, as I pulled away, sprayed into my open mouth. I had been inhaling when some of the water hit me in the back of my throat.

I jerked back in surprise, coughing and spluttering, tripping over my feet and falling on my backside. My head whipped around to see Fox. I was just in time to see him examining similar openings on the opposite wall. Just as I looked back, a jet of water shot directly at Fox's face. Without moving his feet, he leaned to one side and the jet of water squirted neatly over his shoulder.

For just a moment the water felt refreshing to me. The heat in the maze had been oppressive. But that feeling evaporated almost immediately. I was sitting where I had tripped, propped up on my elbows, struggling to stop coughing and catch my breath.

As I fought to control my coughing, all of the other mouths on the wall began spewing water. Some of the mouths were bigger than others. There must have been hundreds of the mouth-fountains, facing each other on the opposite walls. Suddenly, the room was filled with crossing streams of water. Two walls, the original maze walls were just flat stone. But the new walls were now pouring water in. Very quickly, the water began to accumulate on the stone floor of our prison. The high, flat sound of water hitting stone was turning to a deeper sound of water pouring into a deepening pool.

Fox hurried over and helped me to my feet. He clapped me on the back a few times, and I was able to regain my composure, sort of. "Fox! What are we going to do?" I asked.

Fox's eyes were narrowed as he looked around at our flooding cell. Water coming from the hundreds of open mouths in the walls was rapidly flooding our cube. The cold water was a dirty purple gray color. He quickly stepped over to the adjacent wall and rubbed his hand on it.

Since I was standing right next to him, I could hear him speaking, low and fast. "Trapped. Walls move but appear solid… Cube is flooding… Will be to neck level in…" He looked back and forth at the walls spewing water. The accumulating water was already at ankle level. "…two hundred breaths. But can't drown us, since there is no ceiling. We can float to the top. Walls have texture, but not enough for a handhold." Fox turned to me and raised his voice, "Kwan, can you swim?!" I nodded quickly. Father had taught me (and Cho Clei) to swim when we were younger. I was not very fast or graceful, but once I could keep my head above water, Father stopped 'worrying about his children drowning'. Fox was back to speaking to himself, low and fast, "We both can swim, so there is little danger of accidental drowning. At the top, we will mount the walls. Then we can recalculate. This must only the beginning of the demons' plan. But why flood the space, aside from finding us? What is their next step? Focus Fox!" He quietly said.

The water was filling our enclosure faster than I could believe. It was already at our knees, and so far, all we could do was look around. Fox seemed to come to a decision. He began speaking again. Only this time, his speech was louder and clearer, "It looks like they're going to flood the space. Since we can both swim, and since there's no roof, we are not going to run out of air. So we won't suffocate and drown."

I was starting to shiver. The water that was flooding into the room was both cold and dirty. Fox looked deadly serious. He kept speaking, "Since they can't see us, they would need to do something to find us. Our hunters become desperate to find us. But, we are not leaving enough evidence for them to track us. So, it seems likely that they are going to flood this room and use the water to *locate* us. When we swim or tread water, we will have to move the water around to do it. Whoever is hunting us will be able to see that movement. Then they will have our position. The question becomes- what they will do then? Will they send those little demons to get us? Or will they…"

Shui flashed brightly. Fox immediately communicated what is staff had told. "Shui can sense something… aquatic, nearby.

When this place is completely flooded, we should get to the top of the walls as fast as we can. The circlets won't be able to hide us while we are swimming. It's really clever, actually. When we get close enough to the tops of the walls, we will scramble out of the water as fast as we can. After that, we can figure out our plan from on."

The water in the cell was up to our waists and my teeth began to chatter. Just as I was thinking this situation was as stressful as I could possibly manage, water coming from the walls tripled in volume. Suddenly we had less time than we did a moment ago.

Very quickly, the level of dark water was up to our chests. And then, seemingly an instant later, we were swimming. I was gasping for air in the frigid water. Fox treaded water more gracefully, but this was not a time when style mattered. His bag floated on top of the water, but he held on to his staff. I dog paddled, trying to stay as close as possible to the wall, but the water was flowing in and pushing us away.

If there had been places on the wall where we could get purchase, then we could have held the wall and floated up as the water filled in. Unfortunately for us, the side walls did not have any places that we could grip. To my wet hands, it seemed like the walls were smooth. Without a handhold, the only thing we could do was tread water. The cloudy, red-tinted sky overhead completed our sinister surroundings. As the water rose and more of them dropped below the surface, the sound of the fountains lessened.

A few moments later, faster than the chamber should have been able to fill, we were within reach of the tops of the walls.

I tried to lunge out of the water several times to catch the wall but was unsuccessful. Fox said something to me, but I could not hear him over the splashing of my exertions. A moment after that, Shui began flashing brightly and insistently. Fox only said, "Uh-oh." My fear congealed into a ball of terror in my stomach.

Seemingly, A moment later, I was able to reach the top of the nearest wall. I was vaguely aware of Fox crawling out of the water behind me. I heaved myself up, clawing at the wall to throw my leg out of the water. Then, I was able to scramble up on to the wall. Fox was standing on what had been a sidewall of the original alleyway. I was now standing on one of the 'fountain' walls that had come out to 'section off' that hallway. We were only a few feet away, but we were on adjacent walls, perpendicular to each other.

As soon as I got out of the water, I was shaking. Somehow, I had an absolute certainty that there was a terrifying danger coming for us. The hairs on my arms were standing up, and not from the cold water. Deep in my core, I was afraid.

I stood on the wall, panting and shivering (but warming now in the sweltering labyrinth air again). I looked over at Fox on the adjacent wall. His expression back at me showed he was clearly concerned. I must have looked like a drowned man. I glanced to either side and saw an infinite series of flooded rooms just like ours. From up there, I could also see the labyrinth around me. Beyond our corridor of the maze, none of the other paths was flooded. It was only ours.

I had just enough time to catch my breath and let my guard down, when the wall I was standing on vanished beneath my feet. It withdrew back so swiftly that I didn't have time to leap over to Fox's wall.

My arms flailed around and I cried out as I fell backwards into the water of what had been the 'next room'. Time slowed as I fell. Fox yelled something to me, but it was lost to me. As the water enveloped my head, his words cut off completely. My cry had blocked out Fox's words and emptied my lungs.

Time continued to slow. I looked up through the water as I fell in. I could see Fox, standing on the wall above me, staff in hand. He was silhouetted through the dirty water with the red sky and black clouds behind him. Some faraway part of me recognized that, with the partition walls gone, I was now in a long, deep and open channel of water. My terror grew.

Then came a distinct feeling transmitted through the water itself. I felt it as clearly as any other sensation in my life, as clear as a shouted warning. It was the certain feeling of mortal danger. It was the *knowledge* that my life was under threat, not in theory, but actively being hunted. Something was coming to… kill… me. I had never felt the sensation before, but I could immediately recognize what it meant. The thought paralyzed me. My body was frozen rigid by fear. And, unable to move, I began to sink.

Time seemed disjointed as I frantically tried to tell my body to paddle back towards the wall and up to the surface. I had slipped into a blind panic. The feeling of being threatened was overwhelming. Some part of me wanted to close up inside myself.

The cold water seemed darker than it had even a moment before. I realized with a detached feeling of despair that I was slowly drifting to the bottom. Strangely, I didn't feel the need to breathe. I was slowly sinking, and observing. I could feel the building pressure. It was utterly strange.

In my paralysis, I found my body listing, rolling slowly onto its side as I sank. Because of this, I was sinking near the wall, looking in toward the center of the hall. I could hear whatever it was approaching. QUISH….. QUISH….. QUISH….. When it first passed, my disjointed sense of time fed me two different impressions of what was happening simultaneously.

The first impression was fleeting, but still at normal speed. The thing passing by was a massive blur of power and motion. It seemed to take up the whole channel. As the creature sped past me, the water it moved pushed me back against the wall. Then immediately, its passing wake pulled me off the wall to drift, trailing behind it. In that first impression, I could not see what it was. It happened too fast.

The second impression was disturbingly clear and my slowed sense of time fed me great detail. The thing that swam past me seemed made of two different ocean animals. The front half of the creature was the head of a great, flat-headed fish. Its open mouth displaying row after row of sharp teeth. The skin was grey and leathery and had black misshapen lumps all over its body. It's visible eye, a dead sphere, the size of my head, rolled around in the socket, looking for me. It didn't seem to be able to see me. The back half of its body had great tentacles that were ringed with spikes. The creature seemed to move by inflating its body with water, then squirting that water out of the back of its body. When it squirted the water out, it made its body narrow and streamlined by holding its tentacles together and laying the spikes flat. This let it move with extreme speed, jetting through the water. It was fast, and menacing.

Within the first impression, the creature passed in an instant. The QUISH sound it made as it approached, changed into a WHOOSH sound as it streaked before my eyes. It sped through the water, a streak of gray, then it was gone.

With the second impression, the creature's passage took a long period of time giving me the overwhelming conclusion that it was enormous. My eyes saw less as I sank and the water grew darker. Still apparently in shock, I couldn't move.

As I gently settled to the bottom, the thing that kept me immobile, snapped. All at once, forgotten needs and urges occurred to me. My need to breathe suddenly made itself known to me as a burning in my lungs. My need to flee, equally strong, occurred at the same time. Suddenly I was again in control of my limbs. And even though I was able to move again, time remained slow down.

I twisted in the water to get my feet under me, so that I could push off the floor and shoot up to the top. But as I moved my legs around to push off, I instantly sensed my mistake. The creature noticed the movement in the water. I could feel my instinct to survive suddenly start screaming at me as the creature rolled in the water and effortlessly changed direction, now jetting straight at me. My feet found purchase on the labyrinth floor and I gave a mighty push to reach the surface.

It is only because time was slowed down, I think, that I'm able to remember anything about what happened. I remember looking up, seeing Fox's silhouette again. Now, he was pulling his shoulder bag over his head, removing it. His staff, Shui, was standing on end, balanced next to him. I aimed for Fox and pushed off.

As I pushed off from the bottom, immediately sensing the imminent impact coming from my left side. My body was fully stretched out, vulnerable. I was not going to reach the surface before the monster could catch me. I could not resist glancing over to see my coming doom. What I saw was the mouth of a killer fish, filled with teeth, rushing in to eat me. Strangely, I felt intense hatred coming off of the monster, not hunger. It wanted to kill, not actually to eat. I closed my eyes tight, rising through the water, waiting for the killing bite that I knew was coming.

But instead of being bitten in half, I felt myself violently bumped aside. I bounced off the monster like a padded ball, then bounced off the wall, finally drifting, dazed. It felt like I was covered in pillows, like I had a protective covering around me, and *that covering* had been hit. I was shaken, but safe and unharmed inside the covering.

I became aware of the humming vibration coming from the medallion Fox had given me. I could hear it. The medallion made a low sound, clearly vibrating. It sounded like 'MMMMMMM'. Even in the water, I could feel its power. I opened my eyes and looked down to see the medallion floating slightly off of my chest and giving off a faint light.

The medallion had protected me from the attack. The monster seemed as surprised as I was. It had rebounded from the shield just as I had been bounced off of it. Its tentacles spread out in the water behind it, as it held back and recalculated its attack. It seemed to look at me carefully. With a sinking feeling, I realized that it was summoning its strength, and that I would not survive the next attack.

The creature seemed to grossly inflate, and then squirting water from its backside, shot straight at me. Its mouth opened wide in preparation of biting through my medallion's shield. At that moment, I knew that I was about to die.

It was as though the approaching mouth was a killer circle, getting larger as it approached me. Each instant the monster's mouth got closer, a new row of teeth emerged. Row after razor-sharp row appeared out of the shadows in its mouth.

The sudden knowledge was staggering. This monster was going to eat me, then I would be dead. I wished I could have saved Cho Clei. I wished I had been a better son. This was just… too much. I felt so tired and wanted to surrender. My eyes slowly closed.

A brilliant flare, visible through my eyelids, made me open my eyes. I saw a glowing line slice down diagonally in front of me, blocking the killer bite. I dully watched as a pitched battle began in the water in front of me. It took a second to see into the twirling, thrashing maelstrom in front of me. I realized that the glowing line of protection, blocking the attack and coming to my rescue had been Fox's staff. The demonic sea creature was fighting with Shui!

The demon darted in and bit down on Shui. Just before its jaws tried to close, Shui flipped in the water, going from being horizontal across the demon's mouth to standing vertically. The demon bit down to snap Shui in half, but found its mouth propped open instead.

In response, Shui began jerking the creature up and down, left and right. It looked like Shui was the hook of some giant, angry fisherman. While the staff was not curved like a hook, it had the monster caught the same way. The creature redoubled its efforts, and tried to put all of its power into snapping Fox's staff. The creature whipped the staff around like a dog with a stick in its mouth. In response, Fox's staff slammed the creature against the walls of the labyrinth. Each time the creature impacted the walls, a muffled 'THUDD' resonated through the water.

I would have watched to see what happened next, but by that point, I had floated close enough to the surface for Fox to pull me out. I had been watching the battle, floating. Still standing on the edge, Fox reached down and, with one big hand, fished me out. He grabbed the back of my tunic and lifted me completely out of the water, setting me on the wall next to him.

I looked down from the wall. The purple gray water could be seen roiling and churning as the creature fought Shui. The staff was landing tremendous blows on the monster, each time making an impact tremor ripple across the surface of the water. The wall opposite the one we were standing on, shook with another impact. Since I had seen what was happening underwater, I was in awe of Shui. I had no idea Fox's staff was this powerful.

A moment later, the surface of the water broke and the terrible behemoth slowly emerged. Its appearance was both chilling and fascinating at the same time. I was unable to look away. Its shark eyes rolled around as the back-half's octopus tentacles writhed in the air. Fox's eyes grew wide as the monster rose out of the water. This was the first time that Fox had clearly seen the monster. He apparently recognized it. Fox spoke one word, "A Shogatt".

I prepared myself mentally to jump backwards away from the beast. But Fox put a hand on my arm to steady me. We watched as the Shogatt continued to rise. After a second or two, it became clear that the beast itself was not behind its rise. Fox's staff, still clenched between its teeth, was lifting the demon out of the water. The Shogatt's eyes were bulging and showed two things- that it could not quite believe what was happening, and that it couldn't let go.

We watched as Shui hoisted the Shogatt out of the water. It had to be as heavy as 10 horses, but Shui steadily lifted it. Once the Shogatt had been lifted entirely out of the water, it slowly rotated while floating, as if Shui was putting the demon on display. Its tentacles hung down and writhed in confusion. We stood there on the wall, transfixed, watching the Shogatt turn slowly. Then, the staff accelerated its rotations, building up to spin in tight circles. Holding on to Shui with its teeth, the Shogatt was soon spinning along with the staff. As it spun, Its tentacles stuck straight out behind it, limp and forgotten. It was impressive that the monster's jaws were able to hold on. It was able to cling to Shui for five turns. But then the Shogatt was at the limits of its strength and endurance.

With a mighty heave on the sixth turn, Shui flipped sideways again and threw the attached monster off. The beast had been trying to hold on, but Shui's throw was so forceful that dozens of the beast's teeth audibly snapped off. The Shogatt arced over the opposite wall and fell on the other side, on to the next path. Our view was blocked once the Shogatt dropped below the top of the wall, but the sound of its crash was clearly audible. The wall we were standing on shook, as the weight of the Shogatt hit the stone path. A cloud of rubble and dust rose on the other side of the dark canal. Shui dunked itself into the water, emerging a moment later. It spun in the air, flinging off the water. Fox held out his right hand, and the staff flew back to it, clapping into Fox's palm.

"Are you all right?" He looked me over carefully. "I thought we might have been in trouble there for a second." He said. He gave a quick, apologetic smile for the joke. Then he pulled a (somehow!) dry towel from his shoulder bag.

I was still in shock and tried to think. It seemed clear to me that I had just avoided death, and grateful to Fox. "Th- that wasn't... t- trouble?" I smiled back weakly. "Th- thank you for sending Sh- Sh- Shui." I stammered.

Still looking concerned, he shook his head and said, "I didn't send Shui. In truth, I was about to go in after you myself. Shui is a conscious being, a companion, not a servant to command. I can risk my own life, but I couldn't just throw Shui into danger. It wouldn't be right.

No, Shui went in after you on its own. Shui saw you in trouble and decided to intervene.

"It looks as though the medallion protected you from the Shogatt's initial hit, but its power has limits too. The medallion's effects would have enhanced your ability to hold your breath too. Shui could see that you would run out of air soon and not survive another strike. Simply put, Shui saved you." Pausing to consider, he added, "It is the nature of heroes." He held out the staff, admiring it. The metal grain running down the ironwood staff pulsed once in appreciation and agreement.

He lowered his voice conspiratorially as if sharing a great secret, "This is not my first mission Kwan. And from what I have seen in the past, Shui does enjoy a good fight." The metal grain running through the staff flared brightly again, in apparent confirmation. Fox continued, "Truthfully, I doubt I have ever seen a stronger fighting spirit. They say you can take the warrior out of the fight, but you can't take the fight out of the warrior." He gave an appreciative glance at Shui. The metal grain running through the ironwood staff slowly pulsed its appreciation again. Fox smiled back. It seemed like strange praise to give a staff, but after what we had just seen, I agreed.

We only had one direction open to us. We weren't going to swim through the maze, so the path we had been on was no longer an option. We couldn't jump over the water either, so the path on the opposite side wasn't an option. (Also, the Shogatt's carcass was lying on that path.) Our only choice was the path behind and below us. We considered walking along the top of the walls. It gave us a much better view of our destination. But after my experience with the Shogatt, I wanted to be as far away from the water as possible. I said so and Fox agreed.

The wall we stood on was only as thick as my arm was long, but it was three times my height. The question of how to get down would have been a huge challenge for me alone. But Fox reached into his bag and pulled out a small iron hook with a long rope attached to it. The rope had knots tied in it at regular intervals down its length.

He attached the little claw at the top of the wall at our feet. The rope unrolled down and along the wall. We would lower ourselves down, using the knots as handholds. It took a moment to warm my hands up so my fingers could regain their strength. While I rubbed my hands together, Fox secured his staff in the harness on his back.

So, we lowered ourselves down from the top of the wall. When we reached the bottom, Fox grabbed the rope and shook it expertly. The metal hook detached from the wall and fell to the ground at our feet.

After he recoiled the rope and returned it to his bag we got moving on the new path. Fox consulted with Shui to see which direction to go. Surprisingly, when Shui directed us this time, it was the opposite direction that we had been going. But Fox confirmed with Shui that our new direction was correct.

This alley, however, was different from its neighbor. This alley had alternate paths branching off of it. Each time we reached a choice to turn, we consulted Shui and had confidence.

This realm had no end to its surprises though. For example, soon after we started down this new corridor, we came to an open doorway on our right. I stared at it, not comprehending. Turning to the right from here shouldn't be possible. The next corridor over was *flooded*. We had just left that deadly canal, and my clothes were still wet, so I was sure about it! A wall of water should have *blocked* the turn, but instead, we were looking down another clear path. Fox seemed to understand my confusion. "Remember, this place doesn't have the same rules." he murmured. "Come on."

All of the paths began to look the same. The power of the labyrinth to confuse a traveler clearly built up over time. Unless I was being attacked, drowned, or spied on, all of the paths blurred together in my memory. We made so many turns, endless rights, endless lefts, peering suspiciously around hundreds of hall corners. When this labyrinth wasn't terrifying, it was subtly mind-numbing.

That's how it was, when we came upon six of the knee-high demons coming our way. They were carrying several dead logs between them that looked too heavy for their little bodies. I couldn't help but notice deep claw marks on the logs. Fox and I pressed our backs flat against the wall, watching the little demons trudge by.

The character of the labyrinth changed as we continued walking. The stone walls were gradually replaced with thick and thorny, (but apparently dead), hedges. These new hedge walls were only twice our height. I took some comfort from the knowledge that, at least, this place couldn't flood.

The terrifying roar we had heard before, sounded again. I recognized the sound from when we had walked down the carved steps in the cliff face. But this time the sound was not a distant mystery. This time I knew the source. The sound was a chilling threat, and obviously nearby. It made a shiver run down my spine. We tried to peer through the thorny hedges, but couldn't see any creatures. Still, now we knew it was somewhere near us. Fox stopped, and pulled his bag off his shoulder.

He took Shui from the holder on his back and set it on the ground, where it balanced upright, on its own. Then he reached into his bag, and rummaged around inside. He was reaching into his bag, arm buried up to the shoulder, which looked strange since the bag was not deep enough fit his whole arm. "We should take a moment now to go over our strategy." Fox said. I just stood attentively waiting, because 'my' part of our strategy, realistically, would be doing whatever Fox told me to do.

As he spoke, Fox was pulling items from his shoulder bags. "We don't know exactly where the Kaitaur is, but we know it's close. I would estimate we are within 100 paces of it..." Hands occupied, Fox gestured with his chin over his shoulder. "...but the labyrinth is hiding us." I looked around nervously. Having a specific number of paces named, the distance between us and the monster shrunk in my mind. I kept peering over Fox's shoulder.

"Since we don't know when we will come on the Kaitaur, we should get prepared now." He pulled two strange bundles from his bag and handed them to me. It was eight bamboo planks, about a forearm's length. The planks had that strange, rune script carved into them. They were each attached to the next plank by a pale blue silk ribbon that was knotted at either end of each plank.

I untied the silk knots and each package unrolled. Fox explained that the bamboo planks were to fit, like shielding around my calves and shins. The blue silk should be knotted to tie them. They were worn as protection.

Fox explained that we would need to have some sort of defense against the little demons. We had seen how strong they were and how vicious they could be. If they came out and attacked us, they would attack what they could reach- our ankles and shins. It was the area from our knees down that we most need to protect. The runes inscribed on these 'shin shields' would help resist the force of the demons' strikes. Otherwise, I imagine they could break a man's leg with just a kick." Fox had given the first bundles to me. Then he brought out two more for himself.

He demonstrated how I should put them on. I followed his example and soon both of us had our lower legs girded in rune-powered, bamboo protection. He again took up holding Shui.

"Now that we have some small protection, we need to go over our plan. I'll get my flute, so it will be ready when I'll need to play." He was indeed pulling the long flute from his bag, but he never stopped speaking. "You've been tracking what's going on. And you know that our goal is to get past the Kaitaur, so we can reach Cho Clei. So, while I am playing I will need *you* to be our protection." It took a moment before Fox's words' meaning dawned on me. I need to fight? I... I was no fighter!

Fox asked me, "Have you ever fought?" I shook my head, dismayed. If I was our protection, we were in trouble. The memory of the little demons savagely beating the pygmy demon made a shiver pass down my spine. If I had to fight all of them, we were lost!

Fox put up his hand and smiled. "Don't worry, I understand that you are not a warrior. I am asking you to fight. But I'm not asking you to fight alone." My face must have shown my panic. I was confused.

Fox went on, "The strongest fighter I know has agreed to fight with you." Fox held out Shui to me. "It's possible the little demons might not see us, or come in time, but we should be prepared. If you must fight, you will need Shui's help.

"You are a young man with a great deal of promise, Kwan. But if the little demons do attack us, we will need an experienced warrior in this fight. If that happens, trust Shui."

"You... want me to carry Shui?" I asked. I was incredulous. I thought of them as a pair at this point. The idea of them being separated was alarming.

But Fox just smiled and nodded, "Only while we are facing the Kaitaur. Once we have defeated the creature, I will take Shui back. But if we get overwhelmed by the little demons, we would need Shui in the fight.

It was obvious how the plan made sense. Fox's hands were full with the flute, so he wouldn't be able to hold Shui. And now, after seeing how the staff handled the Shogatt, I had no doubts about Shui's power.

"So, you're going to play the flute, while we fight off a horde of knee-high demons. Then your flute will make it drop dead, then we go past and continue to the castle?" I asked. I wanted to show that I understood what he was saying and could plan ahead too.

But I hadn't quite hit my target. Fox nodded, saying, "Almost. I am going to play the flute. But I doubt that the sound of music will make the Kaitaur drop. If you're interested, I have a theory about demons like the Kaitaur and music. My theory is that a being like the Kaitaur will 'see' the music, and that vision will block it from seeing us sneaking by.

You will fight off the knee-high demons. But hopefully, it will be less than a full horde. And after we pass the monster, we will continue to the castle."

Fox held his staff out to me. After a moment of staring at the piece of ironwood, I reached my hand out and grasped the staff just below Fox's hand. The metal grain running down the length of it flared brightly. Several sensations overwhelmed me at once. For just a moment, I heard a clear high tone of a ringing bell when my hand touched the staff. But it was more than just a sound. The tone came with information. The tone came with a… feeling.

The tone and the feeling were hard to describe. This was partly because the impressions came very quickly. It's difficult to be certain of something when it happens as quick as a flash. But it did happen. The feeling, as I can best describe it, was like seeing an uncle that you do not see often, that is both tremendously tough, and cheerful. (and fondly disposed toward you.) The feeling was like getting a warm hug in greeting from that tough uncle. (I did not have such an uncle, but that was the feeling.)

Fox did not take his hand off of the staff. Instead, he looked me straight in the eyes and said, "I have grown to appreciate your qualities, Kwan. But we should be very clear in our communication now. I am not giving you this staff. I am not entrusting Shui to your care. I am entrusting *your* care to Shui. Even though it is an object, this staff is your superior- in experience, knowledge, and power. Do you understand that?"

I nodded humbly. "Good. Now do you remember when you heard that ringing sound in the air whenever you were close to Shui, not long after we met?" I did remember. Fox went on, "If you recall, we were able to harmonize your energy with Shui's energy."

Fox kept looking at me, but I couldn't quite understand the implications of what he was saying. It had been maddening in the beginning, when I first met Fox, how any time he came around I heard a distinct high-pitched sound. When I eventually asked him about it, he figured out that I was "sensitive" to Shui's energy. Fox had performed some kind of introduction and touched my head with the staff. At that point, the ringing sound had suddenly disappeared.

"When we were able to harmonize your energy with Shui's, we found out a few things. It didn't seem useful to tell you about the things at the time. But now, we are far past the point of keeping anything from you." I was intrigued. What haven't they wanted to tell me?

Fox continued, "For one thing, we found out that Shui could communicate with you almost as easily as it did with me. We were able to find out that your mind and your spirit are compatible for direct communication. However, I asked Shui not to communicate with you directly."

"You did? Why not?" I asked, feeling somehow vaguely upset.

"I didn't want you to be frightened." Fox said. "you have a flexible mind, and that is a great benefit in many different situations. But suddenly having an *item* communicate directly with a person's mind could be too much. I'm sure you understand that." I did understand. I could imagine lots of people falling apart if something like that happened. "So, I would suggest that if you feel ready to communicate, open your mind and Shui will do the rest. Part of what we discovered was that your mind is stronger than average. You will have the ability to project your thoughts as well as to receive them with Shui…

That said, Fox nodded and took his hand off of Shui. I thought about what Fox had said and was certainly open to communicating with Shui. "Well… How?" I asked.

Over the next few minutes Fox instructed me on how to clear my mind and then to open my thoughts. In that state, he informed me, I would be receptive to communication. I looked over at Shui in my hand, took a deep breath, and tried to open my mind.

Chapter 17

Shui

It was surprising how easy it was. I had a tremendous amount of momentum. It seems that as soon as I opened my thoughts, I heard a 'voice' in my head. But to call it a voice would not be fully accurate. It didn't have the sound, but I understood meaning from it just the same. It was different from how the Arkyala had been able to give me concepts directly. This was not a matter of giving me an understanding of some body of knowledge. This was active communication between two conscious minds. The voice had that tough uncle character to it. (It was strange that I kept coming up with this idea since I didn't have any uncles, but that was the feeling.)

It had simply been a matter of thinking, 'I'm going to open my mind.' And just like that, a stream of new communication came into my mind. It wasn't like spoken speech, I could hear it in my head. It was a completely different kind of communication. It was like a package that contained the *idea* of sounds, emotional content, the *meaning* of words, as well as subtle tones. And while it is hard to describe, it was easy to understand, even with complicated and specific messages. It felt like Shui's method of communicating was like a fat and comfortable paintbrush that could still, somehow paint thin, precise lines.

The best that I can describe it, Shui sent, **Greetings Batou Kwan. *It looks like we have a fight ahead of us.*** Strangely, the statement had… eagerness to it. Shui was fully confident in his strength. And, in being able to hear the tone to his communication, I knew that Shui was masculine. His thought had conveyed not only confidence, but cheerful eagerness.

I turned to Fox, blurting out excitedly, "We did it! Shui just spoke to me. Or not spoke…" Fox smiled knowingly. "It wasn't like words, or pictures or feelings, it was sort of a combination of all of them."

Fox nodded, "That's good. I expect you will want to let your minds get to know each other, and to formulate your plan for the fight."

Again, I opened my mind and again Shui sent to me, **You don't need to worry Batou Kwan. Every warrior must have their first battle. I am with you and we will fight together!** Again the sense of eagerness came through with the words. There was reassurance and eagerness for the fight to come. **You will find the ability to fight. It is a piece that lives within all beings, even if you haven't used it before. But have no fear, it is there. I will help you in whatever ways I'm able. But if it proves to be too much for you at any point, think to me 'help!'**

It felt as though, now that I was speaking to it, that our party on this adventure had just gotten bigger. A demarcation of the roles occurred to me. I was the young inexperienced student. Fox was the wise scholar and teacher. And Shui was the cheerful and hearty fighter. Both of them had worlds more experience than I did.

Feeling probably more prepared than I was, with Shui in my hand, Fox and I proceeded further into the labyrinth. We had only taken two or three more turns before we heard the bellowed roar again. I felt a cold ball of ice form in my belly. The Kaitaur was closer! If it weren't for the tall hedges in the way, we certainly would've been able to see it.

Just a moment later, when we were walking down the path of the labyrinth, we heard growling and snuffling noises coming from the other side of the hedge. With the chilling certainty, I knew that the Kaitaur was just around the corner. Fox and I exchanged glances. Then he nodded.

We crept closer to where the next hall branched off of our path. We could smell a rotten odor of decay and musk. The tall hedge between us was thick with dead leaves so we looked around the corner. I crouched down, Fox stood above, we both peered around the hedge. We saw a square clearing enclosed by the hedge walls. The clearing had a single dead tree in the center of it. There was an exit door on the opposite side of the clearing from us. But the Kaitaur was nowhere to be seen. Then I shifted my position and noticed it, standing off to one side of the clearing. I don't think that I will ever forget what I saw.

The Kaitaur was a beast pulled from a nightmare. I wondered again at a realm that gave birth to such horrible things. Although, I thought in fairness, there must be monstrous things in our world too. They just weren't *this* kind of monstrous.

The Kaitaur's body was vaguely the shape of a man, in that it had two arms, two legs and a head. But the similarities ended there. For example, the Kaitaur's was far furrier than any human could be. The dirty gray fur appeared oily and matted.

The Kaitaur's furry head had a shape somewhere between a dead bear and a dead wolf. It only had one intact ear. The other one looked like it had been torn off. The Kaitaur only had its left eye too. The eye was a cloudy white, making it look like the monster was blind. But within the center of that eye, a red light glowed. So, it probably could see. The right eye was missing, leaving only a dark, gaping hole.

Next to the blind eye, a split-open patch on the side of the head revealed the pale gray bone of its skull. Its head had a protruding muzzle with long, chipped, yellow fangs. The open jaw hung down at an angle. I looked for a moment and realized that one cheek was missing and that the jaw was badly broken. Only one side of it was properly attached to the skull. A few exposed tendons, unnaturally stretched, were visibly holding the jaw together. Viscous black drool was puddling at the monster's feet.

The Kaitaur's limbs were thick with corded muscle under the long, grimy fur. The skin on its ribcage had been ripped off, exposing the ribs and dead organs underneath. Before my observations went any further, a communication from Shui came through to my mind. It was almost like he was letting me hear *his* observations.

Undead, so strength limits are off... can't be killed... Looks based on the Volmedko- Fangs, but the jaw is broken, so bite may be feeble...Probably venomous... Has claws too, need to gauge speed... Should be slower than a Volmedko, though... Hopefully less power too. No sign of the 'dempheys'.

"I don't understand," I whispered, "What do you mean Shui? And what is a Volmedko? And what is a 'dempheys'? And what does 'Batou' mean?" When Shui responded, I could sense patience and amusement coming through with the 'words'.

First, just 'think' to me. It's faster than speaking. 'Batou' is the word my people used for young ones. It is a name for those who are young, valued by the village, and are being taught. You are young. We value you. And school is now in session... **

The first thing I meant is that this Kaitaur is an animated undead. This means that there is no spirit inside that... golem. It also means that its body does not have any of the strength/safety limits. In a living body, a person cannot use all of their strength. They can keep exerting themselves, but at some point, the body stops feeding them strength. Otherwise, the person would tear their muscles and injure themselves. Since it is not alive, it is not concerned with maintaining its body. If muscles tear, they tear... It also means that there is no 'thought' at work in the Kaitaur. It is only a *simulation* of life, but it will probably still retain acute hunting instincts.

**The Volmedko was a predator from long ago. Whether it was man, Sylvans, or mammots it was hunting, the Volmedko was the supreme killer of its age. It walked on four legs, and was the savage original that many other beasts came from. Bears, grun, wolves, loycans, vargri... all come from the Volmedko. Although, they each only have a fraction of the original Volmedko's power. **

Even though the jaw is broken and it might have a weak bite, we still want to avoid the fangs because it is probably venomous... We will want to avoid its claws too, but we need to gauge its power and speed- somehow, because the

Volmedko was unbelievably fast and strong. I remember the Volmedko from my life... This thing is an abomination, a copy of that noble beast... and it has been used very poorly.

I was going to ask another question, but Shui was pointing something out. ***It is a hollow shell of rage and hate. Look.***

The bellowed roar sounded again. It was an even more frightening sound up close. I looked up just in time to see the Kaitaur charge. It took off running at the lone tree. The Kaitaur was fast, launching itself into the air and landing a tremendous blow on the trunk of the tree. The trunk cracked and the top of the tree fell over. The Kaitaur was apparently strong too.

The beast went berserk, arms flailing, tearing at the tree. Initially, there were deep gouges in the wood wherever the claws touched. But after an impressive berserk moment, the tree had been reduced to a stump, jagged-edged sections of logs, and scattered piles of splinters.

The Kaitaur stood there panting, chest heaving. It turned away from the ravaged tree. I could see its exposed ribs expanding and contracting with each breath. After a few moments, the beast's breathing became more even and it seemed to rest. We crouched there, studying the monster we had to pass.

Good, it is not nearly as fast or strong as the original Volmedko.

There was a wet bubbling sound. My eyes flicked over to look at the tree stump. I can only describe what it was doing as 'growing'. But growing was too wholesome a term for what I saw. Wriggling, gray-black worms emerged from the top of the stump. These worms immediately stopped wriggling and lay down to form the 'new' substance of the tree, making it a little taller. Then the 'new tree' substance would push out more gray-black worms and repeat the process. I watched it unfold with unnerving speed.

In this way, the tree regrew itself to a perfect copy of how it had been before. Even though it was just a 'tree' growing, the process was foul and made me feel unclean watching it. I was still crouching there, peering around the corner, holding Shui, but I realized that I was leaning back as far as I could. The tree finished 'growing.' The Kaitaur was at rest, just standing and staring at the hedge behind it. It was a still moment within the clearing, everything had stopped moving. Then Shui sent a thought.

As for the 'dempheys', here they come. That is the name my people called those little demons. Keep watching, anything we observe about them can help us during the battle.

Many of the little 'dempheys' we had seen practicing to ambush us, walked out through the doorway opposite ours. The little 'dempheys' went into a flurry of motion, cleaning up all of the destroyed pieces of tree. In short order, they had cleaned up the clearing and put it back in its original condition.

Then the little demons took the wood and marched back through the doorway on the other side of the clearing. We waited in position until they returned a few moments later. They must have gotten rid of the wood, because when they returned, the wood was gone. But they brought something else in its place.

Instead of the wood, the 'dempheys' then brought out the bound pygmy demon. It was the masked demon we had seen earlier, the one tied up and savagely beaten. He was being marched out by a large group of the little 'dempheys', each carrying spears or vine ropes. Its mask-face was battered. It was snarling and shouting at its captors. The waist-high pygmy demon was twice the height of the knee-high 'dempheys'. It looked like a pack of tiny people had captured a giant. It was surreal. I was twice the size of their giant!

Vine ropes were wrapped around the pygmy's chest, firmly binding its arms at its sides. More of the vine ropes were tied as choking leashes around the pygmy demon's neck. A dozen of the 'dempheys' were holding the ends of the ropes. They pulled the ropes in opposite directions to control the pygmy demon. A group of the 'dempheys' were carrying their bone spears, jabbing the pygmy in the back.

The little 'dempheys' pushed the pygmy demon into the clearing. Then they split into two groups. Half of the 'dempheys' headed toward where Fox, Shui, and I were crouched.

They still cannot see us, Batou. Hold our position here. Those 'dempheys' came to stand a few paces in front of us, blocking our path. They faced into the clearing, with their backs to us. They were clearly a barrier, so the pygmy would not escape.

The other half of the 'dempheys' stayed in the center of the clearing, poking the pygmy a few last times with their spears, before they released it. Then they retreated to the doorway on the opposite side of the clearing. They stood in the doorway and pointed their spears out. The doorway was now filled with bristling spear-tips, also preventing the pygmy demon from escaping.

When the 'dempheys' released the pygmy demon, the choking vines fell away. The pygmy whirled and snarled at the little demons. It was furious, but wouldn't attack the armed 'dempheys'. The group of 'dempheys' were crouched at knee-height in front of us, raised their spears. We stood behind them, looking over their heads. Beyond them was the pygmy demon and the Kaitaur. And beyond them was the opposite door, guarded by the other group of 'dempheys'.

I experienced a new feeling then. It was like when I was underwater with the Shogatt coming for me. When the Shogatt was attacking, I knew that something was coming to *kill* me. This time, I knew that violence was coming. I could feel it.

Yes, you feel it Batou. Man has senses beyond sight and hearing. Sensing the approach of danger is one of those senses. Violence is coming. Still, hold in place.

The pygmy demon suddenly stopped snarling. It was also aware that it was in danger. Its anger immediately turned to fear. The pygmy slowly turned to see the hulking Kaitaur, still facing away from it. The Kaitaur was staring at the hedge. The pygmy demon backed away slowly. The Kaitaur's head snapped up and it spun to see the pygmy.

The Volmedko could sense fear. That was one of its many senses. It seems this copy can do the same. Still Batou, hold in place.

With a vicious roar, the Kaitaur pounced. I was so scared I thought the beast would smell my fear instead, but it focused on the pygmy demon. It closed the distance between them in an instant. The Kaitaur fell on the pygmy demon. Sinking both teeth and claws into the pygmy, the Kaitaur tore the little demon apart. Each terrible strike from the Kaitaur splashed black ichor across the clearing. When the ichor touched the ground, it began to evaporate into a greasy tar-smelling smoke. Soon the pygmy demon had been reduced to a small collection of chunks covered in viscous black ink. The 'dempheys' were obviously pleased. Many threw back their heads and gave high-pitched snarls. Many pumped their fists in the air. Some made a huffed growling sound that might have been laughter. I had never seen it before, but I recognized bloodlust.

The Kaitaur, panting once more, returned to staring at the hedge again. It seemed to either be killing or resting, but not capable of other actions.

The little 'dempheys' collected the chunks of pygmy demon and took them out from the clearing. Soon the clearing was free of demon chunks. The line of tiny demons that had been blocking our path rushed to join the others. The Kaitaur stood there staring at the hedges. The greasy tar-smelling smoke was still floating through the air of the clearing.

Prepare yourself Batou, the battle is nearly upon us. In this battle, you have only three goals; suppress your fear, try to learn the techniques I will demonstrate, and GRIP THIS STAFF TIGHTLY.

Fox said quietly, "Ready?"

I swallowed the hard lump in my throat and looked around. A hollow feeling in the pit of my stomach was making me feel nauseous. I nodded to Fox and gripped the staff tightly.

Fox raised the flute to his lips. He took a deep breath and began playing. A long, clear note filled the air. To my untrained ear, Fox's playing sounded superb. I was astonished at the mellow tones, perfectly pure and sweet, that were coming out of Fox's flute. At first, the tune was light and playful. It sounded cheerfully diverting, like festival music.

Immediately after that first thought, appreciating Fox's musical talent, I remembered that we were visible again. I looked down at my arms and hands. They looked the same that they had a moment before, but I knew to trust what both Fox and Shomyira had told me.

Fox played his flute and marched ahead, slowing only briefly to peer around the corner. Staff in hand, I resolutely followed behind him. As we turned the corner, the Kaitaur's odor intensified, assailing our noses. Fox, to his credit, kept playing while I gagged on the smell.

The sound of Fox's flute made a strange contrast to our surroundings. The sound was sweet and clear. But the smell in this place was the exact opposite.

As we entered the clearing Fox stayed to the side of the hedge, walking along the perimeter and staying as far away from the Kaitaur as possible. I shuffled my feet. I held Shui across my chest, right hand gripping towards the top, my left hand was gripping the middle of it. My eyes were constantly shifting around.

I knew that we were visible now, and I expected, or at least half expected the Kaitaur to attack. Instead, the beast was having some kind of reaction to the music. It heard the sound of Fox's flute and began to reel drunkenly.

Batou, notice its eye!

I focused on the Kaitaur's face. The red light in its eye was no longer visible! It was just cloudy white. But the Kaitaur's head moved, following something in the air. Did this mean Fox's theory had been right? The Kaitaur could see the music, so it was blind to us now? Taking no chances, we continued to circumvent the beast.

The Kaitaur began lazily slashing at the air. It was clearly incapacitated by Fox's music. I knew the different demons could have different reactions to the music, but I hoped that the little demons might be won over the same way.

But apparently, the little demons were less susceptible to the music. Shui did not send me a warning thought. But I did not need Shui to tell me that the little demons were coming. I could hear their high-pitched yells approaching before they flooded out from the doorway. On the opposite side of the clearing, a horde of 'dempheys' poured out. They were running toward us, screaming, hoisting their spears high.

Ahh! The battle has commenced! Step forward and protect Fox while he plays! And remember your goals here. Luck in battle, Batou!

Before I thought too much, I boldly stepped forward to meet the advancing horde. What was I doing??? What were my goals again? Don't be scared, watch everything, learn to fight and hold on? I was terrified and retreated inside my mind, observing everything that was taking place. Time seemed to slow down to a trickle. It was such a strange sensation that it pushed me out of my fear. I peered at the tiny legs of the approaching demons and saw them actually slowing down. The world was... slowing! This would change everything.

Somehow this extra advantage gave me enough confidence to properly join the fight. The next few minutes were a blur of intense battle. I remember stepping in front of Fox and having the wave of little demons swarm us.

Shui spun out of my hands and landed horizontally, balanced on my right shoulder next to my neck. I reached up to grasp the staff as it pushed me down to one knee. The thick top end of the staff was pointed at the center of the oncoming mass of demons. Their faces were distorted, sprinting and screaming in slow motion. The narrower, butt-end of the staff was pointing over my shoulder, behind me.

I could feel my eyes open wide as the metal grain that ran through Shui began to glow. It grew brighter and brighter until I had to close my right eye and squint with my left. It felt like I was holding a stick of pure sunlight. In my mind and throughout my body, I could feel the power accumulating in the staff.

Then there was a 'THWUMP' sound and I felt an intense bolt of concentrated force shoot out from the end of the staff.

It impacted the demons at the front edge of the incoming wave. The entire horde of demons running toward us were blasted away. Some flew over the hedges opposite us. Some were embedded in those hedges. Some were even driven into the ground, cracking the stone. The resulting recoil bent me back, nearly taking me off my feet. If I had not been on one knee already, it certainly would have knocked me down.

Heh, heh. This is going to be good! I could feel the glee come from Shui and couldn't help but share in it. It was a powerful feeling to have fear convert to confidence. The blow we had just dealt them was so devastating, I was sure we had just won the battle.

But I was very wrong. The battle was only beginning. Another wave of the 'dempheys' immediately came out screaming, ready for battle. The incoming demons slowed briefly, hesitating when they saw their comrades embedded in the hedges. But their frenzied hatred quickly overcame that hesitation.

They were rushing straight at us. This time Shui began flashing rapidly and jumping around in my hands. My arms shook as I held on. This was accompanied by a rapid, staccato, 'THUM-THUM-THUM-THUM-THUM!' sound. In my mind, I compared it to a drummer.

This time Shui fired out smaller shots, targeting individual demons. If time had not been slowed down, I would not have been able to keep up with the action. Individual demons flew back, flicked away by the overwhelming strikes. One flash, one 'THUM', one demon gone, then Shui would target the next one…

We probably would have continued hitting them from a distance, but I suddenly noticed our position. We were on the other side of the dead tree, opposite the Kaitaur. And since we had reached the middle of the clearing, the doorways in or out were now on either side of us. A separate horde of 'dempheys' were rushing out of each doorway.

Good! This will let you learn about close fighting on two fronts!

Shui flipped around again, this time landing under my arm and lifting me back to my feet. Fox was moving, so I kept moving too. The Kaitaur was still reeling, languidly swiping at the air, oblivious to us. I marveled that Fox was able to stay calm and keep his breath so even. The hordes of demons merged and surrounded us. We had only the hedge at our backs. The demons swarmed.

I probably would have panicked and swung Shui around carelessly. But fortunately for me, Shui was an experienced and skillful fighter. The battle began and Shui proceeded to show me how to fight. He demonstrated a number of strikes. The staff began to twirl and spin in my hands, picking up speed and momentum as it did. I felt Shui striking the 'dempheys' with tremendous power. I could feel the concussive force on my end.

As Shui struck demon after demon, they flew off at random angles. Many of them got stuck in the hedges. Sometimes Shui swung low, scooping and chipping the demons up, sending them flying high over the hedges. Other times he jabbed out like a punch, striking repeatedly with the butt end of the staff. Those punch strikes with the butt of the staff made a sharp 'CRACK' sound as it struck each demon's forehead. Shui hit precisely the same spot in the center of their foreheads every time. The demons he hit were knocked flat and sent bouncing and sliding across the stones. At first I felt like I was just trying to hold on to the spinning, swinging, and jabbing staff. But then I gradually became aware that Shui was guiding my posture.

Some part of my mind had been listening to his instruction without realizing it. Of course, that had been the case! I couldn't spin a staff around before this fight! Giving myself over to it, I adopted the unfamiliar poses and found how effective they were.

Several times, the 'dempheys' tried to rush around us. But each time, Shui caught them with wide, sweeping, crushing blows. When they made a break for Fox, Shui knocked them senseless before ejecting them from the clearing. If my feet were in the wrong position, Shui would move one way or another, pulling or pushing me into the correct pose. I felt Shui's subtle coaching, directing my hands where they needed to be. The staff became a blur as I spun it all around me. I spun it on either side of my body, alternating sides, I spun it overhead. But each time, just as I was admiring how the staff was spinning, it would use the collected momentum and deliver a crushing blow to some demon in range (usually at an unexpected angle).

I had been so very afraid at the beginning of the fight. But then, as Shui had more and more success (I don't take ANY credit for this), I began to feel more confident and aggressive. Or at least, I felt less afraid.

But as the fight progressed, I saw that it would not be over quickly. The little 'dempheys' kept coming. What if we lost? When the doubt formed in my mind, it all started to fall apart. I felt unable to keep up with the deluge of little demons. And because I felt unable to deal with the demons, they became too much for me.

I heard a crunching sound and looked down to see a 'demphey' gnawing on one of my bamboo shin protectors. I couldn't feel the impact and felt grateful for the runes. The tide had turned and I was being overwhelmed. In desperation, I thought to Shui, *HELP!*

I was crouching, watching a 'demphey' lunging, spear-first at my face when I called for help. Time slowed down even further until it actually stopped. The 'demphey' froze in mid-air. I looked around and saw that every demon was frozen. Even Fox had stopped moving, still playing the flute, but frozen in mid-note.

Then I blinked and found myself in completely different surroundings. It was almost like waking up from a demon's illusion. I was no longer in the Kaitaur's clearing. I was no longer in the labyrinth. Instead I was standing in the middle of a strange, pleasant room. The change in surroundings threw me out of the battle-panic. The battle was gone. There were none of the 'dempheys' in sight. Now I was just confused.

The room was large, ten paces square. A stone fire-pit was set into the floor on my left. Above it was a painting of a black skinned 'man' with bright green eyes, pointed ears, and shoulder-length, white hair. His features were angular and serious, with a heavy jaw. But there was a twinkle in his eye. His expression showed an abundance of mirth, but even more ferocity. It was a very human expression, but it was somehow clear that this was not a picture of a man. There was a sense of 'otherness', some crucial difference that gave off that impression. This was a picture of a male, but not a man...

On my right, the wall opposite the picture had a large open door that led out to a wooden deck. There were a few pieces of furniture I didn't recognize. For example, there were large pieces that were clearly used to sleep and to sit on, but they were a style I had never seen before. On the other walls were chalked drawings of animals I had never seen either. The animals looked like they were from someone's imagination rather than real life.

I turned in a slow circle and looked at my surroundings. Where was I? Where were Fox and Shui? I walked over to the open door and looked out. Beyond the wooden deck, I could see lush rainforest just outside.

Each of the tree trunks were as big in diameter as my house. Thick vines, the size of large, normal trees curled down around the enormous trunks. I craned my neck, looking up. High above, the leaves made a dense canopy. Suddenly, I was disoriented by the volume of life I heard around me; birds, monkeys, animals! Life! The rich greens I saw were almost overwhelming. I didn't realize how much I had missed seeing other living things. I felt happy tears welling up in my eyes.

Next, I became aware of the sound of falling water. I stepped onto the deck. Apparently, this room was elevated off the ground, a sort of lookout. Interestingly, there were no steps down from this place. It looked like it had been built on stilts nestled against a tree. How did someone get down, and how did a person get back up here? I looked down to the left and saw a green river flowing by 20 paces away. I could see the river flow by for a little distance before my view of it was blocked by a huge tree. It was not visible on the other side of the tree, but clouds of mist billowing up behind it showed the river must fall off somewhere behind it. The river was twice as wide as I was tall, but it was apparently deep, because when it dropped off, the sound of the waterfall it made was clearly audible. Overall the effect was very soothing.

I looked around, confused. What had happened? ***This is unexpected.***

"Shui?" I called out. "I can't see you!" Knowing that I still had connection to Shui gave me hope. "Where are you?"

Try to stay calm Batou. It appears that you have visited my home within the staff. I didn't know that you would be able to do that.

"Wait, this is your *home*? I'm *inside* your staff?!"

When you called for help, it appears that you came to my home for refuge. I do offer you refuge Batou. So, you are welcome here if you want to stay, or you can come to observe the battle.

"The battle!" I cried. The horror and panic of combat came rushing back. "I forgot! We are still fighting?"

Oh yes. But don't worry. Right now, we are communicating outside of time. In this place, time doesn't exist. Everything in the world outside has frozen in place.

"Oh… But what do you mean, I can observe the battle?"

I mean that you are inside your body too. Your mind is anchored to that body while you are alive. So you can always return to that body, even if you don't take control…

"I don't understand." I asked, feeling slow-witted.

Imagine that your body is like a horse. You are riding the horse, but you have your eyes closed. I will take the reins, if you like. And if you want to see what the horse is doing, just open your eyes.

"All right, but Please keep the reigns! But how do I do it?" I asked. "How do I open my eyes?" I could sense Shui smiling, amused.

Simple, Batou! Just tell yourself you are going to open your eyes... Now, it's time to deal with those 'dempheys'.

I could sense his amused smile change into a predatory grin. Even though the 'dempheys' had attacked us, for a moment I felt sorry for them. Then, with certainty, I felt Shui's presence leave this place. I could feel that I was still connected to him. I was sure that I could speak to him if I tried.

But instead, I decided to try to join him in the fight. I willed myself to open my eyes, as though I had just woken up and was lying in bed. I imagined myself in that bed, and simply thought, "Open your eyes."

The process was much simpler than I imagined it could be. The sensation was not quite like opening my eyes. Rather, it was more like being pulled into a room, but it was a room that I knew. It felt like my mind was returning to where it belonged.

Immediately, images and sensations began to appear in my mind that were from the fight, not from Shui's forest home. I was again located in my body. I was again holding the staff. And I was again looking at a little demon, frozen in mid leap toward stabbing my face. The image was scary enough that I almost retreated back to Shui's home.

Luckily for me, Shui was taking control. I watched, astonished, as Shui flipped his own staff around in my hand, knocking the attacking the demon away from us. Then, Shui proceeded to put on a demonstration of stunning martial skill.

The little demons were still attacking. If anything, there were more of them than before. I sat within my mind, looking out through my own eyes, shocked, watching the battle unfold. We were massively outnumbered, and more were arriving every moment. But now, having more weapons, Shui began to fight not only with the staff, but also with my fists and feet.

It was surreal and unbelievable to watch myself instantly turn in to a skillful fighter. Shui was able to twist and turn my body in such unexpected ways that none of the little demons was able to touch me. Strikes sent at us, found us gone when they arrived. Not only that, Fox was completely safe from their attacks so far. Shui destroyed or ejected every demon who rushed at Fox. Out of the corner of my eye, I saw the Kaitaur still drunkenly dancing as the fight raged next to him.

Now that he had temporary control of my body, Shui was able to fight harder than he had before. I had been able to spin the staff very quickly *with his help.* But when he did it on his own, without my clumsy participation, the staff spun more than twice as fast. In fact, it moved so quickly that, even with time slowed down, it was impossible to pick out the staff within the blurred circles it made. I watched him direct my arms and legs into sharp, snapping kicks, crisp blocks, and lightning-fast strikes. Any 'dempheys' that approached us met punches, kicks and expertly delivered strikes from the staff.

I could barely keep up with Shui's speed as the staff became a blur of whirling punishment. The 'dempheys' were like target dummies standing still. If one attacked him (and I was sure Shui was a 'he' now) from a 'blind spot', Shui dealt them crushing blows without even seeming to see them (at least not with my eyes). It was like Shui was always aware of every part of the clearing, even the spaces behind us.

I watched, astonished, as he launched 'us' into a series of acrobatic flips, avoiding a 'demphey' attack and sending three of them flying with a kick. My body flipping, punching, blocking and kicking was something I never expected to see. I had never received any serious fighting training.

Some part of me felt wonderful having the mission, protecting us. I didn't quite feel like a hero, myself. But I felt like I was doing the type of thing heroes do. As a village boy, I could barely believe where I found myself- an action hero?

It felt like every part of my body was reacting and moving at once. Shui's staff, now under the control of Shui's mind, was moving faster than I could easily track. I felt like I was doing some kind of mad dance, spasming, flexing and twitching, but each movement was a strike that ended in broken demons. Shui (moving my body) was spinning and jumping, rolling and ducking, unharmed by the never-ending horde. He was an unbelievable scourge to the 'dempheys'. Only now, did the last few 'dempheys' realize that their comrades were gone. Some hung limp in the surrounding hedges, while others had been sent flying far out of the clearing. Broken, little demon bodies littered the clearing.

Ha! We are still the edge of the blade! Righteous Battle!

What blade? We didn't have any blades. I thought the question toward Shui, not forming it coherently. But apparently I didn't need to, because Shui responded.

It's just an expression, Batou Kwan. Among my people, there were three places that were hardest; the Edge of the Blade, the Tip of the Spear, and the Face of the Club. If a warrior is strong enough, his hardness can equal the Face of the Club. If he is even stronger than that, his hardness can equal the Tip of the Spear. And beyond that, the highest level is the Edge of the Blade- what a true warrior aspires to.

It was only when I felt Shui leave that I realized the fight was over. I was again fully in control of my body. I stood there, dazed and panting, with my heart thundering in my chest. I could hear it pounding in my ears also. My hands were trembling. I was still holding the staff, thinking about the explanation Shui had given me.

Shaking, I looked around the clearing and saw it filled with piles of tiny bodies. None of the 'dempheys' were moving. The only movement I could see (besides myself panting) was from Fox (still playing his flute) and the Kaitaur (still reeling around drunkenly).

As I looked more at the Kaitaur, I realized that its reeling had slowed. It was moving slower, more sluggishly. It was only then that I realized the song Fox was playing had changed. Before it was something light and cheerful and festive. But now, the song had changed to something that was more of a lullaby. The pace of the song was slower now than it had been before. In fact, even I felt the potency of the lullaby. While it did not make me feel like sleeping, I feel like it did help calm the excitement of battle.

The Kaitaur was swaying and turning slowly in place. It was shuffling in small circles, weaving unsteadily. Its slashes at the air had barely any force behind them at all now.

Fox and I watched carefully as the Kaitaur slowed more and more. Eventually, it stumbled to its knees. It weaved back-and-forth, cloudy white eyes looking at something we could not see. A moment later the beast had exhausted itself completely and was lying on the ground. Its chest did not rise and fall with, but then I saw its paw twitch and knew that it had not been destroyed.

Fox played his music a moment longer just to make sure that the Kaitaur was really down. When his caution had been satisfied, Fox stopped playing and slid his flute back into his shoulder bag.

"Outstanding Kwan!" Fox said. I could not help it but I felt myself swelling with pride. There were things that I wanted to ask, and things that I wanted to say. But at that moment, all I could do was smile. I don't know how much of the feeling came from Fox's praise or from the battle itself. I felt… alive. Fox held out his hand and I gave the staff back.

He took a few steps towards the downed beast and made a slow circle around it. Then he planted both hands on Shui and set the butt of the staff against the ground. Then he closed his eyes and began chanting a vaguely familiar incantation. The dirt and stones around the Kaitaur, roughly in a circle, began to sink. I saw immediately that it was the same technique Fox had used it to save us from the fire lizard. It was fascinating watching the process from a different perspective this time. I watched as the Kaitaur was lowered into the ground, still sleeping. Lying on a stone disk that was being pushed into the ground, the beast sank from view. A moment later the ground had sealed up above the sunken Kaitaur. The beast was now hidden within a bubble of dirt and stone just below the surface.

"Both of you did a fantastic job! Kwan, you can see what I meant about Shui's fighting skill!" The staff in his hand flared to light. It was clearly an expression of joy. Shui sent an echo of the same joy directly into my mind. "Now that I've stopped playing music, remember that we are invisible again." I had forgotten but my smile grew- us regaining invisibility was another reason to feel good.

An idea occurred to me. I remembered that we were going to need to pay for our journey back to the living world. I wondered, could we take the Kaitaur? "Do we need the Kaitaur's spirit? Shouldn't you take it?" I asked.

Fox shook his head and smiled ruefully. "We can't. It does not have a spirit or soul to give."

I wondered how long the Kaitaur would be down there. But Fox addressed my question before I could ask, "The beast will be released when it wakes. I can't take responsibility for freeing the Kaitaur from this labyrinth, but I will free it from my trap. Even a mindless undead deserves better than being sealed in a tomb forever."

Oh. It was a sobering thought. I hadn't thought about it that way. Even when it is released from the ground, it will still be trapped in this labyrinth. I imagined being trapped forever in the labyrinth, or the appalling thought of being imprisoned forever underground. I wondered if we shouldn't kill it, instead of leaving it there. It was a killing machine, after all. Now that Fox had subdued it, maybe we should…

But before I could go much further down that line of reasoning, we heard another wave of the 'dempheys' approaching. They rushed into the clearing. I felt a rush that was more excitement than fear, but Shui didn't seem bothered by their appearance. Shui hadn't feared the 'dempheys', not even at the beginning of the fight. And now, after having fought them, my attitude had changed too.

But Fox put his hand on my shoulder and said, "Remember, they can't see us." Sure enough, the little demons were looking around in confusion. When they entered the clearing, they expected to see the Kaitaur, and they expected to see us. But the Kaitaur was nowhere to be seen. Just like we were nowhere to be seen. Instead, the 'dempheys' were greeted with dozens of their fellow demons' bodies.

While they milled about confused and agitated, scratching their heads and chattering at each other, Fox and I edged around them to make our escape. A moment later – Shui flared, and Fox and I stopped moving. The little demons had apparently reached a decision. It seemed that they thought we had run off, and they planned to catch us.

They took off running and streamed past us. Their bone spears bounced at thigh height as they ran by. A moment later they had all run out through the door where we had entered. Again, we were alone in the clearing. "Come on Kwan let's keep moving." Fox said.

We had only taken a few steps when the ground beneath our feet started shaking. The walls of the labyrinth shook. A moment of intense fear gripped me, and I remembered the Shogatt. All I could think was 'What Now???' I hoped that this was not the prelude to another flooding.

The walls shook and rumbled. Dust was shaken free from the stone and clouded the air. Suddenly there was a cacophony of sound and we were surrounded by motion. The sound was made from the rustling leaves of the dead hedges, and from the grating noise of stone grinding against stone. A moment later all of the walls around us began to turn, slide, and pivot.

Fox and I scrambled around, shifting position to stay out of the way of the moving walls. A moment later the walls and hedges stopped moving, then it was silent. Dust was settling to the ground.

The labyrinth had reconfigured itself. Ahead of us, where before there had been a continuation of labyrinth, was now a straight path. From where we were standing, the path led directly uphill to our goal. It was visible, a glowing red castle, straight ahead. It was still several days journey away, but we wouldn't have to find our way through the killer maze. All of the walls in between us and the bone castle had moved to one side or the other. They now lined a wide avenue straight to our destination.

From this distance, I could see movement, showing that the actual castle building was burning. It looked like flames must have been coming out of different windows. There was definitely a flickering yellow-red light surrounding the fortress. It gave an impression, even from a distance. It looked hot… and even more evil than the rest of this place. But that's where we would find Cho Clei, so I steeled myself to approach the demon's lair. After combat with the demons, managing fear wasn't as hard as it used to be. I found it was impossible to be afraid when I felt this tired.

"It looks like we've beaten the Kaitaur and the labyrinth!" Fox said. "Of course, now that we have beaten its guard dog and changed its maze, this demon will definitely know we are coming." I hadn't thought about that.

Even though we were invisible, the changing configuration of the labyrinth showed we were here and had beaten the Kaitaur. "Well, that's where your sister is, so that's where we go… Ready?" He asked. He raised his arm, pointing with Shui up toward the distant castle. I nodded and we set off.

Chapter 18

Fire Fortress

Several times during our journey through this realm, something strange had been happening with distances. For example, we had been travelling toward the castle when the HellFire Road took us under the mountain. Before we went underground, the castle had been visible, ahead in the distance and high above us. When we emerged from being underground and saw the castle, it was closer than it should have been. It was as though every day we walked, even going the wrong direction, the castle got several days closer. I did not notice what was happening at first, but eventually Fox pointed it out to me. "Remember that this place does not have to operate like home." Now we were on a straight path to the castle and nothing stood between us. After an hour of monotonous marching toward the castle, we were suddenly a half day closer. The distance was passing faster than the time we travelled. This allowed me to study our goal.

Right after the labyrinth had changed shape, and we made our final approach, I kept looking up to see new details. At first, the castle was a distant burning building in flickering red and yellow light. Then, as we marched, it was like the ground itself was advancing us toward the castle.

A few years ago, when we were younger, Cho Clei and I would play a game. I would close my eyes and she would creep toward me. Whenever I opened my eyes, she had to stop in place. So the effect was that whenever I opened my eyes, she was closer than expected. The castle was jumping closer the same way.

Whenever I looked up, I could see more of the castle's details. And while there were new details each time, my overwhelming impression was of size. Each time I looked up, the castle seemed to double in size. From a distance, it looked small. But as we approached, the castle quickly took on huge scale. In my mind, I could only compare the enormous building to how I imagined the capital. Even from this distance, I could tell that the walls were too high to throw a rock over them.

There were spaces that must have been large windows, and flames were visible in them, flickering from a distance. Building-shaped red and orange shadows, above and behind the castle walls, showed that there were even larger structures burning inside.

As we got closer, I noticed that the walls of the castle were not quite straight either. As we approached, lines that looked straight revealed that they were actually jagged and angled. Those lines played tricks on my eyes and my mind rebelled against looking too hard at them. Each 'straight' line was made up of numerous smaller crooked lines that looked straight from a distance.

As we got closer and closer, I began to see more minute details. For example, the flat surfaces of the castle were covered in various sized horns. The vast surface of the walls, being covered in barbs, made the 'prickly' building look as forbidding as any place I could have imagined. The building seemed to project menace. It looked like it was almost... alive, like a demon itself. It was hard to explain, but it looked more like the castle had been *grown* there, not built. Then I would look down for a few steps, watching the path in front of me. Then I would look up and notice some new part of the castle.

When I looked up again, the castle looked less 'alive' to me, but still menacing. It was a giant monument from some forgotten age. Being a massive structure made it look timeless. But it's timelessness had been broken, burning now like it was under siege. Of course, I had never seen a castle under siege, but this looked as much like that as I ever would have been able to picture.

The shortest castle walls looked four or five times the height of the Ragyala. At the base of the center section was an enormous iron door. The walls had towers at each corner. Those towers were topped with horned domes. As we got closer, I could clearly see the horns. Each dome had two thick spikes that curved out and up from the opposite sides, like the horned helmet on the demon's statue after the dragon clouds.

Along the top of the walls were wickedly pointed spires, like some type of animals' canines. It got to be a game with me where I would look down, look up, and then notice something new about the castle. Then I would repeat the process. Each time the castle leapt closer. So, each time I had a better view and noticed new details. The smell of smoke in the air intensified. It had been faint before, but it was more noticeable the closer we got to the fortress. Each time we leapt forward, the smell grew more intense.

Before I knew it, we had arrived at the castle. It felt surreal walking straight up to the front door, knowing that we were in hostile territory. But, because we were invisible, I felt reassured continuing. Fox had slowed our pace somewhat, but we were still moving. He seemed to constantly be scanning the front of the castle, also taking in details.

We heard a metallic, thump-clanging sound. It was faint at first, then growing louder. Fox and I turned to see its source. That source immediately made me forget that I was invisible. A group of…metal? … sentries were patrolling the outside of the fortress, and they were heading our way! I stopped moving for a second, paralyzed with fear. There were dozens of silver figures jogging alongside the castle walls. The castle was huge, so they were still some distance away. The sound of their footfalls had traveled ahead of them and alerted us to their approach.

When we saw these new figures, Fox guided me off to the side, off the path. The sentries were on a course that would intercept us at the front gate. We had been following the Hell-Fire Road. It led directly up to, and finally stopped at, the front gate of the castle.

The front gate was a massive door, twice the height of the Ragyala. Although the giant, iron door was closed, smoke still escaped around its edges. Fox and I stood in front of the castle, off to the side of the door. I was keenly aware that if the ShadowLoops didn't work, we were standing in plain sight in front of the huge door.

We stood there diagonally in front of the door, 20 paces away. We watched as the troop of sentries grew clearer as they approached. They looked to be emaciated, but armored demons. It was tough to tell exactly how tall they were because they were in the distance, approaching us.

As the sentries got closer, the repetitive thump clanging noise from their marching got louder. What came into view reminded me of something I had seen in my youth. It was a chart that our family doctor, Doctor Yao, had in his office. I had only been to the doctor a few times in my life, but I remembered the interesting chart. It showed all of the organs in the body, its many muscles, as well as the body's many different bones. That was the comparison that jumped into my mind.

These new soldiers that approached us, reminded me of skeletons. But these skeletons were different from what was inside the bodies of a man. They were similar, but there were some differences.

On their shins, they had spurs that stuck out behind the bone, like chickens. The same went for their shoulders. Spikes jutted out from their shoulders, curving. Their arms looked abnormally long.

But to describe them just as skeletons would not be accurate. Their joints were not exposed. In fact, none of the bones were exposed. It looked instead like skeletons had been dipped in iron. But somehow the iron coating that surrounded their bones stayed mobile and flexible. Between the sound of their marching towards us, the appearance of their iron plated bones, and the dawning recognition of the glowing red lights in their eyes, I suddenly got very scared.

Courage, Batou. Find the stillness

An image came into my mind and I knew that it had come from Shui. It was hard to describe, but what Shui sent me was clearly understandable. The idea was that there was a profoundly calm and secure place within myself. And if I could get to that calm place, I could watch my fear rise and fall without panicking. From that secure place, I could look at the thoughts and feelings I had, without being pulled into them. Shui's advice was not conveyed with words, nor really with images. Instead it was somewhere between a concept and a feeling. And it came with a sample of the actual experience itself. Shui way gave me a piece of that feeling that came from his 'place of stillness'. Without understanding, I began to use his technique, trying to pattern my way after Shui's example.

The advancing demons were still some distance off, but rapidly approaching us. I looked over towards the castle door and surveyed the walls. I craned my neck to see up to the top of them. Aside from the sentries approaching us, I did not see anyone else on the walls or near the door. The billowing smoke coming over the walls, carried burning red embers with it.

"Fox," I said. "How are we going to get in?" When I asked the question, I was feeling firmly rooted in Shui's place of stillness. I could hear the difference in my own voice. I had not asked from a place of panic and worry. I had asked with more calm than I expected, as a secure person with a problem to solve. Fox had been looking at the oncoming sentries, but now turned his attention toward the door. I had already looked around. It didn't seem like there were any other ways that we could get in.

"Right now, we approach and watch. When it comes to actually getting into the castle, I expect the solution will present itself." Fox said. It wasn't a particularly reassuring answer to me, but he hadn't steered me wrong so far, so I put my worry aside.

Just then Fox's staff flashed. A loud boom and a horrendous creaking sound came from the giant Castle gate. A seam of light parted down the middle, and the two massive halves of the great door began to swing inward. The doors themselves appeared to be solid iron, and thicker than I was tall. As soon as the castle doors opened, a wave of heat rolled out. It felt like opening the clay oven in Fong's kitchen.

I felt a faint tingling on my chest and looked down to see the medallion hovering slightly above my skin. Then I noticed a faint blue shimmering in the air. Apparently, the medallion was giving me some protection against the castle's heat. I looked over and noticed a similar shimmering screen around Fox although I had never seen Fox wearing a 'medallion'. Maybe a bead on his rosary worked the same way?

The giant door slowly swung open. The creaking groan of its massive hinges was so loud that I had to cover my ears. I looked over at Fox. He was grimacing at the sound, but didn't cover his ears. Instead, he pointed at the oncoming sentries, then at the door. The soldiers were getting closer and it was clear that when they arrived at the castle door, it would be open.

As the door opened, it granted a view of what was inside. Fox and I moved closer to the huge door to get a better view of the interior. What we saw at first was a massive open courtyard lit with torches on the walls. Inside, the courtyard narrowed down to a wide, but enclosed, hallway. I was surprised that it was not a giant bonfire inside. The inside of the castle was made of stone and iron too, just like the exterior.

The interior stretched away from us, impossibly large, into fire and shadows. I was in awe. I had never seen or even conceived of anything this large.

Then I noticed the floor of that entranceway. After a few paces of stone threshold, the entire cavernous courtyard was paved with different color floor tiles. The patterned floor went all the way down the enclosed hallway. Some tiles were a smooth and glossy black stone. Some tiles were stained a suspicious shade of blood red. Some floor tiles were metallic, and others were a white stone.

The sentries were trotting up towards us. They had almost reached the front gate. Their gait was faster than walking, but not much faster. The sound of their footfalls, though loud, had become a reassuring cadence. But I did not realize that until the cadence was suddenly broken.

When the sentries reached the front of the castle, directly in front of the open castle door, they broke into a sprint. They had been relatively organized when they trotted up, moving in a loose "formation". But when they reached the front of the door, they turned as one, pivoting in unison and sprinted into the castle. Suddenly the reassuring cadence of their steps became a jumbled chaos.

Fox touched my arm. "Look!" He said. He was pointing at the feet of the sentries. They were sprinting, but their legs were moving strangely. Their legs did not move in a straight line as they ran. Instead, their feet darted laterally while running at top speed. The demons ran into the castle, hopping from tile to tile, tapping just the toes of their boots long enough to make contact before sprinting on. I spotted immediately that different sentries stepped only on stones of a specific color. When I noticed that they only stayed with one color, I felt certain that I had seen what Fox was pointing out. I watched one sentry in particular, as the pack ran in. It stepped on black stones, and *only* on black stones. My eyes switched to another. This sentry *always* stepped on the red tiles. None of the sentries seemed to look down as they ran through. I looked at Fox to see if there was something else to notice, but he was watching the sentries.

Their sound of their footfalls had switched from a 'clomp-chink-clomp-chink-clomp' sound when they were outside the castle to a much faster, 'ch-ch-ch-ch-ch-ch-ch-ch-ch-ch-ch-ch' sound as they ran inside.

Very quickly, the demon sentries had nearly finished passing through the tiled courtyard. The sound of their footfalls suddenly reverted to the coordinated 'clomp-chink-clomp-chink' sound. I turned to study them again, but most of the group were already into the enclosed hall past the courtyard.

A moment after that, the sentries had gone. They disappeared into the interior and the sounds of their passage faded out. We stood there a moment in the silence. Then the loud creaking groan of the door's massive hinges broke the silence. Startled, I jumped.

Shui flashed in Fox's hand. I heard the thought in my mind.
This is our chance. We should go. Now!

Apparently, Fox and I had received the same thought from Shui. Fox looked from side to side, considered briefly, and finally nodded. We scrambled through the closing castle doors. They moved slowly enough that it was easy to get inside before they closed.

As we crossed the threshold of the castle door, I looked around and fought a feeling of awe. We had run into the entry, but stopped short of the tiles. The castle inside the walls was beyond enormous. Before us was the courtyard we had glimpsed through the giant doorway. I had to guess how big the courtyard was since its boundaries were beyond the shadows.

Size was distorted here, so the castle looked impossibly big. Some part of my mind knew the castle could not be as large as it appeared, even as I looked around. From my perspective, the castle seemed as large as the maze had been. And I knew that couldn't be possible. The castle had been a spot within the maze, but now that we were here, the castle seemed bigger than the whole maze. Seeming to read my thoughts, Fox murmured, "This place is not as large as it appears…"

White, black, red and gray tiles stretched out on the ground. As I looked at the tiles, some part of me had to admit that seeing the red was welcome. It reminded me of life itself and the vibrant living world. It was not as strong a reaction as when I had visited Shui's 'home' but I could still clearly feel it and identify it.

Now that we were inside, I had a better idea of the castle's layout. We were only entering the outermost level of the castle grounds. It appeared to have concentric rings going around it. The courtyard we were entering was just the entrance to the outermost ring.

I looked up and saw that beyond the courtyard, a series of spire-topped towers rose up to stab into the red sky. At the center of those towers was the taller, central building of the castle. It stood in the shape of a twisted demon. The tower looked like a twisted, half-man half-bat, with arms down at its sides and its head thrown back in mid-scream. I took a closer look at the fanged mouth, horns, and ears like a screaming demon-bat. It was colossal towering above us, silhouetted against the red sky. It was hypnotic. I couldn't look away. I stood transfixed, staring up at it. Black clouds crossed the red sky. Black clouds crossed my thoughts too.

It was only when Fox said quietly, "This castle is different from what you have seen before. The place radiates substantial evil. Don't let it capture your mind." His calm and gentle tone shook me from the place that I had been sliding into.

Now that I had shaken myself out of the trance, I said, "I don't suppose it would do us any good standing here." Fox looked thoughtful for a moment.

"That's true. In fact, it's even possible that it's dangerous remaining where we are, but…" He said. Taking Fox's statement as approval, I took a step forward onto a black square. "Wait! Don't mo-!" Fox said, but it was too late. My foot was already firmly on a black tile. I would have snatched my foot back, but Fox's second direction got through to me in time. I did not move, pinned in place, right foot on the black tile. Fox looked from side to side, nodded resignedly, stepped on to a black square, two paces to my left. "It looks like we are committed." Fox said.

"What did I do? I shouldn't have stepped here? I thought we figured out that you had to step on only one color." I said. Now that I knew I had made a mistake, I was frozen in that spot.

Fox took a step forward onto the next black tile as he responded to me. "We did notice that they were moving on tiles of only one color when they first entered this courtyard. But if you think back, at some point their steps fell back into a regular cadence. They went from running back to a quick march." I nodded. I did remember when the sound of the sentries' steps had reverted from the chaotic '-ch-ch-ch' sound back to the coordinated 'clomp-chink-clomp' sound

But what did that have to do with it? Fox continued, "Which means that at some point, when their steps became 'regular' the one-color-only pattern was broken." He looked at me. I still didn't get it. He went on, "So, whatever trap we are avoiding by staying just on one color tile, will work against us when we are supposed to start walking normally again. I wasn't able to see exactly where that was. Did you?"

Fox sounded genuinely curious and hopeful. A lot of people could have been unkind in that situation since I had put us in danger. Fox had probably wanted to think it through before we stepped onto the tiles. I had put us in danger by being impulsive. But Fox was not being unkind, it was just the conversational teaching method that he had. "No." I replied.

Fox looked over at me with a pitying expression. "Don't feel bad, Kwan. This is a new experience for *both* of us, so we are *both* at a disadvantage here. I received some education before coming here, but I had never actually been to this realm before. In the grand scheme, we will operate in harmony with the Gale, and whatever problems arise will also have solutions arise to meet them." He took another step onto the next black square.

There was a deep 'THOOMMM' sound behind us. The giant doors had fully closed behind us. When the doors closed, sliding into place, they made the tiles tremble beneath our feet.

I looked back and saw that the inside of the doors was intricately wrought iron and white bone. There were also small holes, the size of my finger that dotted the door's interior. They were worked into the bone and iron, pointing into the courtyard.

The sound of the door closing nearly made me jump and lose my balance. Or maybe it was just that the doors were so close to us. They were literally at our backs. I think that I would have jumped, scared like a rabbit, back before I started this quest. But I had changed along the way here. Instead of jumping, I crouched bracing for an attack. I could feel the growth I had done since arriving in this realm.

A blast of sound filled the air throughout the castle grounds. Progress or not, I flinched. The sound was terrifying at first. Eventually I got used to it. It was the sound of… something… demon music? It had pounding rhythms, thumping drums, a distorted screeching and howling. The sound was primal and brutal and it made me think of painful death.

Stepping from black square tile to black square tile, we set out across the courtyard. I winced at the occasionally soaring, screeching demonic vocals. To block out the noise, I tried to stay focused on the immediate goal. Somewhere inside this evil castle was my sister. Find her. It was that simple. Before I knew it we had progressed halfway across the entry courtyard and were lulled into a sense of security.

So, when I stepped on the next black tile and heard a soft 'thwf' sound, I barely noticed it. But I did notice when I saw the wickedly barbed, iron dart hovering in the air. It floated at chest level, on my right, five feet away. At the same time, I felt the familiar tingling on my chest from the medallion. I looked up at Fox. He had only been a step ahead of me, but he already had half a dozen of the darts hovering on each side. More of the darts were arriving each moment, each hitting the shield and sticking there. I focused on a single dart to my right and noticed that it was slightly vibrating, as though it was alive. They were wriggling and pushing to reach us through the shields!

We both froze on our black squares, trying to figure out the best way to go now. "Now walk regularly!" Fox said. We both forced ourselves to walk normally. It was hard since I had been making myself only step on the black tiles. I had put a rigid command in my mind to keep to the black tiles. There was a white tile in front of me, but I forced myself to step onto it.

Fox was doing the same. We were walking on different colored tiles, but it was already too late. We tried walking normally, then marching like the soldiers had. But whatever shot those first darts at us, now *knew* our location. And it appeared to be *tracking* us. The sounds came fast now, like a woodpecker hammering a tree. 'thwf' 'thwf' 'thwf' 'thwf' 'thwf' 'thwf' 'thwf' 'thwf' The air was filled with the screeching, howling music and the (comparatively quiet) sound of darts being shot at us. More and more of the darts appeared, seemingly from nowhere. As they arrived, the darts defined the shape of our shields. It was impossible to ignore. Soon both Fox and I were surrounded by a dome of barbed darts pointing in at us. As we hurried, the darts moved with us. They were held in place, stuck in our shields. But since the shields moved with us, the darts came too.

"Fox?!" I said, panic rising in my voice. We kept walking but I doubted that the shields would last our entire way across the courtyard. Even now the darts were vibrating and pushing closer, slowly and inexorably towards us. They moved with purpose, *alive* with menace.

"Change of plans!" Fox said. "Run!" He yelled. We both took off running straight forward. When it became painfully clear that we would not make it before the shields ran out, Fox performed the technique that had sunk the Kaitaur into the ground. It was the same one that had saved us from the s'la'manda lizard's fire.

He skidded to a halt and planted the butt of Shui into the ground. I slid to a stop next to him. A circle of ground that we were standing on started to sink. But after only sinking to ankle height, the ground stopped sinking. The circle quivered, then shook as though some force was resisting our descent. Fox's eyes were closed in concentration as he (and Shui?) pushed against this resistance. The ground beneath us was quaking and made my footing unstable. More and more of the darts pelted our shields.

And then, there was a CRACK sound underfoot. Fox and Shui had overcome the resistance! Each time Fox had used the technique before, the disc of ground had sunk down evenly, staying flat and level. But this time, something was wrong. The circle didn't stay flat. It tipped. One side stayed stuck, like a hinge, where it stopped, and the other side of the circle dropped. Literally, the ground fell away beneath our feet. As the portion of the descending disc-floor in front of us broke and hinged downward, it formed (to my eye) a crescent moon shaped hole. The circle of tile-covered ground beneath us became a ramp that angled down into the crescent shaped hole.

The unexpected slope made me drop and tumble forward, head over heels. Not only was I disoriented by the fall, but several darts fell to the ground around us. I cringed and covered my head as I rolled, expecting the darts to be pushed through to me. But the medallion shield must have adjusted. The darts tinkled as they bounced off the sloping tiles around me. Fox kept his footing as he slid down the slope. Some darts were knocked out of place as they hit the edges of the opening. But most of the darts stayed in place despite my tumble and Fox's slide. And more darts were still hitting our shields, angling in from above.

The ramp of floor I had rolled down, was pelted with a barrage of darts. Soon, the square tiles were entirely covered by the darts. We were in a wide tunnel. The roof of the tunnel was taller than Shui was long, so it was tall too. It seemed to run underneath the courtyard that we had been in.

We scrambled a few feet further into the tunnel so that no more darts could reach our shields. I noticed with alarm that the protective radius around me had shrunk so much that I could reach out and touch the barbs. (Even though I could, I knew not to.)

"We had better do something about these." Fox said. "Shui, would you mind?" The staff flared to light in answer. Fox stood still. The staff began to spin and twirl on its own. As when we had fought the little demons, the staff was blindingly fast. The spinning staff precisely connected with each of the barbs stuck in Fox's shield. Each of the barbed darts ended up embedded in the walls of the tunnel around us. In only a moment, Shui had cleared all of the barbs from around Fox. Then the staff flipped over to me and knocked away the darts around me. It seemed that when something touched the darts, whether it was the walls of the tunnel or Shui's ironwood, they 'died' and stopped vibrating.

Having cleared the space around us, Shui flipped back into Fox's outstretched hand. The pounding, thumping, screeching demonic music was muted now that we were under the floor. That alone made it easier to think. The tunnel was also cooler than it had been up above. The metal grain running through Shui put off a steady glowing light.

I looked down the tunnel, but without torches, we could only see a short distance. I could see several doors on either side, but then the shadows became too dense for Shui's light to penetrate. I assumed there were more doors farther down the hall, but the darkness made it impossible to see. The doors I saw were divided between being made of iron or white bone.

I reached out to touch the tunnel's wall. It was made from a gritty stone with a rough, scratchy surface.

Fox walked over to the nearest door. It was made of iron, with a thick, iron ring attached to it. Fox took hold of the ring and gave it a pull. Then he tried pushing on it. The door wouldn't budge. I had seen before how strong Fox was. If *he* couldn't open the door, then it was definitely locked.

He made a beckoning gesture and we started down the tunnel. He tried a white bone door next. He checked the doors, but they were all locked. It seemed that there was only one way to go. I stayed beside Fox and Shui. Their power, and Shui's light, represented very real safety. I kept looking over my shoulder, glancing around nervously, but soon stopped. Our moving bodies blocking the light from Shui, cast grotesque shadows all around us. I felt more nervous as I watched the moving shadows, so I looked straight ahead, instead.

I knew that we were close to Cho Clei so I wanted to hurry, but we could only go so fast. We moved cautiously. None of them would open.

Aside from Shui's light, we were in complete darkness. The tunnel contained no lights at all. I knew that I was afraid because my mind turned to trivial issues. I imagined that whatever demons used this tunnel must be able to see in the dark.

I was considering the possibilities, when I noticed a faint red light in the distance. Both Fox and I stopped. Apparently he saw the same light at the same time. And that red light was getting bigger.

There was a flash of light from the metal grain in Shui. Fox mumbled, "That's reassuring." Then, to me, "Shui is reminding us that we are still invisible. So, whatever that is should not be able to see us." We watched, fascinated as the light grew bigger.

The red light we were watching grew, resolving into the figure of a human. It appeared to be a thin (almost emaciated) girl. I panicked for a moment, thinking it might be Cho Clei. But soon I saw a few major details that showed me it wasn't her. As she floated closer, I was able to make out more detail. The more I observed, the less she looked human.

First, it was too big to be Cho Clei. She looked even older than I was. Also, she was clearly floating, moving toward us without touching the ground. Next, the woman was translucent. I could see through her as she cast a faint red light on the walls of the tunnel. She looked how I imagined a ghost looked. As the ghost came closer, she looked like a piece of floating, faintly glowing, female-shaped smoke. Limp arms with elongated hands hung down almost to her knees, lifeless at her sides. The same was true for her legs, hanging and lifeless.

It looked like some invisible hand had picked up the ghost woman's body by the back of the neck, lifted it off the ground, and was moving it through the tunnel. Her head was scanning back and forth as she floated toward us. The most frightening part of the ghost girl was her face.

Where her eyes were supposed to be, instead were two gaping black holes. The red glow that suffused her entire body was conspicuously missing where eyes should be. There wasn't even the glowing dot of red light we had seen in other demons. And, I wondered, if there was no red light, could it even see?

I didn't have time to wonder, as I realized the ghost-woman was speeding up as it floated toward us! The sight was strangely fascinating and for a moment, I was paralyzed. My thoughts felt sluggish. This ghost-woman couldn't be moving as fast as it appeared, could it...?? I didn't have time to finish the thought, before I heard the warnings.

"Down!-" shouted Fox.

Get DOWN Batou!-

At the same time that I heard Shui's command in my mind, I heard Fox with my ears. Fox turned and pushed me down as he dived to the side. I tripped and fell flat on my back. The phantom female figure flew past us, down the center of the tunnel.

I watched the spectral figure get smaller as it raced away. It cast a ring of red light that sped down the tunnel with her. She came to the place where we had broken through the roof of the tunnel. I thought for a moment that the ghost woman would fly up the ramp and end up in the courtyard. But instead, as she came to the ramp of angled floor, she passed directly through the ramp and disappeared.

The entire encounter had only lasted a few moments, but I was thoroughly bewildered. I had just seen... a ghost?

It did not see us. The ShadowLoops still hide us, but even if they didn't, that thing couldn't see us. It has no spirit inside to 'see' anything...

I had the thought, 'But then, why did we have to duck? If it's only a ghost, it would pass right through us, wouldn't it? Just like it did with the ramp down there...' It was then that I heard Shui's thought broadcast into my head.

The power that holds that thing together would be a poison to the living. Touching it would have been the end of you.

"It would have been the end of me too, by the way." Fox said. Shui had opened a channel of mental communication between the three of us. Fox, it seems, had been following along.

We lay on the floor of the tunnel for a few moments longer, waiting to see if something else would happen. I watched the darkness expectantly, listening to the muted demon music, and feeling distant sensations of pain where I had landed. The ground we were lying on was made from the same rough and ragged rock as the rest of the tunnel.

When nothing happened, we got back up and continued down the tunnel. The tunnel went on, unknown, before us. Shui's light penetrated the darkness to a point, but beyond that, we could see nothing. I began to feel like we were floating in a bubble of light. Shui made the bubble, and we were travelling inside it, carrying it with us.

We had traveled a hundred more paces when another distant, spectral figure appeared. This one, however, was not moving toward us. It was floating up from the floor and passing through the ceiling. We froze at first, but once we saw it was rising and not coming our way, we got closer. It was followed by another 'ghost', then another.

We were able to see more and more of these 'ghosts' floating up from someplace below. They were floating up through the floor and then changing their paths so that they split off at different angles, but still rising through the ceiling. So, they all came up from the same point in the center of the tunnel floor, ahead of us, but then changed their course to pass through the roof at different directions.

We inched closer to the spot where the ghosts were emerging. As we crept closer we saw that there was a crude red-black circle drawn on the ground. It appeared that the circle was painted a long time ago. As soon as I had that thought, I recognized that it was naïve. It was a kind of naïveté that was not appropriate to me any longer. When I was just a boy in our village, I would have thought it was paint. But now, with the experience I had in this realm, I knew this was dried blood. This was something sinister, I concluded grimly to myself.

Then I shook my head. Of course, it was something sinister Kwan! This realm was horrible! I tried to study the ghosts, now that I could see them better.

Each came through the center of the red circle. As we got closer, I could see that all of the 'rising' ghosts looked similar to the first one. They all looked female and they lacked eyes. They were all petite, and they were all lifeless. The mouth of each of was hanging open as though emitting some soundless moan.

From a distance away, when we were down the tunnel, they just looked like points of pale red light. But now, closer up, we could see more detail. Each of them was dressed in a tattered shift that barely covered them. But instead of displaying 'skin', the ghosts were only more transparent in those exposed places.

We could also see that the ghosts were now coming through in a rush, several of them passing through the circle at the same time. It seemed that they were rising from someplace and then, in the tunnel where we were, hitting a point that redirected them one way or another.

"Blind sentries?" I asked. But Fox just shook his head. At the same time, I heard Shui's thought broadcast into my mind.

They are travelling kill traps. They cannot see, they cannot think, they cannot fight... and they will not stop. They probably have been patrolling throughout this evil place since it came into being. Move with caution and be poised to jump aside.

As we got closer to the spot where the ghosts were rising through the floor of the tunnel, I began to see that the blood circle where the ghosts were emerging was wider than it first appeared. This meant that to pass it we would need to hug the sides of the tunnel if we weren't going to let the ghosts touch us.

As we got closer it also became clear how fast they were moving when they left this tunnel. The ghosts rose slowly into the tunnel where we were. But when they reached our tunnel, they accelerated and shot off at an angle up through the tunnel ceiling.

We were only about 10 paces away from the blood circle, when another ghost unexpectedly shot straight toward us. Even though I felt prepared for the ghosts to turn toward us, when it happened, my feet felt like blocks of iron. It happened so fast, it surprised us all.

I couldn't move. Time slowed down as I watched the ghost speed toward us. Eyes wide, I started to turn toward Fox.

He was faster than I was, and began moving to push me while I was still frozen. But with time slowed to a crawl, even in that split second, I could see that Fox would not be fast enough. The ghost would squarely hit us both. Then it would kill us, poisoning our lives as it passed straight through us. And we would be too slow to stop it...

Before, when I was underwater and the Shogatt had been hunting me, I had known I was about to die. It took me less time to recognize the same knowledge now. I was going to die. But unlike before, I was not surrendering to death. Instead, this time I had the will to fight. My heart had changed, and my eyes did not close this time.

There was a flurry of action, a burst of movement, and a brilliant flash of light. Shui shot forward, out of Fox's hand, flying forward to meet the charging ghost. The metal grain running through the ironwood of Shui glowed brightly. In the slowed time, I saw the two approaching each other.

From my perspective, it looked like the ghost was growing larger, charging towards Fox and me, and only a thin light of light stood between us. Shui was shielding us. At the moment when the staff had flown into action, there was a burst of information into my mind. It came from Shui, but it did not seem intentional. It was like receiving a burst of communication from Shui, but it was more feeling than thought. It did not feel like the past times Shui had communicated with me. Before, broadcasts from Shui had always been directed, sent with intention. But this felt like a strong feeling that slipped out, like a groan when lifting something heavy.

The information was clear enough. Even though I did not have much experience communicating with Shui, I understood the message. At first, the message came through on one level as a feeling I translated as, **NO!** or **NEVER AGAIN!** Or maybe, **I WILL NOT ALLOW THIS!** But layered beneath that first feeling was a second, stronger feeling that was harder to translate. There was a flash of icy sorrow that immediately changed to a combination of righteous fury and absolute resignation. It was a fierce feeling of being protective toward his... family or tribe? It was the emotional equivalent of a blazing hot furnace. I felt power accumulating like a sound rising in pitch and volume the closer Shui got to the ghost. The light from Shui was blindingly bright.

I tried to see what happened, but at some point, I had to shut my eyes. It was just too bright. What I saw was the blind ghost flying forward at us. Shui was flying fast, charging toward the ghost. I thought the staff was going to keep moving forward and smash into the ghost. But Shui abruptly stopped and held his position, just that moment before the ghost hit.

So at first, I thought Shui and the ghost would collide like goats ramming their heads together. But when Shui stopped, the dynamic changed. Now it was like the goat was trying to crash through a mountain. In the meeting of the ghost and Shui, the ghost fared about as well as a goat would have against a mountain.

Time was slowed-down and my eyes were closed. I heard a hiss like water being thrown on hot coals. Fainter, under the hissing sound was a crackling sound.

While I was listening to those sounds, with my eyes closed, I imagined what my eyes couldn't see. Fearfully, I imagined that the ghost and Shui had both been destroyed, with the ghost's evil and Shui's goodness cancelling each other out.

I was tempted to open my eyes again, but a loud 'CRACK!' sounded and a gale of wind blew back at us. So instead, I squeezed my eyes shut tighter.

I shouldn't have done that.

"Shui!" I was so relieved at finding our companion had not been destroyed that I practically shouted out the name. My voice echoed in the tunnel. I opened my eyes to see Fox standing there, holding Shui in his hand as he always did. My head turned to the left to see what was left of the ghost. But there were no remnants left. Absently, I looked around, expecting to see small pieces of metal littering the ground around us. But the tunnel had been wiped clean.

"What you mean you shouldn't have done that? You saved our lives!" It was just now dawning on me how Fox's staff had saved my life again. "I was afraid that you and that thing had destroyed each other." I said.

I'm not talking about saving you. I have no regrets about that. I just should have stopped at breaking that wretched thing. Instead, I got offended at the nerve of this demon. So, I sealed that portal and destroyed it. No more lost ones will be summoned here... But what I have done will certainly bring attention.

I looked around, but the tunnel floor was empty. Not only were pieces of the single ghost missing, but the rest of the ghosts were now gone too. I focused further back to where the blood circle had been. I saw that Shui had done what he said. Now all of them were gone. There was no blood circle. No more ghosts.

I was going to ask how that could possibly be a bad thing, closing an evil ghost-portal, but a sound of grinding stone behind me, made me turn and jump. A round section of stone, the size of my chest, began to move. Before it had even finished moving, it was clearly an eyelid. The eyelid opened, revealing the huge stone eye and a glowing red pupil the size of my fist.

Startled, I jumped back. Immediately, the huge red pupil followed my movements. Instinctively, forgetting Fox, I scrambled first to my left, then to my right. The giant eye followed me. Horrified, I knew I was visible. "Fox??!" I said, my voice rising.

But as soon as his name had come out of my mouth, the eye closed again. On our right, a door that we had not noticed swung open. Fox held Shui out towards the open door, letting the light from the staff penetrate the darkness.

I thought that Fox was going to stop to ask Shui which way we should go. We could either continue straight ahead or we could go through this new door. But Fox was frowning, reaching out to touch the walls of the tunnel. He looked at the tunnel that was ahead of us. His heavy brow furrowed.

I turned to follow his gaze. We stared in silence at the empty tunnel. It was extended ahead of us.

Just then, at the limit of Shui's light, the ceiling caved in and the tunnel collapsed. The sound was terrifying, and for a moment, I thought the whole tunnel would collapse. Shocked, I took a few steps back. Then I stopped, hearing a second cacophony, and spun around to see the ceiling collapse behind us too. Only the section of the tunnel we were standing in, was not caved in.

We were trapped. The door was now our only way out of here. Fox looked over at me and nodded. "It looks like our next choice has been made for us." Fox gave me an encouraging look, nodded, and stepped through the door.

Chapter 19

Danger, Courage, Growth

The door led to a small hallway, after which was a large square chamber. The room was roughly a cube, and was tall enough that the Arkyala would have been able stand in it. There was a door on the opposite side of the large room.

We wandered over to the door and tried to open it. It was locked, so we were now at a dead end. I was about to say as much, when another ominous rumble sounded behind us. I spun around to see a cloud of dust coming toward us. The 'new' tunnel behind us had collapsed, just like the main tunnel had. I coughed, inhaling some of the dust. It was like before, but this time we did not have a door to escape. We were trapped.

Fox was talking in that quiet, faraway tone that showed he was thinking something through. "didn't crush us in the cave in…has to be a reason it herded us here… (too quiet, something inaudible)… can't be good." I heard the last thing he said and felt a ball of fear form in my stomach.

"Fox, what's happening?" I asked anxiously. We were standing in front of the locked door, turned toward the cave-in behind us. The only light we could see was projected by Shui.

That was when a sparkly sheen of blue flickered into being before us. We started sliding across the floor, being pushed away from the door. I looked down, surprised, to see my feet sliding across the floor. Fox was looking behind us, then around at the room. He said, "Uh-oh."

I turned to see what he saw. When I did, the blood must have drained from my face. What I saw was long sharp spikes slowly (and noiselessly) extending out from the wall. If it hadn't been for our shields, we would have been silently skewered. I looked around and saw that similar spikes were emerging from all four walls.

As soon as he saw what was happening, Fox grabbed my arm and pulled me forward. We hurried to the center of the room. In every direction we looked, spikes were advancing toward us.

Fox spoke rapidly, "It's a trap Kwan. Whatever was behind that eye, led us to this death trap... this cube of spikes. The Valrun Stones protect us to some degree, activating when they are needed, but straight and direct pressure will eventually pierce through the shields. If we are near each other, our shields will overlap and reinforce each other. Our best option is to..."

But as Fox started his statement, we began to rise into the air. It happened so smoothly that we might not have noticed, but the shimmering blue shield had appeared again. This time, however, it was beneath our feet.

Immediately Fox looked down, and I followed suit. There were spikes rising out of the floor! If not for our shields, the spikes would have stabbed straight up through the soles of our feet. But because our shields made a shimmering blue sphere to protect us, they were lifting us up. Or rather, the spikes were lifting up the protective bubble that surrounded us.

I looked around frantically, trying to figure out what to do. Fox looked troubled, brow furrowed and eyes closed in concentration. The metal grain running down the length of Shui flashed brightly twice. Fox smiled broadly. "Of course! Rotation! That should work, Shui! Let's try it!" I looked from the staff back to Fox. Fox was explaining, "When these spikes reach our shield, it is very important that we both hold on to Shui. It is crucial, Kwan. Hold. On. To. Shui. Got it?"

I nodded quickly, not understanding. Fox looked like he wanted to explain more, but the spikes were just reaching our shimmering blue bubble.

We stopped rising as the spikes pinned our bubble and all converged on us. Fox tucked Shui under his right arm and held on with both hands. Then he offered the other end to me and

I did likewise. We were both on opposite sides of the staff, facing each other. We both had the staff firmly held under our right arms. The encroaching points of each lance were now touching our shield. Where each spike tip touched the blue sphere around us, the shield glowed a brighter blue. Each of those points was glowing brighter and brighter by the moment. The spikes threatened to break through any second.

I couldn't imagine what option was still left to us. The shield was going to break and we were surrounded by certain death. Gruesome images came into my mind of what getting impaled would look like, so I closed my eyes. I tried to block them out.

I was going to close my eyes, but then I felt pressure under my arm, against my right side. Shui was pushing. I opened my eyes in surprise. I took me a few seconds before I realized what was happening. Shui was pushing both of us. Fox and I were spinning, revolving around the center of our sphere. I looked out at the shield. It was spinning too, just as we were. The spike tips lit up, glowing with heat. They drew burning horizontal lines across the sphere of our shield. The stabbing spikes had halted their deadly advance! They were unable to penetrate the sphere, turned aside by the spinning surface of the shield. The faster Shui spun, the more the spikes yielded to its force. Sparks flared all around our shield. The skewers that had been sent to pierce us, were now being melted, bent, and *wrapped around our shield* instead.

Shui was spinning fast enough that I had to close my eyes to stop the rising nausea. I was dizzy and disoriented, leaning back inside a ball of fiery sparks. I had to use all my strength to hold on. I closed my eyes, and gritted my teeth to maintain my grip on the staff. The last thing I saw was Fox holding on to the other side of the staff. He was only a dark silhouette on a golden background of glowing, horizontal sparks.

Shui was spinning fast enough that force was trying to throw me backward. The pressure was increasing every second. And if I lost my grip, I didn't know what would happen. Just when

I thought I couldn't hold on any longer, Shui slowed and came to a stop. The shield flickered just as Shui stopped spinning.

I looked down to see that we were standing on, and surrounded by, the harmlessly bent iron spikes, making a metal sphere around us. I marveled at the interior of the bent-iron ball. The ball actually looked pretty interesting now that the threat had passed. We had escaped death, but we were still trapped. Actually, we were now trapped in a much smaller, iron cage. I was about to point this out, when the spikes began to retract back into the wall.

"It thinks we're dead. Well done Shui!" Fox said. Shorter spikes that had not touched our shield were still straight, and retracted fully back into the walls. But the spikes that had touched our spinning shield were severely bent and twisted, so they couldn't fully retract into the walls. They pulled back until the bent spikes' curves stopped their progress.

By that time, the parts of the metal sphere had separated enough for us to climb out of the center. We stepped through the twisted spines and made our way to the door.

The door swung open. Fox and I looked at each other. We nodded and went through the door.

Beyond the door was an unremarkable tunnel. It was not as tall or as wide as the 'ghost tunnel' or the 'spike tunnel' as I now thought of them. This new tunnel was so narrow that we had to walk single file with Fox in the lead.

Fox normally carried Shui straight up, parallel to his body. But this tunnel's low ceiling forced him to carry his staff at a forward angle. This meant that Shui would actually be the first of us to encounter any trouble. Now that I knew some of Shui's ferocious capabilities, I was glad he was at the front of our group. Shui was... the Edge of the Blade.

The tunnel went on for a long way. At first, I expected attack. After a while though, I relaxed my guard. I decided to ask some of the questions I had from this trip. We had been walking long enough that I wondered if we could still even be under the castle. As big as the castle was it felt like we had been walking for hours.

"You mentioned valron stones? What are they?" I asked.

"The Valrun Stones are talismans of protection created by a legendary GaleMaster Immortal." He looked over and pointed at the medallion on my chest. "That is a Valrun Stone." Then he held up a bead on his rosary. "This is another one. We are very fortunate to have them. Master Valrun is no longer with us."

"He died? ... but... I thought he was an Immortal." I asked.

Fox smiled, "It's an expression we use, Kwan. It means Master Valrun has left behind the world of men- not by dying, but by transcending.

"You see, there are different paths on the mountain where the GaleTemple is located. I don't mean that as a metaphor. There are different courses of study taught there, but I'm talking about actual paths you walk on. It is a very special, mystical place.

Some paths lead to treasures you could hardly imagine. Well, after seeing *this* realm, you might be able to imagine. Some paths lead to unbelievable cosmic power, while other paths can break a man's mind.

"One particular path leads to a very special meadow. Several great GaleMasters transcended at that very spot. There, with his fellow masters stationed around the outside as witnesses, Master Valrun began walking across that meadow. A dense, fog rolled in and momentarily hid him from view. There was a light within the mist, and when a gale of wind blew the mist away a moment later, he was gone."

I didn't completely understand what he meant, but I was concentrating. I was going to ask for clarification, but I was taken completely by surprise. If I had been more alert, I might have responded better.

But, in my mind, we were walking, then somehow, we were falling, then I was hanging, swinging over a bottomless pit. In the several seconds after it happened, I was able to put more order to the events that had just happened.

We had been walking down the tunnel. That much was correct. But then, without warning, a trapdoor opened in the flooring of the tunnel. Fox fell through into darkness, and I being right behind him, fell as well. I hate to think what would have happened had it not been for my companions.

As we began to fall, Fox had wedged Shui (or Shui had jammed the small end of itself) into the wall. With amazing reflexes and strength, Fox caught his staff in one hand, and caught my arm (as I was falling) with the other hand.

Shui was lodged deep in a crack in the wall, an arm's length below the tunnel floor. We had fallen into an open, square hole. I looked down, but could not see anything. I had an uncanny certainty that there wasn't anything below us. If we fell, we might be falling forever.

It is illusion. I can see what is being projected at you. This is part of another trap.

I groaned inwardly. Another trap. I didn't want to fall to my death. Even if the hole wasn't bottomless, a far enough fall would kill us! Even if it didn't kill us, at the very least it would break our legs. I was starting to panic. I squirmed. My shoulder was beginning to hurt.

Calm yourself, Batou. Fox is straining to keep his grip right now. When you move, it is much harder for him to hold you.

Immediately, I stopped moving. The last thing I wanted to do was get dropped! I realized that I had been staring down into the darkness, trying to see any details. I looked up at Fox instead. He wore a fierce expression on his face. His eyes were closed in concentration, clearly working hard to hold us up.

Better. Now listen. Fox is hearing us too. Below us is a drop. We will fall several times the height of a man. You will survive, so do not fear that. The danger is not the fall. The danger is what awaits us down below.

My shoulder was aching now. What did he mean? The danger is what is below??? Another monster? After demons, ghosts, the Shogatt and the Kaitaur, I never needed to see another monster ever again.

Not a monster, Batou. What awaits us below are the Gazing Gates.

I heard a gasp, then realized that the gasp had been in my mind, not in my ears. Also, the gasp had come from Fox, not Shui. Fox's mind silently replied, *But I thought that the Gazing Gates had been destroyed!*

It appears that this demon was able to salvage some of the pieces. I suspect he has found a way to the junkyards of creation.

"What are the…?" I gasped, starting to ask, but Shui cut me off.

Questions later! Now Listen! Fox won't last all day. We will need to drop through this hole. We will fall, and survive the fall, but the MOST IMPORTANT thing you MUST REMEMBER is to keep your eyes closed. Keep them closed while you fall! Keep them closed when you land. At the bottom, blindfold yourselves. Then I will help you to navigate past the Gazing Gates.

I could feel Fox agreeing to the plan, mentally. I nodded my assent with my body and mentally. What did they think I was going to do? I didn't want to fall blindly into the unknown! It terrified me, but I had no choice and I was clearly out of my depth. My fate was cast with Fox and Shui long before this.

I was still processing what Shui's instructions meant. I didn't know anything about the 'Gazing Gates'. All I really did know was that I was about to fall a long distance and hopefully not hurt myself, all without being able to open up my eyes. Shui said that we would survive the fall, that meant we would be able to walk after the fall, right? I was going to ask Shui, just to reassure myself. But before I could, Shui sent a communication to me.

You must not peek, Batou. Your life depends on it."

Shui 'thought' to me. I didn't know how I would be able to manage the fall if I couldn't see where I was go—.

And then we were falling.

***

I kept repeating 'KEEP YOUR EYES CLOSED' over and over again to myself. I fell for what felt like too long. At one point, I was sure that we had been falling long enough that we would surely die. I imagined breaking both of my legs, then breaking my hips. I would not have any warning about the impact. I would see a flash of light, feel unbearable pain, then die. Images of landing on my head followed next. I was grinding my teeth and squeezing my eyes shut as hard as I could. I felt like I couldn't contain the panic. I was going to open my eyes. I couldn't resist any longer. If I didn't, I was going to die! But Shui sent me encouragement.

You will not die, Batou. Now is the time for courage. REMEMBER TO KEEP YOUR EYES CLOSED! This is something you must do.

"But I can't!" I yelled the words aloud, hearing hysteria in my own voice. But Shui did not seem to notice. His thoughts came through with calm and patience.

On this path, there are only two ways. The path is forked, and you must choose one. So choose Batou- live, or die? WOULD YOU LIVE?

I nodded, moaning. Of course I want to live! I…I… will try.

Don't TRY to do it. IF YOU WILL LIVE, YOU MUST DO IT.

"I'm trying!" I thought, or maybe cried out. And I certainly was trying, but the fear was too much for me.

I know you feel great fear. But only ONE path will let you live. You MUST do this to continue your life and SAVE YOUR SISTER. There is only one way.

I was lost. I couldn't breathe. I felt like I was tumbling head over heels. I was disoriented and felt utterly vulnerable.

You have only two choices, Batou. The first choice is to die. What is your second choice? You are terrified, but you must do it. What action should you take?

I didn't know what action to take. There was no way out! I shook my head, not even calm enough to send my thought. Tears squeezed out of my eyes as I fought to keep them closed. I couldn't handle it! I wanted to surrender to sobbing.

I might have been screaming. I don't know. There had to be another way!

You have no choice, Batou. You must do this if you wish to live. You must do this if you wish to save your sister.

I understand! Even if I'm scared for me, this is important! This is all for Cho Clei, and I can't let her down! I felt Shui approve of my thought.

Good! My tribe knew the urge to protect those we love, is stronger than the urge to fear for ourselves. Use that power!

I had no idea how to use that power, but I did feel less panic than before. Cho Clei needed me! But I still didn't know what to do!

When you MUST do something, but you are having great fear, there is only one path:

'?' I thought to Shui.

You must DO IT ANYWAY! This is the power of the Edge of the Blade. If you are afraid, you STILL DO IT! The fear is smaller and weaker than you! I believe in you Batou. Don't give up, you're too strong!

Shui thought I was strong??? Maybe I *was* strong? Slowly, the fear began to look more manageable.

Shui's encouragement was working, because now I was listening to him instead of my panic. I did not open my eyes. But how do I 'Do It Anyway'? I cried. As soon as I 'looked' at my fear it was too big to deal with. How could I overcome it?

My people used to say, 'Once you understand *why*, you can deal with the *how*.' What you must do becomes manageable, after you have accepted that it is required. A warrior does what he must.

But it's not enough! I'm still scared! I... I felt like I could have been okay if I had been able to look over and see Fox confidently handling the fall, keeping his eyes closed, and having his composure intact. But I did not have that option. I felt the panic growing again. I was alone. falling, in the darkness.

Kwan. You are not alone. But you have no choice in this. You can do this. We believe in you.

Ok, I have no choice. I *have* to keep my eyes closed. But... but... I couldn't see what it was, but there was something in the way. I was too afraid! I felt like I was going to burst!

For a moment, I thought I heard Fox's voice. No, it wasn't his voice. It was his... thoughts? What was strange was that Fox's thought was soft, barely perceptible, like a whisper. Also, it was clearly *not* directed at me. It felt like I was overhearing a private conversation:

Fox: Shui? The time...

Shui: Yes, but we must cultivate Batou Kwan. This moment is a Point Of Making for him. It is our sacred duty.**

Fox: ...I understand. If he can accomplish this, nothing can ever take it away from him. Very well, you are wise old friend, carry on...

Then Shui was again broadcasting to me.

Breathe, and listen, Kwan. There are two things that people fear. One is pain. The other is the unknown. Are those what you fear?

I... yes... no pain... and... I DON'T WANT TO DIE!

Breathe! Keep your eyes closed, but take a deep breath. You will not die, Batou. Calm yourself. And what scares you about death is the unknown. Listen to my thoughts. The first step is to choose to control your mind. Use your will to calm your mind. Say the words to yourself, out loud, "I choose to control my mind. Hear my intention!"

I forced myself to say it. "I... choose to... c-control my m-m-mind."

Hear my intention! Say it with force! Your Blade is Sovereign! Your will is LAW!

I forced myself to say it. "I choose to control my mind! Hear my intention?" But immediately Shui corrected me.

It's not a question, Batou. You are demanding your rights from all the realms! YOUR INTENTION HOLDS POWER. IT ECHOES THROUGH ALL OF THE WORLDS and THEY RESPOND! GATHER YOUR POWER KWAN! Now, again! "I choose to control my mind! Hear my intention!"

I said it again, but I still had doubts. I could tell that I wasn't there yet. So could Shui. I felt like he was facing me, counselling me, and like this was the only thing I could focus on.

Better! Now do it again, but this time with FORCE Batou! Do that, then we move to the next step.

I steeled myself, taking a moment, even though I knew I was still falling, and concentrated my feelings. I felt them like a ball in my stomach. I gathered up those feelings and channeled them as I intended to say the words again. When the words came out, I heard myself shouting them, "I CHOOSE TO CONTROL MY MIND! HEAR MY INTENTION!"

Again Batou!

"I CHOOSE TO CONTROL MY MIND!!! HEAR MY INTENTION!!!" I yelled, and something changed, somewhere inside me.

I realized that when I was shouting my will, the fear was not there. Each time I said the words, fear was pushed further back. It dawned on me that I felt like I *might* have a chance.

Believe in yourself! Claim your power! State your will! It will push your fear back. Do you feel it, Batou? The fear retreats, doesn't it?

Shui was right. I *could* feel it. I nodded, then repeated that nod as a thought.

Good. Now that you have planted the seeds FOR confidence and belief to grow, you are ready for the next step. You have to let your reason TAKE CONTROL of your feelings. You have to tell your feelings that your mind is in control, tell them when to be quiet. Your MIND is in control.

Again, I nodded, following along.

There are times when your feelings seem all powerful. The truth is that your mind is more powerful. Your emotions are useful tools, but they are not the tools for this situation. Your mind must take control.

I began to see what Shui was explaining to me. Then suddenly, I felt the urge to open my eyes. The pictures of me getting hurt slammed back into my mind even more vividly than before. They were shocking and terrifying. I would be lost! I would be broken! This is the end! I felt more and more sure with every passing moment, that when I landed it would be the end of my short life.

Go back to your will Battou! The fear fights hardest right before your victory! The fear appears larger than it actually is. It is perspective- things appear bigger when a person is afraid of them. Know that and move past it. Tell yourself that you choose to control your mind. Know that you can! You have that power! You know that it is possible to control your mind.

"But what if I die??" I thought to Shui. There was a pause in Shui's mental broadcast. He must have been organizing what he wanted to say, because when he spoke in my mind again, he practically gave a speech.

When facing death, we have to understand that the fight (or the fall) will either kill us or it won't. If It will kill us, then we need not worry. But if it will not kill us, then we need not worry about it either...

I waited, and listened.

Batou, pain comes to every life. Every single life encounters it at some time. But choosing to actively focus on that pain, to hold yourself in waiting for pain... is choosing to suffer. Do not make that foolish choice, Batou.

I began to see that Shui was right. Sometimes pain happened, but suffering is a choice... a foolish choice.

If you are to die today, it is out of your control. So you need not fear. And you must not fear, because you CANNOT change your fate that way, Kwan. With fear, you can only defeat yourself.

Shui was right, I saw it clearly. Then I began to see that I didn't have to let the fear back in. A sense of something settled over me. It wasn't that I had lost my fear. It was like the fear had changed. It had become smaller, something I could look at and push aside. It had become manageable.

AROUUU- HAA!!! I knew you could! You can control your mind! You DECIDED it.

I listened, finally calm, exploring this new feeling.

Your fear does not get a voice! You have done it, Batou! Still, KEEP YOUR EYES CLOSED!

"Shui?" I asked. But I felt curious, not fearful.
Yes Batou?
"How long until we reach the ground?"
Remember to KEEP YOUR EYES CLOSED.
'I understand,' I thought to Shui, 'but how far until-'
Remember, EYES CLOSED!!!
'I've got it! Keep my eyes closed. But how long until we reach the ground?' I thought at Shui. I had been petrified at the beginning of this fall. But now, I could clearly hear the difference in my voice. The panic was gone.
We have stayed in this spot as long as we dare. Stand up.
I didn't understand. Stand up? I reached my hand out to the side and felt hard stone. Confused, I hesitantly stood up, remembering to keep my eyes closed. I was standing... on firm land... shaky and unstable, but on firm land! I wasn't falling anymore. I tapped my feet on the ground to reassure myself it was really there. "Shui? When... what... what happened? When did we land?" I couldn't quite make sense of what had happened.
You landed just after the fall began. Your Valrun shield activated to prevent injury and gently set you down on the ground. You were panicking, so you could not feel it.
I... I was on the ground the whole time? I imagined how I must have looked thrashing around, floating just above the ground, and yelling in panic. I realized how weak I must have looked. I started to feel foolish and ashamed.
Do not feel shame Batou. Every life contains times when we have the option to grow. We find ourselves challenged by a crisis. We either overcome that challenge, that fear- and grow stronger. Or we fail to overcome- and either stay the same, or learn... but eventually the challenge will return. Either way, do not have shame. If you win, feel pride. If you lose, learn.
I stood there, eyes closed, following Shui's ideas. I had never heard these things before. "But, why...?" I said aloud. Shui responded in my mind.
**When we are born, Batou, we are nothing but weakness and divine potential set on a path... Weakness! And the potential to rise! Our

sacred duty is to fight through the challenges we meet, so that we can grow stronger, so that we can learn and develop into something better... our next forms.**

"So..." My thoughts were sluggish, slow to comprehend.

The times like this are the ones that forge our spirits, and let us change into something better. We call these times Points of Making-because they define us and make us who we are. Points of Making come when your Path directs them, not when you want them.

'It was a... challenge... to make me grow?' I thought/asked.

Every challenge is designed to let you grow, if you choose to. The ones who surrender to the challenges... surrender their place in this world... If we do not grow, we contract. Compare how you feel now to how you felt before.

'I do feel different. Better... not scared.'

And you learned, Kwan! You passed the challenge admirably, and have grown as a result. I am proud of you, Batou.

It was starting to dawn on me that I had just come through something... important? I wondered what had happened to Fox. At that moment, a quiet, new thought/voice came into my head. **I am proud of you too, Kwan.** I was startled to hear Fox's thought in my head too. In dealing with my panic, I had forgotten about him.

We have stayed in this cursed spot as long as we dare. It is time for us to push forward. Fox, you carry everything in your magic bag... (Shui was making a joke?) Do you have blindfolds?

I could feel something like a nod, broadcast to us from Fox.

Good. Once you put on the blindfold, I will project sight to you. But remember, EYES CLOSED!!!

A moment later, Fox pressed a strip of soft cloth into my hand. Then, changing his mind, Fox plucked the strip back out of my hand. I felt his hands on my shoulders, turning me around. I faced away from him and he placed the cloth over my eyes and tied it securely behind my head.

Then Fox said, "We are ready Shui."

Chapter 20

The Gazing Gates

I could only compare what happened next to being struck by lightning without any pain. I cried out and stumbled, but in surprise, not pain. Fox's hand on my arm caught me before I tumbled over.

After what felt like an eternity without sight, I could now see! But what should have been a joyful reunion with vision was almost too much to handle. If not for the blindfold, I would certainly have opened my eyes.

I whipped my head back and forth, trying to make sense of what I now saw. I felt dizzy. My head was spinning.

The sensation of being able to see again was overwhelming because I could now 'see' everything at the same time. If I concentrated on what was in front of me, I could see in that direction. If I concentrated on what was behind me, I could see that too, as clearly as the front view, and all without turning my head. The same went for the views on my sides… and above my head. I steadied myself as I saw Fox standing next to me. He was also blindfolded. Slowly I worked out what was happening. I could see… in… all directions… at once!

In a moment of inspiration, I tried to see myself. Instantly, my face came into view! It was like I was standing in front of myself, looking at my own face.

It took me a minute to grapple with the reality that what I was seeing wasn't coming from my eyes. It was so strange.

My first thought was that I looked like I needed a bath. My simple clothes were dirty, and sweat had plastered my hair down onto my forehead. In fact, the only clean part of me was the black cloth blindfold tied over my eyes. I peered more closely at the blindfold. The details of what I was looking at got sharper, resolving into more detail. I could see that the blindfold was made from a doubled over strip of cloth. A shimmer of reflected light showed that the cloth had a sheen.

Then (with my feet firmly planted in place), as I was studying the sheen on the blindfold, the view shifted like I had been moved aside. I had a moment of disorientation as I put together what had just happened.

What I was seeing… came from Shui. I knew that much, and *this* must have been how Shui saw… everything at once! But Fox was carrying Shui. And when Fox had moved his staff, the view projected by the staff also changed. It made sense. But I could change my view… To prove the thought to myself, I tried to see the back of my head. Immediately, I saw my dirty and sweaty hair with the neatly tied knot on the blindfold. Then I switched my view back. So, I could choose to see from anywhere… but if Shui moved… so did my view?

Fox also seemed to realize how he shifted Shui affected what we saw. He planted the butt of the staff firmly on the ground, steadying the stream of images from Shui.

I looked around and saw that there were giant flat panels, like sheets of ice, suspended all around us. We were standing on a twisting path that wound between the panels. Each of the panels had a different shape from the others. They all appeared to be floating and they were pointing towards the path. They showed our reflection like highly polished sheets of metal. We would need to make our way through a new maze now, between rows of irregularly-shaped panels. **Not just flat panels, the Gazing Gates are portals.** Shui filled in. They were different sizes, but even the smallest of them was large enough for me to ride a horse through it.

I tried to shift my perspective to see through the 'portals' from different angles, but my view wouldn't respond. **No, Batou. To gaze into the Gazing Gates is certain death for you. Some would break your mind as you attempted to escape the horror. Some would push you to madness in your desire to join the bliss. But all of them would pull you in after a single glance with your eyes or a single touch from your body. No, Kwan. The only way for you to view them is like this, never directly. I am shielding you from most of the sight of those other* realms. *But if you touch them, you will be trapped in that realm, and neither Fox nor I would be able to get you back. Ever.***

"Ok! ok! I understand! Don't touch the portal/panel things, or they will suck me into some realm and I'll die!" I said.

The thought that Shui gave in response was short, but layered with impressions. ***No, Batou. It would be worse than dying here. You would not die... But you would be lost.*** While the thought was simple information, I felt like Shui said it with sadness, as though he had a head and was slowly shaking it, considering a great tragedy. It was somehow more chilling than if he had 'shouted' at me. I took the warning even more seriously.

Fox and Shui came up with a plan. Fox would walk in front, holding Shui in his right hand. I walked behind Fox, holding on to his left shoulder. I felt like a blind man, even though I was able to 'see' through Shui. The 'vision' that Shui projected to us was just different enough that our steps were halting and slow as we worked our way through the path.

I moved my perspective to a point in front of us. I was taking in our surroundings and trying to see where we needed to go. Before, I was overwhelmed with the fall. Then I was overwhelmed with Shui's sight. But now I was determined to be calm and brave like my companions.

We were standing on a stone platform, surrounded by the reflective panels. It narrowed, leading to a single path. The room itself was not that large, but there was only one direction we could walk. The single path wound between 'mirror-portal' walls.

There is a doorway out of here on the other side... Our path is clear.

With the twists and turns, it would have been impossible to pass through without Shui. To see where you were going, would pull you in. To close your eyes and feel your way through, you would touch a portal and it would pull you in. It was a devious trap.

As we shuffled forward, I heard a 'thought dialogue' between Shui and Fox. At first the thought was vague, and I wasn't sure if I was really 'hearing' it. It was like my thoughts were walking on an empty road, but they had a parallel road that had much more 'thought traffic' going back and forth. And the more that I concentrated on the indistinct 'thought traffic', the clearer it became.

It was communication between Fox and Shui. Once I was sure that I was hearing something, I determined that it was my companions talking. And once I knew that it was them, I had an impulse to stop listening. These were my trusted companions. I shouldn't eavesdrop on them.

But then I remembered that they had discussed me while I thought I was still falling. They had acted with kindness, helping me to learn while they knew I was safe. But *I* hadn't known I had been safe. If I had known, it might have been easier! So, I let myself listen to their conversation. Partially I was curious and… bored? I was blindfolded, shuffling down a path, afraid to touch anything. Also, listening to Fox and Shui gave me a way to distract myself as we traveled the narrow path between portals.

The first thought I clearly heard was from Fox. *I didn't realize it happened so quickly…*

Yes, the bigger animals were still chewing their food. They did not even have time to swallow before freezing solid. It was winds from above the clouds…

But Shui, did they… but the volume of Fox's thought drifted off, too faint to understand.

I tried to figure out what I had just heard as I shuffled along behind Fox. I thought about it, looking around the room at the giant reflective portals. The surface of each one was both moving and out-of-focus at the same time. Shui was blocking me from seeing what they showed, but Shui's screen that 'hid' the portal was moving too. It looked like a furry gray cloth was writhing, constantly shifting and moving. I wondered why, and Shui answered, **It is because I have to keep the shield moving, to adapt to the portal. The portals want to trap us. When I block them,* *they change to get around the block, so I have to move the shield to keep blocking them, then the whole exercise repeats.***

"So, the portals are… alive?" I asked. "I mean, if they can move and change…"

Well… in a way, they behave like living things, but they are not alive like you or Fox.

"Is it… like you, Shui?" I had realized before that Shui was not the same as Fox or me. Obviously, Shui was consciousness inside a wooden staff. But before I had assumed that Shui had started his life as a man. Now, I suspected that Shui had never been a man. He had been… something else.

No, Batou. My kind, the J'nii, lived in the world long ago… after the Yala and the Yira had been placed, but before the time of man. I will tell you about us another time. It seemed like Shui was done broadcasting his thought to me, but then he sent an afterthought. ***There are none left like me, Batou. I am the last.***

The last… the last of his kind. I could not imagine being the last man alive. Just thinking of it, made me feel deep despair. I didn't think I would be able to get over it. But Shui was not pitying himself at all. Not only could I hear it in his thought, but also in the emotional component of his broadcast. His confession was a mere statement of fact. Still, I could sense a rueful smile that came with his response. ***These portals, the Gazing Gates were created long before dragons, before the Yala. They showed different scenes then, but they existed before…*** Then Shui fell silent.

I assumed that Shui was paying attention to our path, and I decided to try to do the same. I returned my attention to looking around through Shui's vision. Shui didn't tell me not to again, so I felt safe to try peering into the portals. I was not able to see through Shui's protection, into any of the portals. But, feeling a little like a mischievous child, I kept trying.

The strange part was that the more I concentrated at seeing into the portals, the more I was able to hear thought conversation between Fox and Shui. I wasn't able to get any pictures from the portals, which was my goal, but I did start to hear 'dialogue' again between Fox and Shui. It was as though being distracted with a completely different task let me tune in on them.

I heard Fox first. *Oh... Source/HighGod forbid. They're reproducing. I didn't know they could do that.* Because I was holding on to Fox's shoulders as we walked, I felt him turn his head away from a (roughly) square portal we were passing. A shudder passed through his shoulders, and his step slowed. It was hot here, but something had made a chill run through Fox. He was clearly disgusted.

Yes, shield your mind. I will protect Batou Kwan. Practice the Ru-kyno Forms, Fox- the ninth form specifically. The third and sixth form are also useful, but less so. These are realms no man was built to see. That realm makes this one look like a paradise. It is frequently thought of as 'hell'- the worst destination possible.

Shui paused, and I assumed that Fox had said something, but I hadn't caught it. Fox's thought had passed me, too faint to understand. But I did hear Shui's response. Fox came to a stop. So naturally, so did I. I kept quiet, sensing it wasn't the time for my questions. With Shui's mental communication, an emotional cue came through, along with the 'words'. The emotional cue was serious, and leaked through in what I could overhear.

I could feel Fox's shoulders tense, then relax.

Good. These portals show places that could break an untrained mind. And even a trained mind like yours can be hurt without protection. Keep using the protections you have learned. Master Ru-kyno taught you the forms. Remember Ru-kyno's ninth Vibration Form, Fox. This is not a place living man was made to see. This location is one of the original anchors of Anti-Life. My tribe called it DarkForce, but you think of it as Evil...

I realized that Fox was able to see through the portals, where Shui was blocking me. Fox saw through the portals, and was talking to Shui about what he saw. I believed Shui about how dangerous this place was, and I felt grateful for the protection.

But Shui, did they... but the rest of Fox's thought/words became too faint to understand. I was again left in solitude, shuffling my feet and following Fox. I tried to concentrate of the portals, but Shui was far more powerful than I was. So, I ended up looking around and occasionally hearing snippets of the conversation between them.

An idea occurred to me. It seemed so obvious, I was amazed I hadn't thought of it before. I asked aloud, "Wait! Won't our shields protect us? I mean the…Valrun Stones. They even stopped metal spikes! Can't they handle the portals too?"

Unfortunately not, Batou. Master Valrun's stones are not nearly powerful enough to block the portals. They would protect you against an arrow shot at you, but they are powerless against the Gazing Gates.

I wanted to trust the shield for this, and argue my point. "But…" I started to continue, but Shui was already sending another transmission.

When you were in the water, you were wearing the medallion from Master Valrun. Why did I go in to save you? Shui's question was simple and unexpected enough that it froze my resistance in place. I had not thought about it before.

"Because… I would have died." I realized it only as I said it out loud. Shui waited. I thought more… "Because the Shogatt was more powerful than the stones?" I asked.

A Shogatt is powerful, but its power is comparable to the stone's shield. I expect that the shield would have kept you safe for two or three bites, at most. After that, the shield would have failed, and that abomination would have eaten you.

After a momentary pause, Shui corrected himself, ***Actually, that's not completely true- they don't* eat. *At least, not the way you are thinking. They are nourished mostly by fear and a few other negative emotions that the ancient GaleMasters called 'looshu'. Beings like you* create *their food, but the Shogatt wouldn't have been able to digest your flesh.***

"Oh!… So, it *wouldn't* have eaten me? It just wanted to eat my fear??? It wouldn't have been so frightening if I knew it wouldn't kill me."

Oh, you misunderstand, Batou. It certainly would have killed you. It just wouldn't have digested you, Batou. But it would have torn you* *apart- without a doubt! It would have killed you on instinct alone, on principle. That was why I joined the fight. The Valrun stone's shield could be overpowered, so your safety was not sure.

A lingering resistance remained in my mind. Before I could voice it, Shui sent another transmission, ***And that same shield would be even less useful here. It would be like expecting a cloth shield to stop a sword thrust. The shield would not help, Batou.***

The direct statement from Shui was simple and honest. This was always the tone of Shui's communication. Shui was tremendously powerful. He had shown different sides of his character that were fierce, or wise, or protective. But Shui had always been honest. It was a simple, earnest statement of fact. 'The shield would not help, Batou.' I believed Shui. My resistance dissolved. I accepted that, at least for now, the shield was useless. I made myself extra wary, and tried to pay even more attention to our surroundings.

I again fell into the same strange place in my thoughts. Shui had gone silent, and I was left to my thoughts. My feet shuffled forward, hands on Fox's shoulders. Shui was projecting vision into our minds, but wouldn't let me see into the portals. Each of the 'Gazing Gates' was a different shape. It was like a giant mirror had been broken, and a handful of pieces had been kept. Some were more circular or angular overall, but the edges of each portal were jagged. Like before, I was looking around and trying to penetrate Shui's protection and glimpse something of what was hidden. And just like before, I began to 'overhear' more exchange between Fox and Shui.

Shui, is that...?

Yes, the Fishmen's Kingdom. Most on land don't believe in their existence. So long has passed since the war, man forgot and makes them into a myth. It became easier for man to feel safe when he forgot certain dangers.

Fishmen? Did that mean they were seeing a portal to under the sea? I tried to imagine what that might look like.

And the fishmen are different from the 'deep ones'? These look different. And I had no idea they were such accomplished builders!

Yes, the fishmen is a term my Tribe used for all of them. But there are several different kinds. You have seen the physical remains of 'deep ones' before. They are different than these 'builder' fishmen. The deep ones' constructions make more use of existing underwater caves and caverns.

I was listening carefully to them, trying to picture what I was missing. I was walking (shuffling) behind Fox. The image that Shui had sent to Fox was full of much more information than his transmissions to me. So, it surprised me when a series of images came through with Shui's response. The first image was of a dark mountain under the water. The image was seen from the perspective of someone under water. There were holes in the face of the underwater mountain.

Some parts of the images were still 'fuzzed out'. Was it possible that Shui's subconscious was still censoring the worst parts of what they saw? I watched, unable to pull my curiosity back.

The next image was a… creature… swimming into one of the holes. The holes in the underwater mountain were apparently doors. The image was immediately followed by a close-up image of the creature, only a few feet away. It had the bottom half of a fish, and the top half was only vaguely like a man. The man half was enclosed in a spiky shell, with arms like a crab's. It whipped its head around, as if to see who was looking at it. Its teeth were black. It's crab arms and claw-hands snapped shut. I could 'hear' the clapping sound of the claws snapping shut underwater! I froze as I saw the thing staring directly at me. Then the image changed to a man with orange hair and blue skin. Aside from the blue skin and orange hair, he had a shape like any other man on land. The main difference I saw was the coloring. He was standing on a tall rock overlooking the sea floor. Behind him was a beautiful city with tall buildings and graceful spires. Behind that city, was a 'forest' of seaweed. Some of the plants even seemed to give off light.

As soon as I had recognition of what I was seeing, the image disappeared. Still, I knew that I had seen a flash of what Shui was showing to Fox! It was a way I could get some impression of where the portals led. But just that quickly, I was left again to the solitude. I continued to shuffle my feet and follow along.

It was amazing to me how much my world had grown since meeting Fox (and Shui). I had been a boy from a village, who had never seen anything amazing. But now, this boy had seen things, and *knew* things existed that no one in my village would even believe. If I told them that demons, dragons, and fishmen were real, they would think I was crazy. Actually, they would just think I was lying to get attention.

We were passing a long, jagged portal. I was peering at it, trying to see inside (with no luck), I 'overheard' Fox and Shui again.

... *city called Atolentus, but it was destroyed several thousand years ago.*

*So, their chariots *did* fly. There was some doubt back at the temple- whether they flew or if it was just a metaphor.*

Oh yes, they certainly flew. They were very clever and figured out how to build many miraculous things. Their knowledge was very advanced. But then again, they brought most of it with them.

*They *brought* it with them?* There was a feeling communicated with the thought. It felt like he was excited and that Fox was leaning in as he asked the question.

Like many beings there, they are not native to our world...

Again, I lost the track of their dialogue. What did Shui mean that they were not native to this world. Did that mean they were like these demons- from a different realm? I wanted to ask Shui to clarify, but I wasn't supposed to be listening in the first place. If I asked him to clarify, Fox and Shui would know I was listening. So, I kept my thoughts quiet and continued to listen. I strained to hear, but I could not pick up any thoughts. I shuffled on in silence.

So it went, with me periodically hearing my companions, while constantly shuffling forward, following Fox. Our path took sharp turns, but Shui directed Fox. In turn, Fox directed me. When I wasn't listening in to their exchange, I was trying to puzzle out what they were seeing and talking about.

Where is that Shui? Are we seeing the night sky? Is that...? I heard Fox's thought begin, but it dwindled down to silence. I didn't hear Shui's response.

It seems to be showing the great emptiness between each world. It is the space above the sky. During the day or night, this emptiness is always... The information from their communication was like a flat stone skipping across the surface of a pond. I only picked up small, interrupted pieces. **...with nothing to breathe and the overwhelming cold...** I wondered at the parts I did hear, but without hearing the full conversation or seeing what they saw, I didn't figure out much. I followed behind Fox, listening and puzzling over what I heard. Time passed, but I couldn't tell how much or how far we had traveled.

We moved along, passing more portals, but I never heard any commentary on them. Shui led us, acting as our eyes, and projecting sight into our minds. Fox held Shui in front of him, and I shuffled along behind.

...I never thought to see it in a pure form...

Yes, even the filtered version you see is utterly powerful. Many can imagine order or chaos, but pure Void inspires awe... Then the thought trailed off. A moment later, the thought picked up again. **And after that, if you stared at it too long, madness would follow awe...**

A moment after that, I picked up a single word/thought/idea. The thought was, **...Unmaking...** A shudder from Shui came along with the idea.

I had fallen back into a sort of stupor. Even though we were in unbelievably dangerous surroundings, I had gotten complacent. I was slowly shuffling my feet along behind Fox, hands on his shoulders. I somehow trusted that we were 'safe', even though we were in such a dangerous place. I was shuffling my feet and looking around through Shui's sight.

Specifically, I had been marveling at the sensation of walking one way and looking behind me (through Shui's sight). I bumped into Fox as he abruptly stopped. At the same moment, I heard the thought from Shui.

There! Above the door! A door?! Shui's tone was warning, but my first feeling was joy. A door meant an exit! I moved my perspective from looking behind us to looking ahead. There was a wide, rectangular stone door ahead of us. It dawned on me that the entire chamber was not really that large. And then, again, specifically to me, **Above the door, Batou! Look!** Shui's awareness directed my sight. He made the area above the door seem closer and larger. There, perched in shadows on top of the doorway, were several of the large black birds (that looked like ravens) we had seen before. In fact, they seemed larger than they had before. It felt like they were at least my height. I jumped, startled, as soon as I saw them. Their red eyes were locked on us as we had been slowly making our way toward them. As soon as I saw them, they attacked.

Seemingly all at once, the battle began. Shui's thoughts came across in short, direct bursts. I immediately recognized it as Shui's 'battle voice'. For the first time, I noticed that temperatures could come through with the thoughts and words and emotions. The best way I could describe it would be that Shui's 'battle voice' came with a fiery chill. There was a merciless, burning cold that came with his words. ***They will go for the blindfolds! Shields up! Protect your eyes! I will deal with these…*** The words were delivered with a clear, but unspoken, distinction. Shui was planning, not to fight, but to kill.

Then I felt Fox turn to face me and pull us both to the ground. We crouched there with our heads lowered. Fox put one arm around my shoulders, covering my head as I ducked down. His other arm and hand covered his own head. I had a fleeting glimpse (from Shui's vision) of Fox and myself huddled there. Then my awareness was drawn to seeing what Shui saw. Several birds leapt off the stone wall and streaked toward us.

Shui radiated a sense of grim efficiency as the staff leapt forward to intercept the birds. It was completely disorienting trying to follow the fight. Everything moved so quickly. The length of Shui's staff spun and twirled, striking the birds and knocking them back as they tried to reach us.

One part of me tried to follow the dizzying fight while the other part of me was aware of my own body. I *knew* that I was crouched on the floor. My eyes were tightly shut under the blindfold. My hands were cradled around the back of my skull, protecting my head. I was curled up so tightly that my elbows and knees were touching. I could feel Fox's heavy arm over my head, adding another layer of protection. I heard Fox's voice, "We don't move from this spot." I nodded but did not reply.

When Fox said this, I gave myself over to trusting my situation. There was a plan, and Shui's recent lessons to me came back quickly. Either the birds would get me, or they wouldn't. If I was going to survive, I didn't need to worry. If I was going to die, I didn't need to worry either.

But more than that, I trusted Fox and Shui. So, I was able to trust that if I stayed in that spot, Shui would handle the birds. If he somehow couldn't, we would find another solution. Fear did not seem like something I needed just then.

I turned all of my attention to watching Shui's fight. And when I put all of my attention into the fight, I noticed several things. One thing I noticed was that the 'blocks' Shui put between me and the portals had become thinner. The blocks were still there, but no longer appearing as opaque and furry, gray cloths. Now they were more like a mesh screen that only kept the worst parts out. Some images began to seep through.

It made sense to me that Shui was exerting himself in the fight with the large black birds. It would make sense that he had less power to use protecting me. But it was fascinating that there was still some essential protection in place. I tracked the live sight Shui was projecting to us.

The birds were at a disadvantage. Even though there were several of them and only one staff, Shui was faster. It was difficult to track the number of birds attacking, because the air seemed filled with black streaks, flapping wings, and feathers. And each time Shui's ironwood made contact with a bird, more feathers were knocked out.

What Shui saw was a collection of streaks and blurs (to me), punctuated with jarring stops, as he delivered strikes or changed directions. I was again amazed at Shui's ability to keep track of so many things at once. It couldn't have been that fast for him, could it? I remembered that time had seemed to slow down as we fought the dempheys. Was that how it always was for Shui? I made a point to ask, after we survived, how he did that. Even trying to keep my body separate and unaffected, I was getting overwhelmed keeping up with Shui's high-speed vision. My body began to get nauseous.

Perhaps he sensed my difficulty, because the view from Shui cut off. My view had been kicked out from seeing Shui's perspective. I could still see though. I could still anchor my perspective somewhere in the room, but not from Shui's location directly. I was grateful for the change in perspective. The nausea stopped. I could still see the fight, but now it was in the third person, watching something *outside of me*, rather than me being *inside* the fight.

My sight was anchored to a space a few feet above my head. A few short paces away, Shui was doing battle with four or five giant ravens. I could track much more from here, than before. But at first, I couldn't see individual birds in the storm of black feathers. Everything, including both Shui and the ravens, was moving at tremendous speed. What I was seeing was still streaks and blurs, but now at least I could follow more of what was happening.

The birds were trying to reach us. Each time one of the birds tried to dart past the ironwood staff, Shui would sense the attack, flip around, and deal the bird a crushing blow. The birds were very resilient as they took strike after strike from Shui but kept coming.

I could hear several different layers of sounds. The first layer was my anxious breathing. The second layer was the sounds of wings flapping, ironwood striking the birds' bodies, their furious squawks, and wind whistling around Shui. The third layer was a layer of mentally 'shouted' sounds from Shui, adding power each time he landed a strike.

The staff danced around, striking one bird after another. Each time, it drove them back towards the door where they were originally perched. I could clearly see the glowing red pupils in the ravens' eyes as they fought with Shui. I had the eerie feeling that that they were staring at Fox and me.

I was watching the battle between Shui and the birds, when I noticed the protective veil flickering in front of a wide triangular portal. I had a moment of apprehension, thinking that I would be sucked through the Gazing Gate. But, luckily for me, Shui had left some crucial protection in place.

It took me a moment before my mind could comprehend what I saw. It appeared to be a land full of ice and snow. Mountains were visible in the background. A group of huge, four-legged, furry animals were turning over fallen tree trunks and patches of snow with their long... arms?... or were those... noses? I didn't know what to call them. But the furry giants had long 'limbs' that came... out of their... faces. Those things were furry and thick, like their legs or like tree trunks.
But these furry 'trunks' were also flexible like tongues, twisting and curling, moving in any direction. They had huge, curved tusks too.

Father had told us about elephants before, but these were furry and larger than I had imagined. They had to be something different.

Then, after uncovering the grasses beneath the fallen trees and snow, they used the 'trunks' to pick up clumps of the grass and feed them into their mouths. They chewed slowly, eating the grasses. I watched as each animal's fur suddenly began whipping around as they were caught in a furious gale. An icy wind tore across the snowy plain.

Before my eyes, all of the animals froze in place. Everything was killed instantly, freezing solid. The scene from the jagged triangular portal was panning across the frozen landscape.

Even though I knew my eyes were closed and my face was covered, it felt like my mouth was hanging open as I stared at the frozen scene. Where… was this?

But before I could spend more time wondering about the frozen scene, Shui's battle shifted closer to us. I turned my attention to the fight against the ravens, shifting my perspective. The birds had gotten through Shui's guard by working together. To protect us, Shui was forced to take position over our ducked heads. The ironwood staff was impossible to follow as it turned aside each peck at our heads. I remember thinking that, while the action was very close, I knew that Shui would be able to handle it.

I saw that the staff was now a glowing rod of punishment. There was a raven on my left side, staying just out of Shui's reach, but trying to snatch away our blindfolds. All but one of the ravens broke off from the fight and stood aside, watching us. They seemed to have decided they were getting in each other's way. They had let a single raven attack.

I realized with a sense of detachment, that it may just be trying to pluck out our eyes at this point. I recognized that glow from the metal running through the staff, but Shui seemed to be waiting for something. Only then did I realize that the bird had shifted position, and was now standing in front of the icy portal. The scene through the portal had reset and was showing the furry animals again. It seemed to be a loop of time. It made a striking image seeing the portal's triangle of white snow and ice contrasting with the raven's black feathers. It also struck me that Shui and the raven were fighting in high speed, while the furry animals were chewing very slowly.

As the bird shifted into position, a feeling of excitement and satisfaction radiated out from Shui. It suddenly felt like Shui had been maneuvering the raven into just that place, squarely in front of the icy portal.

The staff flipped and spun around over our heads, stopping with the large end pointing directly at the raven's breast. The raven was in the process of opening its wings wide. The winds in the scene had just begun. The furry giants in the portal were about to freeze. The glow from the ironwood staff grew brighter. Just then, I heard a thought from Shui. It sounded like, **Duuu-TSKAA!!!**

When Shui yelled/thought, **TSKAA!!!** A ball of light shot out of Shui, hitting the raven in the breast. The giant bird was blasted back off of its feet. The bird hit the face of the portal with wings spread wide, but didn't seem to slow at all as it passed through.

Shui's blast had hit the raven so hard that it was thrown back a dozen paces. But instead of staying in this chamber, the raven was thrown a dozen paces into the freezing arctic air. Shui had angled his blast so that the raven arced upward through the freezing air.

One of the furry giants turned its shaggy head to watch the bird. For the huge beasts, the raven must have appeared out of thin air. The furry animal's 'eyebrows' went up and it paused its chewing to watch the bird's arcing path through the air. Its massive eyebrows went up in a very human expression of surprise. It was only able to turn a short distance before the eyebrows, head, neck and the rest of its body froze solid. It was almost comical seeing the giant animal, mouth open and eyebrows raised, frozen in an expression of surprise.

For a moment, all of us watched the raven's trajectory as it was thrown through the icy wind. Even the spectator ravens drew their heads back in surprise, watching the raven's arcing path through the air. As it rose, and then fell, its black feathers grew rigid and became covered in frost. Its beak froze open in mid-squawk.

While the furry beast was not able to watch the raven's full journey through the sky, we all continued watched from this side. The frozen raven seemed to slow as it fell.

When it struck the frozen ground, the raven shattered. It was even black on the inside. The frozen chunks of shattered raven contrasted sharply with the stark white ice. I stood there with my mouth open, surprised. I had not expected that.

Clearly, the birds had the same reaction that I did. They paused, beaks open, staring at the portal in shock. Fox, however, did not seem surprised. And Shui seemed exultant.

AROUUU- HAA!!! *Righteous Battle!! Which one is next?!* A predatory smile came with the idea. It was a complex feeling… and an understanding- Mercy for crimes of need. Merciless blade for evil.

An image, or maybe a memory flashed into my mind. It was the feeling of being in a room of eight others, grateful to be chosen, repeating our lessons. I knew that I was One of Nine, a future Blade! A flurry of ideas and values came with the thought; life, compassion, strength, justice, respect… I realized that they were Shui's memories. They were the values that had been instilled in Shui. But the next instant, the memory had passed.

ONE BLADE FOR LIFE!!! Shui spun directly over our heads and flew forward to attack the remaining ravens. The ravens didn't seem like they could be stunned, but they were clearly unprepared for Shui's attack.

I was vaguely, peripherally aware that Shui had turned sideways, striking the three birds (simultaneously) in their throats. It was like walking into a line that was hung to dry clothes. All of the birds were knocked flat on their backs. Shui continued fighting.

I was only peripherally aware of what was happening with the fight, because my 'eyes' were still locked on the broken pieces of the shattered raven. Technically, my eyes were still closed and under a blindfold, but my perspective was fixed on the frozen black chunks in the snow. I imagined that I was even starting to feel cold.

Kwan I heard a familiar voice, but couldn't quite place where it was coming from. *Kwan* The call came again. *Kwan!* When the call sounded the third time, it was not only sound in my mind, but also a voice urgently speaking into my ear. "Kwan!"

The prompting from two different directions, in my mind and through my ears, shook me out of the trance I was falling into. I recognized Fox's voice. I also recognized that one of the ravens had turned to look at Fox when he spoke. (Although that raven paid for his gesture, because when he turned back to the fight, Shui greeted it with a beak-crushing blow.)

Not wanting to attract any more attention from the birds, Fox continued communicating, but only through silent mental contact. *Even with the protection that Shui has left us, the Gazing Gates are still extremely dangerous.* His voice seemed calm and soothing in my mind. *And the longer that we gaze at them, the more dangerous they become.* Fox's voice in my mind was very patient. It was like he was *coaxing* me out of that entranced frame of mind, not *forcing* me out of it.

*This is more my responsibility than anyone else's. I am the one who allowed you to come through to this place.** Then, almost to himself, **I should have engaged your mind more throughout *this* part of the process.*

*Let us follow the battle together. Watching Shui in combat is always instructive. He really is a master… But when Shui is *offended* by true evil, its especially impressive.* Just like that, my mind turned away from the icy raven pieces and the 'furry animals'.

Mammots Fox supplied. *Those furry animals were called mammots in Shui's time.* Then, as an afterthought, *Now, the only surface populations live in small groups in the far north. But underground, in the Gartun caverns for example, vast herds of them remain.*

Fox and I turned our perspectives again to the fight. We anchored our sight to a place over our heads, near the roof of the chamber. This gave us a vantage point where we could watch the battle unfold.

Shui was surrounded by the three huge ravens. They had scrambled back to their feet. They clearly wanted to go after Fox and me. But each time a raven attempted to turn away from fighting the staff, Shui quickly punished it. The ironwood of the spinning staff knocked the raven's frail legs out from under it. Then, when the bird was still in mid-air, unsupported by its legs, but before it had fallen, Shui smashed it from above. He struck the Ravens so hard that when they hit the stone floor their bodies bounced and threw off feathers.

So, none of the ravens was willing to go after us. Instead, they all focused their attention on defeating Shui. We watched. *Clearly Shui is in charge of this fight. Learn from this, Kwan- watch how he *acts*, and forces them to *react*.*

Notice that Shui is again leading them into specific positions. Both his fighting technique and his strategies are flawless. As I focused my attention more closely on Shui, I became aware of the portal behind him. I had the impression of a slender line against a reddish orange background. Shui was backed up to it, standing upright. It looked like Shui was trapped. *Do not let yourself stare at this portal Kwan. This one is particularly nasty.*

Shui stood upright, in front of the portal. The bird was stabbing its beak at Shui, trying to push Shui into the Gazing Gate. But, each time, right before the beak was about to make contact, the staff jerked aside, and the raven's beak passed by harmlessly. The raven stabbed at Shui. Shui dodged, the bird missed, took aim again and attacked. That process was repeated over and over, faster and faster, until the ravens head was moving faster than my 'sight' could follow. The raven's beak was a gleaming black point. As it tried to 'stab' the staff, it became clear that Shui was not only faster, but also a narrow target. Both things worked to Shui's advantage.

The surface of the Gazing Gate was right behind Shui. Like the ice portal, there was a mesh barrier over this one. But this portal's mesh was 'woven' much tighter than the last one had been. I was unable to see much of the interior, but a red-orange glow was clear through the barrier. Then I became aware of heat emanating from the portal. The raven had Shui backed against the portal. There was nowhere for the staff to retreat.

The raven stabbing its beak, and Shui dodging the stabbing, was a blur. It seemed impossible that the raven and the staff could go on much longer. Eventually one of them would get tired and make a mistake. I didn't know very much about fighting, but this much at least made sense to me.

There! Did you see that Kwan? Fox pointed my attention to Shui. I certainly had been watching the fight, but it just looked like the position of Shui's staff moved, or slipped a little bit. It was only a small slip, but Fox noticed it and pointed out to me. The bird apparently also noticed. It sped up its attack, seemingly eager to finish Shui. I tracked the sequence of events, but unlike Fox, I still did not see what was coming.

Shui had been poised in front of the portal. The raven had been stabbing at the staff but had not been successful so far. During the next beak-thrust, when Shui dodged the raven's strike, the staff *slipped* again! *The demons see that Shui is getting 'tired' because he has 'slipped'. All things follow patterns on some level, even these things. Shui is projecting the pattern...*

The raven seemed to understand that the staff would have a hard time dodging its next strike. The raven spread its wings and stabbed hard, committing entirely to the strike. Time seemed to slow again.

At that same moment that the raven moved forward to push Shui, the staff dropped to the floor, landing neatly between the raven's spindly legs. Surprised that it had not made contact with the staff, the bird looked down (still in mid lunge) to see the staff between its legs. The staff had landed so that its top was now lying where the bottom end had just been. The bird was leaning forward. *Ah, flawless!* Fox thought came through as undeniable admiration.

Shui flipped up the other side of the staff- behind the raven's back. The rising 'narrow' end of the staff whacked the raven on the back. Shui's blow landed between the outstretched wings, pushing it headlong through the portal. There was a squawk of surprise that was cut off an instant later.

There was a flare of light from behind the mesh screen. I can only describe it as a yellow flash behind the mesh that momentarily overwhelmed Shui's protection. What I saw after that still troubles me. I can barely put what I saw into words.

The scene was hellish. This was no exaggeration, and I came to find out later that many realms called this place 'Hell'.

What I first saw was a nightmarish landscape. The ground was either burning or already scorched. The air itself looked like it was burning. There seemed to be a scorching wind, slowly burning everything that it touched. A lake and wide river of glowing red lava were visible through the, now thin, mesh. The river of lava flowed out of the vast fiery lake before flowing past our viewpoint, on the other side.

I had thought that this realm was like a nightmare when we had entered it to save my sister. But when I saw this actual hell beyond the portal, it struck me how everything was relative. This realm actually seemed *pleasant* by comparison. Through the portal, the sky was on fire. The few dead trees that were visible were also on fire.

But even more disturbing than the environment were the inhabitants. What I saw were numerous creatures prowling the burning landscape. They had different numbers of legs. All of them walked hunched over on both 'hands' and 'feet'. None of them appeared to have skin.

My first thought was that the demons were similar to the animals we had seen before in the woodworker demon village. Like them, these demons had no skin and were covered with corded muscle. Each had discolored patches of muscle, like the demon dogs. But, unlike the demon dogs, these new figures were unrecognizably twisted, each misshapen, but different from the others. The 'dogs' had all been more or less the same design. These beasts were also on fire. Their twisted faces showed expressions of being between fury and agony. It was hard to watch.

They were snarling and screaming. And even though I could not hear the sound, I could feel it. I shudder ran through me (in my real body). My neck and arms were beginning to feel heat. My eyes were wrenched away from studying the grotesque creatures prowling the fiery landscape as the tail feathers of the raven crossed through to that hellish realm. Time seemed to slow.

So, I had some time to work out a theory about what I saw. What I saw was that the feathers began to burn (causing the initial yellow flash), but it did not incinerate the whole raven. Somehow, the Raven could not be burned. I wasn't sure, but I wondered if it could even be killed. Being a demon, the raven's feathers burned, but the injuries seemed superficial, not structural. Instead, it looked more surprised than anything else. It looked around, bewildered, standing there as its feathers burned.

These other multi-limbed demons, prowling around in the background, immediately noticed the raven. It was an intruder into their hellish home, and a novelty. Mindlessly and in unison, the creatures frantically sprinted on their twisted limbs and charged toward the raven. Every one of them, without exception, was faster than I expected.

When they reached the raven, they immediately began tearing it apart. The hell-beasts' vicious claws ripped into the smoking raven and began to fling the dismembered chunks carelessly away. This was a place where everything was suffering. It was a place of anger and pain. I noticed as one particularly large, six-legged demon tore the raven's head off, and threw it into the nearby river of lava. At that point, I noticed the raven's head did burn. It was burning slowly. And I was locked in eye-contact with the burning bird's head.

Kwan! Kwan! Fox was shaking me. Only then did I realize that I had been screaming. It felt like my arms and back had been burned. Just then, I felt Fox's presence in my mind. It was like I was small and was found in a terrible place. I had been lost. But when Fox rescued me, it was the feeling of being taken (by a safe adult) from a bad place to a new place. This area was a place inside of a circle. I could see it in my mind as a circle on the floor. Fox's face was gentle but serious as he led me into that circle. Once we stood inside the circle, it rose to waist height around us in a glowing ring. That ring began to circulate, to rotate and produce a clear high tone around us. We listened what felt like a long time as the note sounded.

The ring of light pulled some of the darkness away from my mind. But before I could consider it much longer, Fox was urging my consciousness to another place. There was the feeling of walking through resistance when I left the ring of light. From there, Fox led me to a triangle that was inscribed on the floor. For a moment, I looked at the floor, or rather I tried to focus on the floor, but realized it was only a gray mist. I tried to inspect the triangle itself that we had just stepped into, but before I could consider it, that triangle rose into the air to head height. This triangle began to rotate and emit a clear low tone.

I would like to say that I remembered more of the ninth form from that first experience, but that would not be true. In truth, a glowing star was the last thing that I remembered seeing, and a sweet, clear tone was the last sound I remember hearing.

That is, until I came back to my senses. I was still in my body, still huddled on the floor, still blindfolded, and we were still facing two remaining ravens. I heard Shui's thought/voice in my mind. **Focus Batou! Observe! Every block should be a strike and every strike should be a block.** He took on the tone of the teacher.

Shui continued the exhibition of battle techniques, but seemed to be ready to finish the fight. The staff got directly between the two remaining birds. Each time a raven tried to peck at Shui, one end of the staff avoided or blocked the first attack, while the other end swung around to strike the second raven.

There it is! Shui's part came through as an excited satisfaction. I thought that he was 'talking' about the fight, expressing that he was pleased with the fight. **The serpent always flees!**

Look Kwan! There! Above the doorway- it's holding very still. Far to the left deep in the shadows. Fox directed my attention to a place above the exit door way. The doorway was a large stone opening with a thick beam above the exit. After a moment, I saw it.

At first glance, it looked like there was only stone above the beam. But 'looking' harder, I saw that there was a shallow alcove above that beam. And there was a single remaining raven perched in that alcove.

That was what Shui was looking for! He knew that there would be one in reserve. I thought that Shui was happy about the fight, but instead he was happy he had found the hidden bird he was searching for.

Now that Shui had found what he was looking for, he allowed himself to attack fully. Fox had been right- it was impressive. And I think that it could have been instructive too, if it happened a little slower. Our perception had to be sped up somewhat. Otherwise, we would not been able to see Shui at all. The staff was *that* fast. But I wasn't an experienced fighter, so I was realistically just watching, wide-eyed. I can't pretend I understood the finer points of staff fighting.

For a few seconds, it appeared that Shui was moving at one speed, and the demonic ravens had slowed their motion. The air itself seemed to have gotten 'thicker' for the ravens. The flying staff would deal a crushing blow to one of the ravens, for example. Then, while the demon was being knocked backwards from the blow, Shui would come to the other side of the bird and deal it another crushing blow from the other direction. **Allow the enemy no time to recover. No time for rest. No time to breathe. No time to regroup.** The ravens were being bounced around through the air, from one of Shui's impacts to another.

Shui was knocking or 'throwing' them across the chamber, away from us. Then the staff would streak down the chamber, get into position, then 'hit' his own throw. Shui was beating/juggling the ravens into position in front of a particularly large and jagged piece of portal. I turned my attention to studying the portal.

The mesh barrier in front of this portal was different from the rest. and while something was definitely there, I couldn't see it. I wondered if it was a different way for Shui to block me seeing something dangerous. I turned my attention back to the fight.

Shui had delivered so much punishment to the two ravens that they were missing clumps of feathers in different places. A thought from Shui seemed to come through, like when I overheard him talking to Fox. **No pressure points...** But it felt like the idea was more a comment to himself rather than to anyone else. There was no swelling or bleeding with either of the ravens, the way I would expect from living people. Still, there was no doubt who would 'win', even before the combat was over.

I was studying the fight as best I could. It could look like Shui was just toying with the birds, but after having seen the way he disposed the last two ravens, I thought I knew what was coming.

First one raven, then the other, lunged at Shui. The staff tilted back from the first attack, and for a split second, it looked as though Shui might be overwhelmed. But then Shui pivoted and sprang back, striking the raven on its side. As it was pitched sideways, the raven tried to twist to lessen the impact of the blow, but it was too slow. The next thing I noticed was the raven flapping one wing desperately.

The other raven and I had the same reaction. We both noticed why the raven was flapping one (and only one) wing desperately. We stood in shock. The tip of one wing had crossed the "surface" of the portal. Instinctively I knew, that raven was lost.

Shui did not waste the opportunity. While the second raven was distracted watching the first, Shui changed directions and spun into a devastating strike. The staff struck the raven so hard that even though all my attention was focused on the 'sight' from Shui, my ears registered the loud CRACK.

Shui had hit the raven's head so hard that its beak snapped off as the head was turned and the raven pitched headfirst into the portal. Its body, realizing what was happening, threw out its wings and tried to push away from the surface of the portal.

The beak was already 'through' the portal, and floated, just on the other side of the Gate.

For this raven, it was of course, too late. The demon bird was pulled headlong into the Gazing Gate. I don't know if it was because the head was pulled in first, but this second raven crossed through to the other side faster than its predecessor.

The realm on the other side of this portal was not as heavily "guarded" as the portal to "Hell". The mesh in front of it was not nearly as thick or densely woven. The more I focused on the plight of the demon birds, the more I could 'see' what was on the other side.

The first raven was being drawn into... what appeared just... an emptiness. I would say that the emptiness was 'black', but even being 'black' would have been something. This place was... somehow... nothing... or rather, it was the *absence* of anything. My mind could not somehow grasp nor understand what it was seeing.

The wing that was caught in the portal was slowly, but, steadily drawing the bird in. The wing that was outside flapped frantically as it tried to escape. Its face, somehow unable to express emotion, now seemed panicked. It let out angry squawks until its head was drawn back through the portal surface. Then its beak continued to open and close, but no sound came through.

I could not turn away from watching the raven's frantic and desperate struggle to escape the portal. I couldn't help but watch. Part of me expected the black raven to be nearly invisible within the empty space. But instead, the shiny black feathers of the raven stood out very clearly. It's difficult to describe, but it felt like the raven was distinct because it was "something" in a sea of nothing.

When the raven first lost its struggle, and was pulled fully into the other realm, its exertions gave it a slow spin as it drifted into the emptiness. What I was able to see, through the protective mesh, was that the raven was still trying to flap its wings desperately.

However, in this other realm, the raven could not fly. Instead, it madly flapped its wings, but the motions didn't change its position. It opened and closed its beak, clearly attempting to cry out.

An instant later my attention was drawn to one wing, then the other. The wings were... dissolving. They seemed to be unraveling, breaking up into smaller and smaller pieces. The pieces broke apart, smaller and smaller. While they did, their black 'substance' briefly became mist, then was just... gone. Somehow it was unsettling to watch. Very quickly the entire raven had come apart, as though it had never existed. I had never seen anything like this. I understood that the demon bird had been destroyed, and that was good. I didn't fully understand why, but it was deeply upsetting to see. *This is the Void, Kwan. What you are seeing is... "Unmaking". Come away, we shouldn't contemplate this place too long.*

My attention turned to the last raven. Its fate was the same as the one before it. This one also flapped its wings. It turned its head violently back and forth, its broken-off beak drifting next to it. The process happened the same as with the bird before. The raven dissolved. It broke into pieces that became smaller and smaller until they were just... gone. I considered what I just seen and became a little nauseous.

Kwan... I heard the sound of Fox calling me and bird's wings flapping. This time I heard Fox's mental call more quickly than before. Or at least I thought I had responded quickly.

But by the time Fox pulled me to my feet, he seemed composed and already had Shui back in his hand. We resumed our journey across the chamber, much faster now. We remained blindfolded, but somehow did not need to shuffle our feet quite as slowly as before.

As we reached the stone exit way, I asked out loud, "Where...where are we going to go now? And can I take my blindfold off?" We crossed through the doorway and immediately turned a corner, heading to the left.

As soon as there was no possibility to glance back and accidentally see one of the deadly portals, Fox let me know that it was safe to take off the blindfold. Eagerly, I reached behind my head and untied the knot Fox had tied.

As I took off the blindfold and open my eyes, I was greeted with the sight of Fox smiling broadly, holding Shui aloft. Shui, glowing brighter than I had seen before, lit the dark passageway.

Sacred are the Times of Making… The tribe regards you, Batou… You have been tested, and have grown… I felt the solemnity of the congratulation from Shui. **Your first form has ended. Now, you are reborn. "A!!h!", always.**

One part of my mind registered A!!h! as just a sound, like a deep voice shouting out a long, almost musical tone. But the sound was just one form of it. The "Aaah!" sound was also a concept, a combination of ideals from Shui's warrior tribe. It was a single idea, with layered meanings. The first layer was a concept that combined; compassion, ferocity, respect, honor, kindness, strength… those kinds of things. It was joy… about virtue.

But on top of that understanding, there was a series of required actions implied. That layer of meaning was made up of directives like; protect the weak, seek then deliver justice, teach the young, speak truth, punish evil… those kinds of things. Shui intoned one last time, **Sacred are the Times of Making.**

I had never heard of that kind of thinking. It seemed overwhelmingly good. It was an idea that was bigger than any I had heard before. I felt tears start to form, making my vision watery. It felt like an idea that was bigger than one person's life. It was the code of… a hero. I felt inspired… and proud. **Hold that pride Batou. Build on it and never lose it, because nothing can ever take this from you.**

I felt amazing, considering the ordeal we were currently in. Even though I was sweating and dirty, I should have been tired or hungry or something, I felt positive very optimistic. I felt bigger than I had been. I had more confidence in my chest and down my spine. I could somehow feel it. I was different from before.

Chapter 21

Cho Clei

"As for your other question, we are going this way. The last of those demon spy-birds flew off when Shui destroyed the others. I suspect the last spy flew off to tell its master." Fox answered as he held out Shui, pointing down the hallway. I realized that it had been a foolish question. Initially, there was only one way we could go.

We continued on our path and whenever we reached a choice in the path, Shui was able to direct us. Fox, always observant, spotted feathers occasionally along the way. It looked like even if we didn't have Shui we would be able to follow the bird's flight. The castle was enormous and soon I was hopelessly lost. We took innumerable turns, like our time in the maze. But being fully enclosed, underground, and in a tunnel made it feel more restrictive than the labyrinth.

We did not really talk after the battle, Shui did not seem interested in talking. I waited to receive a "thought" from him, but nothing came. Fox, also seemed inclined not to speak, as though he was tired from an exertion of his own. I realized then that Fox had actually had to exert himself to pull me back and save me several times. He also had to protect his own mind. Shui probably did not shield Fox as much as he needed to shield me.

So, as we continued along the path in silence, I was left to my own thoughts. Whenever we reached the junction where there was a turn, Fox asked Shui, and Shui would guide us to the right way.

I had some time while we were walking to think about my experiences so far. It occurred to me that there would be no going back after this. I could never 'un-see' what I had seen. The world that I would inhabit after this would be even more dull. I could not imagine how I would go back to making dumplings at Fong's after this. I could not imagine how I could pursue any of the choices that father approved of, now that I had seen myths and legends with my own eyes.

I put that thought away until later, when I could deal with it. Right now, we were following the way that the last Raven had escaped. The thought was that the giant bird would seek out and report to the main demon that was holding Cho Clei.

My lot on this trip was entirely dependent on Fox and Shui, so I kept my eyes open and followed. I noticed a foul odor as we progressed through the tunnel. One of the ingredients that Fong used to make his shiny dumplings was eggs. This odor smelled like a forgotten box of eggs. They were spoiled and smelled like this place.

The smell comes from a yellow rock called 'suulfro'.

It was also getting noticeably warmer as we progressed through the tunnel. Even though I had not been running, I was sweating. But since Fox did not comment on the heat, and Shui did not comment, I did not say anything either. There was a dull pain under my foot. I looked down and saw that I had stepped on a bone.

Fox also stopped. He turned slowly in a circle while holding out Shui, so that the tunnel was fully lit. The ground in front of us was littered with loose bones. We had just stepped on to a 'bone carpet'. It probably would have been more disturbing to me, but we had traveled so far on the HellFire Road that I was used to this.

I didn't even bother to question what kind of bones they might be. I had grown accustomed to everything being strange. A moment of self-awareness stunned me.

I felt different than I had before. This place was changing me. I was changing, growing, in my mind. I was in a fantastic place, and everything had changed- fantastically. I had no idea how much my life would change when I crossed the Pall with Fox.

The heat quickly became oppressive, and the foul odor got stronger. But again, because neither of the others mentioned it,

I didn't either. I had put my head down and was marching forward behind Fox.

As we walked, it got progressively hotter. I looked ahead and could see beads of sweat dripping down the back of Fox's head. It was a surprise to me when Fox began to communicate mentally. I expected it from Shui, but not from Fox. I realized, without having it explained to me, that mental communication would allow all three of us to speak together. It also had the added benefit of not being audible to other people.

We should prepare what's coming next. Fox's thought came through a very serious package of emotions. Before he even continued, I had received different information about how he *felt*. He felt that we should be clear that we were going into a more dangerous situation than we had faced at any point on this trip. His character was honest, and I could sense that he would tell me the truth, but he did not really want to say what he was about to say.

It's strange, but I found myself reacting before I had even received the message. *We don't have all of the information that we need about this demon. But what we do know is cause for concern.* I tensed in anticipation thinking, 'here comes the bad news'. *I have had some time to consider what we are walking into. We know that this demon has taken your sister. We know that we are not leaving without her.* Even though I knew that was our whole reason for being here, it still felt good to hear Fox say it. He was being honest and warning me about our chances, but it did not hamper my enthusiasm. It dawned on me that we had made it this far, despite the odds being against us.

If this demon is as powerful as the warnings have said, however, this will not be easy. There are some at the GaleTemple who say that no man can defeat an ArchDemon... whether he is an Immortal GaleMaster or not. Others disagree. Fox shrugged and spread his hands.

I was dumbfounded. I couldn't believe what I was hearing. Was Fox saying that we did not stand a chance? Have we come all of this way only to find out that there was no hope?

Fox must have seen the expression on my face as I tried to come to terms with what he was saying. A mixture of fear and panic and exhaustion and disappointment welled up within me. Fox went on, "Those Masters would recalculate if they considered the chances of an immortal GaleMaster combined with one such as this!" Fox said the words aloud, surprising me, and held up the staff exultantly. The metal grain running throughout the Ironwood flared briefly, in pride and appreciation.

Then he switched back to 'mental' communication. *With Shui on our side, I would judge that we have very different odds.* My hopes soared hearing this. I expected Fox to go on and tell me that our odds were now good. He did go on. *Now, I would judge our odds at about even, 1 chance in 2. Give or take…*

My mouth opened and closed a few times, not knowing what to say. Our odds were no better than 1 chance in 2? But Fox continued, *To give us reasonable chances of success, we will need to have a plan. We *always* have to have a plan… When a demon captures a living mortal spirit, it needs to be protected not to be corrupted in a place like this…

Oh, don't worry Kwan! I see the look on your face. Our spirits are not being corrupted here. You know some of the benefits of the shield you wear. But one benefit of the Valrun Stone you wear, is that it shields you from the harm of being in this plane. This bead," he said holding up a bead on his rosary. "performs the same function for me. But I'm getting off the point. We have to use this time and go over our strategy. I suspect that this final demon is near.

I nodded, reinforcing to myself how serious this situation was. I felt like a warrior preparing for battle. Righteous battle was what Shui called it. And that probably was a good way to think about it. We were about to go into a battle against a huge supernatural evil. We would rescue my sister, I vowed. Fox continued, *From the beginning of our time in this place, Shui could sense your sister's life. That is what he used to guide us here. He could also sense that her spirit was uncorrupted, so she must have some kind of protection too. I expect that this protection will also be some sort of prison for her. So, I would expect her to be in some kind of cage.

So, we have three objectives. The first goal is to defeat the demon. We would need to do that accomplish our second goal- to free your sister.*

"What's the last objective?" I asked.

Fox smiled broadly, *The last objective is to escape!* He winked, like a boy telling a mischievous joke. I saw that he was intentionally being playful, since all three of us already knew how serious the situation was. I smiled back weakly.

"So how do we…?" I asked, following what he was 'thinking' at me, but not knowing how to proceed.

What is our plan? Well, since we know that it would take a more powerful being than me to beat the demon, our best plan is that Shui and I will attack the demon, while you free your sister. A ball of fear welled up in my stomach for a second. I tried to remember to be brave like Shui had taught me, but the idea of rescuing my sister by myself was terrifying.

There is a combination of techniques that I believe has a chance at overpowering the demon. I won't bore you with detailed descriptions of the techniques, but the idea is that I will use my power and Shui's power to engage the demon with this combination. It must have been clear on my face that I was curious about the attack. Fox noticed, and 'sent' me more. *The combination is; first to engage the demon with a weak strike to draw and absorb its initial fury. Do not worry, Shui is strong enough to withstand the impact of the demon's fury.* The metal grain in the staff flared again, emphasizing its confidence. *But, upon meeting a week strike, the demon will feel the need to press its advantage. It will want to destroy us immediately.* He paused and looked intently at me. *But *our* strikes are special. As I 'said', the first strike will be weak. The second strike will be stronger than the first. The third strike will be stronger than the first *and* the second, *combined*. The fourth will hit harder than the first *three, combined*. In total, we will need do deliver nine strikes that will each vastly increase in power, until the final one renders it powerless.*

"Then what?" I asked.

*We will need to capture it. That is where the SoulCage comes in. A demon like this cannot be destroyed. Well, at least not by beings like us. Imagine that the demon is like a cluster of flies on a piece of filth. If you swatted at the flies, they would scatter. But eventually, the flies will come back together... This is the same as with the demon. The demon can only be *dispersed* by us, like a cloud of flies. So, it can only be 'destroyed' temporarily, at best. Only something powerful, like the SoulCage could hold it.*

I nodded, absorbing that, and waiting for him to go on. *Remember that this is to save your sister. We must do this. And we will not fail.*

Then I 'heard' a thought from Shui **We will prevail Batou. Your strength will arise when the time comes, if you will it. Trust this. You have been the proof of this**

Fox nodded in agreement, *Do you remember me telling how demons are arrogant?* I nodded at his silent question. *They consider themselves evil royalty. This one will consider himself a king and will probably have a 'throne room'. We will continue until we find this demon's throne room. When we reach that place, we will have to locate your sister. Then, once we have found her, Shui and I will attack the demon. We will engage it in combat, striking the nine blows. While we are fighting it, you will be freeing your sister.*

"But *how?*" I whispered. "I don't know anything about breaking a demon's prison! And what if something happens to you two? How would I even get Cho Clei home?" I didn't know why I was speaking out loud. I knew that I could 'think' at Fox and Shui now, but I was uncomfortable and speaking aloud was somehow comforting.

Fox reached up and took the metallic silver bead off of his rosary. He handed it to me. It was surprisingly heavy. *If something happens and Shui and I are defeated, the SoulStone can summon a Yalan on its own. This function of the SoulStone can *only* be used in a very specific situation. Fortunately for you, *if* we failed, you *would* be in that situation. You would need to hold the SoulStone, picture the Ragyala, and focus clearly on a single word. Focusing on the word will focus your mind on the 'call'. Once you focus on that word, the covenant will be invoked and the SoulStone will 'call' the Ragyala. You could call the Arkyala instead, for example. But, in truth, the Arkyala would just end up summoning the Ragyala, since this is his 'area.'

Ah, I see you already wondering why... The power of each of the Yalans is equal, but they each have different duties or responsibilities. Helping mortals trapped in this realm, like you and your sister, would fall to the Ragyala.

My mind was racing. Questions, or things that were almost questions were all competing for my attention. "What... What would I do then?... and... and what is the word that will call him?" I asked.

He held out his hand. *Give the SoulStone back to me, and I will tell you the word. If you say it now, I'm not entirely sure what would happen. But if you were in trouble, we know what it would do.* I handed the stone back to Fox. *The word is 'As-aiy-lom!' if you say that word while you are holding the stone, it will summon the Ragyala.*

"What does 'As-aiy-lom!' mean?" I whispered.

*It is an ancient term. To be fully candid Kwan, beings at your level of development are not usually allowed to visit places like this. Please understand that it is no criticism to note that you are young and lack formal training. It means that you are naturally, and appropriately, out of your depth.

*Because you're out of your depth, because you would not have been able to survive and navigate this realm without us, you will be able to call the Ragyala.

Calling 'As-aiy-lom!' means that you are lost and calling for mercy or help, asking for protection. It is almost as though you were a ship lost at sea. The Ragyala will come to your aid, if you truly need it. He would come to you and search your mind, to explain why he had been summoned. Upon reviewing your memories, he will return you and your rescued sister to your world.

"So, does that mean that after we rescue my sister, we can use the SoulStone to immediately escape? I mean... Since the Ragyala needs to 'let' us back into our world right? We rescue her, summon the Ragyala, pay him, and he will send us back home?" I tried to remember to think to Fox and Shui, but I kept forgetting and speaking out loud.

Well, it doesn't work exactly like that, Kwan Fox said. *Beings like us cannot really summon the Ragyala. The soul stone can summon the Ragyala, but it will only do that in very specific situations. And the Ragyala will only answer the call in those specific situations. Normally, a being like the Ragyala does not appear on command. It *can*, in that it *does* have the power to change its location instantly. But the Ragyala is not an 'assistant' we can call. Our relationship is closer to the *opposite* of that, actually. The first time I summoned the Ragyala, it did not come because of *me*. The Ragyala came because I carried both the SoulStone and the red powder.*

"Oh yeah! The red powder! I had forgotten about that!'

Fox went on, *No, when we rescue your sister, we will need to find a way out of this place on our own. After that, we will have to get to a place where we can access the Pall.*

"And what if the Ragyala is afraid to come around this super-demon?" I asked. I hated to sound like a coward, but it was in my mind, so I said it. "If the Ragyala is chased off by the demon, what should I do then?"

There was a long pause. I waited expectantly in the silence.

The sound of mental laughter, burst from both Fox and Shui, like I had just said something naïve, unexpected and ridiculous. *You don't need to worry about that, Kwan.*

"But..." I started, but Fox cut me off.

Cho Clei needs us Kwan. We don't have any time to waste. Fox was right. None of my questions changed anything. I still had to save my sister, no matter what. I had to trust Fox and Shui. And I did trust them.

"So… where can we access the Pall?" I asked. Fox smiled approvingly. I could feel the approval coming through without him having to speak. I had been paying attention.

Shui and I have been tracking it since we crossed over. An image came into my head. It was a view of a valley, seen from high above. Perhaps it was looking down from a mountaintop? A river wound through the valley, a thin, blue, ribbon meandering through the surroundings. On one side of the river, it was brown and green. It was very pretty actually. On the other side, the surroundings were gray. *The Pall's course does not run in a straight line. Its path is sinuous, snakelike…*

"Like the river!" I whispered excitedly.

Again, the feeling of approval came. Fox looked over his shoulder and winked. *Exactly. Fortunately, there is a place not far from this cursed fortress where we can access the Pall.*

"And if the demon catches us before we find Cho Clei?" I asked.

Then we will have to improvise. In that case, Shui and I will probably attack, and you will stay behind us unless you see a chance to free her. Then, a moment later, *But hopefully we won't have to improvise.*

Right after Fox sent that thought to me, our shields flared to life. The appearance was more noticeable in the darkened tunnel. I could see the faint sphere of sparkling blue light around me. I looked up, but Fox was holding his finger to his lips. I understood the gesture for silence, but I did not understand why the shields had 'turned on'.

It's because of the heat… And it means we're getting close. was all that Fox thought at me. It was strange having communication with Fox like he we were talking face to face, but he was walking away and did not stop or slow down.

The heat? Oh. I *did* feel cooler. Not relaxed, but I was sweating less, and felt a little more secure knowing that the shield was up and working.

We were creeping down the tunnel, walking through it as it curved ahead to the right. For what felt like a long time, we had only had Shui's light to beat back the darkness. But eventually, we saw a faint red-orange glow on the tunnel wall ahead of us.

As we came towards the red-orange glow, the 'suulfro' smell intensified. It was clear that we were nearing the end of the tunnel. I started to imagine the horrors that might be waiting for us. I worried how the demon might attack. I worried about Cho Clei and vividly pictured her in danger.

The time before battle is always the most difficult, Batou. When the battle begins, all of your mind will be present in the fight. But before battle, the mind finds unease, worrying about the future, all in anticipation of when the fight begins. Understand that this is the way before any battle. Understand that you can control it. Remember what you have learned. Understand that the wait will soon be over. Shui's thoughts came through just when I needed them.

Chapter 22

The Nine Strikes

Shui was right. I was worrying. He was right that I was falling into old habits, worrying about the future. Remember what I had learned? What *had* I learned? I tried to review and think clearly.

I suppose that the same things he had said before also applied now. Either I was going to die, or I wasn't, so I didn't need to worry. That fear did not help me now. And because it did not help me, I did not need it now. I could control it.

Okay, I thought. That's fine for me, but what about Cho Clei? This is about saving her. What about being afraid for her? Was that fear different? I 'thought' the question out to Shui?

It is different. It comes at you from a different direction. But, in the grand scheme, your solution is the same. An image came into my mind – It was a stack of pages, each with writing on them. The pages were bound on one side. A breeze seemed to blow through, turning over the pages. The pages flipping in rapid succession.

This is called a 'book'. It is one way for keeping knowledge like a scroll or a tablet. Different things can be written on each page.

Ok… you've shown me a book, but what does that have to do with worrying about my sister?

Every mortal life is vulnerable, like a page in this book. The image of the book changed, pages were being torn out by some invisible force, one by one. ***Just like those pages can be torn out of the book, our lives can be snuffed out at any time. There is no guarantee that we will live to see tomorrow, Batou. Weakness and potential, remember? This is the truth of mortal lives.***

I couldn't argue with that. It seemed clear to me.

*This is true for your life. You have made progress and grown, in part, because you have seen this... But you should also understand that this is true for every life. This is true for your life as well as your sister's life.**

But... She is just...

*All mortal lives are as vulnerable as the pages in that book. Both of your lives. The ancients would judge this quest to be noble as you are 'risking your page' to prevent your sisters 'page' being ripped out. (Or worse, something terrible being written on that page.)**

But... What does that mean? I didn't quite understand how to make the ideas connect.

*You might live through this quest. You might die on this quest. But you understand that worrying about it makes fear that gets in your way.**

I nodded, following at least that much.

*Since you do not know whether you will live through this, how will you conduct yourself now? What have you learned so far? How would you deal with it now?**

I thought about it for a second. Well, if the fear didn't help me, and I saw that it usually wouldn't, I would just have to do my best regardless. I would need to think clearly and try to stay calm. Then... Once I was calm and clear, I could make a plan, then act?

*Is it a question? Are you unsure?**

No, I thought. My mind told me that that was what I had learned. It was the truth. I admitted it to myself. (And in the process felt a small surge of self-confidence.)

*You're absolutely right. That is the way that you should approach a situation that makes you want to worry. And how hard would you fight? How much would you commit to your actions, when it was time to act?**

That answer I absolutely knew. When the fight began, I had to put everything I had into it. Once I was clear on what to do, I would commit to my actions completely. This was for Cho Clei!

*Again, you're absolutely right. And everything that you have thought so far, also applies to your sister. She may live. She may die. It is the same for all of us. So, the worry about her does not help her, or you.**

You do not need that worry now, because you are preparing for action. And that is the most important time to be clear. Fear and worry can enslave the mind, if you let them.

I... yes...

But you know to put those fears aside. You know to only concentrate on what you are going to do. And you will put forth all of your effort, fighting as hard as you can to save her. Choose to put your mind in that place.

I saw that Shui was right. This was the time to be clear. This was the time to put my mind in the right place- to prepare. I *was* going to save my sister, no matter what, I had decided it. That was all I needed to focus on- find her and rescue her.

Then I thought, now is the time to be fully clear. This is not a time to let myself be afraid about anything. I needed to face every truth that I could see. First, there was the unpleasant truth that Cho Clei and I may have to escape this realm on our own. I may have to take Cho Clei, call As-aiy-lom, and plead our case for us to get home. I might have to deal with the great Ragyala itself.

But as we continued to walk, I could watch as the fear started to come up. I forced myself to look at it, and not avoid it. Once I've done that, I could put it aside.

If I had to deal with the Ragyala, so be it. I knew what I would do in that situation. I had been prepared- given instructions. I remembered those instructions. I needed to continue remembering those instructions. And feeling scared did not help me remember what I had to do. It would be a *big* problem if I forgot. Shui was right- worrying about it now did not help.

We were close now to saving my sister. We had come all this way. Whatever it took to save her, I would do. I did not want to have to escape this realm without Fox and Shui, but the reality was that it was out of my hands. It was not my choice to make. If it happened, I would deal with it.

Just then, I felt a great weight lifted from my shoulders. I was able to focus clearly on what it was that I needed to do- what we were about to do. I did start to imagine what we might be walking into. But now, I did not imagine the possibilities as only catastrophic things that would probably happen. I began to see, at least the possibility, that whatever we encountered, we *would* deal with.

For example, I imagined Cho Clei locked in an iron cage. I imagined seeing her and needing to figure out how to open the lock on that imaginary cage. I began to realize that a whole new perspective had come upon me. If I moved the fear aside, a whole new level of agency occurred to me. I saw the problems in my imagination, but I now also saw myself finding solutions to those problems.

This happened just in time. The end of the tunnel came into view ahead of us. From inside the tunnel, whatever was outside was red orange and so brilliant that we had to squint.

As we approached, we slowed. This was as much to let our eyes adjust to the light as to be cautious. As we crept forward to see what was outside, the view took my breath away. It was grand on a scale that I had not conceived of before.

Maybe when I was a young boy, before my imagination had any limitations, if you had asked me to picture the capital palace, I might have come up with something this big. Maybe.

When the tunnel ended, it ended in a short walkway, and then a sheer drop of 30 or 40 paces to the 'ground'. We crouched on the walkway at the threshold of the tunnel, gazing out into an enormous circular cavern. The walls of the cavern were lined with levels of balconies and the doorway openings to shadowy tunnels. This space could hold a massive audience. Below us, on the cavern floor, a statue was in the center of the chamber.

I stood at the edge of the doorway and looked up. The throne room's spire ceiling was impossibly high. I could only see up halfway to the top. The rest of the ceiling disappeared into darkness. I looked out at the expanse, stunned at the size.

My imagination began working, seeing the grand scale. It made me visualize the entire hall filled with thousands of demons watching the central platform. But I couldn't see any demons. The only movement came from the flickering lights around the perimeter of the cavern. Iron braziers, like the ones along the HellFire Road, ringed the chamber.

This had to be what Fox had called the "throne room". I immediately recalled the exterior of the tower. Considering the size of the cavern, I figured that we were directly below the castle's towering, central spire. I vividly remembered the series of spiked towers, stabbing up into the red sky. I was able to picture the tall central tower in the shape of a screaming demon.

I recalled its half-man, half-bat body; it's grotesquely long arms down at the sides, clawed 'hands' clenched, and its head thrown back in mid-scream. It had huge bat ears and curved, demon horns that sprouted from its forehead, visible even from far below. The spire had been colossal, towering above us.

When I looked down at the statue in the center of the chamber, it confirmed my suspicions. Simply put, the beastly statue was clearly showing the demon from the spire. The pose was different, letting me see a 'wing' membranes that connected the statue's torso and its raised arms. The statue in the center of the room was almost as large as the Ragyala. It stood on a wide, raised circular platform.

The bat-demon statue was kneeling on one spiked knee. It held a round container in the air over its head. I looked at the statue's long, gnarled arms. Each clawed hand held a 'handle' on one side of the container. It was difficult to identify what the container was, because it was enveloped in smoke and occasional flares of fire. My first thought was that it was a large soup-pot.

Overflowing from that round thing was a stream of molten metal. At least I assumed it was molten metal. It looked like when I had seen the liquid metal the village blacksmith had been working. But it did not make sense to me because more of the liquid metal flowed out of the thing than was possible. It could not have held that much of the molten material.

Fox and I stood there watching as the molten metal poured directly down onto the statue's head, then shoulders, then down its back before pooling on the platform. I noticed for the first time that there was a circular gap around the platform where there was no floor. When the molten metal reached the edge of the platform, it dripped below.

I tried to gauge how far it would be to jump across the empty ring that surrounded the platform. It looked like I could jump across it. But, I knew that distance changed perspective. Maybe it was too far to jump, but I somehow thought that I could clear the distance.

Clear the distance? Jump across the unknown to approach the terrifying, lava-covered statue? What was I thinking? I don't know why would picture that. It suddenly seemed absurd to me the idea of approaching the statue. I shook my head to clear it of the ridiculous vision. I continued to survey the chamber.

My eye next fell on an impossibly large, red gemstone. It seemed to call for my attention. Otherwise, I certainly would have noticed it, but it would have taken longer. The gemstone stood out, even though it could have been hidden in the fiery chamber. The chamber itself was filled with the glow of reds and oranges from the lava. And those lights were reflected in the ruby. The gem appeared to be impossibly large, larger than I was tall. It was laying at an angle, propped up so that it would be visible from the platform.

And then I saw her.

There was Cho Clei. It took me a few moments before I could understand what I was seeing. My little sister was lying there somehow encased in the giant gem. There was no mistaking her. I would know her little face anywhere. She even had little doll father had given her, tucked under one arm, frozen inside the gem with her. I gasped in recognition.

Be silent from this point forward. Fox thought to me. *I see her too. Stay calm.* I looked over and saw that Fox was intently studying the cavern. *The gem holding your sister is, almost certainly, the shield that keeps her safe in this realm. The good thing is that she, almost certainly, will not be aware that anything has happened. Time does not pass within a within such a stone.*

One of our goals, to find your sister, has been met. But the same problem remains as before. How to 'unlock the cage' to release her.

'You don't know how to unlock the gem?!' I thought at Fox. Somehow, I was sure Fox would have the answer. He had been able to figure out every problem we had encountered.

No, but I suspect the stone is tied to the demon. After we have delivered our nine strikes and captured the demon, the gemstone should open.

I digested that. 'And you have confidence in your nine strikes? The combination, I mean.' I thought/asked soberly.

*Each strike delivers a certain effect. And once the sequence has begun, the outcome should be decided. Each strike leads into the next.

*If you are in a position to 'see' the battle when it begins, you might find our first strike disappointing. Don't be confused… The first strike is very weak, but that is just a formality. As I said, they increase in power…

*They *will* work, Kwan. Once we deliver the strikes, we will beat the demon. I'm honestly less concerned about that part. My concern is *finding* this demon.* Fox thought at me.

'Oh, ok, so how does our plan change?' I asked. While he did not communicate any specific thought to me, I felt approval from Shui. I was staying focused, and he approved.

*Our plan will change in only a few key ways. We will still need to defeat the demon. But since we know where your sister is, it makes sense for you to stay with her while we are fighting the demon.

First, we will need to come down from this ledge. This area was clearly made for spectators. After we get down there, we need to secure your position near your sisters body. That way you will be prepared to collect her when we beat the demon. After that, Shui and I will go demon hunting.* I could sense a fearless, predatory glee from Shui.

I have a rope in my bag. I will secure it... here. He pointed to a large bone that was suspended above the title exit. I had not noticed it before. *Then, we will lower ourselves down the rope, and hope that we are not discovered. Climbing a rope is a vulnerable position.*

And then, as soon as he had said it, he went about doing it. After securing Shui to the harness across his back, Fox pulled a long coil of roughly braided rope out of his miraculous bag. Again, it would've been impossible for the bag to hold the amount of rope that he drew out of it. He tied the rope securely to the bone overhead, pulling on it to test it. Then he turned and gave the cavern one last look. Satisfied that there was no change, Fox flung the coiled rope over the edge.

Somehow the rope was perfectly measured so that it ended, and fell short, just before reaching the ground. *I will go first. And then a few moments later, you will follow me. When we get to the bottom, we go directly to the gemstone.*

And with that, Fox grabbed the rope swung his bulk nimbly over the side and clambered down. I looked down over the edge as Fox quietly receded down towards the floor. A parting thought came into my mind from Shui, **Strength in battle, Batou.**

As I grasped the rope and swung out over the ledge, the feeling of nervousness in my body was palpable. For a moment, I felt like I might be sick to my stomach. Then I remembered why I was here. I glanced down and saw my sister, frozen and asleep, within a demon's gemstone prison. Her face looked peaceful. I tried not to anticipate how she would feel, waking up in this demonic realm. My resolve hardened. I *chose* to push the nervousness down. Cho Clei needed me.

I lowered myself hand-over-hand down the rope. I glanced down. We were all trying to be quiet. Honestly, even though I had seen his strength demonstrated before, I was impressed at how easily Fox moved down the rope.

As we descended, I saw that we had been on the fourth level of balcony in the cavern. as I climbed down the rope, I saw multiple "floors" of ledges. Each ledge had numerous tunnel openings. I could not imagine where all the rest of those tunnels went. Honestly, I did not want to know. Still, nothing moved except the falling lava and flickering firelight.

I tried to be quiet as I scrambled down the rope. And trying to be quiet meant moving slowly. Fortunately, I had always been strong. But I was tired from our journey, and my arms and shoulders trembled as they slowly eased me down the rope. It had been a long trip. Now that I thought about it, I did not actually know how long I had been in this realm. I made a mental note to ask Fox about it later.

Climbing down the rope, I tried to review what I knew, and what I needed to do. Fox's comments from before came back to me, "It would take a more powerful being than me to defeat this demon…"

I felt pretty confident that I was coming to understand Fox's communication. He was encouraging me to be realistic about our chances. That did not mean that our chances were good, but it did mean that we would still have to accomplish our mission. It didn't really change what we had to do, I realized. We were going to rescue my sister!

"Shui and I will attack while you stay with your sister…" The way they lived naturally gave me heroic examples. Both Fox and Shui were willing to risk their lives fighting evil, to save a little girl they did not even know. I was the only one here that had a reason to save Cho Clei. Once again, I was inspired. They were powerful, but humble, and they actually cared.

The plan was straightforward. I would hide near the gemstone, close to my sister. Fox and Shui would do the real work. I reviewed what I knew, my expectations about the coming battle. I knew that Fox and Shui had an unbeatable combination of nine strikes that would defeat the demon. I knew that the first strike would be weak, but by the ninth strike, the demon would be defeated. At that point, the gemstone would open and I would be able to pull my sister out. Then, all four of us would leave this realm together.

Good. I nodded to myself. I felt like I had reviewed and was as ready as I would ever be. I looked down and saw that Fox (and Shui) were almost halfway to the floor.

Soon, we had almost reached the floor. Some part of me could not believe our luck. I hadn't admitted it to myself, but I had been expecting an attack while climbing down the rope.

I felt a thought from Shui. He and Fox had been waiting below, looking around the chamber as I dropped the last distance. Shui sent a brief thought to me. **Do *not relax your guard.***

The attack had never come. We had made it safely to the ground. My senses were heightened as I looked around. I could feel that we had entered a more dangerous area. I nodded, this was not the time for thoughts about our good fortune. Shui was right, it was the time to stay alert and watchful.

It's time to get to your sister! Now! Fox "thought" at me. I did not need to be told that twice. Fox unslung his staff from the harness on his back and we both broke into a crouching run to the big gem.

When I reach the stone, I looked down and my breath caught in my chest. It was my sister. Little Cho Clei! She looked like she had been plucked, still sleeping, from her bed and then frozen in this giant red jewel. Her eyes were closed. She was wearing the same night clothes that she wore at home. I recognize them. I recognized her face. I recognized her favorite doll. I recognized everything. This was *definitely* my little sister. My hands naturally slid along the flat surface of the gemstone, searching for a way to open it. It was hard and unyielding, but cool to my touch. In a moment of exasperation, I balled up my right fist and banged it on the surface of the gemstone.

The only thing that happened was that my hand hurt. And Cho Clei was definitely not freed. Fox crouched down and pulled me down next to him. *You will stay right here Kwan.* Fox said. *Shui and I will go now, find this demon and deliver the Nine Strikes.*

Fox reached out and put a hand on my shoulder. He looked me in the eye. *Hopefully, this won't take long. You stay here, collect your sister when she's free. We will be back.* And with that, Fox stood and stepped out from behind the giant ruby.

He began walking back towards the rope that we had climbed down. I wasn't sure where they intended to go, but it seemed that he and Shui were going to check the opposite side of the chamber first.

I was surrounded by flickering red and orange light. If I let myself be aware of it, I was also surrounded by the stink of 'suulfro'. I was hot and sweating. I could see that Fox was too. As he and Shui set off, I could see beads of sweat reflecting on his head.

Obviously, this was a horrible place. But it wasn't the same kind of horrible that it had been before. Before, this realm was almost unbearable. I had been hovering on the verge of panic, out of my depth, because this place was a huge unknown to me.

Perhaps the biggest unknown, that weighed on me the heaviest, was that I had not known if Cho Clei was even alive. I had not known whether or not she was here. I did not know if she had *really* been taken to this place. I had trusted my instincts... to trust Fox... And my trust in Fox had been rewarded. But until I had actually seen her, I had not really *known*. And that unknown, that missing chunk, had been sitting on top of my mind the entire journey.

Placing that trust had been a gamble, but I had not seen it that way at the time. I had blindly stepped into a completely different world. But now that I knew she was here, it made it easier to deal with every part of being in this place. The fear and hardships throughout our journey here suddenly seemed inconsequential... My gamble had paid off. We had found her! Now we were going to save my sister, then we would all go home.

For the first time, I was able to imagine our success. I could see how we were going to win. We had found Cho Clei! *We actually did it*! And now, we had one last push and then we would all be free. I could fully feel the change in my own perspective. I must have grown.

I watched as Fox and Shui made their way slowly around the cavern. They had only gotten about 20 paces away from me, when we heard a sound that made me freeze in mid-thought.

CAW!!! CAW!!! CAW!!! I did not have to look to place the sound. Before my head had turned to find its source, my mind had identified it. Turning, I was able to see the glowing red eyes perched on one of the balcony ledges above us. The last raven, the one that had escaped Shui's wrath and escaped, had been watching Fox.

I felt dismay in my stomach when I realized that we had been spotted. I reacted, and thought, "Oh no!" But Fox did not seem troubled by it.. He looked up and calmly studied the bird.

An instant later, I got back a response thought Fox, *Stay calm, Kwan. Notice that it hasn't attacked. Shui has taught it that engaging us is a mistake. So, put that fear aside. Instead, think how finding the raven could be useful for us. Remember our initial idea was if we could find the raven, it would be easier to find the demon. We believed that the Raven would report to its master.*

"Oh," I thought. Why hadn't I thought of that? Where the bird was, its master would be nearby.

Now that we have found the last demon bird, Shui and I will continue with the plan. It has seen me, Kwan, but it may not have seen you. Stay hidden.

Chapter 23

Wen-Yi

I have noticed that when something very bad happens, like an accident or something very painful, my sense of time can dilate. This was the case with me at that moment. I was getting ready to let Fox know that I would not move from where I was crouched. But before I could send the thought to him, I felt the world break. I remember feeling time slow, as though it was a wheel that I could *see* spinning slower and slower. I remember looking up, seeing Fox's head lower from looking at the ceiling to the platform. He made an expression of wincing, as though hearing something irritating. I noticed the expression on his face. But before I could process why Fox looked irritated or what was going on, why time had slowed down, it felt like a horse kicked my head.

Or rather, it was a combination of shooting pain in my head, flashing lights behind my eyelids, nausea in my stomach, pain in my testicles, and the feeling of having all of my hairs pulled out. I had never felt pain like it before. It hurt so much I couldn't scream. I couldn't breathe. It came at me in every sense I had.

If I had not already been crouching, I would certainly have fallen and maybe even hit my head on something. Instead, I only fell onto my back and writhed. I was in extraordinary pain, but I had no idea what had caused it.

Whatever had caused the pain, stopped. But it took me a few moments, panting, before I could regain my senses. It was like waking up after a nightmare. I was disoriented and struggled to find my bearings. With horror, I realized that something was happening, but I was barely coherent. There was something large *moving* in the chamber. Some sense I had not been aware of before, knew there was something moving and that it was not any of *us*.

Remembering to stay down, I shook my head to clear it. I struggled back into my crouched position. I was behind the gemstone, so that I could not fully see the central platform. I got ready to crawl forward a little to get a better view. But before I could move, the pain struck again.

A long moment of pain later, I came to my senses on the floor, next to the gem. This time, I fell to the side of where I had been a moment ago. Now, I was in a position to see what I had missed before. I looked up to see Fox staring at the statue with a fierce expression on his face.

My sense of time was still dilated because what I saw happened in slow motion. I saw the grotesque bat demon statue slowly rising to its feet. It wasn't a statue! It was the actual bat demon, Wen-Yi!

In slow motion, it lowered the lava-spewing object it had been holding over its head. I watched as the bat demon rose to its full height. Fox occupied the other side of my field of view, several feet shorter than the demon. And Fox was a tall man.

As the demon stood, I could clearly see what it was holding. The thing it had been holding by two handles, now hung from his right hand. With shock and horror, I realized it was the *severed head* of some evil looking beast.

I can only assume that it was some other kind of demon. The skull's expression looked like a savage beast had been tortured to madness, then decapitated. The "handles" were its curved horns. Wen-Yi had been holding the two horns that were mounted on either side of the beast's head. From where the neck would have, a steady stream of lava was flowing out of the severed head. The bat demon, Wen-Yi had been… bathing… in the burning lava?

The mouth of the severed head continued to vomit out a continuous stream of molten metal. The severed head's eyes showed only black. The bat demon carelessly tossed the severed head down onto the platform. The hideous head bounced before rolling off. The gap encircling the platform was just wide enough for the skull to pass through. It disappeared from view, still spewing the molten metal.

I only then noticed a thin sheet of hot air wavering in between the demon and me. I realized at that same moment, that there was both heat *and* light coming from that gap in the floor. Suddenly I pictured a giant lake of lava below us. Was this room just a thin platform on top of that lake? What else could accept something like the lava-spewing head without it becoming disastrous? As I tried to recover my senses, my imagination ran free.

To my astonishment, Fox opened his mouth and made a series of odd noises. On some level, I recognized it as the strange language of the demons. However, when Fox spoke the 'words', while it was unpleasant to my ears, it did not bring flashes of paralyzing agony. It was clear to me that Fox was speaking the demon's language.

But he was not doing it well. Instantly, without needing to be told, I understood that Fox could never properly pronounce that demon language because Fox was not an evil demon. The demon took a few slow powerful steps forward. As it did, it opened its mouth and my agony began again. Some tiny part of my mind recognized immediately that it was the demon's speech that gave me such pain. But that was only a small portion of my mind. The majority of my mind was writhing in torment.

A moment later (I assume) I again came to my senses. As my eyes cleared, I looked up and saw Fox standing there with one hand up. The demon had stopped speaking. It seemed that the sign to stop was universal.

I was grateful that Fox had stopped the noise. But that immediately turned into concern as the demon, clearly offended at being silenced, made a vicious expression and levelled its gaze at Fox. Fox and Shui were standing there in a battle stance. It was clear that they were ready to fight. ***Same as The Ladders, Fox. Remember.*** I overheard the thought from

Shui to Fox. What were The Ladders? I made a point to ask later.

The demon saw their battle stance and, while keeping its feet planted in place, it jerked to the side, bending its torso at the waist. It looked like a giant had grabbed the statue and snapped the top half, leaving it at a right angle to the legs.

With that, the demon plunged its clawed hand into the side of its torso. The demon's claws pierced its side easily. I watched in disbelief as the demon grinned, working its hand into its belly, then down toward its hips. A moment later, snarling (but not speaking that horrible language), the demon pulled a long black blade out of its leg. It appeared that there had been a sword hidden inside the demon. The sword sliced the demon as it was freed from the body. Black ichor dripped down onto the floor of the platform. When that black blood touched the still-molten metal, it hissed and burned, making the foul 'suulfro' smell even worse. Now it smelled like burnt hair and rotten eggs.

When the demon had finished extracting the blade from its body, it straightened back up. The wound in its side instantly healed closed. Then the bat demon swung the blade in an experimental arc, testing the balance. Viscous black 'blood', still clinging to the blade, was flung off. Some of it flew in Fox's direction. Fox's shield flared brightly as it blocked the flung filth. Apparently satisfied, the demon held its sword with both hands and smiled wickedly.

I wanted to close my eyes, but I couldn't. My eyes were riveted to the imminent battle. **Batou, don't move until we deliver all nine strikes and the prison opens. Count the strikes. Stay focused.** I heard the short and direct advice come into my mind from Shui. It was in his precise battle voice. **What you heard was the demon saying that it had been waiting for us. Now it has more mortals to play with... the foul thing tries to taunt us.** Shui projected.

I had not actually thought about what the demon's 'speech' sounds had meant. But Shui's explanation made sense to me, even in my weakened condition.

The fetid air was charged with tension. Fox stood on one side of my view, holding Shui across his body, ready to strike. The demon's eyes flashed it stepped forward and raised the black blade to strike. Snarling, the demon swung his sword.

Even though I knew what was going to happen, I felt a moment of dread that Fox would be paralyzed and sliced in half. Instead, Fox swung Shui to meet the demon's strike.

Since time was still slowed down, I was able to study the demon's wicked features. Its eyes were glowing red and seemed too small on its large head. It did not have any neck. The head flowed directly into the shoulders and wings. Two large pointed ears, each the size of the rest of its face, pointed forward. The demon's snout protruded forward, ending in two narrow, upturned nostrils. It had a small horn itself that projected upward from the tip of its nose. Its mouth was open, and full of wicked, needle-like teeth. But those needle teeth seemed insignificant compared to its long black fangs. There were two fangs on top and two fangs on the bottom. I noticed that even in this hot place, there was smoke from the molten metal still rising off of the demon's head and shoulders.

I turned my attention to Fox and Shui. Fox, also in slow motion, had his mouth open as well. He wore fierce expression and was clearly making some type of battle cry as he swung the staff. Fox's even, white teeth contrasted sharply with the demon's black fangs.

I knew to expect that Fox's first strike would be very weak. My only hope was that Fox and Shui would not be overwhelmed by the demon's swing.

When the demon's black sword and Fox's staff made contact, the reaction surprised all of us. There was a blinding flash of red light. In the instant when the two weapons touched, the demon shattered. The black sword had shattered too. It looked as though the demon had been made out of pottery and Fox and Shui had smashed the pottery like a huge rock. Its solid form broke into innumerable pieces which then began to turn to smoke.

When the demon shattered, I instinctively flinched. But I was only partly reacting to the demon. When the demon shattered, the gemstone also shattered. My flinching had been an instinctive reaction to the shattering gem next to me.

Somehow, I had imagined it opening like a coffin. I imagined that the surface of the giant stone was just a door mounted on some cleverly hidden hinge. But, the entire gemstone had shattered into dust, bursting like the demon. Unsupported by the evaporating gem dust, Cho Clei's body dropped the small distance to the stone 'floor'. Everything seemed to be happening at once.

Time suddenly slammed back to normal speed. I could not believe my eyes. My sister was lying there. She had fallen the short distance to lie on the rocky chamber floor. Her doll, was still tightly clutched under her arm. I scrambled forward a few feet to reach her. I held onto her, silently vowing not to let her out of my sight until we were back at home. I turned back to look at Fox.

After their first strike, Fox had already committed to the second strike. He stopped the second strike, checking it in mid-swing. He stood there, holding Shui aloft. He wore an expression I had never actually seen before. Fox looked... *confused*. Brow furrowed, he was looking around.

I was confused too. I reviewed what I had been told, *Each strike delivers a guaranteed effect. And once the sequence has begun, the outcome will already be decided. Each strike leads into the next... and *If you are in a position to 'see' the battle when it begins, you might find our first strike disappointing... The first strike is very weak, but that is just a formality. As I said, they increase in power... *They *will* work, Kwan*

Even the weak 'first strike' from Fox and Shui was so powerful that it had utterly destroyed the demon! Joy began to dawn on me. It had worked, just like they said it would! I was so impressed with them that it did not surprise me.

The reality started to sink into my mind. We had beaten the demon. I looked down. I was holding my little sister. "Fox!

I've got her! I've got my sister! Cho Clei is safe!" I was so excited that I had yelled out loud. I had not even bothered to try to communicate mentally.

*This... is unexpected. The *first* strike?* I did not try to reply directly, but my mental response was immediate and enthusiastic. Sure! It might have been unexpected for you, but not for me! You said it yourself... the combination would work! And it did! You two are so powerful! Fox raised his eyebrows as he looked at me, but did not say anything. Then he shook his head and walked quickly over to me (and the still-unconscious Cho Clei). Fox looked at us for a long minute as he took in the situation. *Okay, if we've got her, then we can think it through later. Now we need to get your sister out of here, and back home.* Fox set Shui balancing upright, next to us.

Fox seemed prepared to speak, but stopped as the entire chamber around us began to quake. The rumbling rock all around us would make it hard to hear speech. Naturally, we thought to each other. Fox's sentiment came through to both of us. *That would be our signal to leave. Shui, would you be kind enough to show us the way out?*

Shui responded instantly, **Of course. First, we must escape this place before it falls down on top of us. Then, we must make our way to the Pall.** Fox finally spoke ...out loud, "Can you carry her, Kwan?" He looked around. "We need to move quickly."

Chapter 24

Escape

"Yes! I'll carry her!" I said quickly. Fox helped me to my feet. I stood for a second to clear my head. Then I bent down and picked up my sister. While she would not respond when I tried to wake her up, her eyes were tightly shut like she was in the midst of a nightmare. I imagined that whatever her nightmare was, it must have been better than where we really were. I cradled Cho Clei (and her doll) protectively.

Her body was very light, hardly seeming to weigh anything at all. Despite the danger, I felt a feeling of rising euphoria that we had made it this far. We had found and freed Cho Clei!

Fox again picked up his staff, and without another word, ran back toward the rope. But instead of climbing back up, Fox charged straight ahead into the opening of a different tunnel. Trusting, (as always) that Fox and Shui knew where they were going, I followed. Cradling my sister to me, I ran after Fox.

What followed was a blur of frantic exertion and panic as we tried to escape the fortress. Almost immediately, when we entered the tunnel, it began to collapse behind us. The tall 'bat-demon spire' was collapsing. Unlike the one that we had used to enter, this tunnel had numerous others branching off of it. And each new tunnel had even more branching off it. Our path would have been impossibly confusing if I had tried to keep track of our journey. But I was not trying to keep track the journey. Instead, my mind slipped into a pure animal-sense of fleeing danger to survive.

Our escape was a collection of narrowly avoiding death traps. Our flight was happening with so much haste, in such a terrifying environment, it felt like we were in a never-ending series of pass/fail or live/die choices. If we chose the wrong one, we would die. But Fox and Shui made the choices unerringly.

I was young and fit, but at one point I felt my endurance in doubt. Legs burning, heart pounding in my chest, my breath came in ragged gasps. But Fox kept running, and so did I. I marveled again at the GaleMaster's speed and stamina. He was a big man, but did not seem to get tired.

At one point, it was all I could do to keep my gaze focused on following Fox's feet. We sprinted through the tunnel passages, Shui projecting what little light we had. The mountain itself felt like it was falling down.

Several times the shaking ground threatened to take me off my feet. But because I was carrying my sister, I tried to sprint 'carefully'. Although, I had to admit, you can only be so careful when you are sprinting. I ran on, racing for my life (and my sister's life).

Suddenly, we were running at speed and the tunnel in front of us began to collapse too. Now it was not just the tunnel behind us. The fear suddenly doubled as the danger doubled.

I slipped into a strange state of mind, a trance. My body was exhausted, but all it needed from my mind was to keep me from falling. Otherwise, the rest of me was 'watching' my fear grow, and rise, and try to take over. That fear wanted to paralyze me, to make me freeze and block me from taking action. At the same time, I 'watched' my will fighting back, pushing down that fear. The will was driven by the knowledge of what it was fighting to protect. I finally had my sister. Her unconscious weight hugged to my chest kept me clear about the only point to focus on. I was going to save my sister, whether I was exhausted and afraid, or not.

The crashing and rumbling of the tunnel collapsing let me ignore fatigue and keep running. When the tunnel ahead began to collapse, Fox (with guidance from Shui) would seamlessly divert to a new offshoot-tunnel. It was an exercise in pure trust. Most of the time I could not even see the new tunnels until we were already sprinting through them.

There were several times when I was unable to see a way out. I just wasn't absorbing the details fast enough. But I followed Fox at his relentless pace. Interestingly, while I was running, (my entranced and exhausted mind noticed) I did not really have time to be afraid. I was fully immersed in the flight from danger.

It would be impossible for me to tell how much time had passed. I was suppressing blind panic, but nowhere near where I could judge time. The next thing that I remembered, the tunnel that we were racing through angled upward. I was exhausted, and didn't realize that we were heading towards the castle's main level. Most of my attention was on not tripping while running and carrying my sister.

After we had run up the incline, the tunnel let out onto the ground level, but we were not anywhere near where we had entered.

We were not the expansive entry room, with the checkered floor. Instead, we burst out of the tunnel into a much smaller chamber. There was a stout wall to our left that was shaking.

ial*We don't have time to make it back the way we came in. Through this wall is our fastest way out. Take cover, Batou Kwan. Fox...* Shui's thought came through loudly and clearly. He was obviously sending the thought to both Fox and me. When I was intended to hear them, and not just mentally 'eavesdropping', the difference was noticeable.

Fox did not hesitate. He turned and braced the butt of his staff against the wall on our right. He placed Shui's bottom end at the seam where the wall met the floor. Then, he adjusted the angle so that the top end of the staff was pointing at the opposite 'outer wall' at our height. Then he took his hand off and turned away, covering his head. The staff held itself in place once Fox removed his hand.

I couldn't say which sense I noticed first, the humming sound, or the light. The staff began to glow brighter that I had ever seen before. It was blinding. There was a hum in the air that increased in intensity along with the light. I suddenly remembered from when I had first met Fox. This hum was similar to that sound. It was clearly the sound of Shui gathering power.

Fox saw that I had not followed his lead. I was standing there, mouth open, looking around dully. He pulled me and my limp sister back and turned me away from the outer wall. I not only heard the sound in my mind, but I *felt* it. **DUUUU-UUUUUU-UUUUUUUUUUUU-TSKAA!!!** I shielded Cho Clei's head, knowing what was coming.

There was a blast so powerful that its energy seemed to make the air itself ripple and bend. The rumbling of the fortress breaking apart faded away. Then, gradually, the sounds of the crumbling castle returned.

Still holding my sister, I peered back over my shoulder. The air was filled with a gray dust but little actual rubble. There were the loud sounds of rocks still falling. Then the air cleared enough to show our situation. Shui's blast had blown a hole in the thick wall that was wide enough for us to escape.

My jaw dropped open as I saw how thick the wall had been. It was made of huge stone blocks, as thick as I was tall. Shui's blast destroyed the wall like it was made from a child's toy blocks.

We had been inside the castle long enough that my eyes had adjusted to the darkness. But when Shui blasted the hole open through the castle wall, I found myself squinting. The light outside from the red sky was not bright, but it was brighter than inside the dark tunnels.

Fox stood and tapped me on the shoulder, "Come on, let's go. We don't have time to rest." He hefted Shui, waiting for me to pick Cho Clei up again. Then we were again running.

There was another blur of scrambling and climbing once we got outside of the castle. To my surprise, Fox did not lead us back towards the HellFire Road. Instead, we ran out of the hole in the thick wall and turned to the left. We were going in the opposite direction as we had before.

I stumbled a couple of times, but caught myself before falling flat. Knowing that my little sister would have been injured made me more athletic than I normally was. The terrain outside the castle was similar to 'normal world' mountains. The rocks were difficult to navigate. Treacherous stones would roll underfoot, slowing us down.

What followed was a mad flight. There were several times when I doubted that I could go on. But because Fox never stopped, I didn't consider giving up either. He did slow down when he saw that I needed help, but he always encouraged me to keep going again.

I heard a quiet message from Shui. **This cannot break your body. It is a challenge your mind can overcome. Don't think it, know it. Strength rises when you call it. The same way that you have learned to control fear, you can manage fatigue. If you surrender to the challenge, you die and then she dies. Overcome this challenge, and we can save your sister.*** Shui's encouragement slipped quietly into my mind. It really *was* that simple. If we were going to live, I could not quit. And we *were* going to save Cho Clei! In between Fox's example in Shui's encouragement, I kept going.

Eventually we must have traveled far enough, because Shui signaled Fox that we could stop. We had reached a rocky ledge where a shallow, cave-like indentation gave us a hiding place. Even if some of the metal-skeleton sentries had followed us, it was doubtful that they would come all the way down to this rocky ledge to look for us.

Fox and Shui came to a halt. Utterly exhausted, I set my sister down gently on the ground. Then I flopped down on the ground next to her. I tried to calm my gasping down to just panting. Fox was somehow barely winded. "Has she moved it all?" He asked. I shook my head. I did not think that there was a problem because she was still breathing, but she had not woken up. Fox bent down, frowning and narrowing his eyes as he looked at her. He checked her breathing like I did, but he did not do anything else.

"I will need to consult with Shui to figure out the best way for us to reach the Pall. Don't worry, we are not far now." And then, as an afterthought, "Well, at least not as far as we were." It wasn't as though Fox needed to go anywhere to consult with Shui. He was more excusing the fact that he would not be paying attention to my sister and me for a few minutes. The only thing that really changed was that Fox's eyes took on a vaguely unfocused, distant look. I knew that he and Shui were in mental communication. I should have been paying attention to them. What they were planning would determine our survival. But as I regained my strength, all of my attention was on my sister.

I bent down and said, close to her ear, "Wake up little one. Come back. You're safe now. We're going home. It's Kwan. Please, Cho Clei, come back to us." Tears welled up in my eyes. The possibility was just beginning to occur to me that even though we had found my sister, something inside her may have been hurt beyond repair, or broken during the kidnapping.

I had closed my eyes and was lying there next to her. I was in the process of surrendering to something. It was a combination of exhaustion and despair. But before I could go very far, I heard Fox's voice. "Kwan, look..."

I raised my head and turned towards my sister. Her eyes were fluttering open. As they fully opened, she hissed a sharp intake of breath and looked around, alarmed. She immediately sat up and scrambled backward as she first saw her surroundings. I can only imagine what she must have felt like.

For all I knew she had been having a pleasant dream and suddenly "woke" to a nightmare. She had gone to sleep in her soft bed. She had woken up on the rocky ground. The sky was a deep and menacing shade of red, swiftly crossed by black clouds. Finally, she was waking up to a tall, bald stranger, holding a staff, towering over her.

She was clearly afraid of Fox. But that made perfect sense to me. I had spent a long time on this quest with him, and I had been able to spend time to get to know him at the dumpling shop. But my little sister had either been at home or school, or kidnapped and unconscious. She had never seen him before, and compared to her size, he was huge. As she scrambled backward, confusion grew into full panic. But when she saw me, she cried out and immediately scrambled closer.

I sat up and opened my arms to her. She was babbling, quaking, almost hysterical. I tried to calm her down. But a child of her age needed some understanding of what was going on. I tried to explain to her as best I could where we were, and how we got here. I'm not sure how much she understood, but it was clear that she would never have believed it, if it weren't for her own eyes. The proof was all around her.

Even after I had "vouched" for Fox, my sister was still skeptical. She crushed her doll to her chest the same way that I had held her to my chest fleeing the fortress. Eventually, she calmed down.

Even after calming down, she insisted on sitting next to me. I put my arm around her shoulder protectively. Fox turned to address us.

"Hello Cho Clei. My name is Fox. I have been helping your brother to rescue you. I need for you to listen to instructions and follow your brother so that we can get home. Do you understand?" Wide eyed, she looked over at me and nodded.

He smiled and went on, "Good. I know that you are confused and frightened and unprepared to be here. Are you tired?" He asked. My little sister looked like she was thinking about the question, then shook her head. Fox nodded, "Good. Your elder brother could probably use a break since we ran all the way here. If you don't feel comfortable to walk, I'm sure we can think of some solution. Maybe your brother and I would need to take turns carrying you."

My sister pressed closer to me and shook her head up at Fox. Then she said in a small voice, "We... we'll walk" She hugged her doll to her chest tightly, making it clear who the other part of 'we' was. Fox merely gave a thin smile and nodded.

"This next part is for your elder brother." Fox said. "You're not expected to understand this." He said. Then he turned and addressed just me. "This is our situation Kwan.

As you know we have successfully rescued your sister. But the demon, Wen-Yi escaped. Unfortunately, it was somehow dispatched by the first strike. And since we weren't able to deliver all nine of the strikes, and then catch it with the SoulCage, we are one soul short of our payment to the Ragyala. there's nothing that we can do about it at this point. Perhaps we will be attacked by a new demon on the way home. But honestly, at this point, I have a hard time imagining that is likely.

There is a place where we will be able to summon the Ragyala, but it is a few days' journey from here." I nodded, but knew that I couldn't fully hide the disappointment from reaching my face. I was ready for us to be safely home. "It shouldn't be long from here. We'll take a little time and rest now, then we will get moving again when you've caught your breath." And with that Fox turned away, apparently again communicating with Shui.

On our way to reach the Pall, I found myself preoccupied. Part of me was preoccupied with looking out for my little sister. Now that we had found her, I was determined not to let anything happen to her. I held her hand while we were walking, switching hands if it got uncomfortable for either of us, but always maintaining contact.

Where we encountered treacherous places, I helped her cross. I tried to make the journey as physically easy as possible. To her credit, she did not complain.

At some point Fox offered to carry Cho Clei on his back. He said that she might be getting tired. But she vehemently shook her head, obviously still not trusting him. Fox, shook his head, not seeming to mind. He even left the option open to her, if she decided that she was tired later on. She awkwardly smiled, clearly not trusting him yet.

The other part of me, the majority of my mind, every part that was not paying attention to Cho Clei, was reviewing what had happened on this trip. The reverie I was in, and the new route we took, made it so that traveling back to the Pall was much shorter than the trip out. I marveled at how different my life had been before. I marveled at the new and amazing things I had learned in this realm. I remembered all of my experiences learning from Fox. I remembered the lessons I had learning from Shui. In fact, I reviewed everything right up to the present moment.

I had just reviewed, in my mind and memories, the fact that we did not have enough spirits to pay the Ragyala. It was a mystery how the demon Wen-Yi had escaped. But then, when I looked down at my little sister, I felt a surge of confidence that we would be able to do whatever it took to get back home. We would be able to renegotiate with the Ragyala, or something. We just had to. And as we walked I continued to review everything that had happened.

We were traveling through a rocky clearing when Fox abruptly stopped and turned around to face us. I was a little surprised. "We should pause and have another rest here. I wouldn't mind a cup of tea. Would you like one too, Kwan?" Fox asked.

I looked around. I still had more energy in my legs, but I figured that my little sister could use a break. I nodded but asked, "Do we have time?"

Fox nodded and said, "There is usually time for a cup of tea." Fox said. Then he turned and looked at Cho Clei. "Is that all right with you, young Miss?" Fox asked her, with a wink and a small smile. She looked up at him uncertainly, shrugged and nodded. Satisfied, Fox began pulling implements out of his bag to make a fire and boil water for tea. While he did, Shui was standing guard over us. The staff stood upright, perfectly vertical on its own. Cho Clei eyed it suspiciously.

Chapter 25

Confrontation

Fox walked slowly around the rocky clearing. I assumed that he was looking for wood to burn. He roamed a short distance, circling around where we were. But in the end, he walked back over and took a few pieces of wood out of his shoulder bag.

Fox had soon assembled a small but blazing fire. "Don't worry, nothing has been pursuing us. It was surprising at first- but I thought it might just be good fortune that no demons followed us... So, we don't need to worry about someone seeing our smoke." Fox said. Then he stepped closer.

Fox stood a few feet away, towering over us. He held out his right hand and Shui immediately flew to it, smacking solidly into his palm. Fox looked down at me for a moment, then at my sister even longer. Then he looked around and began speaking into the air, "It really was a brilliant try. I had never even *heard* of such an intricate plot by a *demon*." he said.

He continued looking around and speaking into the air. But I was utterly confused as to what he was talking about. What was a brilliant try? I understood that a demon had made an intricate plot to kidnap my sister, but why was he saying this now? Who was he talking to?

"In truth, I figured it out a while ago. There were only one or two small points that I was unable to figure out. Maybe if I talk through the things that I do understand, I'll see if the missing parts present themselves." Fox was standing in a posture as though delivering information in front of a panel of judges.

"Oh, I did know that you were smart. In truth, an accomplishment like *this* would impressive for any demon, and even more so for a *weak and feeble* demon like Wen-Yi." Fox went on. Was he insulting the demon that… we had already beaten?

"This has been a long journey, and while I did have my suspicions at the beginning, I got more and more confirmation as this journey has progressed.…" I did not understand what he was saying, but I somehow knew that this was important.

He went on. "As I said, I knew that you were smart for your kind. And I also knew the nature of your kind, and that you would try to lie and trick us. But even using our most clever tricks, we can't escape our nature." I was alert now. Something was clearly wrong. What was Fox talking about? And who was he talking to?

He continued, "when we moved in to attack, and deliver our nine strike combination, your plan nearly worked. I suppose it would have worked if it been a traditional attack. If our first strike were a strong strike, it might have been believable that it destroyed you. However, our combination was not built that way. The first strike was not a strong strike. In fact, our first strike was so improbably weak that we would never have used it, in a fighting situation, if it did not lead to the ninth strike.

"When that bat-lava-demon-thing shattered, it was clear that it could not have been you. That… was just a shell. It was merely a hollow shell that we broke in that castle. It was a trick. And it *almost* worked." Then, as an afterthought, almost to himself, "Very nearly."

I had to interrupt. I was confused and didn't understand what was going on. "What are you talking about? How could its body be a hollow shell?"

Fox turned his head to look at and answer me. "It does seem strange doesn't it? The reality is that any being of sufficient power can split itself into parts. It fractures itself into different pieces." He said.

"But why would it do something like that?" I still didn't understand.

Fox smiled patiently. "You have a good heart, Kwan. Guile does not come naturally to you.… Good people rarely see malice coming. Honest people generally don't see a lie, and kind people do not expect cruelty. It is an ironic part of life. — And *every* person has a blind spot."

Shui interjected a thought, **At least, until that person decides to find their 'blind spot' and keep track of it.**

Fox continued seamlessly. "The demon would fracture itself, in this situation, for one reason.…" He waited, but I still did not see it.

"The demon could put a tiny portion of itself into a false copy, but still have most of itself, it's "power", in a completely different place. Does it start to make sense? Wen-Yi put a tiny piece of its power into a decoy…"

"You mean the shattered bat-demon? You mean that was not the *real* Wen-Yi?"

"It is worth considering, Kwan. When the weakest of the nine strikes shattered the demon, I knew it was impossible that we had beaten the *real* demon. If we *believed* it had been destroyed, it could stay around, but our guard would be down. It could be around… even now… and hiding."

There are many ways to disarm an opponent, but guile is the one that a warrior sees last. Shui added as a supplemental piece of understanding to me.

I was appalled at the idea. "It wanted to disarm us… you think it's still planning to attack us? It could *still* be with us? Where???" As soon as I said it, I had a sinking feeling about what Fox suspected. "It's not my sister!?!" I exclaimed.

Fox held up one hand placating me. "No, no. I don't think that the demon is hidden inside of your sister." Fox said. "But that only leaves us with the few remaining options…" He said.

"Where??" I had my arm around Cho Clei looking up at Fox.

"Would you show him, Shui?" Fox asked. The staff complied, and spun faster than my I could track. The butt end of the staff swung through from underneath, and (without hitting Cho Clei) knocked the doll from my sister's hands, throwing it high into the air. Three of us watched the doll's high arc through the air. We were tired and Shui was so incredibly fast that Cho Clei and I took a long moment to react and show our surprise.

Mouths open, we watched its long arc. When it landed neatly in the center of the fire Fox had just made, Cho Clei snapped out of her surprise. She screamed, "My doll!" I clamped my arm down around her, afraid for a moment that she might lunge forward and try to snatch the doll from the flames.

But almost immediately the scream degenerated into miserable wailing. After seeing the doll land in the fire, my gaze quickly flashed at Fox, then turned to look at Cho Clei screaming. My mind was racing. What was happening???

My little sister, the only reason I was here, was now screaming. So naturally, I was focused on her. Another quick glance over my shoulder showed me that Fox was not even looking at Cho Clei. Instead, he was turned towards the fire and the doll. All of my attention was on my little sister. I did not understand what was happening, but I wanted to trust Fox.

But while I was watching Cho Clei, trying to calm her down about the doll, I was intently looking at her and listening to her. I could tell immediately, without having to look over my shoulder, that something had changed.

I had once heard mother talking to a friend of hers, lamenting that a mother could tell what was happening by the sound of a baby's cry. When a baby cries because it's hungry, it sounds very different from when a baby cries out of fear. At least that's what mother said. I had not believed it at the time, but now did.

While my sister *was* still screaming, that scream had changed in pitch and intensity. Before she had been screaming because she was distraught. Now, her scream carried the tone of actual fear. It was a big difference and I instinctively put a protective arm around Cho Clei as I turned around. What I saw when I turned around was something I doubt I will ever forget.

The doll was roughly an imitation of my sister. It had black hair and brown eyes, just like my sister. The 'hair' was made from pieces of thread, and the eyes from two brown stones.

The doll wore a simple, white nightgown over it, the same as my sister.

But what I saw was definitely not a mere doll. When I turned and looked over my shoulder, I barely registered that Fox and Shui were again in a battle stance. What I clearly did register, was my sister's doll - *climbing* out of the fire.

My sisters terrified wailing grew higher and higher as the doll extracted itself from the flames. Cho Clei was hysterical. It was so disconcerting that I actually felt like screaming myself. In retrospect, a doll is not a scary thing by itself. It is a harmless and childish thing.

But when that childish thing starts to burn, and then make its own way toward you, it's not harmless any longer. The face of the doll and the mop of its hair were on fire. Large patches on its cloth arms and legs, as well as its dress were burning also.

The doll had gotten caught on a log in the fire, and had to extricate itself. Once it had clawed its way out of the fire, it stood, looking at each one of us, in turn. Then, it raised a still-burning arm and pointed it at Fox.

The doll did not have a mouth. In fact, there was only a simple line stitched onto the face to suggest a mouth. Because it did not have a mouth, I did not expect the blinding pain.

I was preparing to ask Fox what was going on. In truth, it probably would've come out more like a shriek than a question. But when the pain came again, I knew what it was, even if I still couldn't resist it. It came at me from every direction. It felt as though my world broke, and time slowed down again. The pain throughout my body; the nausea, the flashing lights exploding behind my eyes, the reflexive twitching, were all immediately recognizable. Even worse, some part of me was aware that Cho Clei was spamming also.

But Fox apparently attacked, cutting off the demon's speech in mid-statement. The burning doll leapt to the side as Fox swung Shui at it. Then the little demon doll turned and sprinted away from us. Even though my sense of time was still slowed down from hearing the demon's language, the doll seemed incredibly fast. It's little burning legs moved faster than it seemed possible. When combined with the fact that the little doll was burning, it was especially terrifying.

Somehow, I thought that Fox and Shui would rush into pursuit. I imagine that they would be very intent not to let this demon escape. But to my surprise, they stood there watching the little burning figure run away. Cho Clei had buried her head in my chest, trying to hide from this nightmarish turn of events.

A moment later I saw why they hadn't moved. The burning doll, moving in a full sprint bounced off of an invisible shield that seemed to be surrounding our rocky clearing. "No, I don't think we'll be letting you escape today." The little doll was only smoking now since the flames had burned out. Its little head turned as it looked for a way out.

Suddenly it seemed very clear to me. Fox had not been looking for firewood. He had in preparing for just this moment. He and Shui had placed a boundary around this area so that the demon could not escape. It took off running even faster and tried again to break through the boundary. This time, when the little doll impacted the invisible barrier, there was a flash of light and the doll was thrown back several paces. It even slid a little when it hit the ground. Apparently, the boundary that Fox and Shui had put up was strong.

"Of course, trapping you inside here with us would not be very useful if we did not have any other plan." Fox said conversationally. I was barely restraining my panic, but Fox seemed cool and collected. "As it turns out we need to use your spirit to return back home. It only seems fair, considering that we would not be here if you had not taken *her*." Fox turned his head to nod toward my sister, but never took his eyes off of the doll.

Instead he reached up to his rosary and plucked the metallic silver bead off of it. I recognized the SoulCage. So apparently did the demon. It tried rapidly four or five more times to escape the barrier. Each time the doll was bounced back.

Fox tossed the SoulCage onto the rocks between us and the doll. The demon heard the SoulCage thud onto the rocks behind it. it turned around. When it saw the SoulCage, it made a very human gesture. It through both of the dolls arms up, in a clear sign of alarm.

I expected that the same thing would happen is when I had seen the SoulCage operate before. But instead, the doll did something completely unexpected. The doll ran a few quick steps and dove into the fire. The dolls body hit the coals at the base of the fire. Immediately the cloth of the doll roared into flames. Both Cho Clei and I jerked her heads back in surprise. Neither one of us had seen that coming.

Cho Clei was twitching beside me. Somehow my eyes were drawn to watching the doll burn. I was aware that Cho Clei was twitching and shuddering under my arm. Some part of my mind must have assumed that was because she was choking back tears or screams.

I did not need someone to tell me the doll was no longer a threat. It had burned almost to a cinder. At some point her twitching under my arm became spasms. I tore my eyes off of the doll and looked down at Cho Clei. Her eyes rolled back into her head and I held onto her as her body went stiff and began convulsing. I can describe the panic I felt seeing my little sister in seizures. I looked up at Fox, panicked and pleading. His expression was kind toward me but fiercely stern at the same time. Fox had replaced Shui in the harness on his back.

Fox and Shui were my only hope. I looked down at my sister and felt pure panic. The idea of my good and pure little sister in some kind of torment was agonizing.

Fox shook his head slowly as if disappointed. "I was hoping that it would not come to this. I was hoping you would see that your plan had been blocked." Fox said.

I was lifted off my feet and then dropped back down to the ground. I was confused and tried to figure out what just happened. That was when I noticed my little sister hovering several feet off the ground. Her arms were locked, rigidly at her sides. Her hair was floating, splayed out in every direction. Her eyes were open, but they were not the eyes of the little girl

I had known my whole life. Instead, her eyes held a glowing red light. I had been lifted into the air and thrown off when she had risen, from under my arm, to floating in the air.

She pointed one hand at Fox and began speaking, "Fool! I am far more powerful than you! You are only of the light! You cannot block my plans! Your power does not rival mine!"

The voice was deep and guttural, but in our language. I was stunned hearing these words coming out of my little sister's mouth. I could not believe what I was seeing and now, hearing. The demon Wen-yi had possessed my sister!?!

As the enormous reality of the situation started to set in, I found my mind in a surreal place. If it had not been for the experiences on this journey, with the instruction from Fox and Shui, I probably wouldn't have been so observant. As it was, I glanced away from my floating sister to see what Fox was doing. He did not seem surprised to see my sister floating there a few feet away. In fact, he seemed masterful and fully collected.

I felt reassured by his calm demeanor. It was something that was recognizable to me. It was then that I noticed something. Fox had pulled a small red bottle from his satchel. He had worked the wooden stopper out of it with the thumb and forefinger while palming the bottle with the same hand.

"You imagine to destroy me?! You are powerful for a man, but your power is nothing compared to mine! You cannot hope to beat me!" My sister/the demon bellowed something incom-prehensible. I was still on the ground. When I heard her bellow in that deep voice, I scrambled back startled. But Fox was not startled.

He spoke quietly as he poured a fine, red powder from the bottle into his right palm. with a practiced motion, he replaced the stopper back in the bottle. "Oh, I knew that you were more powerful than we are. I knew that before he reached your fortress. I know it now too." But was Fox saying? Was he giving up, admitting defeat?

"But you see, I didn't to beat you. At least not in battle." The demon possessing my sister must have been confused, because her brows furrowed, in a perplexed expression.

"I can see that you still don't understand. I was giving you credit before for being very clever in tricking us. You used a trick to get around our nine strike combination." The perplexed expression relaxed on my sister's face. She looked somehow... Self-satisfied? Had the demon known what was coming?

Fox went on, "I thought that it was possible you were a demon genius. If you have been clever enough to come up with this plan, maybe you were some sort of anomaly. I didn't intend to test you, but you could see it as a sort of test. Just how intelligent could a demon be?... Or more to the point, would a demon be smart enough to see when it was beaten?" Fox's tone was one of a calm and collected teacher right now, rather than someone fighting a demon.

Chapter 26

Ragyala

"But once your hollow shell 'shattered' and you 'withdrew all of your spirit back into one place, we had you." The demon again twisted my sister's features to look… perplexed.

"As I said before, I was hoping that we could have done this the easy way. Or at least the way that's kinder for that girl." Then Fox said, specifically to me, "Kwan, that is why the SoulCage is not able to capture this demon. By possessing your sister, it is using her soul to 'hide'." Then he went back to speaking to the demon, "I was hoping that you would notice where we were… when we stopped."

I had been asking myself where I recognized that red bottle from. The answer came to me at the same moment as the demon realized where Fox had brought us. I exclaimed, "The Pall!" As I said the words, Fox twisted at the waist and flung the powder he had been holding out behind him.

He began to speak quietly, rhythmically. But this time he did not close his eyes. The hairs on my arms and on the back of my neck began to stand up. I recognized the feeling. It was… unique. I saw a shimmering screen of red light appear a few paces behind Fox. A massive golden shape was vaguely visible behind the screen.

My sister, or rather the demon inside her, made an involuntary sound- a growling yelp. Her body turned and tried to fly away. But Cho Clei's fleeing body bounced off the shield too- she was not able to escape with any more success than the doll had. I winced as I saw my little sister's delicate frame being pounded against the invisible barrier. It was clear that the demon had no concern about injuring her. I heard a sound like dry crackling wood popping in a fire.

There was a flash of green light so bright that I had to close my eyes. It filled the air around us. As I open my eyes, I saw the enormous golden figure walk through the shimmering red screen. Immediately, the familiar feeling of its power became a heavy weight pushing me down.

While the Ragyala was so powerful that it couldn't help but be unnerving, I still felt glad to see it. It was dressed as it had been before, in a white gown with gold embroidery. The gown was tied with a gold strip at the waist. The 'belt' strip of cloth matched the short gold fur that covered its body.

The Ragyala had been twice my height, but since I was lying on the ground when it arrived, it seemed even taller. On top of the Ragyala's thick neck, was the head of a cat. It was proportional to the giant, muscular body, but it was in fact a giant golden cat's head. I doubted I would ever be able to forget the Ragyala. Who could ever forget a giant, golden cat-man?

When the Ragyala first appeared, I caught a glimpse of its face. I saw briefly into its brilliant yellow eyes. They were large and luminous, with vertical slits. Its facial expression was serene.

Its long arms held down at its sides, the Ragyala was holding its black scepter in one hand. Somehow the tool looked especially formidable now. The scepter had a blunt and a pointed spike at the other end. And neither side looked like the giant would use it in a pleasant way.

Fox dropped to one knee as he had before. I would have gotten off the floor, up onto one knee, but I was still exhausted from the flight from Wen-yi's fortress and it took too much strength to rise. I wanted to look up at it, but again, it took too much effort. The being just emanated too much power. As it stepped through the curtain, the Ragyala's stopped and planted its feet wide apart. It radiated not only strength, but also stability. It was like the feeling, when we were little, when Father walked into the room. There was the feeling that 'authority' had arrived.

As soon as the Ragyala stepped into this realm, and its power became palpable, my sister's body was immediately pushed back down to the ground. Her hair was no longer floating out around her head. Instead, it looked like a bucket of water had been poured over her. She was not wet, but her hair lay plastered down like she had just come in from a deluge.

The Ragyala looked down at us for what seemed like a long time. This time, I understood that the Ragyala was looking into our minds. As I thought about it, there could be no better way of finding out what you wanted to know. This was a being who could actually look inside the person's mind to find what happened and to tell what was true.

"Great Ragyala…" Fox intoned. The Ragyala did not look at him however, it continued to slowly survey all of us.

The Ragyala held up his hand, signaling for silence. Fox immediately fell silent. When the Ragyala spoke, the chorus of voices surprised me, just as it had before. When the giant cat-man spoke, it was not the voice of just one person that came out. Rather it was the sound of a dozen female voices saying the same words at the same time. "We regard you… GaleMaster, Immortal, …" Suddenly the way the Ragyala communicated came back to me. The slow speech with long pauses and rumbling volume.

"We can see that your journey… has been productive. You have brought… the living soul you came to find… But you've also brought ─────" I could not hear the words that the Ragyala said. Then I realized that I could not hear any sounds at all while the Ragyala was saying those words. But I was able to look at Fox, and I saw him wince when the words were said. Logically, it must've been demon speak.

"It seems that there are several things to do here." The Ragyala turned and looked at my little sister, but she did not meet its gaze. "But first, we understand… you wish to return… to your realm. We made an exception allowing the living to cross the Pall. Our agreement…spirit payment in full… due on your return. You wish to return, correct?" The Ragyala asked Fox.

Fox pointed at the SoulCage, lying on the rocks a few feet away from him, but he made no move to retrieve it. Instead, the Ragyala held out one hand toward the SoulCage. It spread its three fingers. the SoulCage responded by lifting off the ground and flying directly to the Ragyala's paw. He held the metallic sphere in his hand and raised it to his face. The Ragyala stared at metallic sphere very intently for a few seconds. Then, he dropped the SoulCage back to the ground in front of him.

I tried to look up at the Ragyala but there was still too much power coming off of the giant. I looked over at Fox, but his gaze was locked on the SoulCage. So that's where I looked too.

The SoulCage began to emit a sound I had not heard before. It was a clear bell tone. But this tone was not like the tone I had heard it make before.

In the past, each time the SoulCage was operating, there was the sound in the air. Now however, the sound was different. It was a lower tone. It's hard to describe but I had the impression that the SoulCage was exhaling.

In response, a webbed funnel of light appeared above the top of the SoulCage. It projected outward and upward, like light from a candle. I watched as a crackling cloud of lightning rose from the SoulCage. It rose into the air and hovered above the SoulCage, trapped within the beam of light.

The Ragyala examined it carefully. Then it spoke, "We see… the first." I imagined that the Ragyala would reach out to somehow capture the spirit. But instead, the Ragyala raised its black scepter.

Without hesitation, the Ragyala stabbed the sharp end of it scepter into the ball of electricity. The scepter seemed to absorb the crackling cloud. As we watched, the cloud lightning grew smaller and smaller as it shrank. After a few moments, the lightning cloud had been completely absorbed, and the Ragyala's scepter flashed.

The funnel of light was still present over the SoulCage. The Ragyala turned its attention back to it.

This time, two tiny and grotesque figures rose out of the SoulCage together. They appeared, tiny just outside the surface of the sphere, above it. Then they grew as they rose out of the sphere. Still trapped within the funnel of light, the nightmare "old couple" that I had traveled with on the bridge, became recognizable. The larger they became, the more recognizable they got. I didn't think that I would ever forget their scaly, twisted forms, somewhere between fish and reptiles. The tattered rags that they had been wearing as clothes were now gone. Their entire bodies were covered with sores and patches of hair. Their mouth beaks were opening and closing, but no sound came through. The Ragyala could apparently hear them though. He listened patiently before slowly shaking his head. "We see the second and third." The Ragyala pronounced.

Again, the Ragyala raised its black scepter. Upon seeing the tool, the fish reptile demons tried to flee by going in opposite directions. However, the soul cage would not allow that. Instead, it "reacted" by brightening its light and squeezing the two evil monsters together. When the two evil spirits overlapped, the Ragyala again stabbed the sharp end of his scepter into them. Their beaks opened in what were clearly piteous wails, but we still could not hear anything. Again, the scepter absorbed the demons. The pair of mangled, evil spirits shrank until they were absorbed too. Again, the scepter flashed.

Patiently the Ragyala turned back to the SoulCage. We also turned back to the SoulCage and watched expectantly. This time, even with the Ragyala there, I scooted back a little when I saw the demon emerge. Fortunately, it had taken the shape of a man, and not a giant waterspout. It was the same demon from the statue that we saw in the station once we descended through the dragons.

I remembered the demon when it had arrived as a storm, and become a giant spinning water cloud. Then later when it appeared as a 'man' a full head taller than Fox. I half expected that it would come out of the soul cage glaring at us. But when it emerged, the demon refused to look anywhere except at the

Ragyala. Its eyes, that used to be filled with the fiendish red glow, were only small red pin points now.

It's dirty gray beard and horns protruding from each side of its head were definitely recognizable. But the vampire demon somehow seemed lesser now. It was certainly less confident. It would not dare even showing its teeth to the Ragyala.

"We see the fourth." The Ragyala said. "It was clever of you to use the other demons to capture this one." The Ragyala stepped forward and raised the scepter. The vampire demon clearly knew what was coming. It raised its muscular arms and put both hands out to ward off the strike. It's long sharp fingernails were trembling. Some part of me was very satisfied seeing this demon that had so terrified us, being cowed by something more powerful than it was.

The Ragyala leaned in to pierce the demon. The demon's hands were up at chest level, trying to ward off the Ragyala.

Untroubled, the Ragyala smoothly plunged the scepter's spike through the demon's hands, into its chest. When the spike plunged through the belt, I imagined that I could feel its malice being drained away. After a moment, the demon shrank down until it was absorbed by the scepter.

"But it does not appear that there are any more spirits under the Celestial Mountain." Suddenly I was reminded of the other name for the SoulCage.

Fox elevated his gaze, but did not look at the Ragyala. "Great Ragyala," Fox began. "We have called you in good faith. We arrived with five spirits to repay our return. In our journey to rescue an innocent. But the fifth spirit has taken a hostage."

The Ragyala's feline face managed to look concerned, "These are... very serious accusations..." The weight of the Ragyala's power must have been focused on my sister, because I was able to look up. I looked back and forth between Fox and the Ragyala.

Fox replied solemnly, "Great Ragyala, by the Infinite Light..." Fox reached up and touched his forehead. "By the Sounds of Being..." He touched his forehead again. "And by the Primordial Fracture..." He touched his forehead a third time. "I swear truth. And I request Insight."

The Ragyala gave Fox a long, hard look. "You... request... Insight?" The giant asked. "And you know the cost of deception?"

Fox nodded his head slowly. "I do, Great Ragyala." He spread his arms.

I understood that Fox and Ragyala were discussing something specific. I knew that 'Insight' was when somebody understood something or saw something. But they were clearly talking about something else.

Before I could unravel the puzzle, Fox lifted his head and looked up at the Ragyala. The golden giant looked back and held the gaze for a long time. Fox's body began to glow with a faint golden light. Standing there, arms spread and glowing, he maintained his gaze, locked with the Ragyala. A moment later, the glow around Fox died away. Fox crumpled to the floor, leaving the staff standing by itself.

Fox did not move.

The Ragyala turned his attention to Cho Clei. My sister, dim red light still visible in her eyes, looked up at the Ragyala fearfully. The Ragyala fixed its gaze on my sister and asked, "Any spirit may defend itself against accusation... You have the right... to submit to Insight.... Do you wish... to take it?"

My sister violently shook her head back and forth and snarled at the Ragyala. The golden giant seemed unsurprised. He said, "We did not expect that you would." The Ragyala raised its scepter in one hand, down at the base of the spiked end. He began tapping the other end, the blunt end in the palm of the other upturned paw. Its gaze upon my sister held the promise of imminent punishment.

The giant spoke, "I have found Truth... Honor upon your GaleTemple young Immortal..." The Ragyala made a series of sounds, and the hairs stood up on my arms and neck. My sister's head cocked to the side, rapt. I realized that the Ragyala could speak the demon language, but had just shielded me from the shock.

"Our judgement…" Then the golden giant raised the scepter. I was scared for a moment that the Ragyala was going to stab my sister.

I went to jump in front of my sister's body, but I found I couldn't move. The Ragyala turned to me, "Fear not, little one. Your confusion is expected. You have only begun your studies of the Gale." I had never had the Ragyala's speak directly to me before. It was clear that the Ragyala was trying to be "gentle". But the speech came with such attendant force that even though it was spoken quietly, it felt like thunderous booming. There was so much power behind them that the Ragyala's words were burned into my mind. "Know this, your master will be fine." Then the Ragyala raised his scepter. "This young innocent… your *sister*… will also be fine."

The Ragyala raised the scepter, blunt and towards Cho Clei. The tool was clearly ancient. Its blunt end was an irregular block- roughly spherical, but it may have eroded down from a cube, for all I knew. When the Ragyala held the scepter in the direction of my little sister, she began to howl and twitch. I heard a ghastly demonic wail, but within it, I also heard my sister's smaller and higher-pitched, screaming too. I tried to thrash against the Ragyala's power (to do what I had no idea), but it was impossible. I was an ant trying to push the entire world.

As I watched, a glowing red image appeared. It was in the outline of Wen-Yi, the bat demon! The Ragyala's scepter was like a fisherman that was reeling in the demon. It fought its way back, to overlap with my sister. I watched, terrified, as Cho Clei thrashed back and forth. She whipped her head back and forth so violently that I worried in some part of my mind that she was hurting herself. But the 'fisherman' was too powerful. With horror, I saw the bat demon re-appear. It was not fully solid, so I could see through it, but it was clearly recognizable. It was the same evil figure from the castle. Slowly, the red light diminished in her eyes, and brightened in the demon's.

But the bat demon stubbornly refused to give up the fight. It seemed to have latched on to something inside Cho Clei. The result was that it's back was arched and its claws were sunk into my little sister. The Ragyala did not seem particularly troubled by the bat demon's resistance.

In fact, the Ragyala did not show any emotion at all as the scepter relentlessly pulled the demon out of Cho Clei. My little sister twitched and thrashed, completely at the mercy of the process. Wen-Yi was being extracted out of her through her skin. She also seemed to be retching the foul demon from her nose and mouth. My heart ached to imagine how painful it must be.

And then, abruptly, as if a candle flame had been blown out, Cho Clei collapsed to the ground. Like Fox, she did not move. Tears were streaming down my face as I fought to turn my head toward the Ragyala. What… was happening?

The Ragyala spoke, "We see the fifth. The bargain has been honored." There was a crack of thunder and a flash of blinding golden light. I closed my eyes and cringed.

I tried to open my eyes immediately, but it felt like I was waking up from a dream. Or rather, it felt like I was floating up to the surface from deep underwater. As I floated upward I could hear the Ragyala's voice. It was not booming since it was coming to me in this strange, dreamy place. "You have chosen a clever Master…By the Light… by the Sound… and the Fracture…"

Chapter 27

The Road Home

When I opened my eyes, my new location was immediately clear. The colors of my surrounding were overpowering. I was dazzled by the brilliant blue of the sky. I lay there on the ground, just looking up at the sky, and savoring what I saw. Perfect white clouds contrasted vividly with the blue sky. I couldn't help comparing it to my memories. Fresh in my memory, I easily pictured the red sky with black clouds racing across it. Then I pictured the forest of dead trees, all various shades of gray.

Next, I became aware of the smells of nature, fresh forest smells. A faint breeze wafted gently by. The smells were another clue.

I rolled my eyes to the side, looking to my right, but did not turn my head. I noticed shades of brown on the bark of a nearby tree. White clouds drifted slowly across the blue sky. White clouds... Blue sky... The tree was not dead. In fact, I could see a green leaf on the tip of one branch... I was back in the world of life. Life. Alive! A feeling beyond relief and gratitude passed through me. We had to save my sister! The thought was an echo, a reflex in my mind.

Slowly, tentatively I raised myself onto my elbows and looked around. My sister was lying a few feet away, sleeping peacefully. When I saw her, I knew we had been successful. I stared at her sleeping form for a second as a flood of memories returned to me. With those memories came their emotions too.

I remembered my panic, my profound distress at having my little sister in danger. Portions of our odyssey jumped into my mind. The memories about the first time I saw the Ragyala quickly turned into a stream of surreal visions. I remembered the mythical creatures, demons and dragons, that I had seen with my own eyes.

But that immediately brought my mind to Fox. I turned my head to the other side and saw Fox sitting up with his legs crossed. He had a broad serene smile across his face. Shui was balanced across his knees. but he was not looking at me. He was looking over me, at my sleeping sister.

Seeing that I was awake, he turned his gaze toward me and his smile grew even wider. For a long moment neither one of us said anything. We sat quietly shared that moment of accomplishment. We had set out to do the impossible (at least in my mind) and we had accomplished it! We had gone into unbelievable darkness, and faced pure evil, and returned with what was important. We had saved my sister!

After a moment, as if in answer to our question, my sister opened her eyes. She gave a pure innocent, happy smile when she saw the blue sky. She looked vaguely confused, but not upset.

Cho Clei looked around. When she saw me, it seemed to trigger a similar process in her. She seemed to remember parts of what we had just come through. I could see a number of emotions register and then cross her face. She was too young to properly make sense of what we had just been through, but she clearly remembered that something big had happened. How much she remembered though I could not say.

Seeing me, she scrambled over and threw her arms around my neck. "Kwan!" She said, bursting into relieved tears. "Brother! Where are we?? I had a terrible nightmare! You were in it too! There was a terrible monster! A bat! But you came and saved me...I *knew* you would come for me!" I put my arms around her and hugged her. I let her cry and babble, and tried to make her feel safe. She looked around, bewildered, "And why are we in the woods?!?" I tried to say gentle and soothing things. Quietly she began to calm down. I looked over and saw Fox looking over at me approvingly.

A few moments later Cho Clei seemed to feel better and raised her head to look around. When she saw Fox, she seemed to understand some part of what just happened-some of the role he played in her rescue. The smile that she gave him was one of trust, not the usual skepticism towards a stranger. Fox smiled back at her. I realized that we were all smiling so much that we must look a little simple minded. The thought made me laugh. And then, before I knew it Fox was laughing too, and then Cho Clei joined us.

Fox stood and said, "The Ragyala can place us anywhere as long as the Pall runs through it. This is near where we left. If we start now, we can be back at your home before breakfast. Come on, the sooner we start our trip home, the sooner your parents will know that you two are safe."

***

On our walk home, I asked Fox some questions I had. There were plenty of things that had occurred, that I was unsure about. As we walked, Fox (and Shui) answered my questions and explained a few points about our adventure.

I said, "There... There are so many things about what we went through that I just don't understand." Fox smiled, again seeming like the carefree traveler I had first met. He didn't speak, he just waited for me to organize my thoughts.

So that's what I tried to do. I tried to organize my thoughts so that my questions didn't come out in a jumble. But honestly, they still must have. "Okay! What just happened? I'm not entirely sure that I understood everything we just went through. What...?"

Fox seemed to understand that I couldn't quite organize my thoughts. We had just been through an ordeal. In response, he said, "That demon, Wen-Yi, wanted to escape from that realm we just left. It's probably not difficult to see why. Realms like that, are where dark things like demons have been put, to keep them away from us.

"Still it didn't want to stay there. And because it is cleverer than many of the other demons, it somehow came up with this plan. It needed some way to cross the Pall." Fox made a small grimace. "The 'special problem' I dealt with before coming to your village was, I suspect, in contact with Wen-Yi. I suspect now that Wen-Yi was warned that I was heading this way.

"There are not many beings who could summon the Ragyala and cross the Pall. But certainly, this Wen-Yi knew that a GaleMaster Immortal would be able to, so he likely concocted the plan then.

The demon was not allowed to leave, so it had to find a way to escape. When we got here, your sister was too easy to find. She was too easy to rescue. By that I mean that the path was cleared to reach here. It would have been *infinitely* more difficult if Wen-Yi had been trying to *stop* us. If that had been the case, even the greatest masters would have found it challenging..." Fox said. Then, under his breath as if it was an afterthought, "Well, maybe Master Red Eagle wouldn't have found it challenging.

Any demon that would be capable of kidnapping a human, would be able to hide her better than Wen-Yi did." Fox gestured to everything vaguely. "I expected the whole thing to be harder. Initially I thought that we would have to use different techniques to find her sister. But Shui could see her spirit easily. That was our first clue."

Shui! How can I have forgotten about Shui? "Is...?" I began.

I am here Battou. I could feel the thought from Shui come through, answering my thought immediately. It came not only with the statement that Shui was here. The thought also came with a sense of... pride and affection. Feeling relief that Shui was safe and here too, I returned my attention to Fox.

"It made me wonder – what would be the demon's motive for making it *easy* to find your sister? The only motive that made any sense was that the demon *wanted* her to be brought back. Which brings the next question – why would a demon kidnap a human girl, only to have her collected and brought back?

"Also, on our journey, Shui was able to sense several other demons that had been close by us. More than once, these demons had started in towards us. Clearly, they had plans to attack us. But somehow, most of them abruptly changed their plans. Repeatedly, they charged at us and then turned and ran away.

"That made me wonder – what would make those demons turn around like that? The only cause that made any sense was that something had *scared* them away or *warned* them away. Only a demon that was more powerful could do something like that. Shui could sense that some of the demons that started to attack us were powerful. But all of them were *less* powerful than Wen-Yi. So, it seemed likely that Wen-Yi had *claimed* us and *warned* these other demons off.

"So then, the question became, why would Wen-Yi warn other threatening demons away from us? If it wanted to keep your sister, Wen-Yi would allow the other demons to remove us. The demon would probably even encourage other demons to attack us. It seemed very strange, but the only reasoning that fit was that Wen-Yi *wanted* us to succeed. The demon *wanted us to rescue* your sister. Our path was being cleared for us, as we traveled."

"I had no idea!" I said.

"No course not." Fox said. "There's no way that you would have known. You were not in contact with Shui directly at that point. And besides, there was no reason to worry you.

"The more that I thought about it, it seemed likely that this demon had taken your sister – so that *I would bring it back*. Does that make sense?" Fox asked. "Do you have any questions so far, should I go on?"

"But what about the demons we did encounter?" I asked. "Not all of the demons were cleared out of our way!" I protested.

"That's true." Fox nodded and winced. "This clever demon likely knew that we would need several spirits to pay the Ragyala. It knew that our need would influence our path to the castle. But the demon was impatient. It did not want us to have any distractions. It wanted us to make our way straight to the fortress. By nature, demons are not usually patient.

"I have a thousand questions, but I can't really put them in order." I said. Fox nodded sympathetically, "That's fine Kwan. Let's just go in order of what pops into your mind."

"What happened at the end, with the nine strike combination?" I asked. It had been such a flurry of action to reach the demons castle, I don't think I was understanding much by the time we got there.

Fox nodded. "The Nine strike combination is a real combination, but we never got to use it. The first strike would not defeat any enemy. Only a false actor who is *trying to get beaten*, could be 'defeated' by that. The technique can be supremely useful, but it is only useful once its power sufficiently grows.

"When I saw that the demon shattered, it was expected confirmation, more than anything else. The real battle was far from over. No, the goal then was to get the demon to collect all of its energy in one place. While it was supporting that 'shell' we fought, it was using some part of its spirit to animate the 'shell'. We wanted to make sure that all of its spirit was 'put together'." It must have been clear from my expression that I didn't understand.

"Wen-Yi needed to have its spirit collected together for the next steps of the plan." Fox went on. "It made sense that the demon would need to move its spirit to someplace that would come back with us. That way, when we eventually came back to the Pall, we could deal with the entire demon."

It was beginning to make sense to me. "The demon was really that powerful?" I asked.

Fox nodded gravely. "It was. Together, Shui and I had a chance, but it was a chance with a great deal of uncertainty. No, the way that made the most sense and that was safest for your sister, was to leave this to the Ragyala.

"In truth, the demon Wen-Yi was a genius for a demon. But the demon's genius was outmatched by its impatience and arrogance. As it got closer to its goal, it saw less and less.

"Once I knew what to look for, there were many signs of the demon's plan. The great majority of this process was just observation and deduction. And once I removed the things that just couldn't be, what was left had to be true." Fox said. And then, speaking under his breath, as if he were talking to himself, "Of everything they taught us up at the GaleTemple, I use thinking clearly much more than the energy work."

And then as another afterthought, he added, "And just so that you know Kwan, your stone protected your sister too, after we rescued her. That was another part of the reason I wanted you to stay near her."

"Oh. I see." I thought for a long minute. Some aspects of what we had just been through I understood fully. Or at least I thought I did. Some things I understood partially. And other things, I did not really understand it all. I decided to focus on the things that I did not understand at all. So I asked, "What did it mean when the Ragyala said 'Insight'? What did that mean? And why did you start glowing?"

Fox smiled briefly. "I didn't realize that I have been glowing. To be honest with you, I've only read about 'Insight', never seen nor experienced it myself before.

"To answer your question, Insight is one of the powers or abilities that the Ragyala has. All of the Yala have the power of 'Insight' currently. When the wheel turns and the Yala hand over power to the Yira, the Yira will have the power of 'Insight'. It is an ability to forensically evaluate a person's mind. It is an ability to go to the inside, to the center of a person's being. It is the place that ultimately knows the truth, *before* a being would be able to lie. It is in itself an absolute way for being to testify as to their innocence. It lets the Ragyala determine whether or not there was guilt in a situation.

"The most difficult part about it, is that Insight is a specific kind of process, a specific type of test. The difficulty lies in knowing that it is a gamble. It is a gamble because if a being is judged to be innocent, the Ragyala will help them and restore order to the situation.

"However, if they "fail" that test, the Ragyala will completely remove their mind and obliterate their being. Everything that they have learned and experienced would be gone, as though it had all been burned away."

I interrupted Fox. "So you mean…?"

Fox nodded. "If I had been lying, and if the Ragyala found me to be false, it would have destroyed my mind."

I interrupted again. "But that's not really a gamble. You knew that you weren't false. You knew that you had helped us and were telling the truth."

Fox nodded again, tilting his head to the side. "It's not always as simple as that. The Ragyala, when it is using Insight, is looking deep into the person. It is able to tell whether or not they are being honest. But it is also able to judge whether or not their decisions were right and consistent with the order of the realms.

"It is possible for being to be honest, but to have acted against order in the realms. In that situation, the Ragyala would also destroy the person's mind. So, it was still a gamble.

"But I knew that we had been true to what we thought was right. I also knew the rules that establish order in the realms. I had followed the forms, and I was confident that the judgment would go in my favor.

"And either way, I knew that even if I were destroyed, the Ragyala would take pity on you and return you home regardless. Either way, I was only risking myself. And in truth, I took an oath to do this a long time ago."

I did not know what to say. I had not fully realized the depth of Fox's generosity, and what he had risked to help my sister and me. The realization was staggering, but I forced myself to continue thinking of questions. What did I not understand?

"Oh. Okay. Let me think… All right, how did you know about the doll?" I asked. Cho Clei squeezed me tighter, as a flash of fear came at the mention of the doll.

"It seemed logical for a few reasons. If you choose to study these things, you will learn that it is far easier to place consciousness in an 'object' rather than a person. A person has a mind that resists being 'pushed out'. They fight, and parts can get tangled between them.

"Aside from an object, the next easiest vessel to possess would be a broken mind or a weak mind…"

"The crazy man that sold father the doll!" I interrupted. Fox nodded soberly and continued.

"In the next easiest vessel to possess, after a broken mind, would be a child's mind…" I gasped in surprise, even though I suspected that I knew he was going to say it. I looked down at my sister and hugged her even tighter. "

"You told me about not finding the doll when they were searching for your sister, I started to wonder about it. You had mentioned how your father acquired it. Between its odd origin and its unnatural similarity to your sister's appearance, it was suspicious."

The next question that popped into my mind was, "Will that demon come back to hurt us? Do we need to be on guard for it in the future?" I asked. As I said the words, I realized that before this journey I would have been hesitant and sound frightened. But as the words finished coming out, I recognized from the tone that I was not scared. I was calm and was just asking if I needed to pay attention to that.

"That was actually an interesting question – that is an interesting question, because of how I know the answer. It goes back to the time of Insight. It is exceptionally difficult for me to try to describe what that process was like. The Ragyala is a cosmic being. I invited it to inspect my mind, but I did not know what that would be like.

"In truth, I would probably describe it like trying not to drown while being rushed down a flooding river. The Ragyala's mind is just too big. Its power was just too great. And at the end of the day, I am only one man.

I interrupted again. I didn't feel like Fox was giving himself enough credit. "You're not just one man! You're a GaleMaster!"

Fox smiled in a way that I remembered from when I was young. It was a smile that adults gave when a child said something very naïve. "That's a nice thought Kwan. True, I have worked very hard in studying the Gale, but at the end of a life a man can only reach so high. I was born to parents, just like you.

"My long journey to become a GaleMaster has transformed me into something greater that I was when I started. But even in this form, my power is insignificant compared to the Ragyala. It is like a mouse exercising to grow stronger. It wouldn't matter how many muscles the mouse could put on. Even the strongest mouse in the world would pose no challenge to you. That would be a good analogy for my power compared to the Ragyala.

"But part of the Insight process had my mind and the Ragyala's mind sharing space. So in theory, I would be able to find out information while I was connected to the Ragyala. But as I said, the difference between us was so vast that holding it and attempting to search it felt like trying to drink the whole ocean. There was just too much information on too many subjects across vast distances of time.

"It very quickly became clear to me that I had no power or ability inside the Ragyala's mind. I misspoke before- It wasn't like I was a swimmer in the 'water' of the Ragyala's mind. A better way would be to say that I was like leaf tossed around in a sea storm. Because I had no power to move...

But eventually it did occur to me that the Ragyala *enforced* order. It was fundamentally a being of order. So, in a polite and orderly way I put forward the question/thought wondering what would happen to the demon. The Ragyala did not have to give me any kind of answer. In truth, it was satisfying curiosity. I didn't really *need* to know the demon's faith. I knew that it was only curiosity. And the Ragyala must certainly have known it.

"But, I suppose the Ragyala felt that we had earned the right to know. In truth, your sister is an innocent that was minding her own affairs. That demon was entirely to blame for this whole episode. You did nothing to invite this into your lives. Furthermore, you found courage and took positive action. I imagine that the Ragyala saw your response as noble and could have been influenced by it.

"In response to my thought/question, the Ragyala allowed a flash of understanding to come into my mind. The best way I could describe it would be it was similar to how we first feel telepathic communication."

"Tele- what?" I asked.

"It's just a complicated word for talking to each other but only using our minds. But I'm getting off the point. It was just an analogy. What I meant is that you are used to communicating with words. When you suddenly saw that we could communicate with words, and images, and emotions, and memories, it probably felt like a whole different process." I nodded emphatically that is exactly what it had been like. Fox went on, "We all feel that astonishment the first time. But after a while, when you are accustomed to communicating by thought, it is no longer astonishing. But when the Ragyala uses its telepathy with you, it is astonishing like the first experience. The Ragyala allowed me to understand what had been done with the demon:

"It wasn't as though I "saw" what was done. The best way I can explain it is that there was an "understanding" then, in my mind, of what happened. First, I can tell you that that demon will never trouble us again."

"Did the Ragyala destroy it?" I asked.

But Fox immediately shook his head. "No Kwan. He *Sealed* it. One way to look at this reality is as a *school*. This world is where beings are placed so that they can learn, grow, and develop. And in truth, if you destroy a thing, it will learn nothing.

"That means that the system of life operates with compassion. It does not operate by vengeance. But it does operate by cause and effect. If a being violates the order of life, it is making a cause. And that cause will make effects. Those effects could be seen as punishment, but having seen inside the Ragyala's mind, I now understand that the goal is to *teach* the demon.

I couldn't believe what I was hearing! "That demon couldn't be taught! It should be destroyed!" But as soon as the words came out of my mouth, I felt that they were not quite right. There was a better way to look at this, then just wanting to get even. The fact that Fox could see it and explain it, made him seem even more a hero to me. It wasn't just that he had wisdom. There was also *goodness* there.

Fox went on, "The most wondrous part of it – is that the demon is here to learn and grow as well. It will be many ages until Wen-Yi realizes that, but it is true nonetheless. The Ragyala "placed" the demon inside a stone from this realm, deep in its mountains."

I didn't understand. "I don't understand. Do you mean the SoulCage, I mean the… celestial Mountain? The Ragyala trapped the demon under the mountain?" I asked.

But Fox shook his head. "No, this was something different. I hadn't realized that the Ragyala had this of power. But, the Ragyala somehow merged the spirit of that demon with the substance of one kind of stone in this realm. Apparently, the stone can hold tremendous amounts of energy. And in the final sense, the demon is just energy.

"The Ragyala somehow sealed the demon within the stone, called 'marbol'. I am not unaccustomed to new ways of doing things, but the way the Ragyala communicates and thinks was profoundly… foreign. It wasn't that I saw him place the demon into the rock of the mountain. It was almost like a memory of something that was about to happen. I know that doesn't make sense, but I'm unsure how else to describe it. I suppose it is because the Ragyala operates with a completely different relationship to time. Time and space clearly have different rules for a being like that.

"But that's something that was very positive and life-affirming. The system, and thus the Ragyala was still clear that *every* being, even one is evil as Wen-Yi, is here to improve. But that demon is not ready to move forward. Clearly it still has many lessons to learn. The 'marbol' stone will nullify the demon's power. And Ragyala did place it… so that it could eventually *learn*. After countless oceans of time, when it has learned, it will be released.

"All of us are here to move forward, Kwan. All of us.

"One thing that I did pick up from the Ragyala's mind was very unexpected. It seems that this 'marbol' stone will appear different from this point forward. The Ragyala observed that the stone would have swirling patterns in it from now on. I was able to observe the Ragyala calculating how some of the images from the demon's thoughts and impressions would be pushed forward through the stone. The impressions from the demon's mind would be expressed as swirls within the stone. The Ragyala looked ahead and foresaw that the 'marbol' stone would become more popular in the future. When men dig it out of the mountain, it will show trace images of the demon. It will be harmless, but still, it's interesting

"I tried to get more information to clarify but, the Ragyala's mind was too big. And you can't drink the ocean. There was just too much information. But I did get a glimpse, and that glimpse let me see what ended up happening to Wen-Yi."

"Okay I understand that the demon wanted us to bring it back when you brought my sister back, so it arranged to kidnap her." Fox nodded, and I continued. "So, it… so it possessed a doll to get to her? How did that part work?"

"I did try to find out, but only the Ragyala knows for sure. I did try to get the information from the Ragyala's mind but it was the same situation as before. There was just too much information. To be honest with you, I would have certainly lost my mind, if the Ragyala itself had not kept me safe.

"There were a series of seemingly random images that the Ragyala gave me. But even that was like trying to catch ten thousand pebbles. I have been giving those images some thought though. They correspond to a likely series of events. But as I said, only the Ragyala knows for sure.

"If I had to hazard a guess, I would say it's probably one of the few occult groups that worship demons like Wen-Yi. It might surprise you to know that there are some very evil people in this world, willing to do anything for power. They try to gain the favor of entities like Wen-Yi, and use innocent life as the currency to do it. These evil practices have gone on since before we measured time.

"With people in this world worshiping it, Wen-Yi would have been able to influence their minds. The demon was most likely able to direct one of them fashion the doll. It would've given the follower an image of your sister as well.

"Then the demon would have opened a portal on its side and taught its followers to open the portal on the other side. Then it would be able to send a small portion of its energy through the portal, to inhabit the doll. But as I said, that's only likely- what I deciphered from that deluge of images.

"All we really know about this part- is that the demon managed to get a small piece of its energy over to this realm- into the doll. This could not fully free the demon the way it wanted, but it did let Wen-Yi 'act' in this world. Remember that its goal was to get its whole spirit over to this realm. Only then could it have the full freedom it craved.

"Once the demon was in this world, influencing a weak-minded person would be easy. The people who are mentally ill are particularly vulnerable to influence… The demon would have compelled the "wild man" to get the doll into your father's hands. Then, it would be overwhelmingly likely that your Father would take the doll to your sister."

"Ah… okay, then what?" I asked, processing what he was telling me. I had just come through this whole journey, without realizing much of what had been going on.

"When you saw me before the storm, before your sister was taken, do you know what I was doing?" I shook my head.

I had meant to ask him, but hadn't yet.

"I had been performing a series of tests with the help of Shui. We were able to determine that a very powerful, and sinister spell was at work." Fox said.

"Spell? Like magic?" I asked.

"Not... Quite." Fox said. "But for this point in your education, that works well enough. For now, it's just a word. 'Technique' would work just as well. But what I'm describing- is that the demon was able to use the doll to locate your sister. And after she had been located, the demon could send the storm.

"Why would it send a storm?" I asked.

"That storm was not a natural occurrence. It brought a powerful sleep spell with it. Unless a person had training to resist the demon's trap, they would have been pushed down into a deep sleep.

"And once all of you were asleep, the demon was able to use the doll to transport your sister and bring her to its realm."

"But how could it do that?" I asked.

"You mean the actual mechanism? The way it worked?" Fox peered at me, seemingly pleased that I wanted to know.

"Again, I can only give you an educated guess as to how the demon did it. Once a being fractures itself, it can reassemble or 'recall' the pieces. Since your sister and the doll were inseparable by this point, your sister got 'recalled' too.

Once your sister had the doll, and the village was asleep, the demon would have connected to its energy inside the doll. Then, it could use that energy to enfold your sister and 'wrap' around her. Then it would have summoned that part of its energy and your sister would have been carried back with it. That seems most likely. Then the first part of its plan would be done. At that point, it only had to wait for us to come retrieve her.

I asked, "Why did the demon take us through such dangerous areas like the mirror portals if it needed us to succeed and bring it back?" Fox grinned mischievously and spread his hands.

"Certainly, the demon would have made the way somewhat dangerous so we would not grow suspicious. But there probably was another, greater factor. I suspect the demon had to adapt its plan every time we did something unexpected. When we scrambled, *it* had to scramble. I would guess it never planned to bring us near the Gates. Possession of the Gates is something it would have wanted to keep hidden. In truth, Wen-Yi probably had to change its plan more than once."

Oh. I had almost no idea what I had been getting into! I shuddered, thinking of the dangers we had faced. I tried to think of what other questions I had, but most of the pieces were filling in as I listened. Then I thought of one. "Fox? Why did the Ragyala call you my master?"

Fox stopped walking, and turned to me. I naturally stopped walking also. And my little sister, still under my arm, also stopped. He said, "There are many different studies that are taught at the GaleTemple. They teach us everything from how to use energy, healing herbs, mathematics, calligraphy, martial arts, meditation, even divination."

I must've looked confused, because he explained without me having to ask. "Divination is a word for when you can tell the future." My eyebrows must've gone up, looking incredulous. And then I remembered the experiences I had just finished, and that suddenly didn't seem so far-fetched. "The greatest living GaleMaster who practices divination is the Immortal Master Owl. He has never, to my knowledge, ever been wrong."

"At certain points, in a life of studying the Gale, Masters are sent out to perform missions of teaching or service. I am on a mission of service, to identify and solve 'special problems'. It is part of my path, walking the Gale.

"So back to the infallible Owl Immortal. The one who was never wrong…" He said.

Never wrong? Wow. I was impressed. But I didn't get what this had to do with me. Then Fox said, "Before I left, the Owl Immortal came out of his shrine to see me off. This was unheard of. The Owl immortal was rarely seen by any other than a few advanced Gale Masters. He only took an audience when he needed to look into the future to answer questions, as service to others. I was stunned and humbled, only having seen him once before when I was a young man. He told me that I would meet a worthy apprentice on this trip. It seems clear to me that he meant you. The Ragyala only seemed to confirm that."

I was in shock. I couldn't speak. Was he saying I could become a GaleMaster?

"There are a series of tests that any GaleMaster is supposed to perform before taking on a student apprentice. I'm required to put any potential student through a rigorous set of challenges to test them. These tests determine if a potential student is smart enough or brave enough to study the Gale. But… It's more than that. The tests are looking to see if you have an open and flexible mind and if you have the ability to control that mind. Studying the Gale requires discipline over yourself.

"I did not perform any of those tests on you." Fox said. The part of me that had begun getting excited about the idea of having a life like Fox was suddenly discouraged. I imagined that the tests would be impossibly hard. But then Fox said, "but none of those tests would be nearly as challenging as what you just went through. Nor would they be able to tell me as much about your mind and your character. You have demonstrated, to my satisfaction, that you would be a worthy and capable student." Again, I was shocked at his words.

I was much younger than you when Master Eclipse found me. Because I was a boy, and not ready, he returned when I was your age. Then he made the offer to me." Fox again took on that distracted, faraway look. He gave half-smile and said quietly, "That was a long time ago." His gaze came back in the focus and he turned to me.

"I am planning to make the offer to you after I speak to your father. But since you asked me, I tell you my thoughts. First Kwan, don't answer me now. But be thinking, in the back of your head, if you would be interested in living a life like this.

"It would be very hard work. You would need to learn a tremendous amount. There would be danger, because of the powerful forces you would face. But also, you would learn to wield powerful forces of your own. You would see things very few people would ever have a chance to witness. And, most significantly, you would get to *help* people. Think about it. We will talk about it later." Then he turned and walked away. My mouth hung open. I stood there in shock, Cho Clei looking up at me.

The rest of the walk home passed quickly. When our house came into view, there were no signs of my parents. The sun had risen. The birds were chirping. Their melodic tones were a constant, soothing reminder that we had returned to the world of life. The leaves were a glowing green in the bright morning light.

I was bigger in my mind, or my spirit than I had been before. A whole new range of skills and capabilities had grown in me. Everything looked different to me. I felt much more confident than I had even yesterday.

It seemed amazing to me yesterday was so long ago. When I left, I had been a naïve boy. I had not seen any of the world. Not even the regular world. But now here I was having seen things that no one would even believe. I had seen demons with my own eyes. I had seen dragons… mythical creatures… I had seen the unbelievable!

Fox had explained enough that I finally understood what we had just been through. A demon had kidnapped my sister in an attempt to win its freedom. But Fox, Shui, and I had brought her back!

As we walked, Cho Clei perked up. She was gradually shaking off the effects of her ordeal. I still flabbergasted at the opportunity Fox was offering me. It had been an impossible dream before, the idea of living a life like Fox.

Instead, I had been trapped in the realization that I would have a regular, dull life. I had thought that I would not be able to go back to my regular life, but would have to. After what I had seen, how could I ever be happy in my old life? I would always wonder about what I had seen and want to know more. And now that I was here, the thought of continuing the way that I had been, was suddenly unbearable.

But Fox had offered me a lifeline! My future did not have to be as dull as my past. I felt different. My whole outlook was changing. I no longer had to settle for the options Father gave me. Those were the only choices father could see. I had not wanted to become any of the choices that father had offered me. It had thrown his life into chaos, not being a warrior any longer, but it did not have to challenge me the same way. I had been given an amazing opportunity. *I could do something else.*

Before father had said that strength and courage were our birthrights. He constantly reinforced the idea that we were strong, and courageous. We were supposed to be heroic and good. We were from pure warrior stock. And when war became outlawed, it was a challenge for warrior families. Many were unable to adapt. Now I could clearly see how ours had been one of them.

Before, I could only see how painful it had been for Father. He felt that he had been denied his path and had to settle. It upset and depressed him. He had tried not to show it, but I had seen it. And, in the back of my mind, I felt it would have to be upsetting and dissatisfying for me too.

But now everything looked very different. Now the future looked very different than it did before. I should come up with a strategy. I should have a plan of what I was going to say to father when I saw him. I wanted to present myself as having grown as much as I felt I had.

It gave me some kind of feeling to think about telling my father that I did not want to follow in his steps. I did not want to spend my life in the ways that he thought was useful. I swallowed hard, realizing what I would need to do. I would need to boldly declare the things that I had been too afraid to say before.

I would tell father that I did not want to waste my life being a policeman, and dealing with small problems. I would explain that I wanted to help people by solving big problems. Also, learning deeper or hidden information about reality was an opportunity I couldn't pass. It was what I wanted to do my life.

Still, I had my doubts. I know that I had a lifelong habit of yielding to father's decisions. And then it was like a group of clouds had moved in the block the light of my mood. I realized with a sinking feeling that I might give in to whatever father said if he were angry, regardless of what I thought. And the more I thought about it, the more likely it was that he would be angry.

He was already angry that this had happened to our family. I could tell that he was angry he had not been there to protect Cho Clei. And finally, he would be angry that I had disappeared without an explanation. I did not want him to be angry, but the more I thought about it, it seemed inevitable.

When our new house came into view, Cho Clei surprised me by throwing back her head and yelling, "Mamaaaa!" As loudly as she could. We kept walking, enjoying the rising sun as we made our way down the road toward our house. Before we had made it 10 paces, mother rushed out into the street, her head whipping back and forth looking to see where the call had come from.

As soon my sister saw Mother, Cho Clei ducked out from under my arm. She broke into a run yelling, "Mama!" Hearing Cho Clei's voice, Mother's head snapped towards us, her gaze immediately locking on my sister. Then she was running too. And crying.

Then I noticed Father running out a moment later. He saw Mother and Cho Clei, and ran over wrapping his arms around both of them. My sister was again crying and babbling, now that she had mother here to fuss over her. These types of scenes had irritated me in the past. I had felt, in classic big brother fashion, that my sister was acting like a baby for attention. But now, seeing them, I was just… grateful.

Fox and I had continued walking even though Cho Clei had broken into a sprint. Fox naturally seemed to slow his pace, so

I did too. I understood that Fox was giving Cho Clei and my parents time for their reunion.

But I was slowing down for a completely different reason. I was slowing down out of caution, out of fear. I expected that Father would be angry.

Remember this always Battou. Your family was in danger. You stepped forward and answered the call. You have faced the trials with honor.... And you were victorious. You have brought her home. This is a triumphant return. You cannot throw mud on this thing- it will always shine...You saved your sister. Remember what you have learned. Nothing, and no one, can ever take that away from you.

I sent the pulse of gratitude at Shui. And then, before I was ready, we were approaching Father, Mother and Cho Clei. As we came close, Mother and Father looked up. Cho Clei looked over a moment later. Her hysterical crying and babbling came even more severe. Pointed at us and wailed, "Kwan and that big man saved me!..." She said more than that, but that was the only part that was clear and sensible. Father's brow furrowed as he came to terms with what he now saw, and our sudden change in fortunes.

Mother pressed questions at Cho Clei, trying to find out more about what had happened. But Father seemed to immediately grasp, at least to some degree, what happened. I stepped forward, intending to speak, but unable to. Instead, I lowered my eyes somewhat sheepishly as I stood before him.

I prepared myself to speak, to apologize for having disappeared. But before I could, father had enveloped me in a crushing hug. He squeezed me, pulling me in close. All I could make out where the words, "My son."

I felt suddenly, and with absolute certainty, that it was going to be all right. Father was not angry. He was only grateful to have his children back. Mother was beside herself with joy. It was several minutes before I could speak. I found myself limp with relief.

The enormity of the danger I had passed through was sinking in. As I realized it, Father somehow seem to realize it also. He held me at arm's length and looked at me as if seeing me for the first time. I was startled to notice that Father's eyes were glassy. He had tears welling up in his eyes! I had seen dragons and demons, but I had never seen Father with tears! But even more shocking, he was… pleased with what he saw. I had made him… proud.

I cleared my throat to speak. I had to take the plunge quickly, before my nerves failed me. But Father spoke first. "Who is our new friend?" He asked. Gesturing with his chin toward Fox.

"Father, this is Master Fox, the Immortal." I said without turning. "He rescued Cho Clei. And Father, I'm not going to be a policeman." My tone did not waver. I went on, "But I do have a plan. I know what I want to do."

Father didn't react to my words. Instead, he took a step to the side and released my shoulders. He turned to Fox and said, "Immortal… GaleMaster?"

Fox bowed slightly. I was dumbstruck, mouth agape. Father *knew* about GaleMasters? Father looked more serious and earnest than I had ever seen. (And he always looked serious and earnest.) Father spoke quietly, "You have brought my children home, Mountain Man. I am in your debt.

Fox spoke earnestly, "I did not accomplish this by myself. Your son conducted himself in a way that would make you exceptionally proud. He was brave, intelligent and decisive. At least half of your gratitude goes to him." Father turned and looked at me. I basked in the new look of respect he gave me.

Father nodded and spoke quietly, looking me in the eye. "That's my son." Then he turned back to Fox. My son has grown under your care. Again, I am in your debt, Mountain Man." I had a moment of glorious clarity that Father would accept what I decided. I had not heard him agree yet, but I knew the agreement would come.

Father said 'Mountain Man". Mountain Man? And like a clap of thunder it came to me that the GaleMasters *were* the Mountain men who stopped all the wars! I hadn't put it together before. Fox spoke, "You must have many questions.

I think a long discussion is in order, perhaps over a meal? What time is it?"

Mother answered, "It is breakfast time. I heard Kwan run out to catch you this morning. That was not long ago. I will make us all a meal, while you tell us what happened to Cho Clei. How does that sound?"

Fox nodded and rubbed his belly. "That is an excellent plan."

With real sunlight and birds singing, the five of us started walking. Almost immediately, Father scooped up Cho Clei in his arms and began to carry her. Held protectively by father, Cho Clei quieted down. Mother reached out every few steps and put her hand on my sister's back, reassuring herself that she wasn't dreaming.

All of us were absorbed in our thoughts as we walked back home. I kept marveling that I wasn't going *back* home. Finally, I was going forward.

End

Keep Moving Forward. Always.

Printed in Great Britain
by Amazon